O9-BTI-861

Praise for *New York Times* bestselling author Lori Foster

"Storytelling at its best! Lori Foster should be on everyone's auto-buy list."

—#1 *New York Times* bestselling author Sherrilyn Kenyon on *No Limits*

"Teasing and humorous dialogue, sizzling sex scenes, tender moments, and overriding tension show Foster's skill as a balanced storyteller."

—*Publishers Weekly* on *Under Pressure* (starred review)

"Emotionally spellbinding and wicked hot."

—*New York Times* bestselling author Lora Leigh on *No Limits*

"Foster's writing satisfies all appetites with plenty of searing sexual tension and page-turning action in this steamy, edgy, and surprisingly tender novel."

—*Publishers Weekly* on *Getting Rowdy*

"Foster hits every note (or power chord) of the true alpha male hero."

—*Publishers Weekly* on *Bare It All*

"A sexy, believable roller coaster of action and romance."

—*Kirkus Reviews* on *Run the Risk*

"Steamy, edgy, and taut."

—*Library Journal* on *When You Dare*

Also available from Lori Foster and HQN Books

Body Armor

Under Pressure
Hard Justice
Close Contact
Fast Burn

The Guthrie Brothers

Don't Tempt Me
Worth the Wait

The Ultimate series

Hard Knocks
(prequel ebook novella)
No Limits
Holding Strong
Tough Love
Fighting Dirty

Love Undercover

Run the Risk
Bare It All
Getting Rowdy
Dash of Peril

Edge of Honor

"Ready, Set, Jett"
in *The Guy Next Door* anthology
When You Dare
Trace of Fever
Savor the Danger
A Perfect Storm
What Chris Wants
(ebook novella)

Other must-reads

Tucker
(ebook novella)
A Buckhorn Baby
Built for Love
(ebook novella)
A Buckhorn Bachelor
(ebook novella)
A Buckhorn Summer
(ebook novella)
All for You
Back to Buckhorn
(ebook novella)
Heartbreakers
Charade
Up in Flames
Turn Up the Heat
Hot in Here
Animal Attraction
(ebook anthology)
Love Bites
All Riled Up
The Buckhorn Legacy
Forever Buckhorn
Buckhorn Beginnings
Bewitched
Unbelievable
Tempted
Bodyguard
Caught!
Fallen Angels
Enticing

LORI FOSTER

Cooper's Charm

Recycling programs for this product may not exist in your area.

ISBN-13: 978-1-335-47790-3

Cooper's Charm

This edition published by arrangement with Harlequin Books S.A.

For questions and comments about the quality of this book, please contact us at CustomerService@Harlequin.com.

www.HQNBooks.com

Printed in U.S.A.

Cooper's Charm

1

THE SUN SHONE BRIGHTLY ON THAT EARLY MID-MAY morning. The crisp, cool air smelled of damp leaves—an appealing, earthy scent. A mist from the nearby lake blanketed the ground, swirling around her sneaker-covered feet.

Phoenix Rose stood at the high entrance to the resort and looked down at the neat, winding rows of RVs and fifth wheels in various sizes, as well as the numerous log cabins and the rustic tent grounds. All was quiet, as if no one had yet awakened.

She could have parked in the lower lot, closer to her destination, but she wanted the time to take it in.

Besides, after driving for a few hours, she'd enjoy stretching her legs.

Breathing deeply, she filled her lungs with fresh air, also filling her heart with hope.

It was such a beautiful morning that her clip-on sunglasses, worn over her regular glasses, only cut back the worst of the glare; she had to shade her eyes with a hand as she took in the many unique aspects of Cooper's Charm RV Park and Resort.

Before submitting her résumé to the online wanted ad, she'd

scoured over all the info she could find. She'd also studied the map to familiarize herself with the design.

The website hadn't done it justice.

It was more beautiful than she'd expected.

Dense woods bordered the property on one side and at the entrance, giving it a private, isolated feel. To the other side, a line of evergreens separated the park from an old-fashioned drive-in that offered nightly movies not only to the resort guests, but also to the residents in the surrounding small town of Woodbine, Ohio.

At the very back of the resort, a large lake—created from a quarry—wound in and around the land before fading into the sun-kissed mist, making it impossible to see the full size. Currently, large inflated slides and trampolines floated in and out of the mist, randomly catching the sunshine as they bobbed in the mostly placid water. Phoenix couldn't imagine anyone getting into the frigid water today—or even this month—but the online brochure claimed the lake was already open, as was the heated in-ground pool.

She was to meet the owner near the lake, but she'd deliberately arrived fifteen minutes early, which gave her a chance to look around.

After six months in hotel rooms, and a month familiarizing herself with the park, Cooper's Charm already felt like home. She could be at peace here and that meant a lot, because for too long now, peace of mind had remained an elusive thing.

Knowing her sister was waiting, Phoenix pulled out her phone and took a pic of the beautiful scenery, then texted it to Ridley, typing, Arrived.

Despite the early hour, Ridley immediately texted back, Are you sure about this?

Positive, Phoenix replied. She hadn't been this certain in ages. Hope the interview goes well.

Loyal to the end, her sister sent back, He'll take one look at you and fall in love.

Phoenix grinned even as she rolled her eyes. Ridley had the misguided notion that everyone else shared her skewed but adoring perception. I'll settle for a job, thank you very much.

Keep me posted. Love you.

Her heart swelled. Through thick and thin, Ridley was her backup, her support system, and the person she trusted most in the whole world. Her parents were great too, very attentive and protective, but it was her sister who best understood her. It didn't matter that Ridley lived a very different lifestyle, or that their goals in life were so different.

Phoenix loved working with her hands, staying busy, and took satisfaction from a job well done.

Ridley enjoyed seeing the world, traveling nearly nonstop to posh destinations, had an exquisite flair for the latest fashions and detested being messy in any way.

Different, but still best friends through and through.

Phoenix signed off in her usual way. Love you, too. Byeeeee...

She knew Ridley was still worried, and that bothered her. Much as she appreciated her sister's dedication, she wanted to portray an air of confidence and independence...just as she once had.

She didn't like being weak, and she didn't like allowing others to impact her life, yet both had happened. This was her chance to get back to being a strong, capable woman.

If all went well, today would be a start toward reaching that goal.

Taking her time, Phoenix strode through the grounds, familiarizing herself on her way to the lake. She really wanted to explore the woods and the small, quaint cabins where she would live.

More than that, though, she wanted to be at the lake when Cooper Cochran arrived. She wouldn't be late, wouldn't be nervous and wouldn't screw up her fresh start.

Unfortunately, just as she rounded a play area filled with swings and slides, she saw the lone figure standing along the sandy shore, a fishing rod in hand.

Was that Cochran?

Good Lord, he was big, and impressively built, too, with wide, hard shoulders and muscular thighs. She hated to admit it, but that could be a problem for her.

After all, she'd learned the hard way, on a very basic level, that big men were also powerful men.

Pausing to stare, she pressed a hand to her stomach to quell the nervous butterflies taking flight at the sight of him.

The sunrise gilded his messy, sandy-brown hair. As he reeled in his line, then cast it out again, muscles flexed beneath a dark pullover with the sleeves pushed up to his elbows, showing taut forearms and thick wrists dusted with hair. Worn denim hugged his long legs.

He seemed to stand nearly a half foot taller than her five feet four inches. God, how she'd prayed he'd be a smaller, less… imposing man.

Finding information on the resort had been easy. Finding information on Cooper Cochran…not so much.

She stood frozen on the spot, trying to convince her feet to move, doing her best to conquer her irrational reservations, but she was suddenly, painfully aware that they were all alone on the shore. Logically, she knew it wasn't a problem. Plenty of people were around, though in their RVs or cabins, so there was no reason to be afraid.

Not here, not now.

Lately, though, fear had been a fickle thing, often re-emerging out of nowhere. She'd always been able to hide that fear from her parents, but Ridley was a different matter. Her sister would take one look at her and understand.

But Ridley wasn't here now, and this job was important…

As if he'd known she was there all along, he glanced over his shoulder at her. Reflective sunglasses hid his eyes, and yet she felt his scrutiny and a touch of surprise. She knew his gaze was burning over her and it caused her to shift with nervous awareness.

She guessed him to be in his midthirties, maybe nine or ten years older than her. No one would call him a classically handsome man. His features were as bold as his body, including a strong jaw, masculine nose and harshly carved cheekbones.

Not typical good looks, but he certainly wouldn't be ignored.

She could see that he hadn't yet shaved this morning, and she wasn't sure if he'd combed his hair. The breeze and fog off the lake might have played with it, leaving it a little wavier than usual.

She couldn't look away, couldn't even blink.

His scrutiny kept her pinned in place with a strange stirring of her senses, unpleasant only in its unfamiliarity.

Releasing her by turning back to the lake, he said, "Ms. Rose?"

The words seemed to carry on the quiet, cool air.

Phoenix swallowed. "Yes." She watched as he cast out yet again. It almost seemed that he gave her time to get herself together. Of course, he couldn't know why she was so reserved. Still, his patience, his apparent lack of interest, finally helped her to move forward.

She watched the way his large hands deftly, slowly, reeled in the line.

Her feet sank in the soft, damp sand. "Mr. Cochran?"

"You can call me Coop."

He had a deep, mellow voice that should have put her at ease but instead sharpened her awareness of him as a large man.

"I like to fish in the morning before everyone crowds the lake. Are you an early bird, Ms. Rose?"

"Actually, yes." A white gull swooped down, skimmed the water and took flight again. Ripples fanned out across the surface. By the minute, the mist evaporated, giving way to the warmth of the sun. "You know I had my own landscaping business." She'd told him that much in their email correspondence concerning her application. "In the summer especially, it was more comfortable to start as early as possible. I've gotten in the habit of being up and about by six."

"You won't need to be that early here."

"Okay." She wasn't sure what else to say. "The lake is beautiful."

"And peaceful." This time when he reeled in the line, he had a small bass attached. "Do you fish?"

He hadn't faced her again and that made it easier to converse. "When I was younger, my sister and I would visit our grandparents for the weekend and we'd fish in their pond. That was years ago, though." This was the strangest interview she'd ever had. It was also less stressful than she'd anticipated.

Had Cooper Cochran planned it that way—or did he just love to fish?

"You don't fish with them anymore?"

"They passed away just before I turned twenty. Granddad first, and my grandma not long after."

"I'm sorry to hear that. Sounds like you made good memories with them, though."

"Yes." Fascinated, she watched as he worked the hook easily from the fish's mouth, then he bent and placed the bass gently back in the water before rinsing his hands. "Too small to keep?"

"I rarely keep what I catch." He gestured toward a picnic table. "Let's talk."

Until then, she hadn't noticed the tackle box and towel on the summer-bleached wooden table.

She followed Cochran, then out of habit waited until he'd chosen a spot so she could take the side opposite him—a habit she'd gotten into with men. These days she preferred as much distance as she could manage.

He stepped over the bench, dropped the towel, pushed up his sunglasses and seated himself.

Golden-brown eyes took her by surprise. They were a stark contrast to his heavy brows and the blunt angles of his face.

She realized she was staring, that he merely stared back with one brow lifted, and she quickly looked away. Thankfully, she still wore the clip-on sunglasses, giving her a hint of concealment.

She retreated behind idle chitchat. "I studied the map online and feel like I know my way around. The lake is more impressive than I'd realized. The photos don't do it justice."

"I've been meaning to update the website," he said. "It's been busy, though. We lost our groundskeeper and housekeeper at the same time."

"Someone had both positions?"

He smiled with some private amusement. "No. Either position is a full-time job. But without any of us noticing, the two of them fell in love, married and then headed to Florida to retire."

"Oh." She expected to find many things at the resort, but love wasn't on the list. Love wasn't even in her universe.

Not anymore.

"You said you checked out the map online?"

"Actually, I researched everything I could about the place, including the surrounding grounds, and I'm sure I'd be a good fit for the job."

When he looked past her, she quickly turned her head to find a woman approaching with a metal coffeepot in one hand, the handles of two mugs hooked through the fingers of the other.

Cooper stood. "Perfect timing, Maris."

The woman's smile was easy and friendly. "I was watching."

Long, dark blond hair caught in a high ponytail swung behind her with every step. Soft brown eyes glanced at Phoenix. "Good morning."

"Morning."

"Coffee?" She set one mug in front of Cooper and filled it.

Phoenix nodded. "Yes, please."

Maris filled the second mug, then dug creamer cups and sugar packets from a sturdy apron pocket, along with a spoon wrapped in a napkin. "Coop drinks his black, but I wasn't sure about you."

Anyone who presented her with coffee on a cool morning instantly earned her admiration. "I'll take it any way I can get it, but I prefer a little cream and sugar, so thank you."

Cooper reseated himself. "Maris Kennedy, meet Phoenix Rose. Maris runs the camp store. Phoenix is here about the position for groundskeeper."

Slim brows went up. "Really? I was assuming housekeeper."

Cooper's smile did amazing things to his rugged face, and disastrous things to her concentration.

He explained to Phoenix, "We've never had a woman tend the grounds." Then to Maris, he said, "Ms. Rose used to run her own landscaping company. She's more than qualified and we'd be lucky to get her."

Phoenix perked up. Did that mean he'd already made up his mind to hire her?

"Especially now." Maris leaned a hip against the end of the table. "I don't know if Coop told you, but we're starting this season shorthanded. We were all taking turns with the grounds and the housekeeping, so everyone will be thrilled to take one thing off their list."

Still unsure if she had the job or not, Phoenix said, "It'd be my pleasure to make things easier. If I'm hired, I can start right away." She glanced at Cooper and added, "Today even."

Maris straightened. "Seriously?"

Already feeling a sense of purpose that had been missing for too long from her life, Phoenix nodded. "I'm anxious to get to work."

Cooper put his elbows on the table and leaned forward. "Then consider yourself hired."

Behind the glasses, her eyes widened. "Just like that?"

"You expected a different outcome?"

"Well, no, but—" She could barely contain her excitement. If she didn't have an audience, she would have danced across the sandy shoreline.

"I bet you already packed, didn't you?"

Heat rushed into her cheeks for being so presumptuous, but she admitted the truth with a grin. "My car is full."

"Glad to hear it." He took a drink of his coffee, then said, "You had a great résumé, so meeting was just a formality."

More than a little dazed, Phoenix said, "Thank you."

"So you accept?" Maris asked.

"Of course!"

"Fantastic. So where are we putting her?"

With his gaze on his coffee, Cooper said, "I was thinking cabin eighteen."

Maris paused, subdued a smile and nodded. "Okay then. Give me thirty minutes and I'll get it set up."

"I can do it," Phoenix quickly offered. "I don't want to put you out."

"It's not a problem. I'm just glad you're hired. Now hopefully Coop will find a housekeeper, too—hint, hint." She looked up at the sky and pretended to pray.

Cooper shook his head. "You're the queen of subtlety, Maris. As it happens, I'll be interviewing a woman next week."

In an aside to Phoenix, she said, "He interviews someone every week. Trust me, most don't get hired so easily." Then to Cooper, she added, "If she's not a serial killer, hire her."

He snorted. "You're going to make Ms. Rose think I'm a harsh boss. She'll run off before she ever gets started."

Maris rushed to say, "Coop is the *best* of bosses. Working for him is a dream."

Phoenix laughed. "You don't need to sell me. I'm excited for the opportunity."

"Just because you're a positive person, meaning you'll be fun to have around, I'll make sure you get some extra towels and one of our better coffeemakers." With a wink, she headed off.

As Maris disappeared into her store, her words hung with Phoenix. If most people weren't so easily hired, why was she? She knew she had good credentials, and she knew she could do the work. Was he so desperate to fill the position that a formal interview wasn't necessary?

She wasn't used to things going smoothly these days, but she wanted the job enough not to question it.

Silence dragged on. She was aware of Cooper intently watching her while he drank his coffee. It made her twitchy.

Determined, she turned to him. "I'm really looking forward to the job." Damn it, she'd already said that—or something like it. She didn't want to babble.

"Maris hasn't given you second thoughts?"

Phoenix shook her head. "Actually, she seems really nice."

"She is. I'm fortunate that everyone who works here gets along really well."

Perfect. The last thing she wanted was drama in her life. She'd had enough of that. The plan now was to work hard enough to keep the demons at bay, and otherwise live peacefully. "They all live on-site?"

"Yep." He stood. "Come on. I'll show you around while Maris opens your cabin and gets fresh linen inside." He paused. "You're aware that the cabin is small, right?"

"Yes. It's just me so I don't need a lot of room." In fact, it'd be nice to have less to take care of. Recent events had proven to her that material things were far less important than she'd thought.

"We have some premium cabins, and a few available rental

campers, but I try to leave those open to guests." He carried his tackle box, towel and rod as they walked. "Over there is the cabin you'll be using. There aren't any units around it, but it's close to the lodge, so there'll be a lot of foot traffic going by. We have quiet time from 11:00 p.m. to 8:00 a.m., so no one should disturb you during that span."

She gazed at the small wood cabin that would be her home for the foreseeable future. Screens enclosed a front porch just big enough for a rocker. A lattice skirt circled the base of the cabin. She envisioned some colorful pots filled with flowers to brighten the all-wood exterior, maybe a wind chime or two and a floral wreath for the door.

Decorating it, making it her own, would be fun.

"You're welcome to get your breakfast from the camp store, but you do have a full refrigerator and a small stove. Each cabin can sleep four, but since you're alone, I assume you'll use the loft bed without unfolding the couch. There's only a small TV, but you have Wi-Fi."

She already knew all that from the brochures, so she only nodded.

Cooper paused, his light brown eyes staring down at her. "I know it's not much—"

"I love it. It's perfect."

His gaze lingered. "I think you mean that."

Every word. With a confidence she didn't always feel, she said, "I intend to be very happy here."

"Glad to hear it."

She cleared her throat. "There is one thing…"

"What's that?"

"I'm not very tech-savvy." At her age, it was a terrible thing to admit. "Is there anyone to help me set up the Wi-Fi?"

Looking somehow relieved, he smiled. "We'll make sure you get set up. No problem." He continued on, his pace easy. "My house is up there."

Phoenix glanced in the direction he indicated, shading her eyes as he continued to speak.

"I have two high school boys who come on Mondays to cut the grass. If it's raining, they bump it back to the next day. It's your job to keep track of their hours and to supervise them when necessary. Overall they do a good job, but sometimes need to be prompted to stay off their phones and to clean up afterward."

"I'll take care of it." She looked back at his house again. Situated diagonally from her cabin, it sat atop a rise and overlooked the rest of the park.

"You can see that we've had some recent storms. A lot of cleanup needs to be done. Also, this is the time of year we check trees for dead branches. We don't want any falling on a camper's awning and doing damage."

"I'll go through the park and assess them all." Though she walked alongside him, her attention kept returning to his home. Like the little chapel they passed, it was made mostly of stone with arched entryways and it had a wooden addition on the left side. A path led down to the deepest section of the lake, with posted signs indicating that part was private to him.

"I cut my own grass," he said, as if he thought she was wondering.

"Really? It'd be a simple thing to add that area to the rest." With a riding mower, it wouldn't take much longer to keep the manicured lawn looking great.

"Not necessary." He gestured ahead. "The supply building is this way, and the maintenance building is at the end of the lane."

When Cooper took her arm, she automatically jerked back and would have fallen if he'd let go. Startled, she stared up at him and tried not to look so rattled.

Expression enigmatic, he slowly released her and indicated the limb in her path. "You would have tripped over it."

Because she hadn't been paying attention. *Way to make a good impression.* She forced a smile. "I'm sorry. I was admiring your house."

He looked back at the house as if he'd forgotten it was there—and didn't like remembering. When he returned his scrutiny to her, he looked different, more distant. "Did you catch anything I said?"

"I think so." Not really, but she dutifully pointed, "Supply building, lodge, showers—"

Consideration brought his brows together. "Ms. Rose, you told me you researched the park to get familiar with it, right?"

"Yes." Even without the tour, she probably could have told him where everything was located.

"I did the same."

Not understanding, she asked, "You researched the park?"

"No." He looked away as a woman opened her camper door and carried a bag of garbage to the curb for pickup. "I research all my employees prior to meeting them."

He'd researched...*her*?

Well, of course he had. That was the responsible thing to do. But how detailed had he gotten?

He watched her as if he could hear her breathing, which had the effect of making her hold her breath.

With too much gentleness, he explained, "Social media being what it is, it's not difficult to do."

"No," she said on a sharp exhalation. "I guess it's not."

"With you, I also found multiple news articles after a simple search of your name."

Horrified, she took a step back.

"I do background checks and research on everyone I hire," he repeated.

She wanted to leave...but knew she couldn't. Where would she go anyway?

To her sister? No, Ridley was already too concerned. When

next she saw her, Phoenix hoped to be back to her usual self, a woman her sister could admire rather than one she fretted over.

Her parents? God, no. She loved them dearly, but the last thing they needed was to start worrying about her again. They'd done enough of that already.

Back to a hotel? Though necessary at the time, it had turned into a miserable existence, like a self-imposed exile. Now that she was out, she never wanted to do that again.

She preferred to feel the sun on her skin and the earth on her hands.

This was her chance to make it happen, an opportunity to start over, to reclaim her life. She wouldn't give it up just because her privacy had been breached once more.

Far too serious, Cooper said, "I haven't mentioned your personal history to anyone else, and I won't. Nothing I found factored into my decision to hire you."

Well, that was something at least. "Thank you." She drew a deep breath and, putting it in the simplest terms, said, "I was hoping for a fresh start."

He stared out toward the lake. "I'm sorry for what you went through."

With more accusation than she intended, she asked, "Why do you even bring it up?" She didn't want to think about it, much less talk about it with a stranger. She definitely didn't want his pity.

As if he couldn't help himself, his gaze met hers again; neither of them looked away. "I mentioned it in case you need anything."

Phoenix couldn't blink. The sun behind him set a glow around his brown hair, emphasizing the breadth of his shoulders, his height. It was the oddest thing, but his size didn't really intimidate her. Not anymore.

And it had nothing to do with what he'd just said, but rather it was something about him, some vague sincerity…or sadness?

She shook her head. What exactly did he think he could give her?

And why were they both standing there staring at each other?

Shifting her stance to break the spell, she said with conviction, "I'm fine." Then thought to add, "Thank you."

He didn't look convinced. "If you change your mind—"

"I won't."

Maris called her name, catching up to them. "I have your cabin all ready. Would you like to see it?"

Cooper stepped away. "Thanks, Maris. You'll help her get settled?"

"Sure. Should I finish giving her the tour, too?"

"If you wouldn't mind." Smiling, he said, "Get her set up for our Wi-Fi, too." He glanced at Phoenix. "You can start tomorrow, Ms. Rose. I'll email you the names and phone numbers of your helpers, along with our usual schedule."

Phoenix realized she must have offended him to have him walking off without finishing his instructions, but she wasn't sure how to fix it. "I'll be ready."

He flashed her a subdued smile. "Welcome to Cooper's Charm. As the sign says, it's a good place to get away."

What the hell just happened? Cooper blindly headed for his house, disconcerted over the tension in his muscles, the hot rush of awareness. True, he'd been intrigued by Phoenix Rose since first reading her unusual name. Everything after that had only heightened the curiosity. Then there was the compassion, too, taking him by surprise, he felt it so strongly; he'd blamed it for his early decision to hire her.

But neither of those emotions explained his reaction when he'd *felt* her behind him, when he'd turned and met her eyes, widened behind her glasses.

He'd been all set to meet her, to treat her with gentle indifference. But she'd gone all still and quiet, which in turn had dredged up a heated rush of protectiveness.

And something else.

Something he hadn't experienced in so long, it was almost unfamiliar.

Blocking that thought, refusing to examine his reaction too closely, he headed for his house. He had plenty to keep him busy today. Every day, actually. Phoenix Rose would be one more employee. Nothing more, nothing less.

Somehow before the day was over, he'd convince himself of that.

June arrived hotter than usual, which meant the park was already packed. He still hadn't found a housekeeper, but now that Phoenix was with them and helping to split the extra work, the complaints had dwindled.

He wasn't surprised that she'd fit right in, at least with the women. With all men, him included, she seemed far more reticent. Polite always, friendly enough, but lacking any real warmth.

He understood why, of course. He'd read the awful details of the attack, of what she'd suffered. What he didn't understand was his continued fascination with her, a fascination that had grown each day.

Everything about her drew him. With no encouragement from her, he thought of her too often. When she was near, or hell, even just in view, he couldn't look away.

He recognized his interest as protective, concerned—the same things any moral, normal man would feel toward a woman who'd been hurt. But it was more than that, too.

It was personal.

That shouldn't be a surprise given her ripe curves, compelling pale blue eyes and air of quiet vulnerability tinged with pride.

The surprise was that it was more than just physical attraction. He wanted to seek her out, talk with her more, get to know her better.

With every other female employee, he'd had no problem drawing a professional line. It was only Phoenix who pushed him past a comfortably detached relationship.

However, her "do not touch" vibe, along with his respect for her privacy, kept him from showing any overt interest.

He'd lied when he told her that her background hadn't factored into him hiring her. It absolutely had. His routine research on a potential employee had taken him well beyond the usual superficial work record and into personal, life-changing issues. Of course he'd sympathized with her.

And admired her.

The woman was a fighter.

Caught in a web of his own interest, he stood at the kitchen door overlooking the park, coffee in hand, and waited for her to emerge from her cabin. Like clockwork, she stepped out promptly at 7:00 a.m. and started on her walk. She always went around the park first thing, checking for problems and getting her equipment out so she could start her work when quiet time ended.

Wearing modest shorts and a loose T-shirt, her inky-black hair in a clubbed ponytail, she headed for the maintenance building.

He studied her, not quite smiling but definitely… Hell, he didn't know what to call it. Enthralled?

Though she didn't seem to realize it, Phoenix Rose was a sexy little thing, short at five-four, especially when standing next to him. Most women would consider her plump, but most men—himself included—would focus on her big soft breasts, rounded hips and beautiful legs.

Definitely enthralled.

Her purposeful stride made her ponytail bounce. Made her breasts bounce, too. When her sleek hair was loose, the ends teased over her chest right where her nipples would be. She had a dimple in her chin, dainty but strong hands, a surprisingly narrow waist, and eyes the color of a summer sky.

Never before had he considered glasses sexy. But now… Maybe he liked them on Phoenix because he knew she used them to hide—much like a superhero. Whenever she got nervous, she touched them as if to remind herself they were there, adjusting them needlessly.

He could have told her that the glasses didn't conceal a thing. Neither did the loose shirt.

At his age, after what he'd had, what he'd lost, he didn't indulge relationship games—or even relationships, really. Those had ended with the death of his wife six years ago. These days, if he found a woman attractive, he let her know it. She either reciprocated and they had sex, or she didn't and he let it go. Neither outcome troubled him much.

Either way, he didn't get involved.

Phoenix was different.

Her vulnerability was as obvious as her hope. She wanted to make this work and because, in some ways, her reasons for coming to Cooper's Charm were the same as his, he'd been happy to give her the chance.

Smart move on his part.

She did a great job with the grounds, keeping everything tidy, well-trimmed, and adding a professional flair that really classed it up. Flowers bloomed in every bed, the walkways were cleanly edged, and even the trees looked healthier after she'd removed several branches.

Did she throw herself into her work to help her forget, as he'd once done? At twenty-four, she'd run a successful landscaping business. That is, until the incident six months ago. So maybe she was just a workhorse by nature.

Admirable for someone so young.

When Phoenix disappeared from his sight, he turned back into the kitchen and went to the computer station at the end of the counter. The laptop was already open and on, an image frozen on the screen.

Phoenix stared straight ahead, battered, her glasses missing, her eyes wide and vacant with shock as paramedics tended her. A moment that personal and devastating should have never been posted, but in the social media world of today, a lot of things were online that shouldn't be.

Coop didn't sit and he didn't need to read the accompanying story. He'd looked at the story so many times, he already knew it by heart. It still drew him far too often as he struggled to understand her better.

Six months ago, when Phoenix was alone at the business during a frigid day in November, two men had broken in armed with a handgun and an AR-15 style rifle. It had been such a successfully busy day selling Christmas trees and wreaths, the till was likely full.

The men had taken all her money along with some personal items—and then they'd assaulted her.

His muscles tensed as his hands fisted.

Not rape, thank God, though apparently one of them had tried as the other kept watch. Overall, they'd badly manhandled her, thrown her around, hurt and robbed her. It wasn't until a prospective customer stopped in to see if the shop was still open that she'd finally escaped.

The men had run away and to this day, they hadn't been caught.

Her security cameras showed the attack, but revealed only two very large men wearing ski masks.

Coop closed his eyes. For too long he'd existed in a state of numbness, functioning but unable to feel anything real.

Now he felt Phoenix's pain and fear, and so much more. It brought back his own pain—and the rage.

But at the same time, it gave him a purpose.

He couldn't help his wife, but he could help Phoenix.

Not easy to do when she rarely got comfortable with men.

From what he could glean off social media, she'd gone to a hotel after the attack and stayed there, surrounded by people—protected—until she'd moved to Cooper's Charm. Her Facebook page, once filled with fun memes, silly videos, and comments from family and friends, had gone silent except for things others had posted—encouragement, words of strength and the occasional note about missing her.

Eventually, despite her brief, undoubtedly obligatory replies, the posts from others had waned, too.

At first he'd wondered about the timeline being public instead of private. But she'd admitted to being tech-challenged, and he imagined she'd had other things on her mind than social media.

As if she'd forgotten all about it, it had taken months before she'd posted on her wall again, and then she'd shared a photo of herself, making a goofy face while holding a cup of steaming coffee. The text had read: Everyone relax, I'm still here.

Hundreds of replies poured in. Phoenix Rose had many people who cared about her, yet she'd moved two hours away to the park.

It didn't take a genius to realize she wanted to reclaim her life, and moving to his resort was the first big step. He hoped she found what she needed, but as he'd discovered, you couldn't be alone at a crowded resort, yet you could still be lonely.

The knock at the door drew him out of his thoughts. He closed the laptop and crossed the kitchen to the door, seeing through the glass pane that Phoenix stood there.

A new sensation broke through the gloom. Damned if it didn't feel like anticipation.

Shirtless and barefoot, dressed in only his jeans, Coop opened the door with a barely banked smile of welcome. "Good morning, Ms. Rose."

Her startled gaze went over his body first, then locked desperately to his face. She hastily straightened her already-straight glasses. "Mr. Cochran. I'm sorry to bother you, but I have a problem."

Maybe he should have pulled on a shirt…the hell he would. He was in his own home and if she planned to stick around, she'd have to get comfortable with him. Throughout the summer, most people dressed down, with women in halters and shorts or bikinis, and men more shirtless than not. People were in and out of the water all day, from sunup to sundown.

Maybe if he hadn't just been thinking about her and all she'd been through, he would have handled things differently. Instead, he corrected her for the tenth time, saying, "You know, everyone else calls me Coop." He couldn't very well call her by her first name if she insisted on boss/employee formality. Not that there was much about the resort that anyone could label as "formal." It was all about fun, relaxation and getting away.

She stared up at him.

"Try it," he urged. "I promise it won't hurt."

2

AFTER A FEW BREATHLESS SECONDS, PHOENIX'S GAZE flickered away. Ignoring his request—hell, pretending he hadn't even said it—she explained, "The mower won't start. I tried to find Daron, but apparently he's off today."

Coop stifled a growl of frustration. She needed time, not pressure, so he concentrated on the reason she'd come to see him. If he couldn't get her to relax, he could at least be helpful.

Daron Hardy was the twenty-five-year-old handyman extraordinaire who worked for the park. He could fix anything, which made him valuable, but he was also a huge player. Coop had no doubt that Phoenix had already caught Daron's eye.

The good thing about Daron, though, besides his skill at repairs, was that he could be trusted, and he was a gentleman at heart. Daron would never deliberately make a woman uncomfortable. He didn't hear it very often, but he understood the word *no*.

Coop stepped into his kitchen, saying, "Come on in."

"I..." She hesitated at the door, then looked behind herself as if checking for avenues of escape.

Pretending he didn't see her uneasiness, Coop said, "I'll have to give him a call. He stayed out last night but said he'd be back sometime this morning. Coffee?"

She glanced at the pot with the same intensity she'd given his chest. Coop wasn't sure if that was a good or a bad thing.

Assuming he'd convince her, he got down another mug, filled it, set it on the table and pulled out a chair—all without looking directly at Phoenix again. He reached for the phone near his laptop and dialed up Daron, then leaned back on the counter.

Cautiously, leaving the door open behind her, Phoenix entered the kitchen and eased into the chair. She wrapped both hands around the mug as if chilled, which was impossible given the warm morning. While Coop waited for Daron to answer, she sipped the hot coffee.

The phone stopped ringing.

"Shh, hang on," Coop heard in a whisper, and then, in a normal tone, "Hello?"

It didn't surprise Coop to hear a woman giggling in the background. Daron was an active, healthy young man. Working at the park shouldn't hinder a social life. Daron seemed to have found the right balance.

"Sorry to interrupt," Coop said.

"No problem, boss. 'Sup?"

Watching Phoenix, seeing how she avoided looking at him, Coop briefly explained the issue.

"Damn," Daron said. "That thing's been on life support for a while, but it was purring just fine after the last time I tweaked it."

"It's probably past time for me to—" Coop heard the woman say something else.

Daron started to shush her, ended up laughing, and said quickly into the phone, "Give me twenty minutes or so and I'll head back."

"You don't have to rush."

"See ya soon, Coop." The call disconnected.

Easily imagining why Daron had left so quickly, Coop looked at the phone, shook his head in amusement and then put it back on the desk.

Not bothering to hide his amusement, he sat opposite Phoenix. "He should be back in another hour…or two."

"He didn't say for sure?"

"He's a little preoccupied with a date."

"Oh." Smiling, she looked up—then at his shoulders and chest—and quickly tucked back a tendril of hair. "I forgot about his date."

"He told you about it?"

"Daron mentions all his dates." She sent him a crooked grin. "He's hilarious sometimes."

As long as she was laughing at Daron, Coop figured he had nothing to worry about. "That's probably not how most women describe him."

"True." She chuckled. "He doesn't lack female attention, that's for sure."

"But you see him differently?"

She sipped her coffee. "He's young."

Coop lifted his brows. "He's twenty-five, the same age as you."

"Ah, but my sister says I'm an old soul." She wrinkled her nose. "And that's nicer than when she calls me a stick in the mud."

Cooper grinned. "We can't all be the life of the party."

"Right? That's what I tell her." She traced a finger around the top rim of the mug. "I hate that I'm interrupting Daron's plans."

"He was due back soon anyway." Coop studied her. Those small smiles of hers packed a hell of a wallop. "I assume it's that ancient rider that won't start?" They had two push mowers, too, but they weren't for the big areas.

"Yes."

To keep her around a little longer, he asked, "Was it acting up yesterday?"

"Pretty much always. I don't have Daron's talent, but I can usually get it to start with a little tinkering. This time—nothing."

"Dead battery, maybe?"

She shook her head. "I checked that." With a lot of concentration, she looked at him again, her gaze fixed only on his face. "Mr. Cochran—"

"Coop."

She paused, then dutifully said, "Coop, have you considered replacing it?"

Finally hearing her say his name gave him a deep sense of satisfaction. At thirty-four, smiles, glasses and first names shouldn't have affected him at all, but then, something about Phoenix had struck a nerve from the moment he'd seen the first article on her assault. "Every time it quits on me."

Damn, he wanted to kiss her.

And she couldn't even look at him.

It was an odd sensation not to recognize himself and his reactions. After a year of his life lost to a mournful rage, it had taken him a long time to regain his control, to tamp down those useless emotions. In the four years since then he'd stayed busy to keep himself in check.

Now, those volatile feelings seemed misdirected, still there, simmering deep inside, but with an entirely different motivation.

"You have?" Phoenix sat forward, an elbow on the table, enthusiasm in her eyes. "I know it's a big expense, but a zero-turn mower would be ideal."

Inspiration struck, and he said, "At the end of the month, we could check them out together if you want." Before she could deny him, he added, "I'd need you to help me choose the best one for the park."

She retreated back in her seat. "I'm sure any would do."

True. Plus, he wasn't so inept that he couldn't choose a

damned mower. That wasn't the point, though. "Why have a landscaping expert around if not to get an expert opinion? We wouldn't have to go far. There's a dealer in Woodbine with everything from massive farm equipment to small push mowers for tiny yards." He saw the indecision in her pale blue eyes, made larger by the lenses of her glasses. "You're the one who will be responsible for it, so it makes sense for you to help choose it."

"But—"

"You'd be on the clock, of course."

Fascinated by the visible process, he watched as she debated with herself, stiffened her spine, nudged her glasses farther up the bridge of her nose and nodded.

Amused by her, and impressed with her fortitude, he asked, "Yes?"

"Okay, yes." Her attention dipped to his body, then shot back to his face. Her eyes narrowed in concentration. "We can do that."

Her agreement released the tension in his muscles, when he didn't even want to admit to being tense.

He definitely shouldn't have been tense.

"Great." Did that mean she trusted him, at least a little? He knew he was losing his grip on his carefully tempered emotions; he'd deliberately kept himself from feeling too much, because feeling hurt had turned him into a person he didn't recognize.

For the first time in years, it didn't alarm him. These feelings weren't chaotic and hard-edged. If anything, they were… soft. And enjoyable.

A twinge of disquiet went through him, but he ignored it. "I'll go over the calendar, talk to the dealer and let you know well in advance what day we'll go."

"Sounds good." She finished off her coffee and stood.

Coop stood, too—and this time her attention went all over him, even the fly of his jeans. He fought back all natural inclinations in an effort to keep the moment casual. Phoenix wasn't a woman to rush, and he doubted the look had been an invitation. Probably more like curiosity, and he'd take what he could get. "Let me know if Daron can't get the old mower going, okay?"

"We could get by with the push mowers for a few weeks."

He didn't want her to have to *get by*. "Let me know, Phoenix."

As if the use of her name no longer fazed her, she nodded. "Will do." She surprised him by carrying her cup to the sink. Once there, she noticed the photo near his closed laptop. For a long moment, she stared at it, her head slightly tilted.

He didn't explain. He *couldn't* explain.

Something softened in her expression. Without a word, she turned to go.

Relieved, Coop moved toward the door with her. Talking about his wife was always difficult and now, with those strange emotions gripping him, he didn't dare go down that road.

"Thanks for the coffee."

"You're welcome. I'll check in with you later to make sure Daron has things going. If you need anything else, let me know."

When she stepped outside, the bright sunshine put blue highlights into her smooth ebony hair. With her eyes squinted against the glare, she stared toward thc lake. "That's your private dock?"

"Yes. The buoys mark the no-swim area for guests, making it safer for me to take my boat out to the main body of water, and for me to swim away from the resort guests."

"I've seen other boats way out there."

"People ski or go tubing. But you haven't even swum yet, have you? You know the water's warmed up a lot. You should take a dip." He wouldn't mind seeing her skinned down to a bikini.

She gave him a look bordering on horror. "Not me."

Propping a shoulder against the door frame, he asked, "Why not you?" Was she worried that a bikini might invite male attention? He sorted through the idea, and realized that, after the assault, she wasn't only uncomfortable around men, she actually feared a man's attention.

A man's touch.

The thought brought a frown. A woman like Phoenix Rose should be enjoying every aspect of life, not shying away from the physical—

"I can't swim." She scowled with the admission.

Not buying that for a second, he asked, "So you never swam in your grandparents' pond?"

"The fish were bigger than me. I mean, when I was a kid." She held her hands apart about two feet. "The carp and catfish were huge."

He liked the image of her as a little girl awed by the size of a fish. "You know they're more afraid of you than you are of them."

"I know that now." She took a few steps away and hesitated. With exasperation, she admitted, "I can swim."

"Yeah?" Damn, she was cute—and obviously honest. An irresistible combo. "So why the fib?"

Would she be honest with him now? Was she afraid of intimacy?

She rolled one shoulder, then swatted the air. "Because admitting that I'm not comfortable in a crowd is lame. But then I realized that saying I couldn't swim sounded just as lame, so..."

The admission twisted his heart, and turned his tone gruff. "I'm glad you can swim, and I understand about crowds." Was it *only* crowds? He wished he had the words for more specific questions.

She actually laughed. Just for a second, then she quickly cut it off.

Coop studied her face, the way she flattened her lips to fight the grin. *Really nice lips.* "What's funny?"

"If you don't know, maybe I shouldn't tell you."

Teasing—that had to be a good sign. If she feared him, would she do that? He didn't think so.

He pushed away from the door. "Come on, now. Don't leave me guessing."

She grinned. "Well…you realize that you hired me to work around crowds, right?"

"True." As if lit from the inside, her eyes were beautifully bright when she laughed. "But working around them is not the same as mingling."

"No, it's not." She scrunched her nose and again looked at the lake. "I could maybe swim without mingling."

He could tell she wanted to. "It wouldn't be easy. Between the scuba divers, the paddle boaters, the flirting adults and the splashing kids, you'd pretty much be in the thick of it."

"Yeah, probably." She gave a wistful sigh. "It's not crowded early on the weekdays."

A slow burn started through his blood, and to his surprise, he easily accepted that it was both physical…and emotional. "Would you like to swim early one morning?"

"Maybe." As if she only just then realized the direction of the conversation, she said, "Oh, I don't mean with you."

Cocking a brow, he asked in mock affront, "Why not with me?"

Her dark lashes fluttered in nervousness. "You're part of the crowds."

Damn, he did not want to be lumped in with the masses. He wanted to be different. He wanted to be more.

Softly, he said, "Not if it's just me."

"But I…" Her words trailed off.

"You what?" he prompted.

Defiant, she whispered, "I don't look that great in a bathing suit."

His imagination went into hyperdrive. "I find that very hard to believe."

At his inadvertent husky tone, pleasure colored her cheeks. "I'm…" She gestured. "You know. Maybe a little thick?"

Coop nearly choked on a laugh, but he knew she wouldn't understand so he turned it into a cough. Here he was, getting semihard thinking of her stripped down a little, and she thought he might be disappointed.

His gaze went unerringly to her breasts. "That's not how I'd describe you."

A little breathless, she said, "No?"

He looked at her closely, watchful for fear or anxiety. Instead, he saw interest in her eyes.

"Can I be frank?" On the heels of that, he explained, "I don't want to overstep or…make you nervous."

Pride lifted her chin. "I'm not nervous."

Though she didn't say it, he heard the unspoken qualifier: *Not with you.*

Pleased that some of the barriers were crumbling, he smiled. "All right then. I'd say soft, curvy." His gaze moved over her body. "Sexy." As he looked at her, her breathing hitched and her color intensified.

She blinked, nodded and let out a breath. "Thank you."

He was probably pushing too fast, way too fast, but he heard himself say low, "You don't ever have to be afraid of me, Phoenix. I swear, there's no reason."

Her eyes flared, then narrowed in defensive annoyance. "I'm not."

Hoping that wasn't a lie, he said, "Good. Then we can swim sometime?"

She shook her head. "I'm *not* afraid, it's just—" With an agitated huff, she reached back to flip up her ponytail, letting the humid summer air kiss her nape. After a quick peek up at the sun, she put clip-on sunglasses over her lenses. "I'm sometimes uneasy. That's all."

"With me?"

Immediately, she shook her head. "No." Her frown deepened, this time, he suspected, with confusion. "No, not with you." As if realizing what she'd said, she rushed into new conversation. "It's going to be crazy hot today. I better get to work before the sun starts roasting everything in sight." She turned away, taking two fast steps.

"Phoenix."

She stopped, waited and finally glanced back.

With the sunglasses in place, he couldn't tell if she looked at his face or his naked upper body. Either was okay with him. "You're doing a great job."

"Thanks." A small smile came and went. "For the compliments and the nice visit."

"Anytime." Coop watched her leave with a long, purposeful stride. He thought of everything she'd gone through.

The bruises had healed, but some of the wounds remained.

Still, they'd gotten to a first-name basis. She'd smiled. She'd chatted.

She'd more or less admitted that she felt differently with him.

He'd call that progress.

I saw his wife.

Phoenix sent the text to Ridley, then waited for a reply.

Her phone rang instead. She was alone in the maintenance building, so she answered. "Hey, Ridley."

"What *wife*? When did he get a wife? All this time I thought we were discussing a single guy!"

"He is single, but he's widowed." She thought of the image on his desk area and grew wistful. "She was beautiful."

"I didn't know," Ridley said. "How long ago did she die?"

"Maris told me about her. You know, the woman—"

"Who runs the camp store, yup. I have all the characters clear in my head."

Phoenix laughed. "They're not *characters*."

"Well, I've never met them because someone won't invite me

to visit, so for me, they're not yet three-dimensional, regardless of your great descriptions."

Ridley had been using that sarcastic tone since Phoenix was four years old. It stopped working on her when she'd turned twelve or so, but Ridley, three years older, had never given it up.

Now, it merely seemed a part of her sister's personality of snark tempered with love.

Giving a credible snort, Phoenix said, "It's beautiful here, and loads of fun, but you know it's not your style."

"My style is ever evolving," she said in lofty tones. "So when did he lose his wife?"

"Maris said it was six years ago, before he bought the park."

"Do you know how she died?"

Phoenix tucked the phone against her shoulder so she could continue prepping for work. "No. Maris isn't really the gossipy type."

"And neither are you, so I suppose you didn't ask?"

"Of course not. It makes me feel so bad for him, though. He's a great guy. Can you imagine going through something like that?" As soon as she said it, Phoenix cringed. "I mean—"

"No worries, sis." Ridley adopted her best *I don't give a shit* tone. "My situation was entirely different and I know it. I may have lost a man, but he's still living."

True, but Ridley's ex had been so cruel in how he'd left her and the reasons he'd given…

"Stop it," Ridley commanded. "I'm loaded, thanks to that dick, so I get to live the life I love. That is, the life I love minus seeing my sister who won't let me visit."

Phoenix rolled her eyes. "I'll visit you on my next day off."

"Now where's the fun in that? I want to ogle the man candy."

Phoenix choked. She definitely didn't want Ridley doing that. "Daron is too young for you. Heck, he's too young for me and he's my age!"

"I wasn't talking about our studly repairman, fun as that

sounds. It's the head honcho I want to see. The way you've described him… *Rowrrrr.*"

Phoenix felt her face go hot. In a low whisper, she said, "I haven't!"

"Oh, it comes through, sis. Pure lust."

"It's not!"

"You're screeching. That's a telltale sign of lust, you know."

Phoenix exhaled a deep breath and said more calmly, "I'm not lusting."

"I hope you're fibbing, because I was totally jazzed over the possibility."

"Ridley," she warned. *Was she lusting?* Maybe a little bit. And that was a huge deal. For a while there, she'd only been able to see men as threats first, and once that faded, with indifference.

There were so many other priorities that required her focus…

"Men and sex and all the good stuff in between are things you should be enjoying," Ridley said. "I know you think you can't right now, but I promise, it's just like riding a bike. Once you've learned it, you never forget. It all comes back in an instant."

Phoenix burst out laughing.

"Let me guess," Ridley said, her voice deadpan. "You're imagining pedals and those narrow seats?"

Sputtering with her hilarity, Phoenix added, "And ten-speeds!"

Ridley laughed too, then snuck in, "So you *do* like him, huh?"

Sudden caution washed away her humor. Ridley was like a bloodhound on the scent. "Who, Daron? Yes, he's nice and he's good at what he does."

"I'm not dumb and you're not dumb, so give over already."

She sighed. "Yes, I like Cooper, but like is not lust, Ridley. And I don't know when…or rather *if*, I'll ever again be comfortable with that."

"You will be." Ridley said it with conviction. "I think you're almost there already, and I have that resort owner to thank for it."

"Rather than debate it," she said, "I have to get to work."

"Okay, sorry for calling. I just needed to hear your voice."

Phoenix softened. What would she have done without her sister? Ridley was more than a sibling, more than a best friend.

Sometimes, Ridley was everything.

Smiling, Phoenix said softly, "It was nice to hear yours, too."

"Smooches."

"Smooches back atcha." As Phoenix slipped the phone into her back pocket, she heard a sound and whirled.

Daron stood at the entrance to the maintenance building, his not-quite-six-foot frame lounged against the opening. He wore a ball cap backward over his shaggy brown hair, loose board shorts, an unbuttoned shirt and a playfully leering smile. "Did I just hear you making kissing sounds with a guy?"

Relieved to see a familiar face rather than the boogeymen who haunted her dreams, Phoenix grinned. Daron she could handle. He was never serious, didn't push, and she had no real problems being around him. "Actually, that was my sister."

"Yeah?" His brows climbed. "Younger or older?"

"Older by three years."

Suggestively, he asked, "Does she look like you?"

"Chubby? No. She has some red in her hair, but we have the same eyes."

Daron pushed away from the wall. "Just so you know, you're *chubby* in all the right places."

She looked down at her chest, laughed and said, "Well, yes, Ridley and I have *that* in common." It was so odd that she could joke with Daron in a way she couldn't with Cooper. How she felt about Cooper made all the difference, but it still surprised her that she could be so easy with Daron.

"If she ever visits, I want to meet her."

"Trust me, Ridley would insist on it." She gestured at the

riding mower. "I think it died, but if you can revive it for a few more weeks, that'd be great."

"Why just a few weeks?"

"Because after that, Cooper says he'll look into a zero-turn."

"Whoa." Daron rocked back on his heels. "How'd you talk him into that?"

"I just mentioned it."

"Yeah, well, I've mentioned it to him a hundred times but he always just tells me to resuscitate the poor old thing." He lifted the hood on the mower and began tinkering. "Because it came with the park when he bought it, Coop considers it nostalgic."

Thinking of the photo of Cooper's wife, Phoenix asked, "Were you here already when Cooper bought it?"

"Nah. I was working part-time in town at the grocery while going to school for an associate degree in business. Coop was in buying groceries when this older lady's car died on her. I went out to the lot to get it going. I guess a few customers told Coop that I had a knack because after watching me work, he offered me a job—and I agreed. Best decision I ever made."

Probably one of Cooper's better decisions too, Phoenix thought. She knew Daron was invaluable to the running of the place. "Has it changed much since he took over here?"

"Are you kidding? It's all different." He rolled one shoulder. "Better."

"New employees?"

"For the most part." He grunted as he twisted something. "Most had already moved on or retired."

Fascinating. She watched Daron's arms flex, then something gave way. Frowning, he switched positions.

"I guess he changed the name after buying the resort?" That was the one thing that surprised her. Cooper didn't seem the type to flaunt ownership, or to draw attention to himself.

Daron grinned. "I did that. The big sign up front used to say Cherry's Charm."

"The previous owner was named Cherry?"

Shrugging, he said, "That, or the name came from all the weeping cherry trees." He adjusted a few more things inside the hood of the mower. "The sign was all but falling off the pole, so Coop told me to take it down. Talk about nostalgia—it was a vintage sign, shaped like an old camper, you know? I couldn't see pitching something like that, so I removed the rust, repaired the lights, repainted it with Coop's name and hung it properly."

What a wonderful thing for him to do. "And the name stuck."

"Much to Coop's annoyance." He raised his head from the engine to flash her a sheepish grin. "He eventually forgave me."

Phoenix tried to resist, but curiosity got the better of her. "He'd already lost his wife when you met him?"

Daron paused, his expression troubled. "Yeah, that's why he came here." He glanced up again. "I think it was like a fresh start or something. A way to move forward instead of just…suffering."

Her heart squeezed painfully at the idea of him hurting. She thought of the sign and whispered, "Cooper's Charm. A good place to get away."

"I guess Coop thought so, since he bought the park and he's been here ever since." Stepping back, he said, "Give her a go."

Trying to reclaim her light mood from moments ago, Phoenix sat on the riding mower seat and, after inserting the key, she pressed the clutch, checked that the mower was in Neutral and turned the key. It fired right up.

"There you go," Daron said with a bow as he closed the hood. "My work here is done."

"Actually," she said over the engine, "there's some issue in the laundry."

"Always is." With a jaunty walk, he saluted her on his way out.

Phoenix sat there a moment, then she withdrew her phone and opened the ongoing text conversation with her sister. She typed in, Cooper's Charm is a good place to get away.

Ridley replied with a smiley face.

They both knew that no matter where she lived, if she truly wanted the past behind her, she had to fully face the future.

A week later, Phoenix darted through a drizzling rain and into the camp store. It was still early, but she saw lights on and figured she'd join Maris in a cup of coffee. The two of them got along well and Maris was friendly without being intrusive.

Unfortunately, as she rushed in, her wet sneakers met the tile floor and came out from under her. She flailed in the air.

A strong pair of hands caught her under her arms. "Easy." Those same hard hands got her upright and then lingered as she turned to see who owned that deep voice.

The shock of his touch hit her first, followed swiftly by a stab of…well, not exactly fear, but definitely uncertainty.

She was reflecting on the progress she'd made, pleased that she could think calmly enough to know she was in a room with friends, when she looked up—into vivid green eyes framed by sun-bleached blond hair, all wrapped up in muscled perfection.

Her tongue stuck to the roof of her mouth.

Beside her, she heard a chuckle and turned her head to see another—more familiar—vision, this one with darker hair in a perpetually tousled state, rich brown eyes and a huge smile.

"Daron." She straightened and stepped away from the man holding her. "I… Sorry, the floor is slippery."

"Especially in the rain," the man agreed.

"Don't worry about it, Phoenix," Daron teased. "All the women ogle Baxter. He's used to it."

Baxter said, "Shut up, Daron," without any evident animus. "It was mutual ogling."

Oh, *no, no, no.* Accepting his assistance without fear was one thing. Anything else was out of the question.

Daron whistled. "And the day just got more interesting."

This time Phoenix glared at him. He pretended to lock his lips. *Right.* Like she'd believe that.

Daron might be a fun-loving, harmless guy, but he was rarely quiet.

Baxter, she knew, was the scuba instructor. She'd visually admired him from a distance several times—after all, she might be damaged but she was still a woman. She'd already known that Baxter was lean, strong and undeniably gorgeous. However, that hadn't prepared her for seeing him up close. The man was put together very finely.

Rather than continue looking the fool, she pushed aside the nervousness and, putting on her most polite and purely social expression, she held out a hand. "I'm Phoenix Rose. We haven't had a chance to meet."

"Phoenix. Interesting name." Thankfully, at least from her perspective, he picked up on her lack of personal attraction. "Baxter McNab. I'm the scuba instructor and director."

"I've seen you with groups at the lake." She looked down at the wet floor. "Thanks for the good catch."

His gaze slanted to Daron. "Dumb-ass over there did the same thing, only I didn't bother catching him."

Daron dramatically rubbed his sexy behind. "I think I broke my...pride."

From the other side of the counter, Maris asked, "Coffee?"

"You read my mind." With a fleeting smile toward the men, Phoenix headed for a stool. "I hope this rain doesn't last."

To her surprise, Baxter took the seat right next to her. Until Maris refilled his cup, Phoenix hadn't noticed it. Now it was too late for her to get up and move without looking rude, which would draw unwanted attention.

"It's going to rain all day," Baxter predicted. "Long as there's no lightning, it won't interrupt my day."

"Wetsuits," Daron said, taking the seat on the other side of her, "are impervious to rain. But you and I—" he gestured at Phoenix and himself "—won't be able to get anything done."

Hunks as bookends. Not that long ago, she would have been

crawling out of her skin, but now—although a little uncomfortable—she accepted the situation as harmless.

She was congratulating herself for that small coup when Maris slid a cup of coffee in front of her, already doctored with creamer and sugar. "Thank you." Phoenix couldn't imagine a better way to toast her continued improvement than with fresh, strong coffee.

Sounding glum, Maris said, "Odds are it'll be a thunderstorm that shuts down everything."

"I don't mind storms." In fact, she usually liked them. For Phoenix, they helped to insulate her in her own little world, away from memories that could still cut deep.

"Storms mean you can't work," Maris explained. "But it also means everyone in the park is going to try crowding in here or the rec center for indoor entertainment."

"If I'm not working, I could come by and help you."

Maris gave a look to Daron and Baxter. "Notice neither of *them* made that offer."

Daron leaned over the counter. "You want me to keep you company, Maris?" His eyebrows bobbed. "Be happy to oblige."

Baxter shook his head. "She's turned you down...what? A dozen times? Give it a rest already."

"When I can sense victory? No way!"

With a slight flush to her skin, Maris rolled her eyes, then concentrated on Phoenix. "I just took some scones out of the oven. Cranberry orange. Want one?"

"Oh, that sounds delicious."

Baxter scowled past Phoenix at Daron. "I'm blaming you for us not getting scones."

"Me? What'd I do?"

"What haven't you done?" Maris asked.

He grinned. "Not much."

"You brag like a high school boy," she accused.

"Any high school boy who's been with you probably had reason to brag."

Maris fried him with a look. "What the hell does that mean?"

"Yeah..." Sheepish, he rubbed the back of his neck. "That didn't come out quite right. I didn't mean bragging rights because they scored."

Maris's expression darkened further.

"I meant because you're a catch. You know, if you gave them any attention, it was reason to brag."

This time Maris rolled her eyes. "If you have to explain it—"

"Should've kept my mouth shut, I know."

Phoenix couldn't help but laugh. Serious come-ons, even when not directed at her, could still make her fidgety, but ridiculous teasing only amused her, and Daron was all about the ridiculous.

Maris didn't appear to have the same reaction as she set the plate on the bar counter. "I suppose there's enough to go around."

"You see?" Daron said as he reached for a flaky scone. "Deep down, she adores me."

Right before his fingers touched the plate, Maris snatched it out of his reach. She put two on a napkin in front of Phoenix, and two in front of Baxter. With her nose in the air, she headed into the kitchen.

Undaunted, Daron turned puppy dog eyes on Phoenix.

Grinning, she took one and scooted the napkin with the other over to him. "You're shameful." Using the excuse of following Maris, she slipped out from between the two men.

The phone in her pocket buzzed with a message.

Knowing it would be Ridley, she withdrew it and saw, Good morning, doll across the screen.

Smiling, she texted back, Good morning. Storms here. You?

Sunny skies. As usual, Ridley added, I miss you.

And as usual, Phoenix replied, I miss you, too. I'll visit soon.

You keep saying that.

Yes, she did, but she wasn't yet ready. She wanted to be herself when she saw Ridley again. She needed to prove that she was strong enough to reclaim her life.

Soon, she promised herself. Very soon.

Rather than explain all that to Ridley, which would have her big sister sweeping in for a rescue, she quickly texted, I'm at work. Gotta go.

Love you, Phoenix.

Her heart swelled. Love you, too.

Caught by the wind, the door slammed opened again and Cooper stepped in. More powerful than the storm, he commanded attention in his calm, take-charge way.

The rain had darkened his sandy-brown hair, leaving it stuck in thick hanks to his forehead and neck. His wet T-shirt clung to his wide chest and shoulders. None of that seemed to bother him.

She'd thought Baxter was devastating, but now that Cooper joined them, the room felt smaller and far steamier. He had that type of presence about him, whether he intended to or not.

When it came to her reactions, no man could make her more physically aware than Cooper Cochran.

3

PHOENIX DRANK IN THE SIGHT OF HIM. HOW A MAN could look so appealing, even when drenched, she didn't know. She was a frazzled mess, her damp clothes drooping, and he only looked sexier because of the rain.

She thought of his invitation to swim privately, and the idea teased her. He'd made a point of letting her know that he appreciated her curves, which seemed odd since his wife had appeared to be very slim, yet she didn't doubt his sincerity. She'd seen the admiration in his eyes and heard it in his deep voice.

She'd never obsessed much about her body. She'd "blossomed" early in life, which meant she'd gotten jibes, and then a ton of interest, from boys and later men. Her weight fluctuated depending on her life, so there were times when she was slimmer, and times when—like now—she'd put on pounds.

Of course, living in a hotel room while binge-eating takeout for an extended time explained her current weight gain. For too many nights she'd shut out the real world, even her family, and soothed her fears with food. She'd always been an outdoorsy person, but after the attack…instead of taking her comfort in sunshine and hard work, she'd consumed milkshakes, pizzas and loaded burgers with fries while watching whatever movie played on the television. Overall, she had amazing physical health with no medical issues, so if the scales fluctuated, she didn't care.

She also didn't expect to draw male appreciation. But she had—from Cooper.

His interest hit her on two levels, spiking her own sexual response, which hadn't happened since before the attack, but it also struck an emotional chord because she knew he'd loved his wife, and yet he'd lost her.

How very difficult that must have been for a man like Cooper. Anyone could see he was a natural leader, and that went hand in hand with being protective.

She'd like to know how he'd lost his wife, but she also didn't want to overstep.

With him now in the camp store, a heated mix of subdued wariness and unfamiliar exhilaration shimmered together through her blood. He brought with him the scent of the rain and the energy of the storm, making the other two men fade from her awareness.

Under one arm, Cooper carried a rolled, rubber-backed rug. Before fully entering, he spread it out on the floor and then used it to wipe his feet.

When he looked up and saw Phoenix, his entire demeanor changed, or so it seemed to her.

But maybe she was the only one getting flustered.

Maris emerged from the kitchen with a large towel. "Thanks, Coop." She tossed the towel to him. "We already had two slips, Daron in a full wipeout, and Phoenix in a near miss. Luckily, Baxter caught her."

For some reason, a blush stung her face. No one seemed to notice—except Cooper.

As he ran the towel over the back of his head and neck, his eyes never left her. "You're not hurt?"

She shook her head. "No, not at all. But the rug's a good idea."

"It's usually there," Maris said, "but right before I closed last night a camper brought in his dog—and he peed on it."

"The camper did?" Daron asked.

"No, his… Oh, hush." While Daron snickered, Maris filled another cup of coffee and reached over the counter to hand it to Cooper. "The guy was horrified, but luckily he didn't yell at the poor dog, who he said was still being trained." As she headed back to the kitchen, she said over her shoulder, "I promised him it wasn't a problem."

"We're pet friendly for most breeds," Cooper told Phoenix, right before he stripped off his shirt and laid it over the back of a booth seat. Using the fluffy towel, he dried his impressive body—at least, impressive to her. No one else seemed to pay any attention.

Yet Phoenix couldn't look away. Dark hair sprinkled his chest between his brown nipples, thickest in the middle between pronounced pec muscles. His skin was taut, firm over his midsection, more muscular at his abs. The hair teased around his navel, then cut into a thin line that disappeared into his low waistband.

Realizing where she stared, she desperately grabbed her own coffee to give herself a different focus.

Something other than his sleek skin, his firm muscles, his scent—and his overwhelming presence.

Did no one else feel it?

She glanced up again as he raised an arm, still drying off. Why did it feel so intimate to see the lighter skin on the underside of his biceps, the tufts of hair there? Lightning flashed through the windows and only a second later, thunder shook the floor, drawing her from her fascinated scrutiny.

Baxter lifted his coffee in a toast. "Looks like I'm off for the morning, too."

Cooper moved to a window to look out. "Damn, it's really coming down. Hopefully it blows over." The wet waistband of his jeans hung low, and she could just see the top of dark, snug boxers. The tanned skin of his back glistened from the dampness.

Her palms tingled at the thought of touching him...

"More ogling?" Daron whispered, leaning close so no one else heard him.

Phoenix jumped as if goosed.

"I won't tell," he said, then grinned hugely.

"Nothing to tell," Phoenix whispered back, but damn it, she knew her face was red.

"Uh-huh. That was a hungry look I saw, almost as if you were imagining him *nekkid*." He tsked, his tone playful. "Does he know you're—"

"Daron." Neither of them noticed Cooper's approach until he spoke. "Get hold of Joy and see if she can get some extra stuff set up in the lodge."

"Sure thing." He pulled his cell from his back pocket. As he stepped away, he said, "I'll see if she needs any help, too."

Phoenix had only met Joy Lee, the entertainment director, a few times. Her impression was of a tall, elegant woman with light brown hair, vivid green eyes and a cute five-year-old son that she adored. Joy took great pleasure in organizing activities for adults and children alike, and she did it with flair.

Baxter said, "I need to email folks that we're canceled for this morning and iffy for the afternoon. After that, just let me know what you need." He withdrew his own phone and headed to the back of the store to the dining tables.

Left alone with Cooper, Phoenix struggled to keep her gaze on his face, but it wasn't easy. Even after toweling off, his skin looked dewy and his sparse chest hair fascinated her. It looked soft, a little darker than the hair on his head, but then, his brows and lashes were dark, too.

"Phoenix?"

It'd be easier not to stare if she wasn't eye level with his chest.

Someone turned on music, and suddenly one of Kid Rock's

country songs filled the air. The way Daron grinned, she assumed he was the culprit. Even as he spoke on the phone, he winked at her.

The music ensured she and Cooper wouldn't be overheard while speaking, and that somehow made his closeness more intimate.

Needing a distraction and fast, she dared a quick look up at Cooper. He stared down at her as if they weren't in the middle of the camp store with three other people. His wet eyelashes created a compelling frame for his direct, amber eyes. He said nothing, just continued to look down at her.

Almost like he might kiss her.

Whoa. The air got thick enough to choke her.

Obviously, nothing in his lambent gaze would help her heartbeat slow down, so she hastily removed her glasses on the pretext of cleaning the lenses on the hem of her T-shirt.

While she couldn't see him clearly, she asked, "I was thinking of helping Maris, unless there's something else you want me to do?"

"Such a loaded question."

She peered up at him, seeing only a blurred outline of his face. "What?"

"Never mind." She sensed his smile as he shook his head. "Are you any good on the computer?"

Her tech skills sucked, but she could type, copy or print, so she said, "Depends on what you want done."

Suddenly his fingertips touched under her chin, freezing her to the spot. "Are you going to put your glasses back on, or clean them until I leave?"

The challenge helped her catch her breath. She slipped on the glasses, then frowned up at him. "Better?"

"Definitely." His voice deepened as he tipped her face up even more. "At least now I know you can see me."

Yes, she saw him, and crazy as it seemed, she couldn't stop thinking about leaning into him.

"Damn," he whispered. His thumb brushed her jaw, then he withdrew his hand and looked around, almost as if he just realized they weren't alone.

More thunder boomed. With a disgusted look at the window, he snagged his coffee and took a long drink. "Mmm, I needed that."

Given the direction of her thoughts, he sounded far too sensual saying that. She cleared her throat. "Maris makes good coffee." It's why she often joined her instead of making it in her cabin, or so she told herself. But maybe the truth was that she didn't want to drink her coffee alone.

Not anymore.

She picked up her own cup and sipped.

After half a minute, Cooper seemed to recollect himself. "If you wouldn't mind, once Joy has a plan, you could put it on a flier and print out fifty copies. We'll leave a stack up here on the counter for anyone dropping into the store."

If he could be business as usual, then by God, she would, too. She forced a bright smile. "Great idea." She glanced at Daron again, hoping he'd have the details from Joy, but he had a shoulder braced on the wall and was still talking—or, knowing Daron, it was more like flirting. "Soon as he lets me know what to print, I'll take care of it."

"Sounds good." He finished off his coffee. "Will I see you at the lodge?"

The lodge aka rec center aka activity center was the largest building in the park. It was the main site for all activities from weddings and dancing to crafts and yoga. But that involved large groups of people and she preferred the solitude of her little cabin.

Before she could answer, Cooper said, "We could use your help tonight. It'll probably be busier than usual."

He'd just put her on the spot, and she had a suspicion he'd

done so on purpose. Of course, she did work for the park, so it made sense that he'd want all hands on deck. "What if the weather clears up?"

"You still won't be able to do more than clean up debris. The ground is saturated." He crowded closer and lowered his voice. "I know you're not keen on joining in, but it would be helpful."

He didn't leave her much choice. "Then of course I'll be there."

Daron joined them. "Joy has it under control."

"Took you that long to find out?" Cooper asked.

"Nope. But after I hung up with her, I got another call." His mouth tipped into a crooked grin. "Now that I have a date, I know how I'll be getting through the storm tonight."

"Tonight," Cooper repeated, "but today we'll need you around."

"Count on it."

The first group of people dashed in, five of them together.

"Get those fliers done," Cooper told her, before turning to talk to the guests.

Daron joined Phoenix in Maris's small office space, giving her info on evening bingo for the adults and special games and crafts planned for the kids throughout the day. She had to admit, it did sound fun—though she'd never played bingo before and had no real interest in starting now.

In no time, they had the fliers out. Daron headed off to help Joy set up, Baxter stuck around and helped take orders from a big morning crowd, and Phoenix happily ducked away to the kitchen to help with prep.

Cooper seemed to be everywhere, in and out of the rain as often as he was in the store, often helping campers with one problem or another. Each time she saw him, he'd obviously gotten drenched again with his hair plastered to his head, his shirt to his back. A look of deep concentration darkened his face, yet he remained friendly to all the campers.

Still, she couldn't help but notice that there was something different in how he spoke with others compared to how he spoke with her. She couldn't pinpoint the distinction, but she sensed it all the same.

Was he as interested as she was?

If so, would she be able to do anything about it? Given her recent history, she didn't know.

By midafternoon, the rain had finally let up, but the skies stayed dark and the lightning continued as muted flashes behind thick clouds in the distance.

While she could, Phoenix went out to remove fallen branches from the road. That proved to be a bigger job than she'd anticipated, keeping her busy right through dinner. She was just storing the wagon when her phone buzzed.

Knowing it'd be Ridley, she pulled it out and read the screen.

You sent the shitty weather my way.

Sorry, she typed. It's still drab here, too.

Does big sexy like the rain?

Grinning at the nickname Ridley gave to Cooper, she replied, Probably not, since it brings a lot of unique issues to the park. He's been running all day.

So no time to woo you, huh? That sucks.

Phoenix bit her lip in indecision, but this was Ridley, the person she was closest to in the whole world, and damn it, she wanted to share. She took a breath and typed, Actually, he touched my chin.

As the seconds went by without a reply, her tension mounted.

Finally, her screen blinked with ::Gasp:: Your chin? Seriously? That lecher.

Laughing, Phoenix replied, Shut it.

Does he need me to give him pointers on better places to touch? Your big sis is here for you so just let me know.

Telling the truth, Phoenix replied, It was... She had to stop to think of the right word.

Yes?

Intimate. After sending the text, she waited in an agony of suspense.

Like a prelude to a kiss?

Yes. Thrilled that Ridley had understood, her fingers flew as she texted, But we weren't alone.

So no kiss? Ridley included a sad face.

No kiss, Phoenix confirmed. And I'm not sure I'm ready for that anyway.

Ten speed, Ridley shot back. Lots of pedaling. You've got this!

In the off chance a kiss became an option, Phoenix hoped her sister was right. She didn't relish the idea of freezing up and making a fool of herself in front of Cooper.

While locking up the maintenance shed, she replied, Thank you for always being my cheerleader, but now I have to get back to work.

If a kiss happens, I want to be the first to know. Promise me.

Laughing again, more than she had in months, Phoenix typed in, I promise! Now I really do have to go. Love you, byeeee...

Still grinning, she returned the phone to her pocket and stuck her head out the door to peer up at the thick clouds in the sky. It was getting darker by the minute, but the rain continued to hold off. Deciding she had enough time to grab a quick sandwich and a five-minute shower before heading to the lodge, she hurried to her cabin.

On her way in, she noticed the smeared clumps of muddy footprints on the small porch and frowned. She checked the bottoms of her own shoes, and while she had a few leaves stuck to the soles, she'd avoided the mud.

Cooper, maybe? Had he looked for her? The thought added to her aberrant bubbly mood, sticking with her while she ate and rushed through a shower and a fresh change of clothes.

The outside lights flickered on as she made her way to the lodge. Long shadows followed her. Very few people were around the usually busy lanes, but those who were outside waved at her and offered greetings, undaunted by the miserable weather.

Only one man, probably in his early thirties, continually gave her sly glances, making her uneasy with his furtive interest. She tried a friendly smile but he quickly looked away rather than speak to her. For a moment that stymied her, but he went into his camper, so she dismissed him from her mind and continued on her way.

Hugging her arms around herself, Phoenix looked over the park. Many people had set out lights to counter the gray day, or they had small blazes going in their fire rings. Music carried on the humid air, not intrusive but rather soothing. She could see the lake in the distance, turbulent from the storm. Lights from the shore danced over the surface. Two men hidden inside rain slickers fished off a dock. The buoys bobbed wildly in the water.

On impulse, Phoenix captured the scene with a photo and loaded it to her Facebook page, tagging her sister in it. She captioned it with: *Even on rainy days, Cooper's Charm is beautiful.* It was the first post she'd made in a while, and it felt good to do something so mundane.

As she continued on to the lodge, the wind buffeted her face and shook rain droplets from the wet leaves overhead. A couple of kids ran past her, followed closely by more sedate adults. She watched them go into the lodge and a few seconds later, she did the same.

Without realizing it, as soon as she stepped inside she looked for Cooper—and didn't see him in the crowd. A little deflated, ridiculous as that seemed, she edged around the perimeter of the room to avoid the most congested area.

She was in a good mood and didn't want to risk the usual tension-coiling effect she got from crowds. She should have been over it by now, but large groups still brought back memories of that eventful day on the lot, with so many people coming and going as they purchased holiday supplies and Christmas trees. After closing, she'd been rejoicing over the profitable day, happy at her success, oblivious to everything else…until the door to her small shop had crashed open and the armed men had rushed inside.

She assumed they'd been there earlier in the evening, when one of them rasped, "You did a lot of business today, didn't you, honey? Should have a full cash drawer, so hand it over."

Of course, terror-stricken at the sight of the weapons and masked faces, she'd done so immediately. She hadn't given a thought to the money she'd lose. They'd also taken the engagement ring off her finger and the beautiful, delicate necklace that her sister had given her, and still she hadn't protested.

Unfortunately, they weren't satisfied with those things.

One of the men had stood in front of her, lingering, leering, until finally he'd said, "Take off the sweater."

With his face hidden, all she'd seen was the icy anticipation in his eyes. His cohort's laugh sent terror up her spine. She'd tried to run, but—

"Hey, Phoenix."

Snapped back to the here and now, Phoenix realized that she'd been standing near the wall, staring blankly as she rehashed events she'd dearly love to bury.

"I didn't mean to startle you." Joy stood before her, compassion and concern reflected in her gaze. "Are you okay? You look a little...dazed."

Mortification sent a rush of burning heat into Phoenix's face. Happy commotion churned around her as people jostled for seats to play bingo; they were enjoying the night, talking with neighbors, making new friends...and she'd been reliving a nightmare.

Pushing the memories aside, she tried to smile, reminding herself that she was a strong woman forging a future here. "Yes, I'm fine." Other than being horribly embarrassed. "I just—"

"It's okay." With a gentle touch to her arm, Joy said, "I've been there a few times myself."

Phoenix sincerely hoped Joy had never gone through anything remotely like what she'd suffered, but then again, there were a variety of troubles to go around, some less in severity, some far, far worse.

Despite the craziness of the night and the raging storm, Joy looked as cool and elegant as ever. Her long hair was undisturbed by the humidity, and her chic sleeveless dress was soft and fresh.

Next to her, Phoenix felt like a sack of dirty laundry.

"Can I get you anything?" Joy asked. "Maybe a drink?"

Phoenix rushed to say, "I came over to help *you*, not take up more of your time. I should probably warn you, though, I'd be better with the kids than with adults."

Joy watched her a second more before smiling. "That would be wonderful, thank you. Follow me." She turned and led the way to a slightly separate area where more than twenty kids sat at very low tables with paper plates, glue sticks, uncooked pasta and washable markers.

Joy paused next to her son, a cutie with pale blond hair and big brown eyes. "Jack, this is wonderful." She lifted the plate with colorful macaroni glued haphazardly around the edge of the plate and a burst of spaghetti in the middle. "I love it."

Jack gave it some thought. "It needs more blue."

Joy's brows went up. "I believe you're right." She set the plate back in front of him, stroked a hand over his fair hair, then answered a little girl calling her name. Before she was done with that, another girl had a question, and then a little boy needed the bathroom.

Laughing, Joy clapped her hands to get their attention. "Kids, this is Ms. Rose and she's going to help out while I get some other things done."

The boys and girls, in a variety of ages, reacted with smiles, questions or total disregard.

Joy said, "Ms. Rose, Amanda has been a big helper. Amanda, you won't mind helping Ms. Rose?"

Amanda looked around nine or ten, was tall for her age, and she beamed with the responsibility.

The little boy who needed the restroom left with Joy, but she returned him a few minutes later. He immediately ran back to his craft. Luckily, the kids wore stick-on name tags and that made it easier for Phoenix.

She had so much fun that she barely took note of shouts and laughter from the nearby adults. Ninety minutes later, she sat cross-legged on the floor at the kid-height table, absorbed in a new craft with the kids while also snacking on juice boxes and cheese crackers, when she became aware of the shadow cast over the table.

Her heartbeat went a little chaotic, but it wasn't fear doing that to her; instincts caused the reaction because she knew right away it was Cooper behind her. Tipping her head back, she found him smiling down at her.

Phoenix didn't know what it was about him, but he stole her breath away.

"Beautiful artwork, Ms. Rose." He glanced at her elephant made from a foam cup and construction paper.

"Hi." She set aside her craft and, flattening her hands on the table, started to stand.

"Let me." Cooper caught her under the arms and lifted her upright. Once on her feet, she quickly turned to face him.

He wore a dry T-shirt and jeans, but his hair was still damp. Though he'd finger-combed it back, already thick locks fell forward again.

Before the attack—and prior to her engagement—Phoenix had been like any other woman. When faced with a man as compelling as Cooper Cochran, she could have flirted and teased as easily as anyone else. Now she adjusted her glasses and tried to think of something to say.

As if she weren't awkward, he asked, "Did I interrupt?"

Reluctantly replacing her glasses, she glanced at the kids. Their small bodies crowded over the table as they alternately ate handfuls of crackers and worked on their creations. "There's no interrupting snack time."

"Or creative genius?" he asked, taking in all the various pieces of artwork drying on tables, shelves and along the wall heater.

"Exactly." *Why did he always smell so good?* "You finally caught a break?"

"It's been busy," he agreed. "I've seen you running a lot, too. Did you eat?"

"I—"

A flash of lightning illuminated every window, followed by a great boom of thunder—and the lights went out. Night had rolled around without her realizing it, and it was very dark inside the building.

Pandemonium ensued.

She heard a crash, someone shouted, one of the kids cried out and landed against her legs. Since she'd been facing Cooper, she stumbled into his rock-solid body.

Hard, warm, and that intoxicating scent… His hands clasped her shoulders.

"I'm sorry," she started to say, her palms against his chest to balance herself, but she got jostled again and almost fell.

Her glasses slipped off her face. She made a wild grab for them but it was already too late. Where they went, she didn't know, but the child squeezing the back of her knees drew her attention. "Oh, honey, it's okay." Blindly, she reached back and found the top of his head. "I'm right here." Then louder, for all the children, she said, "Everything is okay. Just stay still a moment until—" She felt the crunch beneath her foot and froze.

Another child shrieked.

"It's like a game," Cooper said, his voice strong and soothing, naturally calming the children. He kept one hand on her shoulder while addressing them. "Count to ten and we'll have light again, I promise."

As he started to count, so did the kids.

"I'm on it," Joy called out, just as emergency lights flickered on. A second later, she lifted a bright lantern.

Phoenix realized she was standing very close to Cooper although she couldn't see him clearly. "My glasses…"

"Damn." He knelt down and said with regret, "Found them."

Having Cooper Cochran at her feet was a little disarming, especially with his large hand now burning against her waist. Trying for a note of levity, she said, "Please tell me I'm not standing on them."

"Wish I could."

She groaned theatrically, but inside she was cringing. Just her luck.

He urged her back a step, then stood again. "Can you see without them?"

"Big blurry shapes, but not details."

He took her hand and placed the glasses in it. "I don't know if it helps, but you only stepped on one side."

They felt mangled, one plastic arm completely missing and the lens on that side cracked.

"I guess one lens is better than none." She lifted the broken glasses to her face and, closing her right eye, peered through the remaining lens. Now that they weren't in darkness, most of the kids merely seemed concerned. The child holding her legs, however, squeezed tighter, making her stumble.

Slipping an arm around him, Phoenix maneuvered him to her side, then went with him back to the table. The other kids huddled closer to her. Making a joke of it, she looked at them comically out of the broken glasses, earning a few giggles.

"Help me out, kids. If you're still here, call out your name, okay? Right now I can't see so great."

Jack was the first to shout his name, followed by the rest of them, each trying to be louder than the other. Behind her, she heard Cooper laugh.

She liked that he was patient with kids. Had he wanted children of his own before his wife passed? She had a feeling he'd have been a terrific father.

Just as suddenly as the lights had gone out, they came back on. Now that they could safely navigate, parents came to collect their children. Apparently, it was late enough to call it a night, because everyone began dispersing.

Cooper hung around with her as she spoke to the different parents. When they were finally alone, he asked, "Do you have another pair of glasses anywhere?"

"In my car." *At the top of the lot.* She sighed. Getting there without her glasses would be tricky, especially in the dark.

Cooper curled a finger under her chin and tipped up her face.

"Let me pick up real quick, then I'll get them for you. I'll only be a minute."

She saw him move away and knew he was gathering up the supplies left behind from the rushed mass exodus. "I can do that," she said, using the glasses like a monocle.

He laughed at her. "I think it'll get done quicker if I just take care of it."

True enough, he was just about finished already. Joy had supplied bins for the crafts, so most everything just went back into those, sorted by paper, scissors, then markers, paint and crayons.

After he wiped off the table, Cooper took her arm. "Let's go. I'll take you to your cabin and get your keys, then I'll get the glasses."

"I can do it." She didn't want to impose on him, especially after he'd had such a busy day. "I still have one lens to see."

He hesitated. "I'd feel better about it if I walked with you."

There was that protectiveness again. "If you're sure you wouldn't mind, then I'd appreciate it. But we don't need to go to the cabin. I have my keys on me." Since she kept her cabin locked, her keys hung from a clip on a belt loop.

"Great." His fingers wrapped gently around her arm just above her elbow. "Come on." He led her through the building, pausing to talk with Daron and Joy to explain where they were going.

Daron laughed at her, but Joy was apologetic.

"It's not your fault that I was clumsy."

With Jack leaning against her hip, Joy said, "But you were helping me."

"I had fun. The kids were great."

Daron hoisted Jack up to his shoulders. "I'll help her close up," he said. "Go get Phoenix's glasses before she runs into a wall. I want her hale and hardy tomorrow to help with all the cleanup we're going to have to do."

"I'll start early," Phoenix promised.

Daron groaned in feigned dread. "Give me until nine, at least."

"Oh yeah, you have a hot date, don't you?"

He nodded. "And I'll probably need to sleep in."

Joy rolled her eyes. "Go on, you two. We won't be much longer, especially with Romeo here anxious to be on his way."

Outside, they ran into Baxter, who'd stopped by to see if they needed anything else before he left for his home away from the park.

If he noticed Cooper's hand on her arm, he didn't mention it.

"Maris is doing okay?" she asked.

"Already closed up shop, and I saw her to her RV. She's in for the night."

Cooper thanked him, and then they started the long walk up the drive to the top parking area.

4

COOP STRUGGLED WITH HIMSELF EVERY STEP OF THE way. The air was dark and thick around them, sounds muted by the night. The beams from the security lights didn't travel far in the fog. It was only ten, but felt more like midnight. Though he'd worked all day, he wasn't tired.

Far from it.

Beside him, Phoenix remained quiet, concentrating on where she stepped. The loss of her glasses gave him the perfect excuse to touch her, but with every heartbeat he was mindful of what she'd been through. Slow, he reminded himself. Considerate, cautious and *slow.*

Beneath the loose, long-sleeved shirt she wore, he felt the warmth of her arm against his palm.

He wanted to kiss her.

And he felt guilty because of it.

"Watch it." He steered her a little to the right. "Daron was right. The park is a mess."

"I cleared up what I could earlier, but with the wind still blowing, more branches are going to come down."

"I know. Just as everyone helped out today, we can all pitch in tomorrow to get things back in order."

"I imagine you'll have your hands full with other things. Besides, I don't mind the work. I like to stay busy."

Without meaning to, Coop caressed her arm with his thumb. "It helps you to forget?"

Though she kept walking, a kind of stillness settled around her. When the seconds ticked by, he thought she might not reply.

Because he didn't want to pressure her, he said, "I didn't mean to—"

"Yes."

Nothing else. Just that single word. The urge to pause, to pull her in close and hold her, burned inside him. But that was not what he did. No, he did something far worse. "I understand."

She glanced his way. "Do you?"

Damn. He didn't want to talk about his wife and everything he'd lost. Shaking his head, he sidestepped. "You're in the right place. There's never a shortage of things to be done here."

She released a tight breath. "Daron told me about the sign."

That made him huff a laugh. "I still owe him for that stunt."

"It's a good name for such a nice park. And if the sign is vintage—"

"Vintage my ass," he muttered. Phoenix's husky laugh unfurled some long-dormant emotion inside him. "You think that's funny?"

Playfully, she bumped against him. "I think you're too modest to enjoy having the park named after you."

"I'm not modest."

"Yes, you are, otherwise everything here would be named after you. Like the camp store would be... I don't know, maybe Cooper's Corner Store."

He grinned. "What about the scuba shop, the beach and the lodge?"

"Let me think on it." She nudged her shoulder against his

again. "It is pretty awesome, you know, having the place named after you. You should be proud. It's beautiful and so well run."

"I hire good people."

"Yes, you do."

"That includes you, Phoenix." He looked at her profile, at the way her dark hair trailed down over her chest. She had a stunning figure, like an old-fashioned pinup. Her large breasts and generously curved ass only emphasized the narrower dip of her waist. She had a body that made it damned hard for him to concentrate. "I haven't missed what a great job you're doing."

"Thank you." Oblivious to his carnal struggle, she playfully peered at him through the single lens of her broken glasses. "It's more about you, though. You're so good with everyone, always helpful and welcoming. I know the visitors appreciate it."

"I'm not always that involved, but sometimes it's necessary."

"Right," she said in a disbelieving drawl. "From what I've seen, you're far from an absentee boss."

"Well, I do live here," he said by way of explanation. "Makes it hard to dodge people when I'm a resident."

Her mouth twitched. "You can't tell me you don't enjoy it. I've seen you in action."

Accurate. When he'd first bought the park, it wasn't to mingle.

It was more about saving himself.

These days, though, he did enjoy the vacationers more often than not. He definitely loved the area, too, with the scenery, fishing, scuba diving and walks in the woods…

Huh. It occurred to him that while he'd been thinking of himself as the same old angry, aloof man, he'd actually changed.

Bemused by that realization, he said, "You've interacted with enough of the guests to know how it is. The majority of them are friendly, which makes the occasional jerk easy to tolerate."

"True." To avoid a puddle, she stepped closer to him. He breathed in the scent of her shampoo, and the subtler scent of her skin. "Thank you for convincing me to go to the lodge tonight. I actually had fun."

She sounded so surprised by that. Apparently, fun hadn't been on the agenda much lately. "Even though your glasses got broken?"

"Yes, even with that." They reached the top of the lot. "I'm parked over there. The yellow Ford Focus."

He started down the row of ten cars. Large sycamore trees continually shook rain off their leaves, sprinkling them with every step they took.

"I'm sure you could tell I had reservations," Phoenix continued, "but the kids were great."

"They liked you."

"And you." She smiled. "You're a natural with them."

He took that like a blow to the heart—and he knew she noticed. Here in the upper lot with the security lighting brighter, how could she not?

Fighting off things he didn't want to feel, Coop said, "If you ever want to talk about it, I'm a good listener." Focusing on her, on her needs, was so much easier than dealing with his own.

They reached her car, and she stepped away from him, unhooking a key ring from her belt loop. "My sister says the same thing."

He'd seen mention of her sister on her Facebook page. "What do you tell her?"

"That I'd rather work through it on my own."

Since he'd felt the same, he understood that, too. "And are you?" He took the keys from her.

"Working through it? I think so."

As he unlocked the door, he asked, "By working hard?"

"In part."

The interior car light showed her tidy tendencies. "Where are the glasses?"

"Center console." She crossed her arms and leaned against

the wet side door. "You have such a…presence about you, like the alpha dog or something."

That made him straighten, and he smacked his head on the ceiling of her small Ford. *Damn.* Trying to sound only mildly interested, he asked, "Alpha dog?"

"Leader of the pack. The guy who steps up and takes charge."

Those sounded like compliments, but after what she'd been through, he couldn't imagine her being a fan of bossy men. He found the glasses and backed out of the car. "I think you're imagining things."

"Adults feel it," she claimed, "and they react to it. But the kids didn't seem to notice."

He opened the glasses and carefully set them on the bridge of her nose, taking the time to move her hair back so he could slide the arms into place on her ears.

For her part, Phoenix didn't move, not to help—and not to stop him.

His hand lingered, toying with her thick, silky hair. He liked that she didn't fuss with it much. Usually it was in a ponytail, but sometimes, like now, she left it loose.

Being so much bigger, his body cast her in shadow. He could still see her eyes, big behind the lenses of her glasses. The frames were bigger than her usual pair, a little dated but still cute.

"What about you?" he asked softly.

"I'm no alpha."

Smiling, he took a step closer. "I mean, do you feel it? Whatever this presence is you're talking about."

She nodded slowly. "I do." Her gaze dropped to his mouth. "Big-time."

He was a goner, his guilt evaporating as if it had never been. He forgot all the reasons that he shouldn't come on to her. He forgot that he still missed his wife. All of his attention was on Phoenix.

"Does it bother you?" The last thing he ever wanted to do was intimidate her or make her nervous.

"Maybe it did at first, but I'm getting used to the effect." The tip of her tongue slipped out over her bottom lip. "Now, I might even like it."

That was his last clear thought as his instincts took over. Coop tunneled his fingers into her hair close to her scalp and leaned down to take her mouth.

Tentative at first, he kissed her lightly, slowly. If she showed any reserve at all, he'd stop.

Hard as that would be.

With a small gasp, she slipped her hands up his chest to his shoulders.

Heat. Softness. Kissing her was somehow *more* than he'd imagined, and then she parted her lips, an invitation he couldn't resist.

As he drew her closer, he tilted his head to the side for a better fit. No longer tentative, he delved into the sweetness of her mouth.

Inching nearer, Phoenix made a quiet sound of surprise and acceptance. Her fingertips slid along his nape, making his skin burn. He felt her lush breasts against his chest, and his cock stirred.

Need exploded, red-hot, primitive. He forgot that he should use care, that she might get spooked. Going strictly on instinct, he lifted his hand to her breast—

Like a dousing of ice water, headlights suddenly hit them. Squinting, Coop raised a hand to shield his eyes and moved protectively in front of Phoenix. The sleek BMW didn't immediately move to a parking space. He waited, his irritation growing as the lights stayed in his face, then finally the car swung into the nearest opening.

"What the hell?" He tried to press Phoenix farther behind him.

She looked slightly dazed…and very ready.

Damn it.

A woman, taller and slimmer than Phoenix, stepped out of the car, bathed in smiles. "Phoenix, you're cured!" She opened her arms.

He heard a gasp, followed by grumbling. "I'm sorry," Phoenix huffed as she strode out from behind him. "That's my sister."

"Your sister?"

In a louder voice, she accused, "You have rotten timing, Ridley!"

Ridley laughed. "Are you kidding? Seeing you get it on with Big Sexy—that is him, right?"

"Shut up before I kill you."

"It's him." Smug, Ridley sent Coop two thumbs-up. "Seeing that made my day, sweetie. No, week. Hell, maybe my entire month." She gathered Phoenix in close and squeezed. "I'm glad I didn't miss it."

Coop felt like he'd stepped into a comic play without knowing his lines. "Your sister?" he said again. "Here?" *Now?*

Phoenix turned, her smile tight. "Cooper Cochran, this is my sister, Ridley Rose."

He remembered the name as one of her Facebook friends, but he didn't think he'd seen any photos. She looked a lot like Phoenix, just as chesty up top but not as curvy below. Same nose and a similar shape to her chin. Beneath the security lights, he saw that her hair was more of a reddish brown, long but styled.

She didn't share Phoenix's fashion sense, which leaned toward casual and comfortable. Instead, Ridley wore a shirt that draped off one shoulder, skintight jeans and open-toed lace-up ankle boots. It was a sexy outfit. *She* was sexy. He made the casual observation without any personal interest.

Not surprising, since he burned for Phoenix.

Ready to take charge of the bizarre situation, he stepped forward, hand extended. "Ms. Rose, it's nice to meet you."

Ridley tsked, stepping past his hand to embrace him in a tight hug. "Any guy who's had his tongue in my sister's mouth has to call me Ridley."

"Ridley," Phoenix gasped, clearly horrified.

Coop laughed. Hell, he wasn't sure what else to do. "I agree with Phoenix—you have lousy timing, Ridley." He patted her back then set her away from him. "Here for a visit?"

"Indeed. Extended." She headed for her pricey car. "Since you're here, Big Sexy, maybe you can help me with my bags."

"Bags?" Phoenix repeated. "Plural?"

Coop was more interested in hearing how he'd gotten such a ridiculous nickname. Had Phoenix helped in choosing it?

If so, he wouldn't mind it so much.

"You wouldn't come see me, so I had to come to you." Ridley shrugged. "Don't tell me you're surprised or I'll think you don't know me anymore."

Phoenix stomped over to her.

It was somewhat satisfying, seeing her so put out over being interrupted. Didn't help blunt the sharp edge of his lust, but at least it showed him another aspect of Phoenix's personality, namely her temper.

Phoenix jerked around to face him, her demeanor all businesslike. "You can go on, Cooper. I'll help Ridley with her bags."

That sounded distinctly like an order...which he ignored.

Hadn't she just told him he was an alpha?

"Guess you don't know me either, huh?" He reached past her and accepted the overstuffed case Ridley struggled to hand him. Damn, had she packed for a month?

He watched in surprise as she got out an enormous purse, a smaller overnight case and another, smaller suitcase.

The last she shoved at Phoenix.

After hiking the straps of her purse and the case over her shoulder, Ridley asked, "Where are we staying?"

Phoenix seemed to take evil delight in saying, "I *told* you my place is tiny. *Very* tiny. You'll have to sleep on the couch."

Vindictive. Another trait he hadn't seen before. Enjoying himself, Coop stepped back and watched the sisters interact.

Ridley laughed. "You act like I haven't roughed it before."

"Sleeping on a short, narrow couch is not roughing it."

"Then why are you acting like it is?"

"Because for *you*, it will be pure torture." Phoenix dropped the small suitcase in an act of defiance. "I told you I would visit, Ridley. You knew I wanted time alone."

Ridley's gaze swung to Coop. "Had I known you weren't really alone, I might have heeded your wishes."

Throwing her arms wide, Phoenix said, "This is where I work!"

"Get paid much for making out?"

Cooper laughed. God, they were hilarious together. "You two should take that show on the road."

"Or," Ridley said, "we could at least take it inside?"

"Do you two always squabble?"

"No," Ridley said.

Phoenix countered, "Yes." Then she added, "Because Ridley always thinks she knows what is best for me."

"I am older," Ridley pointed out.

"Only by three years."

"Still older." She smiled at Coop. "Lead the way, BS."

"BS?" Had he just been insulted?

"Big Sexy? Never mind. It does lose something when it's just initials, doesn't it?" She looked up at the sky and shivered. "Let's get out of the dreary weather before my hair starts to curl."

Coop turned to Phoenix. "She's going to your cabin?" He wouldn't make any assumptions, even though he assumed her pique was over the timing, and not any real animus toward her sister.

Phoenix opened her mouth, and Ridley cut her off. "Of course I'm going to her cabin. She can't give me hell if we're in two different places."

"Exactly." Phoenix tried to take the lead, all but marching down the long drive to the resort.

Catching up with her in two long strides, Coop took the smaller case from her. She gave it over with a huff, and then carried on.

He followed, Ridley at his side.

Behind her sister's back, Ridley kept smiling at him.

"You really are a big one, aren't you?" she whispered.

"Don't talk to him," Phoenix growled without looking back.

With a roll of her eyes, Ridley mimicked her, her mouth moving as she mimed, *Don't talk to him.*

Coop grinned at her antics, but at the same time, he wondered if his size was a problem for Phoenix. The men who assaulted her wore masks, so the only clear description was *big.*

Like him.

He frowned, bothered by the thought, until Ridley spoke again, her voice carrying on the night air.

"She always sulks like that. Been doing it since she was in diapers. I ignore it."

Phoenix snapped, "You have *never* ignored it. Instead you egg me on—as you're doing now."

Ridley grinned in satisfaction. "And it always works." Then to Coop, she added, "She's hiding it well, but she's happy to see me."

Phoenix snorted. "So what if I am? Doesn't change anything."

Coop asked politely, "How long will you be with us?"

"I haven't yet decided." Then louder, obviously to tweak her sister again, she said, "I'm thinking a month or so."

Phoenix stiffened, but didn't respond.

"We could use the comic relief," he promised, "but if you do decide to stay, I can set you up in a fifth wheel or a cabin. Just let me know."

"Give her a tent," Phoenix said, and she even glanced back with a big grin. "Ridley loves roughing it, remember?"

"Actually," Ridley said, looking around as they walked down the center lane, "I had no idea an RV could be remarkable. Some of these are huge, and they look really posh."

Phoenix unbent enough to say, "You should see the insides."

"Could I?"

"Tomorrow I'll show you around," she promised. "Everyone here is friendly, so a few campers might be happy to let you in."

It amazed Coop that Phoenix could be so annoyed one minute, then let it go the next. Nice that she didn't hold on to a grudge. He smiled when he thought of his wife's temper and how she could stay mad for a week when it suited her. Never at him, but over any injustice—

He drew up short, appalled at himself for that observation. *I will not draw comparisons.* Jesus, he felt disloyal for the brief thought.

Kissing Phoenix was one thing; he was human after all, and she was smokin' hot with her lush body and shy smiles. He didn't blame himself for not being able to resist her.

But to draw parallels between her and his wife? That was as taboo as it got, and unfair to both of them.

Ridley bumped her hip into his, much as Phoenix had earlier. "Solving world peace?" she asked in a whisper.

Damn it, Ridley was as perceptive as her sister. He shook his head. "The few campers we have for rent aren't the nicest, but they're clean and functional."

"Hmmm. Is there any place around here to buy one?"

Phoenix whirled on her. "No!"

Ridley sniffed. "I will if I want to."

"It would be a ridiculous expense."

"Robbie left me a ridiculous amount of cash. You know that."

"Robbie?" Coop asked.

Phoenix brushed a hand through the air. "Her scumbag ex."

"You're divorced?"

"Very much so. I ditched his name, so I'm back to being Ridley Rose." She leaned toward him as if in confidence, saying low, "But I saw no reason to ditch his money, you know? The bastard wanted out, his parents wanted him out, and together they paid a small fortune to see it happen." She shrugged.

"I take it he was wealthy?"

"Disgustingly rich, yeah."

Phoenix moved closer to Ridley, as if in support. "What Robbie Rhodes had in financial riches he completely lacked in character."

Coop wondered what had happened, but he didn't ask. "I see. Then it sounds like you came out ahead in the deal."

"Absolutely," she said with conviction.

But he heard the hurt.

Frowning in worry, Phoenix hooked her arm through Ridley's, saying, "Maybe a nice long visit is a good idea after all."

Rolling her eyes, Ridley turned to Coop. "See, now that she thinks *I'm* the one who needs to unload, it's all fine and dandy for me to be here." Sotto voce, she added, "Phoenix doesn't like to look needy."

"She mentioned that once."

Eyebrows raised, Ridley pulled back. "She did?"

He nodded.

"Well, well, well." She slanted a look at a silent Phoenix. "Looks like you'll be riding that bike in no time."

Phoenix tried to frown, but ended up laughing, and that got Ridley laughing, too.

Coop smiled. He didn't understand the joke, but he liked the sound of their mingled amusement. "Here's Phoenix's cabin." He gestured at the small wood structure just ahead.

"Oh, uh..." Ridley stared in horror.

Phoenix hauled her on. "There's no backing out now."

To ensure they got inside safely—or so he told himself—Coop followed. When they got to the front door, he frowned at an excess of mud on the deck boards. "What happened here?"

Phoenix slanted him a look. "What do you mean?"

"It looks like you entered a mud wrestling competition."

Ridley looked back and forth between them.

After clearing her throat, Phoenix said, "I assumed you stopped by—"

"And cleaned my shoes on your deck?" Not a good impression to give her sister. "I wouldn't do that."

Now she frowned, too. "Well, I didn't do it. It was like that when I stopped by here earlier to grab a shower."

Suspicion brought his brows together. "Stay put a second." He stepped off the small deck and cautiously walked around the building. Where there used to be a dirt border circling the lattice skirt, Phoenix had planted flowers.

Beneath one window, those flowers were trampled.

More quickly now, Coop finished the inspection. Though most vacationers left the windows open for the fresh air, Phoenix had them secured. If that was because of the rainy weather or her past, he wasn't sure.

He returned to the women and saw by the porch light that Phoenix's expression had tightened with some unnamed emotion. As casually as he could, he asked, "Mind if I take a look around inside, just to be sure…?"

"That no muddy-footed goons broke in?" She handed him the keys with a grand gesture. "Be my guest."

Ridley, no longer teasing, put her arm around Phoenix, and together they stepped back to wait.

There weren't many hiding places in a cabin so small, so Coop unlocked the door, flipped on an inside light, and glanced around. Tidy, just as he'd suspected it would be.

She'd brought the outdoors in by placing plants on all available surfaces, including the mantel over the small fireplace, the shelf at the bar-type eating nook and the counter between the sink and the microwave.

In the bathroom, she'd exchanged the utilitarian shower curtain with a puffy one the shade of butter that matched the towels and floor mat. In the corner, another plant hung from the ceiling.

He went two steps up the ladder to the loft and saw she'd also exchanged the bare bedding with a soft quilt and matching shams on fat pillows. Other changes were obvious in the loft, like the hanging light and lap desk with a book still on it, the low storage trunk she used as a nightstand and the wicker laundry hamper.

Phoenix Rose had taken a small vacation cabin and turned it into a cozy and functional home.

"Do you see something?"

He glanced down and found Phoenix standing very close by, her face turned up to his, her eyes worried behind the lenses of her glasses. "Only a decorator's touch." As he climbed down, she moved back—and almost fell over one of Ridley's suitcases.

The cases alone crowded the small space. With a muttered complaint, Phoenix moved them to flank the fireplace, clearing them from the center of the floor.

She'd have her hands full tonight getting her sister settled—and that on top of a busy day.

Plus a brief foray into lust.

If he thought about that much, he'd get primed again. Not good with two women standing there watching him in such close quarters.

"Everything looks secure. Maybe it was Daron looking for you..." Although he couldn't imagine any of his employees leaving mud tracks behind. It was almost as if whoever had come up on her deck had first tromped through the woods during the storm.

He didn't like that notion at all.

"Well." Phoenix laced her fingers together and smiled up at him. "Thanks for checking."

"Seriously," Ridley said. "It's always nice to have a big stud around for the dangerous stuff."

Phoenix looked horrified, but Coop found her hilarious.

"Been a long time since anyone called me a stud."

"Bull." Ridley had been peering into the bathroom, but now she turned his way. "You're too confident to be unfamiliar with outrageous flattery."

"And you, Ridley? You're rather confident yourself. Does that mean you get outrageous flattery heaped at your feet?"

She gave him a shark's smile, all teeth, attitude, and yes, confidence. "Absolutely."

Before the banter could go any farther, Phoenix dove in. "I guess we should call it a night."

Coop hesitated, but with Ridley now inside the bathroom, complaining about the minuscule proportions of the shower, he scooped a hand around Phoenix's nape and drew her up on her tiptoes to brush his mouth over hers.

The sensation was electric, especially now that he knew how good she tasted and how quickly she could ignite. He stepped back slowly, resenting the distance that had to be between them, even while knowing it was for the best.

He had a hell of a lot to think about, and she needed time to decide just how far she wanted the physical attraction to go.

To keep Ridley from knowing, neither of them said a thing until he reached the door and opened it. "Will I see you tomorrow at the store for coffee?"

She drew a slow breath and smiled. "I'll be there."

Hopefully, her sister wasn't an early riser. Coop would enjoy the chance to talk to Phoenix alone…and if things went right, maybe taste her again, too.

5

RIDLEY WOKE WITH A STIFF BACK AND A DESPERATE need for coffee. There were no familiar sounds. Sunlight poured in through the thin curtains over a small window.

It took her a second to orient herself, and then she realized she was in the cramped loft of Phoenix's new digs.

God, the mattress—if you could call it that—was just *too* lumpy.

She turned over and found that Phoenix had already ditched, leaving her alone, and she hadn't heard a thing.

That shouldn't have surprised her. After all, she'd always been an owl to Phoenix's rooster, but last night they'd been so physically *close* in the bed; every time she'd moved, she'd bumped Phoenix. Little sis hadn't complained. Ridley had, repeatedly, but Phoenix had stoically concentrated on sleeping.

Or more likely, she'd been concentrating on that big, hot-and-sexy hunk she called a boss. *Whew.* Cooper Cochran had that indefinable thing that drew women like flies. Call it machismo or a sexual aura; it gave him the power to dominate a room.

It made a woman ultra-aware of his presence…but could also make her feel safe.

In Ridley's opinion, he was exactly what Phoenix needed—and the last man Ridley would have expected to draw her interest. Clearly, big men were no longer off the list for little sis.

She smiled, seeing that as a positive sign, an indication that Phoenix was getting back to her usual self.

Now, if only they'd capture the bastards who had savaged her…

With an effort, Ridley unclenched her fists and turned to her back, staring up at the exposed boards of the loft ceiling. It was so low in some places that she couldn't stand upright.

This is where Phoenix has chosen to escape—rather than come to me.

It broke her heart to know she'd let down the person closest to her, that, for some reason, Phoenix wasn't comfortable using her for support and backup when she needed it most.

Even though she'd gone running to Phoenix when her scum ex had dropped her like a hot, barren potato.

Groaning, Ridley forced herself to sit up and, using both hands, shoved her wild hair out of her face.

First things first: she needed coffee.

Where had Phoenix told her she could get a cup? Oh, yeah, the camp store. Hopefully that wasn't too far away, or too crowded with other people.

They'd talked for a while last night, after Ridley had insisted on sleeping where Phoenix slept, not only so they *could* talk, but because in the rustic resort with woods all around and numerous big trees, any number of bugs could be lurking.

Ridley didn't do bugs. Not ever.

It had seemed far more likely that the ground floor might suffer a bug attack, so she'd gone to the loft.

Did bugs climb ladders?

Still sluggish, she crawled across the awful mattress and peered over the side.

The bathroom was down there.

Her clothes, her makeup…everything she needed so she could then go fetch coffee, which she needed the most, was down there.

Resigned, she turned and carefully descended the ladder. The wooden floors were cool against her feet, but once she stepped out of the air-conditioning, it would be smothering hot, probably muggy too from all the rain last night.

Wearing only her nightshirt and panties, she went to the bathroom, brushed her teeth and looked at the disaster of her reflection in an oval mirror over the sink.

She was contemplating the phone-booth-sized shower when the knock came at the door.

She stared at it for a full ten seconds before deciding to answer. It could be Big Sexy and if so, she had some questions for him.

Glancing down, she saw that her shirt covered all things vital; no need to delay while she dug through a suitcase.

Shoving her hair back again, she turned the knob and opened the door—then gawked. "Lord have mercy. You might be better than coffee, and that's saying something, you know?"

More than six feet of tanned, chiseled body stood before her. If that wasn't enough, nature decided to go for overkill with dark blond wavy hair, a sensual smile and laughing, vivid green eyes. *My, my, my.*

She'd had a lot of conquests, but none as stunning as this walking turn-on.

"Thank you—I think?" The vision grinned down at her. "And actually, I have coffee, too." He lifted a foam cup. "Phoenix sent me, so I assume it's the way you like it."

"Delivered by a gorgeous man? Oh, Phoenix knows me so well." She took the cup and sipped, her eyes closing in bliss as the warmth and taste—and yeah, maybe the caffeine, too—penetrated the fog surrounding her. "Wow, that's good."

Tall, blond and sexy propped a rock-hard shoulder on the door frame. "So you're Phoenix's sister, Ridley?"

"Mmm." She was functioning, but not enough for manners. "And you are?"

"Baxter McNab, the scuba instructor."

Her eyes flared. "This joint has scuba diving?" More to herself than him, she whispered, "Fascinating." Maybe it was time she took up lessons.

"We have a great many entertainments, Ridley."

Oh, there was something quite delicious in the low, suggestive way he said that. She stepped back. "I probably shouldn't keep standing in the doorway."

He made no move to leave. "Looking like you look, probably not."

She wrinkled her nose at his rudeness. "It's called bedhead and lack of caffeine. Since I just woke, and I've only drank half the coffee, it's to be expected."

"Not exactly what I meant, but okay."

She eyed him. *What had he meant, then?* She enjoyed confidence in a man, but his was a bit overblown. "Did you want to come in?"

"One hell of a temptation, but I'm making up a scuba class that I missed yesterday. I've only got a few minutes—and that wouldn't be nearly long enough."

If dictionaries were picture books, *cocky* would have an image of this dude next to it. "What did you say your name was?"

"Baxter McNab." He gave her a knowing smile. "Feel free to ask around about me—or to look me up."

She planned to do exactly that. "I'm not usually good with names, but I doubt I'll forget yours."

"Good to know."

Waggling her fingers at him in dismissal, she said, "Run along, then."

Instead, he straightened away from the door. "I take it you're used to giving orders?"

Cocky *and* sexually charged. Her temperature rapidly rose a few degrees. "As a matter of fact—"

"Because I'm not great at taking them," he said softly, deliberately interrupting her.

"Is that so?" She hadn't been awake long enough to accept a challenge—but accept it she did. "Strong women threaten you, do they?"

His gaze went over her. "Is that what you are?"

She stiffened at his skepticism. "Yes."

As if placating her, he nodded. "Orders tend to get lost when they come from half-dressed women who look like you—and no, in case you're still not clear, that's not an insult."

Obviously, he was a player.

Since her divorce, so was she. Trying not to look affected, she cocked out a hip and sipped more coffee. "Okay, I'll bite."

"Better and better," he murmured.

She had a little trouble breathing. "If it's not an insult, what is it?"

"It's me trying to figure out how a woman wakes up looking so fucking hot."

Well, damn, he just might be better at this than she was. More dangerous, too, given the provocative glitter in his stunning green eyes. "You have me at a disadvantage," she said—and hastily gulped more caffeine.

The smile turned predatory. "In what way?"

Setting the now-empty cup aside and donning her best, boldest smile, she stepped toward him. "I have no idea how sexy you might look first thing in the morning." She braced one hand on the doorknob, the other on the door frame where he'd been leaning.

He reached out and touched a long lock of her hair. "We could remedy that."

Against her intent, she swayed toward him. "I suppose we could." She eased the door halfway closed. "As a strong woman, I'll let you if—or when—I'm interested." She grinned. "Goodbye, Baxter. Thanks for the coffee."

She shut the door in his face—but not before she saw his eyes narrow…and his mouth curl into a smile.

If she wasn't mistaken, he'd just accepted the challenge, too.

★ ★ ★

Phoenix felt utterly limp. After coffee with the gang this morning, she'd gotten right to work. Hour after hour, the temps rose and the sun baked down through a cloudless sky. The humidity was through the roof, but she still had an area to work on.

Most of the vacationers were in the water—either the pool or the lake. Even from where she worked near the more primitive tent camping, she could hear the splashing and laughter.

More than ever, she wished she felt comfortable taking a quick dip.

Twigs and branches were everywhere they weren't supposed to be, flowerpots were overturned, some plants damaged. She had at least two more hours to go before she could call it a day.

Waking before Ridley had given her a chance to have coffee with Cooper in relative privacy. They'd sat on the picnic bench out by the lake and talked quietly. That hadn't lasted long, though. They both had a lot to accomplish today.

"There you are."

Phoenix glanced up and saw Ridley walking toward her. Her sis had her hair gathered at the top of her head in a casually sexy topknot that no matter how she tried, Phoenix couldn't replicate. She looked great in a loose sleeveless top with a floral print, light blue shorts, flip-flops and big sunglasses.

As Ridley went past, vacationers stared. Her sister had always gotten that reaction. There was just something about Ridley that drew immediate attention.

Standing, Phoenix used the back of one glove to wipe her brow. "Did you get the coffee?"

"Yup, thanks. The delivery boy was nice, too. At least, nice to look at."

Uh-oh. "Did Baxter do something?"

"Nothing I can't handle."

Phoenix couldn't see Ridley's eyes, but she had the odd feeling her sister was insulted over something. "He's always been really nice to me—"

"He's nice to you because Big Sexy already staked a claim."

"—but I understand he flirts with every woman."

Ridley pushed her sunglasses to the top of her head and scowled. "You mean I'm not special? Gee, I'm crushed."

She said it sarcastically, but Phoenix suspected there was a hint of truth behind the words.

Had her sister finally met her match?

That is, her match since the divorce?

Before that, before Robbie shredded her confidence and stomped on her devastated heart, Ridley had been a fun-loving, happy, very sweet woman.

With a sarcastic wit, sure.

But there'd been more to her than that. Now it felt like the sarcasm was all Ridley cared to share. It was almost as if she packed away her other, softer emotions…and only unpacked them for Phoenix.

"Last night was nice."

Ridley smiled. "Smooching with Big Sexy?"

"I meant talking with you in bed, just like we used to do as teenagers." Growing up, they'd equally squabbled and confided, competed and shared. In the end, though, no matter what, she knew Ridley was her backup.

Ridley dusted off a landscape boulder and sat down. "It felt like old times, especially with you falling asleep first, and getting up earlier than me."

Memories had her mouth twitching with humor. "You were always a terrible slug in the mornings. I remember how hard it was to get you up for school."

Ridley grinned. "It was cruel of Mom to go off to work and delegate the chore to you."

"I think that's why she liked the early shift."

They laughed together. Ridley sobered first. "It really was nice. I've missed you a lot."

"I know, and I'm sorry. I just… I needed that time alone."

"You're feeling better now, though?"

Lifting a hand to shield her eyes, Phoenix looked up at the blazing sun. It was easier than looking at her sister. "I'm not yet where I want to be, but I finally feel like I'm getting there."

In a burst of anger, Ridley growled, "It'd help if they'd catch those miserable—"

"It might." Phoenix bent and started picking up the debris she'd raked into a pile, dropping it into her wheelbarrow. Knowing the men were still out there, still a possible threat, plagued her. She couldn't deny it, but she didn't want to think about that right now.

Usually, she didn't want to think about it at all.

Sometimes she didn't have a choice.

Maris drove up in a golf cart, pausing beside the sisters. "I hate to interrupt your visit, but with all the rain, guests need extra towels and we still don't have a damned housekeeper. I swear, if Coop doesn't hire someone soon, I'm going to do it for him."

Phoenix grinned. "He's been trying, right? But no one works out."

Ridley cocked her head to the side. "I can help. Just tell me what to do."

Alarmed, Phoenix said, "No, you don't need to—"

At the same time, Maris said, "Seriously? That'd be terrific. Hop on and I'll show you what to do before I have to get back to the store."

Ridley got to her feet. "I'd hug you, Phoenix, but, yeah…you're a mess."

Phoenix looked down at her dirt-stained shorts, her sweat-stained tank and dirty work boots. "Truth."

"Will we be able to have dinner together?"

"Shouldn't be a problem."

Ridley blew her a kiss. "Then I'll see you tonight."

With a sinking feeling, Phoenix watched her sister and Maris ride off on the golf cart, chatting like old friends.

Ridley was wonderful—everything a sister could ask for and more. Caring, supportive, hilarious, always there when needed... She possessed all the very best qualities, but she was not a manual labor-type worker.

Thinking of all the things that could go wrong, Phoenix got back to her own chores. If she could finish early, she could check up on Ridley.

Forty minutes later, she was in her own golf cart looking over the rest of the resort when Cooper flagged her down.

The sight of him quickened her pulse and made her lips curl in an automatic smile. She stopped beside him.

To her surprise, he climbed into the passenger seat. The small cart swayed before settling again.

"There's a tree down at the edge of the woods, caught up in the branches of other trees but hanging over a play area. I closed that section off for now, but I want to go by the supply shed to get the chainsaw, then we can remove it before it falls and hurts someone."

"Wow, I'm sorry I didn't notice it." She drove the golf cart with the attached trailer toward the maintenance building. "I did a cursory check of the area and started in the places I thought were worse, but I never thought to check the woods."

"No reason you would." He relaxed beside her, one arm along the backrest, his face tilted toward her. "You're a little sunburned."

Phoenix wrinkled her nose. "I put on sunscreen, but that was a while ago. I thought I was almost done."

He reached out to tuck back a damp wisp of hair, loose from her ponytail. "We'll be shaded in the woods, and afterward, you should call it a day."

"I don't have that much more to do." Tomorrow she could

get back to her regular routine. Driving straight into the maintenance building, she parked the golf cart and started to step out.

Cooper stopped her with a light touch to her shoulder. When she turned toward him, he slowly smiled.

"What?"

"I don't know how you do it, but you look really cute with a burned nose and sweaty hair."

"Right." She bumped her shoulder to his. "Don't let the glasses fool you. I'm not *that* blind."

Far too serious, he studied her face as his fingers moved from her hair to her cheek.

He looked so intent, she asked, "What?"

"I want to kiss you again."

Her heart tripped. In case he didn't realize, she whispered, "I wouldn't stop you."

That made him smile again. "It occurs to me that I should explain a few things first."

Okay, so maybe she needed to get comfortable. Phoenix half turned toward him, crossed her legs and removed the clip-on sunglasses. "Ready."

"Took some preparation, huh? I promise it won't be anything too profound."

During her and Ridley's talk last night, they'd covered all the pros and cons of her getting involved with Coop, so Phoenix guessed, "Is this about me working for you?"

Surprise showed in his amber eyes. "In a sense."

"I'm an employee."

"Yes, but this isn't a conventional boss/employee situation."

"You don't have to convince me." It was her turn to touch his face. She traced the high angle of his cheekbone down to the firm line of his jaw. Light beard stubble rasped her fingertips, causing a bloom of heat inside her. He was so *much* a man, carelessly taking his strength for granted. Yet he was considerate, too.

Long-dormant instincts told her that he would never use

his strength to hurt her. Until the attack, she hadn't thought in terms of safety, but she did now, and she knew she was safe with Cooper Cochran.

He turned his face to kiss her palm. "I want you to know that no matter what happens between us, it won't affect your status as an employee."

Humor got the best of her. At first, she thought he might want to talk about his wife and how he still loved her. In comparison, this topic wasn't so bad. "Honestly, I wasn't that concerned about job security." She fought off a grin. "Who else would do as good a job as I have?"

"No one. The place looks better than it ever has before." Chagrined, he rubbed the back of his neck. "None of that came out quite as I meant it to."

"I understood all the same, and I appreciate the reassurance."

"Do you?" Before she could reply, he muttered, "Forget I asked." Then he leaned down and put his mouth to hers in a kiss that managed to be both gentle and hungry.

It was perfect—except it didn't last long enough.

His forehead to hers, he said, "Let me try this again."

She thought he meant the kiss. "Yes."

Instead, he drew a breath. "You're smart and motivated. You could have a job anywhere. Doesn't mean you want to start looking right now, not when it seems you're settling in here."

Settling in. Yes, she really was, settling into her job, her cabin—and the reality of what had happened.

Things were finally coming together for her again, and he was right, she didn't want to have to change jobs. As long as they were in agreement…

She looked up at him through her lenses. She should probably explain that she couldn't get too involved. She was working through a lot and a relationship would only complicate things. But maybe he wasn't thinking along those lines anyway. After seeing the photo of his wife, she'd sensed that he was still grieving for her.

Most likely, they were both looking for the same thing: distraction, comfort, even companionship.

And sexual satisfaction.

Content with her internal rationalization, Phoenix closed the inch that kept his mouth from hers. His lips were warm and firm, slightly parted. She teased over his top lip, then the bottom, gliding her tongue just inside before taking the bottom lip between her teeth for a gentle tug.

He made a sound like a low, soft growl, but didn't move or in any way attempt to take over.

Knowing she'd surprised him, she asked, "Anything else?"

His gaze burned. "*Everything* else."

Everything else…carnal? She hoped so.

He said, "For now, we better get to that tree—before I convince myself that this is the most appropriate place ever to have sex with you for the first time."

The idea gave her a shameless grin. If she knew they wouldn't be caught, she wouldn't mind at all. Then again, she definitely needed a shower first.

"Amazing." He glanced at her face while he got the chainsaw and a few other supplies. "I think I read every thought, and that final decision."

She should have been embarrassed but she only laughed. With Cooper, she felt free in a way she hadn't even before the attack.

In a way she hadn't with her fiancé.

That gave her a twinge of shame. She knew David had loved her, maybe loved her still, though she hoped he'd moved on.

"What?" Cooper asked. "You've gone too quiet."

Shaking it off, she emptied the small trailer. "I was just thinking."

He waited, but when she didn't confide in him, he let it go. "Before I got sidetracked, I meant to ask if tomorrow afternoon would work for us to go pick out that mower? It's a little sooner than I had planned, but Daron says he might not be able to keep the old one going. We should both be caught up by then."

"I'd like that." It'd only be for a few hours, but by then Ridley would surely have realized she didn't like stocking towels and cleaning cabins and she'd be at loose ends without much to do.

Then again, knowing her sister, she'd probably find a way to get near Baxter again.

A startling thought…but also entertaining.

It fascinated Coop, how easily he could read Phoenix's thoughts. That she'd been tempted by the idea of sex in the maintenance shed told him that she felt the chemistry, too, and wasn't hampered by foul memories. Like him, responsibility had guided her in the end.

That, and vanity.

She was sweaty, a little dirt-stained and sunburned. It hadn't been a turnoff for him. Hell, she could be layered in mud and he wasn't sure he'd want her any less.

Side by side, they worked to cut back the fallen tree so that it wouldn't be a danger to anyone. Coop made a point of keeping her in the shade as much as possible, and he did all the heavy lifting. But it wasn't easy to hold Phoenix back. Whatever she did, she did it to the best of her ability.

Made him wonder if she'd be that tireless in bed.

Actually, every damned thing she did or said sent his brain toward thoughts of sex.

They'd cleaned up the best they could when Phoenix paused. "Listen."

"To what?"

"Do you hear water?" She turned to take several steps into the woods. "I know there's a creek back here somewhere."

"You haven't seen it yet?" Cooper pulled the keys from the

golf cart and stuck them in his pocket. Taking her hand, he said, "Come on. I'll show you."

And maybe, if they had some privacy, he could even coax her into the water.

He led the way. The trail had grown over, which wasn't a bad thing considering the abandoned train trestle over the creek. The significant drop to the shallow creek bed made it a hazard for kids, not just those in the resort but from the local area, as well. Without a path, they were less inclined to find it.

Coop didn't need a path. He knew the area well, having come to it multiple times when he'd first bought the resort. He'd walk the creek for hours, thinking about his life, what he'd lost—trying to find a way back from the anger.

Carefully, he moved aside branches and weeds, and one very nasty spiderweb, constantly aware of her smaller hand in his. She was a slight, delicate woman—and stronger than she realized.

The woods smelled rich, mixing with the scent of her heated skin, sending a pulse beat of need to thrum through his blood. He lifted aside a spray of wild roses from a prickly bush, and there it was.

"Wow." Phoenix paused as she took it in. "This looks like a painting."

Coop agreed. Sunlight glittered over the moving water of the creek. Wildflowers and small trees grew along the shore. High overhead, the trestle loomed, a profusion of ivy growing up the iron braces. Birds flittered around from branch to branch while insects sang.

Smiling, Phoenix moved past him and hurried down the slope to the water, sliding on loose dirt a few times. For a moment, Coop just stood there, watching as she paused to unlace her boots—inadvertently giving him a spectacular view of her ass in the snug shorts.

God, he wanted to explore those killer curves.

His palms twitched at the thought of holding her still beneath him while he thrust deep…

"Are you coming?" she asked.

From fantasizing…maybe. But he knew that wasn't what she meant, so he said, "Let me know if it's cold."

She laughed, taking out her cell phone and a ring of keys that she set nearby on a rock.

Cautiously inching into the water until it came to midcalf, she said with a laugh, "It's *freezing*." She turned to face him. "Come on in—ack!"

Coop watched as her foot connected with a slick, moss-covered rock and she flailed. He was already hurrying down the slope when she landed in the water with a great splash.

Sure that she'd hurt herself, he reached the edge of the creek—and her laughter stopped him. She roared with it, reclining on her elbows, her head back with her hilarity.

His mouth twitched…but his gaze zeroed in on her body. The icy water trailed over her hips and waist, lapping at her breasts, making her shirt ten times more interesting because of how it exposed her figure.

Again, she reminded him of a luscious pinup.

Squatting down near her small, pale feet, he asked, "You're okay?"

Flipping her toes in the water, she splashed him. "The shock of the cold about did me in, but now it's refreshing." She gave him a coy smile. "Care to try it?"

Yeah, he would.

Sitting back on the slight incline, he removed his shoes and socks, then waded in next to her.

Phoenix stared up at him, water droplets on the lenses of her glasses, her nose pink, her soft lips smiling. She lazily stirred the water with her hand. "Down here, Cooper."

So damned tempting. Keeping his gaze on her body, he knelt down beside her, cupped his hands in the chill water, and slowly poured it over her belly. Phoenix shivered and went still, but didn't protest.

Coop felt himself reacting and it amazed him. He hadn't felt like this since the passing of his wife—the rush of churning desire caused by just a look. True, he'd eventually sought out physical encounters, but it hadn't been like this. He'd been slaking a basic need only. There'd been no teasing, no laughter. No casual conversation, no real enjoyment beyond release.

He hadn't gotten to know those women because he'd had no interest in knowing them.

Things were very, very different with Phoenix.

What had started out as sympathy, encouragement to help her heal—or so he'd told himself—had in no time at all morphed into something more powerful that overshadowed his altruistic motives.

Now, even the guilt he felt wasn't enough to hold him back.

With one wet finger, he traced the waistband of her shorts beneath her shirt, trailed up to her navel, then further still until he brushed against the full under-curves of her breasts.

She inhaled a slow, shuddering breath.

"Okay?" He didn't want to cause her even a twinge of uneasiness.

"Yes."

At the huskiness in her voice, Coop lifted his gaze to hers. Her eyelids were lowered, her face flushed. "You are incredibly sexy, Phoenix Rose." Sexy and more. So much more—but at the moment he couldn't begin to define it.

Her eyes, filled with curiosity, held his. "It's odd, but you make me feel sexy."

Cold water washed around his legs, hot air drifted over his torso. Pebbles, smoothed by the current, shifted beneath his feet.

Her nipples were tight, taunting his restraint as he cupped a hand around her breast. Firm and full… Fuck, he wanted her. "Did you not feel sexy before?"

She idly lifted one shoulder. "Sometimes, I guess, but not like this. Not—" she looked at their surroundings with a smile "—in a stream after working all day."

"You were sexy the day I met you, and every day since then." Especially now, with the sunshine stroking her dark hair, and her relaxed attitude.

She hesitated, her gaze slipping away.

"Phoenix?"

"When I first met you, I was intimidated." Her brows scrunched as she considered that, then she added, "And very *aware*, if that makes any sense."

Because this was serious, he moved his hand to her shoulder, making it easier for him to concentrate. "I never want you afraid, not of me."

"Intimidated," she stressed. "Not afraid."

Knowing the distinction was important to her, he nodded. "And since then?"

She slowly smiled, reaching up to touch his chest, her fingertips first lightly stroking before she flattened her palm over his heart. "I've been very, very curious."

Coop held himself still. Her hand was small, wet and cold from being in the creek, and the simple touch sent tension spiraling through him. "About?"

Again she looked away—but her hand remained firm against him. "I've wondered about your life, why you moved to the resort." Her gaze flickered back to his. "About your wife and how she passed."

Automatically, he shook his head. He couldn't discuss it, not now, maybe not ever.

"I think you must have loved her a lot." Pale blue eyes searched his. "She was beautiful, and she had a gentle smile."

Closing his eyes, shutting out her tender sympathy, he warned, "Phoenix—"

She half sat up, her hand gliding up to the back of his neck, the chill of her palm a shock against his sun-heated skin. "I'm not trying to pry. You asked and I answered. That's what I'm curious about."

"Not sex?" Even as he asked it, he felt like a coldhearted bastard.

But she grinned. "Oh, definitely that, too." Her fingers stroked the nape of his neck. "That most of all, actually."

He was contemplating ways to take her, how to make it work here, *right here*, when the baying started. They both looked up, searching for the source of the awful sound.

Laughter carried through the trees, followed by another pitiful cry.

Coop scowled, starting to stand, but Phoenix beat him to it. She was on her feet in an instant, trudging barefoot along the stream, going from rock to rock at a precariously fast pace.

He jogged after her.

They both spotted the dog on the trestle at the same time.

Some asshole was there, threatening it, laughing at its terror.

Phoenix stiffened on a sharp inhale, one hand covering her mouth. "Oh, my God."

She whispered the words, so faint that Coop barely heard them.

But the man must have heard their splashing approach because he moved to the side of the trestle, scowling down at them. "Mind your own business."

At the harsh words, Phoenix jerked back, her gaze jumping back and forth from the man to the dog, painful indecision in her eyes. She opened her mouth, but said nothing.

Abuse of any kind had always set him off, so Coop was already pissed. Seeing Phoenix like this, reserved in her fear, really pushed him over the edge.

6

WORRY HAD CARRIED PHOENIX TO THE BOTTOM OF THE trestle. She'd expected kids and had fully intended to reprimand them. Instead, she found a rough-looking man.

Sudden fear turned her blood to ice…but the poor dog. "You're scaring it," she accused, meaning a forceful shout and only managing a weak protest. *What am I going to do?*

He threw another rock, which thankfully missed the poor animal. "He killed one of my chickens."

She was trying to find her voice, trying to think of a reply, when Cooper stepped up behind her, saying over her head, "Hurt my dog again and you'll be sorry."

Until that moment, she'd forgotten he was with her. She looked up, seeing him as the man might: big, solid, pissed off.

A massive deterrent to abusive jerks.

Oh, thank God. She faced the man again, then looked for a path up to the trestle. Cooper's hand on her arm kept her still. "Stay here."

Ignoring his bare feet, he climbed the slope, up and around weeds and bramble, then she saw him emerge at the edge of the trestle. Wooden ties were missing in places, leaving gaping holes big enough for a body to fall through. Paying no attention to the seething creep, Cooper maneuvered easily until he reached the dog.

He glanced down at Phoenix. "He's okay. Just scared."

It meant a lot that he'd take the time to reassure her, but she badly wanted him and the dog away from the threat. "Can you get him?" she asked. If the dog lunged away, they could both end up falling from the trestle.

"Yeah, I'll get him."

The man stood at the other side where the trestle butted into the hill and stopped. "You owe me for the chicken."

Still Cooper ignored the guy and, stripping off his shirt, carefully bent to the dog. Moving slowly, he bundled up the muddy animal, then stood with it cradled in his arms. The dog tucked its snout against his neck.

Cooper said, "Come by the manager's office at the RV resort tomorrow and I'll give you what you're owed."

Phoenix heard the menace in the words, but either the creep didn't notice, or he was too stupid to take heed.

He spit toward the creek. "I want my money now."

Ignoring him, Cooper turned, making his way carefully back to land.

Finally regaining rational thought, Phoenix turned and hurried back down the creek where they'd left their things. She tucked the phone into her pocket and hastily donned her socks and boots. Leaving them unlaced, she snatched up Cooper's things, turned, and almost ran into two more men.

Her heart shot into her throat. She couldn't see past them and had no idea where Cooper had gone. She didn't mean to, but she backed up.

"You heard him. Harry wants his money now."

She heard a rushing in her ears and realized it was her own

racing pulse. Cooper couldn't be far away, but how much help would he be against three men while holding a frightened dog?

She carefully inhaled, then asked with admirable calm, "How much?"

"Fifty ought to do it."

Outrageous, especially since she didn't believe that small dog had eaten a live chicken—not that it mattered. She'd left her purse in her cabin and only had five dollars in her pocket, put there in case she needed a drink or a sandwich from the camp store.

Unsure what to say, she backed up another step, stumbled over her laces, and barely kept herself from falling. Her glasses slid down her nose and she made a frantic grab to keep them in place.

The man speaking to her grinned.

They were both dirty, boldly looking her over. The talkative one was shirtless, the other wore a too-big, greasy black T-shirt.

This is not like the attack at the store, she promised herself. *It's not night, I'm not alone, and—*

"Ah, look. I think you're making her nervous, Frank." The second man gave her a malicious smile. "Cat got your tongue, baby?"

Frank stared at her mouth. "Speaking of tongues—"

Suddenly Cooper was there, his big body casually moving between them, forcing the men back as he handed her the dog.

"I don't think it'll try to run, but be careful just the same as you head back to the park."

He wants me to leave him? Rationally, Phoenix knew it made sense. If she left, she could at least send others to help—if it wouldn't already be too late. She should hurry…yet she couldn't seem to get her feet to move.

The dog, a smallish beagle mix with a bloody ear and big, frightened brown eyes, immediately stuck his nose over her shoulder, crowding as close as he could. The animal's need for comfort helped her composure. She automatically crooned to him, backing up again to give Cooper some room while she tried to decide what to do. Stay or go? Try to help or keep out of the way?

She had no idea where the first man had gone and that worried her enough that she gave a quick look behind her, but all she saw was the rushing creek and woods.

They were well away from the resort…with three thugs threatening them.

Trying to be subtle, Phoenix cradled the dog in one arm and bent down to pick up a round, fist-sized rock. It wasn't easy juggling everything, but the dog helped by curling as close as he could get.

No one paid any attention to her.

Cooper, his posture loose, his attitude unconcerned, faced the men. "I strongly suggest you boys run along now."

Boys? That had to be a joke, but then, to a mature, responsible man like Cooper, they might seem young. She guessed them to be her age, maybe a little less, which would make them around ten years his junior. Still, men in their early twenties weren't boys, especially when they reeked of trouble.

"Did you pay Harry?" Frank asked.

"Your chickenshit friend who likes to mistreat animals?" Cooper shifted closer to him. "Is that who you mean?"

Both punks bunched up.

Cooper continued, "I gave him a time to come to the RV resort tomorrow to get what he's owed. Until then, I'm done talking to any of you."

Had he and Harry spoken again after she'd run back to get their things? If they were politely conversing, maybe the worst of the threat was over.

Sadly, she realized it wasn't when Frank, copping an attitude, poked a finger hard against Cooper's chest.

Sneering, Frank said, "I suggest you—"

Before he could finish, Cooper kicked at his lead leg, sweeping it out from under him, and the shirtless fool went crashing to the bank, half rolling into the creek. He clutched his knee, groaning.

Almost at the same time, Cooper snatched up the other jerk by his shirt, saying close to his face, "You seriously don't want to do this."

The explicit warning hung in the air. Somehow, Cooper looked even bigger, bulkier—and all congeniality had disappeared in a poof.

Hands up, the leaner man said, "Okay, dude. Relax."

Behind them, Harry finally showed up. "Let's go," he said, his tone sullen. "I'll get my money tomorrow."

Phoenix stared at the abuser. Along the left side of his face, mud caked in his hair and ear and was smeared across his jaw. His eye was slightly swollen and bloodshot. A rip in his T-shirt ran from the neck down to his sternum, causing the material to hang on his frame. He looked defensive and…

Small.

Physically and emotionally.

The realization surprised her, but now, with Cooper in charge of the situation, they all appeared far less threatening, more like the boys he'd accused them of being.

Residual fear kept her legs quaking, but her heart had slowed from its frantic beat.

She watched as the other two helped Frank from the creek. He limped badly. Together, shoulders hunched, grumbling among themselves, they departed.

As soon as they were out of sight, Cooper turned and, as he started to take his shoes from her, noticed the rock. One dark eyebrow shot up. "Were you planning to brain someone?"

Feeling horribly self-conscious now, she dropped the rock into the creek with a splash. "Maybe."

A smile flashed over his face as he stepped into his shoes, then knelt to tie the laces. "You should have left when I asked you to."

Anger vibrated in his tone but she didn't know if it was aimed at her or the men. She'd wanted to go—and he deserved the truth. "I…couldn't." Reaction settled in, making her voice tremble.

He shot her a look, and his stern expression softened. After tying her shoes, too, he straightened. "Come on." Easing the dog back into his own arms, he made sure his shirt stayed tucked around the poor thing. "I don't want to stick around to see if they find their balls."

No, she didn't want that, either. Anyone heartless enough, cruel enough, to torment an animal was, in her opinion, capable of anything.

Cooper adjusted the dog in one arm, keeping it close to his chest, then wrapped a big hand around her wrist and started them on their way.

Phoenix licked her lips, her thoughts flying. "That man—Harry they called him—he was muddy and the side of his face was red."

"He tried to take the dog from me."

A simple statement, that said so much. "You hit him?"

Shrugging, he kept them going at a fast clip. "I wasn't going to let him have the dog."

No, of course he wouldn't. She went the rest of the way silently, not sure what to say, anxious to get the dog to safety so she could assess his injuries. Minutes later, they emerged near the golf cart. Kids were close by, shooting baskets. A man was in the process of parking an enormous RV. Two women walked by, involved in friendly conversation.

It all seemed so normal, but Phoenix faced the truth: she wasn't. Not yet.

Would she ever be?

Cooper turned the golf cart and instead of heading for the maintenance shed, he drove it to his own home. Phoenix was quiet, too damn quiet, as she idly stroked the dog's head resting on his shoulder.

It had taken every ounce of control he had not to annihilate the punks who'd mistreated the dog and frightened Phoenix. Rage, familiar in its intensity, shimmered just beneath his calm facade.

"You shouldn't pay them."

Hearing her speak, regardless of what she said, relieved him. "They won't get a dime from me." The words emerged gruffer, angrier than he'd intended, but he was still so fucking furious…

Phoenix tipped her head. "But you said—"

"I want them to show up tomorrow." He wanted that bad. "How else can the police talk with them?"

"Oh." She released her breath on a faint smile. "I like that plan." Then she frowned. "You'll keep him?"

"Her, and yeah, I will."

Her brows rose above the rims of her glasses. "He's a female?"

Despite his volatile state, Coop laughed. Talking about the dog helped tamp down his turbulent mood. "Yes, *she* is—and why are you so surprised?"

"I dunno." She eyed the dog skeptically. "He…*she*…just looks like a male, don't you think?"

"Not where it counts, no."

She choked, then gently stroked the dog's head. "What if someone claims her?"

Shaking his head, Coop rejected that idea. "She's a stray." He glanced at Phoenix again, glad that she was loosening up even if he couldn't. "Didn't you see all the bloated ticks on her?"

"Uh, no." Snatching her hand back and scooting a few inches away, she asked, "Ticks?"

"Likely fleas, too. A bath is on the immediate agenda—and since you had her against you, you should leave those clothes outside until you can wash them."

Looking a little queasy, she asked, "What about her ear? It's bleeding."

"Hard to tell the problem under all that mud, but I don't think it's serious. Might've just been a tick that broke—"

"Eeww." Her face scrunched in disgust.

It belatedly occurred to him that she might want some time alone. Her clothes were wet, her hands still trembling in reaction. Just because the dog was a priority for him, didn't mean she felt the same. "I wasn't thinking. Did you want me to take you home first?"

"No." She firmed her mouth, and probably her resolve. "I'd like to help, if that's okay."

More than okay; he wanted to keep an eye on her, at least for an hour or so. After that…well, he'd have to see. "If you're sure?"

"Positive." With one finger, she tentatively touched the dog's head, and said softly, "It's the least I can do."

Coop didn't like the sound of that. Keeping his voice even, blanking out all frustration, he asked, "What does that mean, Phoenix?"

She whispered, "At the creek, with those men…" Her breath shuddered in, back out. "I was no help at all."

"You held the dog when I asked you to."

She shook her head. "I went deaf, dumb and blind, just like…" Her gaze shifted away, but she turned back to him seconds later as if facing her demons. "Just like before."

New anger surged through his blood, further tensing his muscles until he thought he might break.

What the hell was a woman supposed to do against three men?

What could she have done against armed robbers?

Not a damn thing…just as his wife couldn't.

The fury churned, bubbling up, harder and harder to suppress. Staring straight ahead, he clenched his hand on the steering wheel. A dozen retorts came to mind, none of them appropriate.

"I thought I was doing better—until that happened."

"You had a rock," he reminded her.

"That I'm not sure I could have used."

"Well, thank God you didn't. I had it under control."

She teased, "It's those alpha tendencies of yours."

Cooper snorted.

She was quiet a moment, then softly admitted, "I was so scared."

His jaw clenched. "Sometimes fear is commonsense."

"Not if it paralyzes you." She leaned her head against his shoulder in a brief show of affection, then straightened again. "I don't know what would have happened to the dog if you hadn't been there."

The dog? It bothered him even more wondering what might have happened to *her.*

"You were really impressive, by the way."

One more compliment and he'd lose his tenuous hold on control. "I was fucking furious." *Still was*—not that she noticed. "I almost wish they hadn't left so easily."

"You wanted to fight?"

He gave a sharp nod. God, how he'd wanted to demolish them. Only his concern for Phoenix and the poor dog had stopped him.

"You're confident you'd have handled them okay?"

He was, but… "Not confident enough to risk you."

Her gaze moved over his face, and she smiled a little. "So if I hadn't been there?"

He stopped the golf cart in front of his drive and stared down at her. "If you weren't there, what would have happened to the dog?"

"You saved her."

"I can't fight and hold the dog, too. She'd have run off, and we might never have found her again. Imagine what a life that would have been for her."

"But we did find her, and now we'll make sure she's happy."

Coop stared at her, stunned by the idea of "we."

As if she didn't understand the significance of what she'd just said, Phoenix dug out her phone. "I saw some pet supplies in the camp store. I'll ask Ridley to see if they have flea shampoo, okay?"

Knowing she wanted to help, he banked the rage and managed another curt nod.

She didn't notice his struggle. Was she that comfortable with him? Or was she just that drawn into her own recriminations?

Dog first, Coop decided.

And once he had the animal settled, then he'd deal with Phoenix.

Ridley glanced at the lake, thinking how nice a dip would be in the cool water. She'd been working all day and, seriously, it sucked. Her shoulders ached, her hair was a mess and her hands were chapped.

Tomorrow, for sure, she'd find gloves.

Tomorrow? Did she really plan to do this all again?

Maybe.

Tired as she might be, she also felt a sense of satisfaction. Daron had come into one cabin to repair a leak in the sink just as she'd finished cleaning. He'd whistled low and said, "Spick-and-span. I don't think I've ever seen it this shiny."

Pleasure had almost made her blush. When was the last time she'd scrubbed a floor? Eons, it seemed. But she'd done it, challenged by Phoenix's skepticism, as well as a need to keep busy.

She'd glanced around too, and realized she *had* done a nice job. Score one for her. "Thanks. I don't believe in half-assing anything, you know?"

A true comedian, Daron had replied, "I'm all about the full ass."

They'd laughed together and she'd felt an odd sort of companionship—wrought from shared work?

For sure, what she felt with the fun-loving Daron wasn't nearly as intense as the punch of sensation from Baxter.

So here she was, multiple areas now cleaned, a bucket full of supplies in her hand, and she wondered where Baxter might be.

Shielding her eyes, she searched the beach around the lake, finally spotting him in a wet suit, the top rolled down around his lean hips leaving his upper body bare. She soaked in the sight of him, blond hair slicked back, tanned chest glistening in the sun, white teeth showing in a big grin as he talked…to two attractive women in bikinis.

She scowled. *What a dick.*

Would he go off with one—or both—of them? He could, she supposed, judging by their body language. One even stroked a finger down his chest, through a sprinkling of chest hair, down almost to his navel.

Never mind that other people crowded the beach, Baxter didn't stop her. Hedonist. Exhibitionist.

Show-off.

She sighed. *Confident men are so damned sexy.*

As if he felt her dark scrutiny, his gaze suddenly shifted to hers and locked there. He slowly turned to face her.

Busted. Ridley told herself to put her nose in the air and walk away, but instead she cocked out a hip and smirked at him.

It wasn't easy, showing attitude while holding a scrub bucket, but she hoped she managed it.

Without looking away, he said something to the women. Seeing their disappointment, she wasn't surprised when he started her way.

Well, hell.

When facing off with superstuds, she preferred to look her best, not her worst. Using a wrist, she pushed a hank of hair from her face, loosened her sweaty tank from her boobs, and curled her lips into a big fat smile, determined to exude her own share of confidence.

His stride was long enough that, even though he didn't appear to hurry, Baxter reached her in no time. Sunshine lightened the green of his eyes, making them look like emeralds as he studied her from her messy hair down to her feet and slowly back up again.

It felt like he'd just stroked her, and damn the man, she liked it enough that her nipples tightened.

A small, satisfied smile quirked one side of his mouth before he finally, reluctantly, lifted his attention to her face. "You made it through the whole day."

Umbrage unfurled. "You thought I wouldn't?"

"Many people don't."

Oh. So maybe that wasn't a specific insult aimed at her, but rather the expected norm. Ridley shrugged. "The Rose sisters always rise to a challenge." And Phoenix had definitely challenged her. Had she done it on purpose, just to egg her into leaving sooner? She couldn't wait to talk to her sister, to let her know that she'd not only stuck it out, but somewhat, sort of, *maybe just a little*, enjoyed exerting herself for a change.

Baxter said, "Good to know...in case I ever want to challenge you."

The two women he'd left behind walked past them, and along the way they cast frowning stares of disbelief at Ridley. She almost laughed. "It seems your adoring audience is confused."

He didn't look at them. "They're interested in classes."

"Uh-huh." *Shut up, Ridley.* "They're interested in *you*."

Lowering his head in assent, he murmured, "That, too." He rubbed a hand over his opposite shoulder and glanced up at the sun broiling down on his bare back. "Thing is, I don't fool around with customers."

"Well, shoot," she heard herself say. "There go my lessons."

His gaze locked on hers, and holy moly, some powerful tension arced between them.

He took a step closer. "It's hot as hell out here."

Hotter by the second. Nodding at his hips, she said, "'Specially in that suit, I bet."

"I have a place just outside the park." His gaze dropped to her mouth. "I'm heading there to shower if you want to join me."

Yes, she most definitely did. "Is your shower big enough for two?"

"Long as we stay real close."

Heat gathered at her core, making her breathless. "Works for me."

He took the bucket from her with one hand and with the other at the small of her back, turned her toward the scuba shop. "I have to change, then we can take my car."

Excitement, hot and heady, coursed through her. Ridley didn't even care about retrieving her purse or, as per her usual insistence, her own car.

She followed him to the scuba shop building. After setting the cleaning bucket on a bench, he used a key from a coiled band around his wrist and unlocked the door. Standing aside, he gestured for her to enter.

The interior was cool, dim and cramped with equipment.

"Give me two minutes to change." He disappeared past a curtain into a back room.

With anticipation riding her hard, Ridley busied herself by looking around. Rows of tanks filled the bottom shelf of a tall square table. *How long has it been since I had sex?* She couldn't remember, and that said something about the quality, right?

Snorkeling sets hung from standing racks. *How long since I wanted the sex this much?* Pretty sure the answer was *never.*

Regulators, goggles and fins filled various pegboards. Wet suits hung in the back. *Hurry up, Baxter.* If he didn't get a move on, she just might join him back there…

A stack of T-shirts caught her eye and she read the slogan on the front.

DIVERS GO DEEPER AND STAY DOWN LONGER.

"Oh, I hope so," she whispered, clenching her thighs in reaction.

She heard the swish of the curtain and looked up to see Baxter coming toward her. He wore a snowy-white V-neck T-shirt that stuck to wet spots on his chest and shoulders—proof that he hadn't taken the time to really dry off. Loose cargo shorts hung low on his lean hips and he wore unlaced sneakers.

All in all, he looked impossibly casual, sexy and in a hurry.

He got close and said, "I shouldn't have waited to do this."

"What—?" His mouth settled on hers before she could finish the question, answering with a demonstration that made her heart thunder.

His hot tongue teased along her lips, and she gladly opened, welcoming him in, curling her own tongue around him and giving up a soft moan of pleasure. His big hands framed her face, gently angling her one way while he tilted the other so that their mouths aligned perfectly for a hot, deep, wet kiss that curled her toes and tightened her womb.

He pulled back, drank in two deep breaths, then gripped her hand. "Come on."

They stepped back into the humid air. He locked the door behind them, took her hand again and headed for his car. They'd gone only a couple of feet when her cell phone buzzed in her back pocket. While keeping pace with him, she withdrew it and glanced at the screen—then stopped. "It's Phoenix," she said by way of explanation. Never, ever would she ignore her sister's call.

He paused with her, waiting, his expression hungry.

Ridley cleared her throat to remove the husky need from her voice, then said, "What's up, Phoenix?"

"We found a dog."

"We?" she asked.

Phoenix rushed out, "Cooper and me. We were down by the creek—"

"There's a creek?"

"*Ridley.* The dog might be hurt."

Something about this felt very off. She heard that odd note in her sister's voice—a note that meant *she* was the one hurt, scared or upset. *No, no, no.* Phoenix had already been through too much. "What can I do?"

"Some a-holes were picking on it, so we brought it back and it needs a bath. Will you see if there's any flea soap in the camp store, and maybe some dog food?"

"I'm on it, honey. Everything will be fine." Or at least, she prayed it would. The idea of Phoenix encountering people who'd mistreat an animal made Ridley want to put on her whoop-ass attitude and annihilate some jerks. "Where are you now?"

"Cooper's house. You know where it is?"

She looked at Baxter. "Cooper's house?"

A new alertness had entered his expression, as if he recognized a problem, and knew it would lead to his frustration.

To his credit, he picked up on her angst and didn't complain. "It's there." He pointed at the stone house on the rise. Putting his hand on her shoulder, his thumb caressing the joint, he asked, "What's wrong?"

Ridley shook her head and said to Phoenix, "I'll take care of it and be there in just a few, okay?" She'd rush because she needed to see for herself that Phoenix was okay. She'd *just* gotten her sister back. No way in hell would she let her go again. "Don't worry."

"Thanks, Ridley."

Blowing a kiss into the phone, she disconnected and, with a ton of regret, looked at Baxter. He stood there, tall, tense, and oh-so-ready. "I'm *really* sorry."

His eyes closed. "Well, damn."

Briefly, she explained what she knew while heading for the camp store. "I could have asked someone else to do it, but—"

"She's your sister."

How awesome was it that he understood? *Pretty damn awesome.* "Right."

He kept stride with her, saying, "If Maris doesn't have it here, I can run into town to grab what's needed."

She flashed him a smile over her shoulder. Not only did he not complain about their thwarted plans, but he offered to help. "A knight in shining armor."

"Let's not get carried away."

She paused just outside the store door so that he almost bumped into her, then whispered, "Not yet, anyway. Later, I plan to get very carried away."

Clasping her hips, he aligned his groin with her bottom. "I'll hold you to that."

Ridley drew in a shuddering breath. "That?" she asked, pressing back against him and the erection she felt. "Or my comment?"

"Both."

Before she expired of need, Ridley hurried on inside.

Fortunately, Maris had everything she needed, and to Ridley's surprise, Baxter didn't leave her once she had it all in a bag. He took the bag from her and started with her toward the hill.

Slanting him a look, she asked, "You're coming, too?"

"Might as well." He stared straight ahead. "I'm in need of a distraction."

Despite her worry, it pleased her that she wasn't the only one deeply affected. "Can I ask you something?"

If Ridley hadn't been watching him, she might have missed the very slight way he tensed.

"Something personal?"

"Relax. I'm not going to ask if you have dreams of marriage." God knew, she didn't. "Actually, it's about Cooper."

His shoulders loosened. "What about him?"

"Does he often take employees to his house?"

He shrugged. "For a grill-out every now and then, or to discuss a problem, sure." He put his hand on her back as the hill got steeper, giving her a little boost. "But if you're trying to find a roundabout way of asking if he gets involved with the women he employs, no, he doesn't. This thing with Phoenix is a first."

"So everyone has noticed that he's interested?"

Baxter snorted. "It'd be hard to miss. Surprising, too. Not only does Coop not date employees, far as I know he doesn't date. Anything he does with women he keeps strictly private." He nodded at the house. "So private, that I've never known him to bring anyone here except, like I said, as a group thing."

"Wow."

"Don't look so worried. Coop's a good guy."

"It's not that." She chewed her bottom lip, but she hadn't had anyone to talk to, and for some ridiculous reason Baxter suddenly felt like a good confidant. She glanced at him. "Do you know anything about my sister?"

He shrugged again.

"What does that mean?"

"It means I can guess." His brows pulled together. "I'm not exactly obtuse when it comes to women."

Oh, hell no. He wasn't...he wouldn't... "You were interested in *my sister*?" If she was second choice, she'd—

"What? No." He shook his head. "I mean, of course I noticed her. Any straight guy with a heartbeat would *notice* her. But from the start, she looked at Coop differently."

Mildly appeased, Ridley said, "So let's hear it. What do you think you know about her?"

Without hesitation, he said, "She's not shy, though she comes off that way because she's so reserved. Seems to me that's something new for her, like she probably used to be more outgoing."

"Very true." It killed Ridley to know how much damage those bastards had done.

Baxter continued, saying, "She's a little... I don't know. *Wounded.* Divorce maybe?"

"No," Ridley said without thinking. "Getting dumped is my shtick." The second the words left her mouth, Baxter paused to stare at her. She didn't want to go into those details, so she coasted past it real quick. "Phoenix was assaulted. Robbed, threatened." Her throat tightened. "Hurt."

"Jesus," he breathed. "Tell me the fuckers are locked up."

She wished she could. "They got away." Shaking off the worst of the memories, she added, "Phoenix is one of the strongest people I know. You could tell that girl to move a mountain and somehow she'd make it happen, but since the attack, she's had a hard time finding her inner Amazon. She's still in there, I know it. Phoenix knows it, too, and she's impatient to get back to one hundred percent. I think coming here is a great first step for her. But if things go wrong between her and Coop—"

"Give your sister some credit. Would an Amazon, even one in hiding, let a guy get the best of her?"

She frowned. "No, probably not. I can't help feeling protective, though."

"My guess is Coop is feeling the same." They'd almost reached the yard when Baxter said, "You know his wife was murdered, right?"

Ridley stopped so suddenly, she almost tripped herself.

Baxter turned to face her. "From what I heard, she was in a convenience store picking up bread and milk. There was an attempted robbery, a fight broke out, guns were involved, and Coop's wife got caught in the crossfire before the police arrived and killed both men."

Ridley stared at him, horrified as possibilities flew through her thoughts. "You think he sees a parallel with Phoenix?"

"I didn't say that. If anything, he's drawn to Phoenix because she's hot and sweet, and she looks at him like she wants to devour him. But knowing Coop, he's aware of her background and feeling some protectiveness, as well. Hell, I felt that way even before you shared. There's just something about her."

That made Ridley scowl. For someone who professed not to be interested, Baxter had already given more meaningful compliments to her sister than he ever had to her. Ridley knew he wanted her, but he sure seemed to like and respect Phoenix more.

And damn it, I will not be jealous of Phoenix. More than anyone else, Ridley knew what an amazing person her sister was. Of course everyone who met her would like her, too.

However, no one could like or respect her more than Ridley did.

"It seems odd," she grumbled, "that the first woman he gets involved with is someone who has a similar background to his wife. How genuine could that be?"

His widened eyes mocked her. "Are you trying to marry her off?"

"Of course not."

"Then what's the problem with two adults having some fun? You didn't strike me as a prude."

She made a rude sound. "Far from it."

"Same here. So let it go."

She countered that, asking, "Why did you tell me if you didn't think it was important?"

He opened his mouth, then closed it in a grim line. "Believe me, I wish I hadn't."

"But why did you?"

His hand fell away from her back. "You asked about other women. One thing led to another. But I fucking detest gossip so I hope you'll forget what I said."

Not likely, she thought. "I won't repeat it."

"Thanks." He looked at the house. "You can trust Coop. That's the important thing."

The door opened and Phoenix said to them, "Come on in."

7

BAXTER'S MOOD LIGHTENED AND HE GRINNED. "HEY, Phoenix."

"Baxter." Her gaze zeroed in on the bag.

"Everything you need." He held it out to her.

"Thank you."

"I'm just the mule. Your sister got it all together."

Phoenix turned to Ridley. "I appreciate it." She carried it quickly to the kitchen table and emptied the contents, putting out the food and two dishes, then unwrapping the soap.

Baxter saw Ridley staring toward the photo of Coop's deceased wife. She looked aloof, annoyed and so fucking hot, he hurt.

Phoenix affected him differently, in a nicer, lighter way, so he focused on her. She was more wet than dry, and too much sun left her nose and cheeks pink. Her glasses were a little crooked.

Overall, she looked sweet in a natural, earthy, very approachable way.

Total opposite of Ridley, who was more striking, polished and not all that approachable.

He burned for her.

Getting that thought out of his head, he asked, "Who's getting the bath, you or the dog?"

Phoenix flashed him a smile. "We were in the creek earlier, but most of this is from the dog." Heading out of the kitchen, she asked, "Want to meet her?" and gestured for them to follow.

In the laundry room, Coop stood at the tub, picking bugs and burrs off a young beagle and dropping them into a waste can.

Ridley had started forward but at the sight of a tick, she backpedaled and hit the wall.

Coop glanced up. "Thanks for coming by."

"Ridley wanted to help." He shifted his gaze to her. "Isn't that right?"

She carefully leaned forward, looked in the wastebasket at what they'd removed from the dog's fur and swallowed convulsively. "I don't like bugs."

So there was something that could unnerve her? Maybe she wasn't made of heated steel, after all. He couldn't resist saying, "Wow, look at that one. It's huge, and it has all those little legs still wiggling."

Phoenix swatted at him as she turned to her sister. "Ridley, would you wash and dry the food dishes you picked up? I think she'll be hungry once her bath is done."

"Glad to." Edging out of the laundry room, her gaze averted from the can, she darted out.

Smiling, Baxter watched her go. Even in a rush fleeing already dead bugs, her hips swayed and she kept her head high. The way that woman moved…it was enough to get his pulse tripping again. "I guess I shouldn't have teased."

"She'll get even later," Phoenix promised. "She always does."

Intrigued by that notion, Baxter held his hand out to the dog, let it sniff, then lightly touched under her chin. "Either of you want to share what happened?"

Phoenix spoke up, giving him a ridiculously brief rundown

of how they'd come to have a dog that mostly centered on Coop as a daring hero.

"He saved the day," Phoenix claimed. "You should have seen him, he was so impressive."

Biting back a grin, Baxter said, "Sorry I missed it."

Coop frowned while keeping his gaze on the dog. He'd lathered her up with the flea soap, something the dog seemed to enjoy as she lifted her nose and half closed her eyes in an expression remarkably like bliss.

"If you saw the three idiot kids, you'd know it wasn't impressive at all."

"*Three* of them," Phoenix stressed. "And they were men, not boys. Cooper was awesome."

"However it rolled out," Baxter said neutrally, "I'm glad you were both there to rescue this poor girl." He rubbed one knuckle under her throat and her eyes closed the rest of the way.

"She's cute, isn't she?" Phoenix crowded in next to him so she, too, could stroke the dog.

That got Coop's attention. He glanced first at Baxter, then at Phoenix standing so close. "While I finish up here, why don't you go help your sister?"

She carefully worked loose a mat in the dog's fur. "I doubt she needs any help washing a food bowl or opening a can."

His frown darkened. "I could use a cup of coffee, if you don't mind making it."

She straightened. "Actually, that sounds good to me, too."

Coop looked relieved. "Coffee is in the cabinet next to the fridge."

"Got it." She bent to the dog again. "Enjoy your bath, sugar."

Coop waited until she'd gone, then looked up at Baxter. "That's bullshit about me being a hero."

Folding his arms, Baxter leaned against a cabinet. "Not from her perspective." He glanced out the door, but Phoenix was gone. "Ridley told me what happened to her."

Coop shot him a look. "I don't think she'll thank her sister for that. Phoenix is private."

"Guess Ridley needed to talk, too." He shrugged. "You know I won't say anything."

Gently, Coop rinsed the dog—while telling a very different story about their conflict at the creek.

Baxter had to admit, Coop's version, complete with rage, sounded more realistic. "Damn. Thank God she wasn't there alone."

Though fury burned in his eyes, Coop kept his tone even, calm, when he said, "You have no idea how badly I wanted to take those punks apart."

"I have a good guess." Baxter knew he would have felt the same.

"Phoenix is stronger than she realizes, but even when she has good reason for caution, she thinks she's being weak." Coop snorted. "Like she would stand a chance against three men."

"Maybe it's not that she couldn't take them on, but that it brought up old memories for her. She probably wants to put that in the past, where it belongs, so when something happens to bring it back—"

"She feels out of control." Coop paused in thought. "I can understand that." He rubbed the lather along the dog's back... and her tail went wild. "Happens to me occasionally, too."

After a long look, Baxter nodded. "To everyone, I suppose." That was as close as he'd come to admitting he sometimes still dealt with his own shitty memories. "You think they'll show up tomorrow?"

"I hope so, but it's doubtful. For one thing, none of them wanted to take me on."

"Going up against a guy your size is a little different than kicking around a stray, or scaring a woman."

"Makes them cowards to do either, and I can't see a coward

facing me man-to-man for any reason." He met Baxter's gaze. "Sneaking around, though, that I can imagine."

Would the creeps dare to slink into the park after hours, maybe to commit acts of vandalism? It seemed possible.

"Let Daron know so we can all keep an eye out."

"I could go back to the creek." He'd relish the excuse to burn off some energy. "Maybe cross the trestle, take a look around. They probably live nearby."

Coop was already shaking his head. "It'll be dark soon. And when I speak with the cops, I don't want them to think we were looking for trouble."

Much as Baxter hated to admit it, he had a point. "You're calling them tonight?"

"I had to prioritize. The dog was covered in mud and too many ticks and fleas for me to want her in the house without cleaning her up first."

And no doubt, Phoenix had been shaken. "I'll call Daron soon as I leave here. I'll let Maris and Joy know, too."

"Thanks." Coop lifted the dog out onto a towel spread over the top of the dryer. When she shook, she sprayed them both—as well as the walls and cabinets—making the men laugh. The dog barked in what sounded like happiness.

Baxter smiled at her. "You like being clean, do you, girl?" Clean and safe.

"She has a cut on her ear," Coop said, drying around the area very carefully, "but I think it's okay. My guess is she scratched it while running or hiding from those assholes, maybe on a piece of fencing or something."

While Baxter checked the ear too, the dog's butt swayed back and forth in bliss. "Yeah, a small cut. Doesn't seem to bother her." He saw the gentle way Coop dried her and guessed, "You're keeping her?"

"Yeah." He set the dog on her feet. She stared up at him with enormous, adoring brown eyes, still wiggling, waiting for direction. Coop shook his head in amusement, then led her to the kitchen by patting his thigh.

They entered the room, and Baxter stalled.

Phoenix was just opening a pizza box. She smiled at the dog while saying, "Guess what? Maris brought us a pizza, plus cupcakes for dessert. She said it's her contribution to the dog rescue." Phoenix set down a food dish and the dog attacked it. "Guess that proves she didn't eat a chicken!"

Coop didn't seem to see anything wrong with the impromptu dinner. "Smells good." He got down plates, handing one to Ridley and shoving one at Baxter.

He automatically took the plate, but said, "I need to get going."

Ridley shot him a disbelieving look, but he avoided her gaze. He didn't want this, didn't want to sit around the table taking part in cozy conversations with friends.

That reeked of something more than hot sex.

More than superficial.

Ignoring his statement, Phoenix dropped a slice of pizza on the plate. "You've got a few minutes to eat, right?" Holding his gaze, waiting for an answer, she pulled out a chair and sat.

He felt put on the spot big-time—and damn it, she did it deliberately. He stared back at her. "Maybe one piece."

Approval curled her lips. "Great."

Ridley, her back now stiff, gave her sister a dirty look as she took the seat beside her. Mouth tight, eyelids half-closed, she affected a brooding expression. It seemed she didn't like the situation any more than he did. For reasons he couldn't understand, that added to his pissed-off mood.

While Baxter stood there arguing with himself, Coop snagged the chair next to Phoenix.

Now he had no choice but to sit by Ridley.

And why the hell was that such a problem?

Because I wanted to fuck her, not engage in social chitchat.

"I can keep her tonight, but let me know if you want a turn."

Baxter's gaze shot up, a scowl in place, a protest ready…and he realized Coop was talking to Phoenix about the dog.

Luckily, Coop was watching the antics of the animal, and Ridley had her attention fixed on her plate.

But Phoenix didn't miss a thing, and she gave him an evil grin.

How had he never noticed her mean streak?

Bright moonlight spilled through the window, painting soft shadows on the ceiling. The air-conditioning kept the small cabin cool. Phoenix and Ridley were up in the loft, side by side, neither of them sleeping yet.

She felt her gaze the moment Ridley looked at her, and she almost sighed. Truthfully, she was surprised her sister had held back so long.

Phoenix's body was tired, but her mind wouldn't settle. *What-ifs* ran through her thoughts at Mach speed—and in every scenario, she came up lacking.

"You made yourself at home in Coop's kitchen."

Well, that was an innocuous enough comment, not at all what Phoenix had expected. "He asked me to make the coffee."

Ridley turned on her side, propping her head on her hand. "He keeps a photo of his wife on his desk."

"I'm sure there are photos in other places, too." His TV room…and his bedroom. When Phoenix thought about the image of his wife, *soft* was the first description to come to mind. Soft blond hair, soft dark blue eyes, soft smile. Cooper's wife was a lovely woman—and he'd lost her. It made her heart ache for him.

It made her think about her fiancé, the man she'd pushed away.

She would always feel bad for what she'd done to David, but she knew in her heart that she'd made the right decision when she'd broken the engagement. David deserved someone who would love him as Cooper had loved his wife.

She wasn't that woman.

Oh, she'd cared for him. A lot. But that she'd wanted *away* from him after the attack spoke volumes. He couldn't console her because she hadn't wanted him to. She hadn't wanted anything from anyone. Not even her future husband.

Letting him go was the kindest thing to do.

"It didn't bother you to see the photo?" Ridley asked.

She shook her head. "I think he's still grieving for her."

"You," Ridley said, "are an amazingly wonderful woman."

Phoenix turned her head to see her sister, not sure what had brought that on. "Thank you. You're pretty wonderful yourself."

Ridley was silent a moment, then asked, "Do you know how she died?"

"No." Phoenix also rolled to her side, but she was too tired to prop herself up and instead just snuggled into her pillow. "Do you?"

"Baxter told me."

Her sister's hesitation bothered her. "And?"

"There are…similarities." She held Phoenix's hand. "To what you went through, I mean."

Catching her breath, Phoenix half sat up in denial. "What are you saying?"

Ridley squeezed her hand tighter. "She was shot during a robbery. It was an accident, I think."

Her heart slammed in her chest. "Shot?"

"Caught in the crossfire is how Baxter put it."

"How tragic," she whispered, reclining to her back again. In only minutes, a senseless act of violence had upended Cooper's life, changing it forever. She couldn't imagine the heartache he'd suffered.

The sudden urge to go to him, to comfort him, chased away her tiredness. Not that he struck her as a man who would take comfort. No, he was the type of man who would suffer in silence, then push forward through sheer will. A strong man.

A gentle man.

As he'd proved today, a hero.

"Has he ever mentioned her to you?" Ridley asked.

"No." Phoenix studied the shadows on the ceiling. "Why would he?"

Ridley loomed over her. "Because he's interested in you, that's why."

Maybe he was, but probably not like that. Not for anything beyond a physical relationship. She was okay with that. She couldn't get involved anyway. A week or two of sex? That sounded about right. Actually, it sounded incredible.

But anything more wasn't on the agenda.

Right?

That thought was so unsettling, she asked, "What about you and Baxter?"

Ridley sighed dramatically. "We'd been well on our way to getting down and dirty, and I have a feeling it would've been sublime."

Phoenix turned again. "And? What happened?"

"No idea, really, except that Baxter is a dumbass who's afraid of conversation," Ridley complained.

Phoenix snorted a laugh. "What does that mean exactly?"

"You didn't notice how he froze up at dinner?"

"He was a little quiet," Phoenix admitted.

"Oh, the man was all about getting horizontal, but hanging out together with family and friends? He turned into a silent, withdrawn jackass."

Dumbass, jackass. The rapid-fire insults led Phoenix to believe that Ridley was hurt, and that fascinated her. "Did the two of you—?"

"No." Ridley shook her head. "We were headed that way before you called."

Phoenix could almost hear the regret in her sister's voice. Gently, she said, "I'm sorry I interrupted."

"Don't be." Her jaw worked. "I've decided he's not worth the trouble."

"Sex is trouble now?"

Ridley almost snarled. "With Baxter?" She punched her pillow a few times. "Apparently."

Phoenix had difficulty sorting out the problem. "So you think the idea of getting to know you better actually scared him off?"

"What else? He woofed down a slice of pizza, ate an entire cupcake in one bite, then ran off as if he thought I might wrestle him down and jam a wedding band on his finger." She huffed. "*So* stupid."

"Clearly, he doesn't know your history—or does he?"

"Not much of it, and it's just as clear that he doesn't want to. He wants sex, period."

Phoenix studied her sister's face in the pale glow of the moon. Sudden awareness dawned, bringing her more alert. "And you want more?"

"No," Ridley said with heat—and a touch of desperation. "Absolutely not."

Sadly, Phoenix knew that wasn't true. Her sister had loved being a wife, and had looked forward to being a mother. It still broke her heart to know what Robbie had put her through. In a cautious whisper, she asked, "Then what's the problem?"

"He got me all primed then just..."

Gently, Phoenix probed, "Just what?"

"He abandoned me!"

The outburst took her by surprise. "Well, we did have a little catastrophe with the dog, so..."

"No, it wasn't that," Ridley insisted. "He was fine when we first found out about the dog. I figured we'd hang with you guys a bit, then carry on with our plans. But noooo. That was asking too much."

"Maybe it wasn't that," Phoenix said, trying to find a way to make Ridley feel better. The problem was, she didn't know Baxter well enough to know what motivated him, how he felt about women.

How he might feel about her sister.

"Didn't you see how he cut me out?" The sound of Ridley punching her pillow again gave away her frustration. "He was downright cold. I doubt he'll ever follow up on those sexual promises he made. What type of a jerk gets a woman all hot and bothered and then bails?"

A jerk with his own history, Phoenix was thinking, but instead of saying so, she pointed out the obvious. "You were awfully quiet over dinner, too."

"I was annoyed. Know the difference."

Oh, she knew the difference—because she *did* know her sister. Nine times out of ten, when offended, Ridley went for the jugular. With Baxter, she'd withdrawn.

Her sister was in deeper than she wanted to admit, but Phoenix let her off the hook, saying, "We're a pitiful pair, aren't we?"

"Not you." Ridley took her hand again, lunging into the switch in topic. "Look at all the changes you've made! I'm so proud of you, Phoenix. So damn proud."

Her sister's praise only reminded her of how badly she'd reacted earlier. "There's no reason to be proud, believe me." She told Ridley everything that had happened at the creek—including how memories had glued her feet to the ground and muddled her thoughts, how she was useless and didn't do a damn thing to help.

"Oh, my God," Ridley groaned theatrically. "That's such a load of crap and you know it." Sitting up in a rush, she poked Phoenix in the stomach.

"Omph. Hey!"

"You deserved that poke!" She started to do it again.

Phoenix quickly rolled out of the way, coming up with her pillow as a weapon. "Stop it!"

"No, *you* stop with the melodramatic self-recrimination."

"Melodramatic?" Phoenix gasped.

"It's ridiculous! I've never been attacked, but I know I would have been just as cautious under the circumstances. You're not Superwoman, you know, so give yourself a break already."

Her frown faded as she realized that Ridley's argument was very similar to Cooper's. "What if Cooper hadn't been there?"

"I hope you'd have had enough sense not to confront the men!"

Sense had nothing to do with it. It was all about fear. "So I should have just left that poor dog to—"

"No," Ridley said with impatience. "You call for backup instead. What good would it do the dog if you *both* got hurt? And that's probably what would've happened if you'd done things any differently."

She had a point. "The problem is that I'm not sure I could have thought that clearly, I was so terrified."

"With good reason. But look how far you've come." This time Ridley stroked her hair. "I see a world of difference, even if you don't. You're here in this crowded resort, mingling every day. You're actually planning wild sex with Big Sexy."

"I didn't say it would be wild."

"And you're arguing with me!" Ridley threw out her arms. "You're well on your way, so stop rushing yourself. Even Amazons need time to heal."

Phoenix didn't know what she was talking about with Amazons, but she felt like she *had* made progress, so perhaps she should give herself a break. "You're a pretty awesome big sister, you know?"

"Yeah, I am. You definitely got lucky in the sister department." She grinned, her teeth showing white in the dim light. "But then so did I."

A yawn interrupted Phoenix's smile. Finally her brain was

as tired as her body. "Maybe we can solve our man problems tomorrow."

"For sure we won't figure it out tonight." Ridley stretched out on her back and pulled a sheet to her waist. "Good night, Phoenix."

"Night." With most of her remorse lifted, Phoenix closed her eyes…and thought of Cooper.

It was a nice way to fall asleep.

The impromptu dinner had helped to curb Coop's simmering anger. Having Phoenix at his table, seeing her relaxed, knowing she enjoyed playing matchmaker, had all reassured him that she was okay—no doubt still berating herself, but he'd eventually get her over that.

He wasn't sure if Baxter or Ridley had realized her intentions, but he'd caught on right away when he noticed how she watched the pair. It amused him, seeing this other facet to her personality.

Through her actions, Phoenix had made it clear that she felt part ownership of the dog, but Coop wasn't sure how that would work. Was she ready for that type of relationship, where they shared a mutual responsibility?

Was he?

He wanted her, yes—wanted her sexually, wanted her happy, wanted her to feel secure. But beyond that…it'd be such a big step for both of them, a step that could lead to more.

He feared he was already on the way to that, so it could be a moot point.

He'd wanted Phoenix to maintain that happier mood during dinner, not dredge up the conflict again by calling the cops in front of her. Because of that, he'd waited until everyone left before notifying the local police.

The timing worked out, actually. He reached one of the men he knew, Officer Gibb Clark, who worked evenings. Coop explained to Gibb what had happened, and the arrangements he'd made to meet with the men tomorrow.

Not surprisingly, based on Coop's descriptions, and where the conflict took place, Gibb felt sure he knew the men.

"Picking on a mutt sounds like their MO," Gibb said. "I'll go by there tonight to see if any of them are still out and about, and if so, I'll talk with them. As to them coming by to see you tomorrow, I don't see that happening."

"I had the same thought," Coop said. "Seems more likely they'll show up at night to cause trouble."

"Afraid so. Let me know if anything happens, and I'll be out tomorrow just in case they show."

Coop thought about Phoenix and her sister in the cabin alone. He knew Phoenix locked up every night. Besides, with all the cabins, tents, RVs and fifth wheels, the bastards would have no idea where she was.

He'd paced the kitchen as he talked to Gibb, the dog trotting along behind him. Whenever he stopped, the dog sat, her eyes alert in expectation. It was like having a shadow…with a tongue that hung out and a butt that constantly wiggled.

When he finished the call, he replaced the phone on the desk and turned to look down at her. She jumped to her feet, ears up.

"Ready for bed?"

The question earned him a bark, then she ran three tight circles—looking far from tired.

"I have a feeling it's going to be a long night." Coop fetched an old blanket and put it in the corner of the kitchen opposite the food and water dish, then called her over with a soft whistle.

Curious, she sprinted to him, ears flopping, butt moving counter to her shoulders. Coop grinned. She really was a cute little thing.

He gestured at the temporary bed. "What do you think?"

She sniffed the blanket, looked at Coop and waited.

"Sorry, but Phoenix isn't set up for a dog. Her place is too small and she sleeps in a loft—"

Rearing back on her haunches, the dog yapped at him.

Somehow, though it came from a small, adorable pup, that yap felt like a reprimand. "I couldn't invite her to stay over. Her sister—"

Another yap.

Coop sighed, recognizing the ridiculousness of carrying on a one-sided conversation with a dog. "If we're going to have these talks, you at least need a name."

As if she understood, she tipped her head, one ear flopping down, the other cocked in interest.

Kneeling, he offered a hand for her to sniff. "I'll have to give it some thought. Before your bath, I would have named you Mud. I'm not sure Phoenix would approve, though."

Butt wiggling, the dog crawled into his lap. With a lusty sigh, she put her head over Coop's forearm, then looked at him with dark, worried eyes.

"You'll like it here in the kitchen. It's cozy and quiet."

The dog appeared far from convinced. From her perspective, the large kitchen might seem lonely.

Coop glanced at the photo of his wife on the desk area. So often, Anna's image had kept him company while he worked on accounts, paid bills or researched equipment or employees. Having her near hadn't filled the emptiness; to the contrary, it had kept the emptiness fresh, as if he'd wanted it to last.

In that moment, it struck Coop that the hollow pain he'd learned to live with was no longer quite so hollow, or quite so painful.

Phoenix, with her smiles, her attitude of determination and her own soft need, had blunted those familiar aches.

His chest constricted, but with a deep breath that he slowly released, everything inside him loosened. It was as if he'd also released the old rage...and the loneliness.

The change had happened so slowly that he hadn't noticed it—and yet so suddenly that it left him reeling with surprise.

He was different now.

Whatever happened between Phoenix and him, he'd never go back. Hell, he wasn't even sure he *could* go back.

As he stared at his wife's smiling image, he smiled, too. He'd kept photos of her everywhere as if by seeing her, she wasn't really gone. Somewhere along the way they'd become painful reminders of what he'd lost.

Now, he found the photo soothing, like the whisper of a cherished memory…one that no longer hurt.

He stroked the dog, saying, "She loved animals."

A tiny voice in his head said, *So does Phoenix.* Hadn't she rushed to the dog's rescue? Despite her fear, she hadn't suggested that they leave.

No matter what she believed about herself, Coop knew that if he hadn't been with her, Phoenix would have found a way to save the dog. He just hoped and prayed that, if ever put to the test, she'd know to call for backup before doing anything reckless on her own.

He'd wanted to talk with her, to explain that the situation had warranted her caution. There was no reason for her to think she'd acted cowardly. In fact, he hoped she would stay cautious.

But Ridley had shown up with Baxter in tow, and the tension between them had been like a live thing. Every time Baxter had looked at Ridley, sparks flew—even though Ridley refused to look back. Despite the way they'd tried to ignore each other, it was obvious that Phoenix's call had interrupted their plans.

Coop would have found it funnier if his own plans hadn't gone off course.

He wanted Phoenix, now more than ever, and if it hadn't been for the dog, he'd probably be in bed with her right now.

That realization brought its own concerns.

Her bed was out; Ridley was staying with her and there was only the loft.

And his bed…

With another sigh, the dog closed her eyes and pretended to sleep. Coop knew it was a pretense because every couple of seconds, she looked up at him—as if to ensure he hadn't budged.

One more glance at his wife's image—and he made a decision.

"C'mon, girl. Let's see if you need to do any business before I turn in." He carried her out, ignoring the idolizing way she licked his chin.

Since it was dark, he kept a close watch on her after sitting her down. Tomorrow he'd need to get a collar and leash, and he supposed a trip to the vet was in order.

While the dog sniffed every blade of grass, Coop stared toward Phoenix's cabin, then around the resort. All was quiet. Security lights lit the grounds, as well as exterior lights on the campers. There were enough guests that no one could be truly isolated.

Indicating she'd finished, the dog sat on his foot and leaned against his leg.

Coop scooped her up and they went back inside. He locked the door, then carried the dog to the bed he'd made on the kitchen floor. "Be good," he told her when she started to follow him.

She sat back, her eyes huge, somehow conveying worry.

"It'll be fine, and soon you'll prefer sleeping alone." Hoping she believed him, he turned out the light and went down the hall.

When he reached his bedroom, he undressed and turned back the bed. There on the nightstand was another photo of his wife. She'd been gone five years now, and there had been times that he'd felt like he'd lived a lifetime without her.

Tonight was different.

Because of Phoenix.

Because what he felt for her was different.

He picked up the photo, brushing his thumb along the edge of the frame. "I will always love you, Anna."

Her image, so serene, gazed back.

He wanted Phoenix to move on, and because of her, he was ready to do the same.

He smiled at the photo and slipped it into a drawer.

The bedroom, he decided, was not a place for dwelling in the past.

With much on his mind, he turned out the light and stretched out on the bed.

Seconds later, the dog started howling just outside his door.

8

THE NEXT MORNING, WHILE PHOENIX INHALED HER usual cup of coffee at the camp store, Coop came in, the dog held in one arm. Her ears bounced with each step he took, and she appeared to be smiling as she looked around at everyone and everything.

Such a happy little dog. Seeing her made Phoenix happy, too.

She needed a leash, a collar and probably a dozen other things.

As soon as the pup saw Phoenix, she wriggled to get down. There were very few people in the store this early, so Coop set her on her feet, and she came charging over, her ears blowing back, her frantically wagging tail visible in her whole body.

"Hello, sugar." Phoenix crouched down and hugged the dog close, accepting the doggy kisses to her face.

"Sugar?" Coop asked. "Is that what we're calling her?"

One more thing the dog needed: a name. "It was just an endearment."

"She is sweet," Coop said as he considered the dog, then he mumbled, "When I'm not trying to sleep, that is."

Uh-oh. "She kept you up?"

"No, she slept fine—once I let her into the bedroom with me."

Picturing that brought a smile to her face. "She slept with you?"

"In my closet, actually." Coop gratefully took the cup of coffee that Maris handed to him, thanking her before taking a drink.

Making a sound of appreciation, he pulled out the chair next to Phoenix and sat. "She refused to sleep in the kitchen, as I originally planned. You should have heard her howling. It was pitiful."

"Awww." Phoenix cuddled the dog closer, then kissed the top of her furry little head.

"I couldn't take it."

"Of course you couldn't. Neither could I. I bet she was scared."

"After what she'd been through, then coming to an unfamiliar place, I'm sure it was all spooky to her." He took another drink, then sighed. "Soon as I let her into the room, she ran around all crazy, on the bed, under the bed, into the connected bathroom. She kept going until she found the closet door open enough for her to burrow in." He shrugged. "She didn't come back out."

Phoenix reseated herself, then lifted the dog into her lap. "She probably had to hide at night, you know?" *From cruel men, as well as natural predators.* God, how she hated that thought.

"That's what I figured." He reached out to scratch the dog behind the ear. She tipped up her face, let her tongue loll out and half closed her eyes. "I checked to make sure she wasn't destroying anything, but she was just curled up tight in the corner behind my hanging clothes and a pair of work boots. I don't think she needed it, but I got the blanket out of the kitchen for her, moved a few things around and let her get comfortable again. She slept there until I got up this morning."

Not a bad compromise. "You were tired, weren't you, sugar?"

"Let's hope the good behavior holds out, because I got an early vet appointment for her today."

Wow, that was quick. "How'd you manage that?"

"Small town." He made a vague hand gesture. "Everyone knows everyone, so the vet is a friend. He fit me in before his regular business hours start."

"That's so nice." One more way that showed how special a small town could be. Not that she needed another reason to love Cooper's Charm—after her first week she'd been sold on the place. Now, knowing Cooper so well…

He reached over and tugged lightly on her ponytail. "While I'm gone, don't go near the woods, or to any of the more private areas of the property."

Well, that sounded ominous. Lifting her brows, she said, "Define private."

Though his tone was mild enough, his jaw tightened. "If you have to go to the maintenance building, take someone with you."

Incredulity brought out a laugh. "Like who?" Until Ridley had stepped in as housekeeper, they'd been shorthanded. Now they barely broke even on workloads.

"Just wait for me to get back, and I'll go with you."

The last thing she wanted was another person worrying about her. She had no one but herself to blame, of course, not after how she'd reacted yesterday.

"Should I point out that there are several campers using the primitive tent area near there?"

He leaned closer. "I don't care who's camping, I don't want you alone that far from the congested areas."

She frowned. Maybe it was more than her reaction that had him concerned. "You expect trouble from those men?"

"Actually, I don't." His hand lifted to her face, curving around her cheek. "But I'm not willing to chance it."

Whoa. What he said, how he looked at her while saying it, felt so intimate, it brought a flush to her face. After all the touching and teasing yesterday, she knew they were on the fast track to a sexual relationship. Knew it and anticipated it.

But she hadn't expected so much emotional involvement, all the casual public touching and…and the concern. Caring for someone, worrying for them, had nothing to do with uncommitted sex.

She'd come to Cooper's Charm to reassert her independence—but could she do that if she immediately fell into a relationship?

Phoenix hugged the dog closer, knowing that what bothered her most was how much she liked the idea.

How much she liked *him*.

To escape the lure of his golden eyes, she turned her attention to the dog.

Aware of Maris peeking at them, and Daron just coming in, she nodded. "Okay." Giving in to him was the easier path to take, but she didn't feel cowardly—just prudent. After all, if he thought there could be danger, it didn't make sense to push. "I promise."

She heard the wry note in his muttered, "Thank you."

Had her promise sounded less than sincere?

Now that he'd gotten his way, he sat back and lifted his coffee cup again.

One thought led to another and she asked, "When are we meeting with them?"

The cup plunked back to the table. He didn't pretend not to understand. "We? I don't want you anywhere near them."

That got her back stiff. "Why not? I have as much right to confront them as you do." She thrust up a quick hand. "And no, don't say it. It'll be perfectly safe this time and you know it."

With his jaw tightening again, he stared at her. *Into* her. "I'm the one paying. Unless you want to?"

She snorted, not about to fall for that nonsense. "Neither of us would give that Harry creep a dime, so don't try to sell me that. Have you contacted the police yet?"

Cooper sighed. "Last night, actually."

She leaned closer. "So you're setting a trap for him?"

"If I say yes, will you stay away?"

The dog stirred, looking up at her worriedly, before gazing at Cooper.

Though Phoenix had just given herself a pep talk on uncommitted sex, it hurt that he wanted to cut her out.

That he didn't trust her enough to let her be a part of it.

He probably figured she'd freak out again…and in all honesty, she couldn't promise him that she wouldn't.

Keeping all emotion from her tone, she said, "When it comes down to it, you don't have to make up stories. After all, you're the boss."

Cooper stared at her, his expression even harder. His lips curved in a terrible attempt at a smile. "Maybe we could step outside for a minute?"

She shared her own attempt at smiling. "Of course." She started to rise, but he surprised her by taking the dog from her first, then putting a hand to her back.

That meant she had to go first. Maris watched with amusement. Daron stood beside her, arms folded, a big grin on his face.

Did they both know she was in trouble?

That irked her so much that she ended up striding more rigidly than she'd intended. Once outside, she turned on Cooper—but he stepped around her, heading for a picnic table on the sandy lakeshore. The dog stared after her.

Huffing, Phoenix followed him until he finally stopped and set down the dog, his back still to her. She had a finger up to make a verbal point when Cooper suddenly turned, scooping an arm around her lower back and drawing her close.

"First…" His mouth lowered to hers, and despite the heat in his eyes and the grim set to his brows, the kiss was light and gentle. He put his forehead to hers.

"First what?" she managed to whisper.

"First I had to get that out of my system." His warm breath teased her lips. "I've been thinking about kissing you since..."

"Since?"

He quirked a bemused smile. "Since the last time I kissed you, actually."

"Oh." Since she'd been thinking about it too, she savored the admission.

"Second," he continued, his tone more stern, "this isn't about you being an employee. And even if it was, you're more than that now and you know it."

Yes, she did, and it didn't bother her as much as it should. "You write my paychecks," she pointed out, softly now since he'd so nicely kissed her.

"That's separate from this." He kissed her again, not so light or gentle now.

The dog barked.

Cooper leaned back and, with a smile, straightened her glasses for her. "Now, could you tell me why you want to be there?"

That felt suspiciously like a trick question. "If you'll tell me first why you *don't* want me there."

To her surprise, he agreed. "All right." Taking her hand, he led her the rest of the way to a sun-bleached table. The dog, playing a few feet away, dug in the sand.

After they'd both taken seats, he said, "As you know, I called the local police. Officer Gibb Clark, a friend, is going to join me. We're hoping the bastards show up, but it's doubtful. If they do, it could get ugly."

Her eyes flared. "You would fight with them in front of an officer?"

"That's not my plan, but anything is possible. What I meant is that Gibb will likely take them in—one way or another—for some answers. That's if they even show. Either way, I'd as soon the men not focus on you more than necessary. If they do put in an appearance, things won't go the way they're hoping and I'd prefer they see me as their problem, not you."

Actually...that all made sense. Even without the past that influenced her reactions, he was certainly better able to handle them than she'd be. "All right."

"Thank you." He caught her chin. "Now tell me why you wanted to be there?"

The urge to look away made her heart beat faster, but she didn't want to be a coward anymore. "Mostly I wanted to prove to myself..." *What?* She shook her head. "Something. *Anything.*" That sounded so lame she groaned. "I don't want them to know that they intimidated me."

Cooper slowly nodded. "Okay, I get that."

Because he would feel the same? She couldn't imagine anyone intimidating him. He seemed so self-possessed and sure of himself.

"You understand, though," he continued, "that anyone in that type of disadvantage would feel intimidated?"

"I do now, yeah." She cracked her first genuine smile. "Ridley gave me hell last night. She called me melodramatic and a few other things." When he started to scowl, she laughed. "It was her way of telling me the same thing you're saying. Plus, she insisted that I'm doing great now, much better—and she's right. For a while there, I'd...lost myself."

"You weren't used to being afraid."

"No, and believe me, I don't like it."

His brows pulled together. "Yesterday was a setback."

"Maybe a little. But I realize that, most of the time, I don't even think of the assault anymore." Which meant she really had come a long way. For a while there, she'd lived in the memories, unable to escape them for more than a few minutes at a time. Now the opposite was true. She thought of it less and less—while she lived more and more.

Relief showed in the loosening of his shoulders. His frown eased. "I'm glad to hear it."

She watched the dog jump after a butterfly. "Will you let me know what happens?"

"Yes. Right afterward, we're supposed to go for the lawnmower—and dinner. We can talk about it then."

Very aware of his warmth beside her, his big powerful body and those beautiful eyes, she leaned closer but kept her gaze on the dog. "Mmm. And after that?"

He stilled, but then his hand slid under her hair, clasping the back of her neck. "After that I'm hoping to have you alone."

She glanced at him, then away, struggling to look blasé. "For sex?"

"Eventually." Proving he was aware of her game, he growled, "I want to get you naked first. Seeing you at the creek, your shirt and shorts clinging to your hot bod..."

Warmth spread inside her.

"That was a hell of a tease, Phoenix." His hand moved over her shoulder, down her arm to her elbow, then onto her waist. "I'm going to need at least an hour just to look and touch."

Anticipation nearly sucked away her breath. "Sounds like a plan." She turned and kissed him, fast and hard. She had to go now—while she still could. "I should get to work."

He stood with her, and she saw that his eyes were brighter, his nostrils flared.

He really did want her, and it thrilled her.

He clasped her chin. "We'll leave at five."

"I'll be ready." She'd have to finish early enough to shower and change. For once she wanted Cooper to see her dressed as a woman, not just as the head groundskeeper.

He continued to look at her, the tension mounting—then he tore his gaze away and whistled for the dog. "C'mon, Sugar. Time for your appointment."

The dog tipped her head, letting one ear touch the ground

while the other flopped over her forehead. Then she lunged, racing toward Cooper, stopping short, darting away again.

He shook his head. "She has these running fits..."

Phoenix laughed. "You'll really name her Sugar?"

"Why not? She's pretty damn sweet." When the dog ran close again, he caught her up against his chest and she immediately started licking his face.

So far, Sugar had gotten more kisses than she had, Phoenix thought.

But tonight, that would change.

The issues of a relationship faded away behind ripe anticipation.

Now that she'd already done this once, Ridley discovered a pattern and so she did very little backtracking, which meant she finished the chores more quickly. Plus, after the thorough cleaning of yesterday, today was mostly upkeep of the areas she tended, with the addition of two locations where campers had just checked out of cabins.

When she finished early, she made a decision.

Throughout the day, she'd only seen Baxter from a distance, but with every second that passed without him seeking her out, she stewed with indignation...and her determination grew.

She would have him, hotly, thoroughly—and then she'd be the one to walk away. Let him be the one left wondering.

Oh, she'd make it so good, so outrageously incendiary that he'd want her again and again...but she would decline.

It was a powerful fantasy, very unlike her usual risqué dreams, which focused more on the activities, not the ending of them.

But for now it'd do.

In order to play that out, she needed privacy. No way would she be trapped at Baxter's home—wherever that was—and she definitely couldn't see a sexual marathon happening in Phoenix's small, low-ceiling loft.

Especially with Phoenix living there, too.

Mind made up, Ridley put away her gear, grabbed a quick shower and headed up the long drive to where she'd left her car. She wasn't exactly sure where she'd go, but a gas station attendant could probably give her some direction.

Along the way, she passed Daron, the flirt, and asked him, "You're going the wrong way, aren't you?"

He grinned. "Coop asked me to watch his new dog while he wined and dined your hottie sister."

Making a theatrical display of it, Ridley looked around. "And yet I don't see the dog. Lost her already?"

"Maris kept her for me while I helped a camper get everything stored away. He's new to RVing and wasn't sure about… anything."

"Like?"

"How to park it, how to hook it up to the water and electric, how to turn on the fridge or television—all basic necessities."

So Daron knew how to do all that? It didn't surprise her. He was an incredible handyman with a knack for tinkering that, according to Phoenix, could make anything run.

"Fascinating," she said, already thinking ahead.

Ignoring her observation, Daron nodded approvingly at her fitted summer dress and strappy sandals. "And where are you off to, looking so fine?"

Yes, she did look fine. She'd specifically chosen the peach-colored casual pull-on dress because it hugged her figure and came close to matching her skin tone. Now if only Baxter would notice…

She no sooner had the thought than she turned and saw him, a good distance away, staring at her and Daron with arrested attention.

Oh, now, that was nice. "Thank you for the compliment." She sidled closer to Daron and touched his chest. "So you know all about the setup and running of RVs, do you?"

"Sure. They're easy once you get the hang of it."

"Then maybe, if you wouldn't mind, you could assist me?"

One brow lifted and he grinned. "Assist you in making Baxter jealous? Sure."

His accurate insight made her laugh. "Not exactly what I meant, but that'll do in part." She wrinkled her nose. "He is rather obtuse, don't you think?"

"Nope. I think he sees everything. My guess is that you're both playing the same game." His grin widened. "Can't wait to see who wins."

"I will." She resisted the urge to look at Baxter again. "Now, I need to buy myself a camper of some sort. Can you direct me to the nearest location selling them?"

Blank surprise filled his handsome face. "You're buying a…?"

"Yes."

Both brows lifted. "Planning to stay on?"

Her brows came down. "Why not? I'm good at this housekeeping stuff." At least *she* thought so. "And the position is open, right?"

Jumping on that, he said, "Yes, and you're hired."

"Is that your decision to make?"

"Trust me, Coop will be thrilled. Everyone else quits after the first day."

Ridley gave an elegant shrug. "Everyone else is a wuss."

Skepticism stole his good humor. "You're sure you're not just doing this to spite Baxter?" Pretending a pleading look, he said, "Don't toy with me, doll."

"Oh, I'll spite Baxter, count on it." And she planned to get started on it right away. "But the job has nothing to do with him." No, the job had to do with her sister—and the strange self-satisfaction she felt in the work. She let out a breath. "So… I need some digs and there's no time like the present."

He worked his mouth to the side, then asked, "RV? Fifth wheel?"

Ridley waved her hand, unsure which was which and simply said, "Yes, one of those."

"For *here*?" Daron clarified.

Definitely here. How else could she provoke Baxter? "I'm going to reserve that nice spot over there—" she pointed "—with the woods behind it. I already checked and it's available."

Daron turned to stare at the spot she indicated. "There?"

She shrugged. "It's not the ideal location, I admit. I'd much prefer to be near the creek. Fewer bugs, and the sound of water moving is so soothing. But the spot by the woods will have to do."

Bemused, he asked, "So you're going to live here, permanently?"

Why did he keep saying it as if she'd be moving into a cave? Maybe there was something she didn't know. "It'll be a..." she pursed her lips, looking for the right words "...long-term reservation."

"Huh." Daron glanced toward Baxter, then shook his head with a huffing laugh. "Poor bastard."

Ridley affected a look of affront. "Are you insulting me?"

"Nope. Just admitting that you're a ruthless player of the game." Hands on his hips, he asked, "Have you ever driven an RV? Or pulled a fifth wheel?"

"No, but it's not a problem because I'll have it delivered."

"When?"

"Tonight, if possible."

His face went blank, but he quickly recovered. "*Tonight?* Not unless you're paying cash—"

"Oh, I am." Few benefits remained from her disastrous marriage—lots of money being one of them.

"Do you have any idea what a nice RV costs?"

"I searched the internet, so I think so."

He chewed the corner of his mouth a moment. "You want it as soon as possible?"

"Yes." She was most anxious to start her provocation of Baxter.

"I want to show you something."

Teasing, she said, "Oh, honey, I've already seen it all."

"Ruthless," he muttered with a grin, then gestured. "This way."

"Oh, all right." She really wanted to get on her way, but she could indulge him for a moment—especially since she felt Baxter still watching them. Was he closer now? Getting the wrong impression?

She hoped so.

How dare he ignore her after they'd come so close to—

Daron stopped in front of a massive RV with a FOR SALE sign in the window of the entry door. "Here you go."

"Here I go?"

"You want an RV, this one is for sale, it's by the creek and already paid up for the rest of the summer. If you stay on as housekeeper, Coop will reimburse you some of the rental fees—a perk of the job."

"It's yours?" For some reason, she thought he lived outside the park.

Daron laughed. "No, but I'm taking a commission for showing it to interested people." He dug keys out of his pocket. "Come on. Check out the inside."

"I don't know." She wasn't keen on buying anything used.

"It's only a year old," he hurried to say, as if he'd known her thoughts. "And it's in pristine condition."

"Then why is it for sale?"

"It's a divorce situation."

"Ah." She waited while he unlocked the door and automatic stairs came down. Then she gasped, blindly following Daron as he stepped inside. The interior was… "Decadent."

"Right?" He stood back while pointing out obvious features. "Four-door refrigerator, full dinette, leather couch and wing chairs—and the driver and passenger seat swivel, so when you're not traveling, they become part of the living room."

Ridley had no idea a moving house could be so plush. Daron was waxing on about the engine and auto-leveling or something, but she wasn't concerned with that.

Heading down the hall to see the rest of the interior, she passed a microwave oven, three-burner stove, solid-surface countertops and lots of kitchen storage.

In the moderate bathroom, which was still far bigger than what Phoenix used in the cabin, she found twin vessel sinks and a shower curved to fit into the space. The shower wasn't large, but then, she wasn't a large woman. "No bathtub."

Daron leaned close. "You're welcome to use mine when you feel the need to soak."

Grinning at his cheesy—and surely playful—come-on, she headed into the bedroom. "Hmm. This is tight." The king-size bed took up most of the space, with drawers built underneath and a stationary dresser/clothes closet on the opposite wall, a TV in between.

Lounging in the door frame, Daron said, "I hate to break it to you, but they don't make them bigger than this. If you want more room, you'll have to go custom, and that'd be months before it was ready."

The idea of months made her wrinkle her nose. "Really?"

"Afraid so."

Not all that disappointed, Ridley ran a hand over the padded headboard, the surface of the nightstand, and then the velvety soft coverlet—and made her decision. "I'll take it."

Blinking, Daron straightened from his lounged position. "You'll take it?"

"Everything has been cleaned, yes?"

"The bedding, yeah, but you're now the official housekeeper. I'd go over it all again if I was you."

"Of course you're right." She ran her finger over a layer of dust.

A little disbelieving, he looked around. "Do you want to know the price?"

"Is it fair?" she inquired.

"A bargain, actually."

She thrust out her hand. "If I pay you now, how soon can I move in?"

Appearing dazed, he accepted her hand, his brows up so high they disappeared under his tumbled brown hair. "Er..." He looked around again, then shrugged. "Whenever you want."

"Perfect. If you'd like to ride with me to the bank, we can get it taken care of right now."

A grin slowly spread over his face. "Let me see if Maris can keep the dog a little longer." He pulled his cell phone from his pocket.

While he made the call, she started back through to the living area, admiring the tasteful decor while also making a mental note of the things she'd like to buy. New throw pillows, a rug for the entry, maybe some fresh flowers for the dinette. She opened the cabinets and found most empty, but dishes and glasses remained in a few.

"Maris is a go."

Of course she was. Not only was the dog adorable, but Ridley suspected Maris would do just about anything for Daron, even though they appeared to have a contrary relationship. "The dishes stay?"

"Sure, if you like them. Matching towels in the bathroom, too."

She nodded, thinking that she'd have to go to the BMV next, then the grocery, and of course she'd have to call her insurance agent—

"One question," Daron said from behind her.

Absently, her thoughts full with her to-do list, Ridley asked, "Yes?"

"How rich are you?"

At the open front door, she turned to face him with amusement. "My ex had scads of money—and so I took what I could when he filed for divorce."

"*He* filed?"

A smirk hardened her smile. "Hard to believe, huh?" She gestured down her body. "Me being such a catch and all."

"Actually, yeah." Daron folded his arms over his chest. "So what happened?"

"Nosy much?"

"Curious, yeah. I admit it."

She shook her head, denying him. No, she wouldn't go into it. Not here, not now.

Maybe not ever.

"Let's just say he wanted more than I could give him, and leave it at that." Before he could press her any further, she took the first step out—and almost ran into Baxter.

Judging by his expression, he'd heard every word.

No. No, she definitely didn't want him to know of her rejection so instead she said with sugary politeness, "Baxter, what a surprise. I'm afraid Daron and I weren't expecting…company."

Baxter's gaze went past her and she knew Daron stood right behind her.

When the slightest hint of amusement narrowed Baxter's eyes, she looked behind her and found Daron shaking his head in the negative.

She glared.

Daron grinned, then said to Baxter, "I was showing her the RV, nothing more." He sent an apologetic glance to Ridley. "Not from lack of interest, understand. But I do like for that interest to be reciprocated."

She lifted her chin. "Who says it's not?"

"My intuition?" he asked. "My eyes? My sense of self-preservation?"

Baxter, the ass, actually laughed.

"Thanks for nothing," she growled at Daron.

Shrugging, he explained, "Baxter is bigger than me."

She knew that had nothing to do with it. More likely, it was some stupid male code of honor or something. Daron had sensed the chemistry between them, so he wouldn't get involved. "Whatever. You're useless." *And she was losing her touch.*

"Hey," he objected. "I did show you the RV, right?" He coaxed her, adding, "That has to count for something, right?"

"Not really."

"Are you buying it?" Baxter asked.

Before she could tell him to mind his own business, Daron chimed in with, "She is. The lady has good taste, and apparently deep pockets."

Incredulous, she glared at him again.

Daron drew on an expression of innocence. "Was it a secret?"

Baxter spoke up again. "So you'll be around for a while?"

"I'm obviously not needed for this conversation." She gave Daron a small shove. "He has all the answers, after all."

Theatrically, Daron grabbed his shoulder, saying, "I'm injured."

"Keep it up," she warned, "and you might be."

Baxter gave her a long look—a look that seemed almost tender. "I'll let you two finish settling things." He hesitated before adding, "Welcome to the park, Ridley."

Trying to disguise her trembling anticipation, Phoenix sat at the table across from Cooper toward the back of a quaint, family-run restaurant. They'd already bought the mower, arranging for delivery to the park by the first of the week. Now they'd almost finished their dinner at a local steakhouse.

Soon they'd be on their way to Cooper's house.

God, she could hardly wait. As if she'd already indulged in foreplay, her breasts felt heavy, her skin too sensitive, and throbbing heat gathered at her center.

"Dessert?" Cooper asked her.

She wanted *him* for dessert. "No, thank you." Mostly, she wanted to be alone with him. She forced herself to say, "But if you do—"

He shook his head, then to her consternation, ordered coffee for them both.

He didn't seem in much of a hurry.

Trying for some normal conversation, she asked again, "Nothing else happened with the goons? Officer Clark didn't find out anything—"

"I'm not keeping anything from you. Gibb and I waited, but they didn't show up." He shrugged. "Gibb went by the neighborhood where they live, but he didn't see them. He only knows one address, but no one answered the door when he knocked. He said he'll drive through there a few more times, and of course if we see them again, we're to call him."

"That seems like an awfully simple story."

"When there's more to tell, I'll tell you. So far, that's it."

She didn't like it. She wanted some sort of resolution…

"What?" Cooper gently asked, studying her frown.

Not much got past him, she thought with a sigh. "I detest open-ended problems." It was a rare thing for her to share, but tonight, with Cooper, the words just came out. "The men who assaulted me are still out there somewhere, an unknown threat. And now this."

They both went silent as a server set steaming cups of coffee in front of them.

Once she was gone, Cooper reached for Phoenix's hand. "I'm sorry."

Even that simple touch made the need inside her flare. "Don't be. I'm fine." This was not a night for negativity. Tonight was for moving forward. For living. She wanted to make the most of it, and thinking that had her smiling. "Better than fine, actually."

With his thumb, Cooper explored the back of her knuckles, then her blunt nails.

"I have calluses," she said, self-conscious with her work-rough hands. She couldn't remember the last time she'd had a manicure. Why bother when she spent her days digging in dirt?

Cooper smiled. "Everything about you fascinates me."

Because she was so different from his wife? She wouldn't ask… but she couldn't stop from wondering.

He seemed to debate with himself before finally saying, "I don't want you to be uncomfortable tonight."

Having no idea what that meant, Phoenix said softly, "I'm not." Not anymore. Not with him.

His fingers curled around hers and his gaze lifted to her face.

God, she loved his eyes, so calming with the whiskey-colored centers encircled by a rich brown. Golden striations made his eyes very unusual—and oh, so appealing.

When he said, "My wife died five years ago," she snapped out of her musings.

Tension added angles to his face, rigidity to his shoulders; she felt it in the grip on her hand. The conversation might've been awkward with any other man, but this was Cooper: natural leader, defender of puppy dogs, friendly boss to a resort that made everyone feel welcome.

To let him know it was okay, she squeezed his hand in return and asked softly, "What was her name?"

The question threw him for a moment. "Anna."

"She was beautiful." His hand was big and warm…*he* was big and warm. A powerful man, capable—but she knew he'd suffered and it killed her. "I can't imagine what you went through, but I know it had to have been terrible. You loved her."

His mouth tightened. "We'd only been married two years. In a lot of ways, it still felt like a honeymoon—" His gaze shot to hers.

His uncertainty brought out her encouragement. "I'm sure it did. Were you the same age?"

He shook his head. "She was a year younger."

"In her photo, she looks like a happy person."

"She was. Very happy." He stared off to the side and said low, "Everyone loved her."

"You lost her suddenly?" She knew the story her sister had relayed, but sensed Cooper needed to tell her himself.

"She called to say she was on her way home but that she was stopping for a few things from a convenience store. She was killed there in an armed robbery. I was expecting her home any minute…and then police were at my door."

Tears burned the backs of her eyes. "I am so sorry," Phoenix whispered. No one should ever have things change so drastically, in such an awful way.

He hesitated, still reluctant, before meeting her gaze. "What few people know is that she was pregnant."

Dear God. It felt like she took a blow to her heart, making her hand go slack in his.

He held on, his gaze locked on hers. "I've not shared that with anyone else."

Emotion choked her and she swallowed hard, doing her best to hold back tears. "It's private. I understand."

He nodded. "I just wanted to explain—"

"You don't owe me any explanations." She leaned forward, holding his hand in both of hers. "You loved her, Cooper. A part of you will *always* love her." She gave him a sad smile. "Just as a part of you will always mourn."

After a long look, he seemed to settle more comfortably in his chair. "For the first year I was a complete bastard. I hated everyone and everything. I raged often, even at my own family."

She understood that. Hadn't she turned away from everyone who loved her? "I'm sure each person reacts differently to grief." Hers was to hide away. "Yours was a show of anger."

"I got into too many fights—or more like brawls." With a short laugh, he said, "I'd frequent all the local dives, but I rarely drank. Mostly I waited for an opportunity..."

To let go of some of his hurt. She nodded. "Go on."

"I almost got arrested once, but the guy I'd knocked out was a serious asshole who needed it, so instead the cop told me to go home and not return."

Wow. She'd felt his confidence, especially when he'd faced off with three grown men he'd called *boys*, but she'd never imagined that he'd honed his skills with actual bar brawls.

"The second year," he continued, "wasn't much better, but at least I got my temper under control. I was still pissed at the world, but I kept it in check."

"That took a lot of willpower." Did he know that she admired him?

Apparently not, given his shrug. "The third year... I came here."

"Cooper's Charm?"

"That's not what it was called then, but yeah. Giving up my nine-to-five job was a relief. I could hide here."

Sadness stole her breath. "Surrounded by people?"

His gaze bored into hers, seeing far too much. "Sometimes that's the best place to hide, because others don't realize what you're doing. For a proud person, the perception matters."

Knowing he meant her, she sucked in a breath, and her glasses slipped down the bridge of her nose. "I suppose it does."

With a small smile, he reached out and straightened them, then smoothed her hair before sliding his fingers around to cradle her skull. "When we leave here, we'll go back to my house."

For sex, she reminded herself. "Okay." It was important to remember that this was about sex and only sex—especially after he'd just shared such a private history with her.

His hand fell away and he sat back in his seat, no longer touching her at all. "When I said I didn't want you to be uncomfortable, I meant that I put away most of my wife's photos."

A tidal wave of shame washed over her. She felt like an interloper. "But you didn't have to—"

"I know, but I did it for me, too." Withdrawing his wallet, he pulled out several bills and laid them on the table. "As you said, I'll always love Anna."

"Of course." Why did the assurance make her so gloomy?

He stood to pull back her chair. "But I don't want to mourn anymore."

9

"SHOULD WE CHECK ON SUGAR FIRST?"

Cooper glanced at her, maybe gauging her mood. "Trust me, like all other females, she adored him at first sight. She immediately rolled over so he could rub her belly."

Phoenix felt her face go warm. "All females, huh?"

Without taking his eyes from the road, he reached over and clasped her knee. "Present company excluded—I hope."

It seemed wicked to enjoy his small show of jealousy, but enjoy it she did. "Daron is handsome, funny, and yes, sexy." *But he's not you.* "He's also a giant flirt, so I'm not sure any woman should take him too seriously."

"That's another reason he willingly agreed to dog-sit. He said cute puppies are like chick magnets."

She laughed. "Like he needs any help with that."

As he pulled up to his house, he said softly, "Phoenix?"

"Hmm?" She looked down at the park, now cast in the glow of the lowering sun. The reflection off the lake seemed to glimmer everywhere, on each RV, the maintenance building, the creek.

He turned off his truck and shifted to face her. "You're not nervous, are you?"

Nervous, anxious, impatient…all of those. "No," she lied.

She could tell he didn't believe her, but he got out and circled the hood of the truck. She already had her door open and stepped out as he reached her.

A child shouted happily from the lake, drawing their attention.

Cooper started them toward the house. "I still need to get you into a bikini."

"Don't hold your breath." He'd made several comments about her physical appeal, and while she liked her body just fine—extra pounds and all—she couldn't help but worry that he might be disappointed. Not worried enough that she wanted to have sex in the dark or under the covers. No, she wanted them both naked with enough light for her to study him all over.

She shivered.

Unlocking the kitchen door, which he almost always used rather than his front door, he asked, "Why not a bikini?"

They stepped into the interior, and Phoenix said, "It's just not me." She set her purse on the counter, then laced her fingers together to keep from reaching for him. "Besides, I don't swim very often, so my ancient one-piece will have to do—"

In a single move, Cooper turned her and pinned her to the door, his mouth coming down on hers, ending her explanations. With one hand beside her head, he braced himself. With the other he cupped her face, gently holding her captive as he took the kiss from soft and exploring to hot and hungry.

She needed no more prompting than that, spreading her fingers over his shoulders, down his solid chest, his waist, to the hem of his shirt—and then inside.

God, his skin was hot, and she pushed the shirt up as she explored. She loved the soft hair in the center of his chest, how his small nipples tightened as she touched them.

He groaned into her mouth, then lifted his head, his breath coming fast. "Here." He reached back and stripped the shirt away.

Phoenix made her own small sound of pleasure. "You are a feast for the eyes, Cooper." Watching the progress of her hands now, she stroked him, lightly grazing her nails over him, squeezing muscles and tracing firm contours and dips.

She looked up into his eyes, heavy-lidded now, dark, and whispered, "Take off your pants, too."

Briefly, he closed his eyes. "Not a problem, but let's go to the bedroom. If anyone knocks on the door..."

"I don't want to share you," she agreed—then her gaze automatically went to his wife's photo on the desk.

Either Cooper didn't notice or he didn't care. He already had her hand, tugging her out of the kitchen and down the hall. They passed the now familiar laundry room and a bathroom, went through his living room—which she saw for the first time—and then past a guest bedroom that he'd set up as a workout room, filling it with weights, bars and other equipment—all of it neatly organized.

He moved so quickly, Phoenix was nearly running to keep up, but that suited her fine. He drew her into a large, sparse room at the back of the house. A king-sized bed dominated the area, with dark wood nightstands flanking it, a matching dresser and armoire. Blinds covered the windows, but no curtains. The closet door stood ajar, and the door leading to the connecting bath was wide-open.

It was a masculine space, but bare in the extreme. No decorating, no woman's touch...and no personal photos.

He removed his wife's photo for me.

No, she would not let regret intrude. Not now. Drawing breath, she faced Cooper and said succinctly, "Pants."

"First, this," he murmured, and slowly—maybe to make sure she wouldn't protest—peeled her laced tank off over her head.

She'd dressed more carefully for the date, in the nicest tank top she owned with slim-fitting Capri jeans and slightly heeled sandals. Underneath she wore a matching bra and panties in a soft shade of blue that complemented her eyes.

She quickly straightened her glasses, not wanting to miss a thing. And wow, was it worth seeing.

Cooper stood back from her, his gaze touching everywhere, lingering in places as his breathing deepened. Beneath the fly of his jeans, she saw the heavy ridge of an erection.

His shoulders flexed, as if he held himself back. "Damn, you're gorgeous."

Phoenix felt silly and happy…and insanely turned on.

While he stared at her, she brought her hands to the snap on her low-riding jeans. She let her fingers play, taking her time, aware of his expectation, until finally she popped the snap free.

He tipped his head back a little. "Go on."

Oh, she loved how husky his voice had gone.

Still teasing, she eased down the zipper and stepped out of her sandals. She hooked her thumbs in the waistband.

Cooper watched her with eyes barely open, his mouth firmed, his big hands curled into loose fists.

Knowing what it would do to her boobs, she leaned forward and pushed down the jeans, struggling a little to get the tight material off her ankles. She felt awkward—until she straightened again.

Cooper had a hand on his fly, fingers splayed so that his palm fit firm and flat against his cock beneath the denim.

Her heart started punching and she said, "Let me."

She strolled to him, brushing his hand aside, opening his jeans, being careful as she drew the zipper down over him. He wore dark gray boxers, the material soft beneath her fingers as she traced his length.

Knees locked, chest working, he stood there and let her explore—but not for long. Suddenly, he toed off his shoes, shoved down his jeans, taking his boxers and socks away at the same time. He kicked the clothes to the side and reached for her, scooping a hand into her bra to cup her breast.

"You're more than a handful."

"Yes." She wrapped her fingers around him. "So are you."

His mouth landed on hers again, open, hot, his tongue searching as he cuddled her breast. Her glasses went askew and she didn't care. She pulled them off, holding them in one hand.

He kept kissing her even as he opened the front clasp on her bra, as he took her arms from him so it would fall to the floor.

Both of his large, hot hands slid into the back of her panties, palming her cheeks, lifting her to her tiptoes until her panties fell to the floor, too.

With an arm around her back, the other beneath her bottom, he easily lifted her onto the bed, coming down beside her—still kissing her.

Her lips felt swollen and sensitive and she loved it. She loved the smell of his body, the taste of his mouth, the strength and gentleness in his hands.

"Let me look at you," he whispered against her mouth. "Don't move."

Since she wanted to look at him too, that worked for her. She slid her glasses back into place.

Braced on a forearm, he loomed over her. "Do you want to put them on the nightstand?"

"No." She shook her head, staring up at him. "I want to see you clearly."

His smile looked wickedly sexy. "I can work around them, then." He kissed her again, this time tenderly, careful not to disrupt the frames. Next his mouth brushed her jaw, her throat, her collarbone…

Knowing he was on a specific path, her breathing labored and when he reached her breast, she held her breath.

His tongue licked gently over her nipple and she couldn't suppress a groan. Then he latched on to her, sucking her in, drawing on her while his other hand moved down her belly, over to her hipbones and thighs.

He drew her legs apart.

When he raised his head, she was almost panting. "Cooper."

"Shh." He looked down her body, his nostrils flaring again, dark color slashing his cheekbones. "You're fucking perfect."

With him, she felt perfect.

He looked at all of her, his hand following his gaze, raising her temperature, especially when he cupped a hand over her sex. "You're hot." His fingers probed, his body still positioned over her, watching. "And wet."

"Cooper..." She reached for him.

"No. Don't move or you might lose those glasses."

"I'll take them off," she offered after all.

But he grinned. "No, I like them on you." With his fingers still between her legs, he bent and licked her nipple. "This body." He pressed a kiss to her lips. "This face." He nuzzled her hair. "You're all soft curves and sexy sweetness—and then the glasses." One finger pressed deep into her.

Contracting around him, she breathed, "You're teasing me."

He growled near her ear, "I want to tease you until you come."

It wouldn't take much, he had her strung so tightly.

He started kissing her again, the sensitive line of her neck, the rim of her ear, while his hand worked between her legs, opening her, spreading her slick excitement. He pressed two thick fingers inside her, then raised his thumb to her clitoris and she arched in acute pleasure.

"Mmm," he whispered around her nipple, biting carefully, tugging, then sucking again.

Phoenix sank her fingers into his hair, holding him close. She closed her thighs around his hand, ensuring he couldn't leave her. Against her will, her hips rolled with his fingers. Heat expanded, and she felt those first twinges of a climax, climbing higher and higher, getting sharper—

On a gasp, her body bowed, trembling, soft moans crawling from her throat, her teeth clenched, her head back. The orgasm ebbed and flowed, built and receded, until finally, boneless, she sank into the bedding.

Her heart continued to race and she breathed heavily, her body weighted with a buzzing lethargy.

Cooper, she thought. That happened with Cooper and she couldn't help but smile.

She realized she still clutched his hair when he carefully untangled her fingers and pressed her hands at either side of her head.

"You with me, Phoenix?"

"Mmm, yes." The second she got her eyes open, he pressed his mouth softly to hers. His hand rested on her belly, and she suddenly realized that her legs were sprawled.

"No," he whispered, his fingertips drifting over her inner thigh, making her go quiet again. "I'll let you catch your breath, but I prefer for you to stay just as you are."

An emotion swelled in her chest, fulfilling her heart, making her smile big and her eyes glisten. "I don't want to catch my breath. I just want you."

He left his scrutiny of her body to stare into her eyes. "You're sure?"

"Very, very sure." To prove it, she levered up while pushing him flat to his back. "Condom?"

He gave her a long look, then nodded at the nightstand.

She snatched up the small packet, flapped it twice then held it in her teeth while she crawled over his thighs. God love the man, he did it for her.

"When you lean over me like that," he rasped, "your tits look incredible."

Ripping open the condom, Phoenix grinned. "Like this?" One hand flat on his shoulder, she arched her back.

"Yeah." He reached for her, but she leaned away.

"Now, Cooper. It's my turn." She'd never been overly timid with sex, but feeling this free, feeling this sexy, was new and she wanted to take advantage of it. "If you start touching me again, I'll melt and we won't get anywhere."

Those amber eyes stared at her. "All right."

The way she sat low on his thighs, her legs tucked under her, kept her exposed and she knew he looked at her there. Pleasurable little sparks continued, keeping her ready for more.

She liked the way his chest hair swirled around his small brown nipples, how it trailed down his body, leading to the goods.

And how good it was.

Scooting farther back, she dropped the open condom packet on his stomach and took his erection in both hands. A man couldn't be any harder, she thought, stroking up the length, squeezing, stroking down again.

Beneath her bottom, his legs stiffened more.

She played with him, breathing harder as he pulsed in her hands. A drop of fluid appeared at the tip and she used her thumb to spread it around.

Cooper's hands fisted in the sheets and he murmured, "Jesus."

She would have liked to kiss him, to taste him, take him into her mouth—but he looked as if he'd reached the end of his rope and she badly wanted him inside her.

"Let me get this on you." She withdrew the condom, then tortured him further with the precise way she rolled it down his cock. "Now we can—"

He flipped her to her back and kneed her legs apart.

"Wait!" Her glasses definitely had to come off. She folded the arms and handed them to him. "Nightstand, please."

She felt him move, the bed dipped, then he settled over her.

"If I'm this close," he asked, his breath on her lips, "can you see me?"

"Yes." She wrapped her legs around his waist to keep him there.

"Perfect." Reaching between their bodies, he positioned himself, then nudged in—little by little.

Until her heels dug into his ass, urging him on.

Until her arms tightened around his neck, demanding.

His mouth took hers and he thrust in hard and deep. They both groaned, bodies already straining together, in sync.

The slick friction seemed to spark every nerve ending in her body. His belly rubbed against hers, his chest against her nipples.

He wedged a forearm under her, lifting her so he could go deeper, adjusting her so that every stroke glided over her clitoris. He thrust hard and fast, making the headboard bang against the wall.

She felt the heat pouring off him, felt the coiling tension in his shoulders and back and in her own body…

"Cooper."

Pressed firm inside her, his big body shuddered as he put his face in her neck and let go.

A few minutes later, as her breathing began to calm, Phoenix eased her hold. Odd that she'd clutched him so tightly, almost desperately, but he didn't seem to mind. Gradually, her legs loosened and slipped to the sides of him. He rested over her, and she relished his weight, kissing his damp shoulder, breathing in his scent.

"Am I crushing you?" he muttered, his tone drowsy as he started to rise.

She managed a hug. "Don't you dare move."

"Another minute then." He licked her neck. "Any longer than that and we're taking chances."

True, the condom would stay in place for only so long now

that he wasn't erect. It was daring of her, pushy even, but she asked, "Can you get rid of it and then come back to me?"

He pressed up to his elbows, his now-relaxed face very close as he ran his fingers through her tumbled hair, smoothing it back. "If you'd like that."

She'd more than like it—and that made it risky. Even knowing it wasn't wise to need him, she still wasn't ready to let him go. Not yet. "Please."

His lips moved over hers in a heart-melting kiss. "Be right back."

In the small connected bathroom, Coop stretched. He felt good—relaxed, spent, but also, on some primal level, triumphant.

Phoenix hadn't feared him, hadn't shied away from him being over her. With what she'd gone through, he'd had a very real concern that bad memories would hamper her pleasure.

Not so.

She'd demanded, taken, enjoyed. And she gave.

Phoenix was...*more* than he'd expected. Free, sensual.

Sexual.

And confident.

That had been the biggest turn-on. She was a woman who knew what she wanted and didn't hesitate to go after it.

Hearing her quiet voice order him to remove his pants... He'd hold that as a favorite fantasy for a good long while.

It occurred to him that, after years of being dead inside, existing in a robotic void, he was now stunningly, alarmingly alive. Being with Phoenix had sharpened his senses, awakening them to every small nuance of her touch, her scent, her taste, and the soft, husky sounds she made in her pleasure.

Phoenix's reactions had drawn out his own.

He'd started by wanting to help her, and instead, she'd helped him without even knowing it. She'd brought him back from the dead. Truthfully, he enjoyed living again.

He'd have to take it slow. Just because he loved feeling again, didn't mean she was ready to do the same. Each person had to take his or her own path. For Phoenix, that path was first to independence. She wanted freedom from her fears, autonomy over her life. It was important to her, and that made it important to him.

Knowing she waited for him—another circumstance he liked—he removed the condom, and then dampened a washcloth for her. He was wondering where the night would go, how long she'd stay, when he heard a phone ringing. It wasn't his ringtone, so that meant it was Phoenix's.

When he stepped into the bedroom, he saw that she was still utterly limp.

And gorgeous.

"That's your phone," he said, watching as she got one eye open. "I'll get it for you, okay?"

She stuck out an arm, palm up, and wiggled her fingers.

He'd planned to wash her himself, but gave up the idea with the imperious way she requested the cloth.

As he handed it to her, she said a prim, "Thank you," then closed her eyes again when the ringing stopped. "That was probably Ridley on the phone. Usually, she just texts me, but I wouldn't have heard it, so—"

"I'll get it."

She opened her eyes again. "I'm sorry for the interruption."

Standing beside the bed, looking down at her body, he said, "It's fine."

"If you're going into the kitchen like that, maybe you should pull on your shorts?"

The way she stared at his dick, he'd be hard again in no time. He headed for the door. "Stay put."

"Oh, believe me," she murmured, "I'm not budging."

A glance back showed her gaze now on his ass. Coop laughed as he went down the hall.

He found her purse on the counter in the quiet kitchen. The sun now sat on the horizon, sending brilliant color to waver over the lake. One night, he'd sit outside with Phoenix and they could watch the sunset together.

But not tonight. He had other plans in mind.

When he reentered the bedroom, she was sitting up against the headboard, glasses in place, the washcloth gone, and the sheet to her waist. Damn, that was fast.

She took the purse, dug out her phone and settled back again to flip through the screen. "Yup, Ridley texted three times."

Coop got into bed beside her, but didn't bother with false modesty. "Anything wrong?"

As she read, her brows pulled down, then shot up. "Oh, my God."

She sounded more incredulous than alarmed, but still it worried him. "What?"

"Ridley bought an RV."

Not at all what he'd expected. "An RV?"

She was already hitting numbers for her sister, so Coop bided his time.

Suddenly, she said into the phone, "What do you mean you bought an RV?"

With no other noise in the room, Coop heard Ridley say, "I can't very well seduce Baxter in your loft, Phoenix. So I bought my own place."

Somehow, despite Baxter's aloof behavior at dinner the night before, Coop didn't think any seduction was necessary.

Phoenix sputtered. "But you already have your own place."

"It's not here, though...and Baxter is."

Phoenix cast an uneasy glance at Coop.

He winked.

"Ridley," she said, her voice low, "do you want him that much?"

"I want him to want me, sure. It's all part of my evil plan."

"I'm not sure—"

Ridley interrupted with, "Shouldn't you be gettin' it on with Big Sexy?"

Phoenix's brows came down again. "You called me!"

"In case you don't stay over with the hunk, doing the nasty all night long. I didn't want you to worry about me if you found out I wasn't there."

"But…where are you?"

As if speaking to a dunce, Ridley repeated, "I bought an RV."

"And you have it already? Where is it?"

"Here in the park, by the creek. It's used, but you'd never know it. Daron was helping the owners sell it, so once he knew I was looking… It's perfect for me."

Coop whistled low. "I know which one she means, and it's top-of-the-line."

Eyes widening, Phoenix looked at him, then back at the phone. "You bought *that* one?"

"Coop is there with you? Nice. Please tell me you're both in bed naked."

Because she'd hit the nail on the head, hot color rushed into Phoenix's face. Coop just laughed.

"Ooh," Ridley said. "You *are*. Excellent." Then to Cooper, she said loudly, "Please forgive my sister's faux pas in lingering on the phone. She hasn't ridden that particular bike in a while."

Phoenix said, "Good night, Ridley," with firm insistence.

"Come by my new place tomorrow!" Ridley made kissing noises and then the call disconnected.

Dazed, Phoenix leaned over the side of the bed to drop the phone back into her purse.

"So." Coop casually stripped the sheet down to her knees. As he feathered his fingertips over the lush curve of her breast, he said, "Your sister really is loaded?"

It took her a second to reply, then she only nodded. "Remember, she told you she was."

"Yes, but I didn't know that meant she could afford the extravagance of buying an RV just to be near Baxter."

Phoenix swallowed heavily, her eyes starting to close. "Somehow he hurt her. I don't think he meant to, but since the divorce, she's sensitive."

He replaced his fingers with his mouth. Her skin was satiny smooth and fragrant, and he already wanted her again. "I'm sure Baxter will enjoy her efforts to make him miserable."

She laced her fingers into his hair. "I just hope she doesn't make herself miserable in the bargain."

Drawing her nipple into his mouth for a leisurely suckle, he ended the conversation. Phoenix was quick to respond, which made it more difficult for him to pace things slowly, but he managed to keep control of them both. Kissing his way down her body, he enjoyed her sensitive nipples, her softly rounded belly, the curve of her hip and the supple strength in her thigh.

Needing to taste every inch of her, he lifted her left leg over his shoulder.

She tensed all over, but not in a bad way. He heard her whisper, *"Oh, my God."*

Glasses askew, head back, bottom lip caught in her teeth, she waited.

Coop nuzzled against her, growling at the incredible scent of her musk, feeling her wetness against his fingers—and then his tongue. He licked carefully at her lips, nibbled delicately, then opened his mouth around her.

"Cooper." Her fingers clenched painfully in his hair.

He urged her other leg up and over his shoulder, then lifted her hips in his hands. "I could eat you all day, Phoenix." He blew softly against her, opened her farther with his thumbs, and licked into her.

Legs going taut, she pulled him closer.

"You like that?"

A small whimper was her only reply. Nice. Everything about Phoenix turned him on, but this, seeing her lost to lust, scorched him.

He trailed his tongue up and over her swollen clit, again and again until her hips followed the movement and her body strained for release. She was so wet that he slid two fingers easily into her, pressing them deep.

"Cooper," she breathed.

"Tell me what you want." Knowing she was ready, he continued his rhythm, pushing her closer and closer.

"I want..."

He waited.

"Suck on me."

The ragged request damn near made him come. He pressed his erection against the mattress and did as she asked, drawing on her the same way he had her nipples.

She gave a low groan, her heels digging into his shoulders, then she lifted high on a cry, her body shuddering, her breaths gasping. He wrung every small moan from her that he could before hastily sitting up to roll on another condom.

"This is going to be fast and hard," he warned, again lifting her ankles over his shoulders.

She swallowed, nodded, but her eyes stayed closed. They hadn't removed her glasses but she'd pushed them to the top of her head. Her cheeks were damp, flushed a dark pink...like her nipples. Her lips were soft and swollen.

He covered her breasts with his hands, catching those stiffened nipples between his fingers for a subtle pinch.

That got her eyes open.

He stared down at her face, watching her as he entered her with one hard thrust.

She clenched tight around him, squeezing his cock in silky wetness.

The position had her thighs pressed high and wide, leaving her totally open to him. He asked, "Okay?"

The slightest of smiles reassured him, but she also purred, "Very."

"Good. Then hold on tight." Coop adjusted slightly, withdrew, then thrust in hard again.

Phoenix lifted her arms above her head, wrapping her hands around the rails of the headboard.

So fucking hot.

It was deep this way—and she seemed to love it.

Spurred on by the small sounds she made, the way she matched his thrusts, he pounded into her.

Her skin grew dewy. Her inky dark hair tangled around her face.

Too soon. Far too soon. Much as he wanted to make it last, he knew he couldn't wait. "Phoenix." He latched on to one nipple, sucking strongly, using his teeth to tug—and she climaxed.

He gathered her close, his face beside hers, and let himself go.

He was glad his wife had never been in this house, never been in this bed—because now, whenever he was in it, he'd think of Phoenix.

10

HOPING THE EVENING WOULDN'T END YET, PHOENIX listened in as Cooper called Daron to see if he needed to come get Sugar. To her relief, Daron assured him they were fine. In fact, he and the dog were with Maris at her shop. They'd just taken the dog for a walk and were now settling in for a snack.

Cooper played it cool, but he grinned at Phoenix while thanking Daron.

After he disconnected, he said, "That's an interesting turn of events."

She shook her head. "Maris pretends to dislike Daron, but I think that's just a front."

"Meaning?"

"She's super committed to her business and future, and Daron is..." The right word eluded her.

"A knucklehead?"

She laughed. "You know he's not, not really, but most of the time he's the opposite of serious."

"True enough." Cooper stepped closer. "Since we have some time left, you want to watch a movie?"

Teasing, she said, "Depends on the movie."

"We'll find something." His gaze moved over her, lingering on her boobs. Typical man. "I have some ice cream if you're ready for dessert."

Leaning forward, Phoenix took a soft love bite of his chest. "Mmm, dessert."

"Keep that up, and we won't make it out of the room." He snatched up his T-shirt and dropped it over her head, then stepped into his boxers. "I don't want to cover you up, but I'm not into torture, either."

Loving his playful mood and all the compliments, she laughed. "Ice cream sounds great." By silent agreement, they moved to the living room. While he fetched the ice cream, she explored the space.

A big couch and two chairs faced a large television. Sports magazines littered an end table. A bookcase filled with biographies, mysteries and crime novels drew her.

On the first shelf, between a stack of books on the left and a row on the right, was another photo of Cooper's wife, this one of her in jeans and a T-shirt, her hair windblown, her feet bare.

She'd just moved away to peruse his magazines when he returned.

"Sorry it's a little messy," he said, bowls of ice cream in hand.

"Actually, it's really nice. You've set it up for your comfort, and that makes others comfortable, too."

"Good." He sat on the couch, patting the cushion beside him. "Come here."

She settled beside him, half lounged against him, her feet up beside her. Cooper kept one arm around her, his feet crossed on the coffee table.

She accepted the bowl from him, agog at the massive scoop of chocolate ice cream.

"Did you ever want a house?"

The question caused a pang of remorse. To give herself a minute to think, she shoveled in a bite, waiting while the ice cream melted on her tongue. Should she be brutally honest with him?

What would he think of her once he knew?

"Phoenix?"

There was that perception again. She put the spoon in the bowl, but didn't look up. "I had a house. Or rather, my fiancé bought a house for us. I helped to pick it, but after the…" Most people called it a robbery, but it had been so much more than that. If the men had *only* wanted money, *only* wanted her jewelry, would her world still have fallen apart?

Would she, right now, be in that house with David, happily married with her planned future ahead?

For the first time since it had happened, she didn't regret the loss of that future—because it hadn't included Cooper.

Quietly, determined to be as upfront with him as she could be, Phoenix said, "After the attack, I withdrew. You know that much. I couldn't seem to face anyone and that included David. He didn't understand. How could he? At first he postponed the wedding, thinking I just needed time."

Cooper said not a word, and though he barely moved, somehow both their bowls ended up on the coffee table and his arms were around her.

She burrowed closer, glad for a way to hide her face.

To hide her shame.

"I hurt him so badly," she admitted, her throat suddenly tight. "I know that, just as I know he deserved better."

With his chin on top of her head, Cooper said, "I think you did what you had to do to cope. There's no disgrace in that, honey."

Oh, how she wished that were true, but facts were facts. "Strangers destroyed my world…and then I destroyed his."

Though she tried to refuse, his hand lifted her chin, relentlessly insistent until she met his gaze.

"That's nonsense. You and I are both proof that people are

resilient. If he hasn't recovered by now, he will soon. Life goes on, you know, sometimes even when you wish it wouldn't."

The stark words made her heart skip a beat. Had Cooper wanted to die after he lost his wife? She hated that thought.

"And," he said, his mouth touching gently to hers, "if it wasn't meant to be, it's better that you ended it before marriage."

She'd often told herself the same, but it was small solace when she thought of David's face, of all the ways he'd tried to convince her to stay with him. She groaned at the image. "I hope he's found someone else. Someone better."

"Shh. Don't say that."

"It's true." She'd face reality even if he wouldn't.

"Some people belong together and some don't. It's not about being better, it's about finding the right one."

That was a sober reminder that Cooper *had* found the right one—and she'd been taken from him. "I'm sorry. I don't mean to have a pity party." God knew he'd lost so much more.

"Hey." He drew her face up again, this time so he could kiss her until she softened. "I'm glad you shared with me. I want you to. Anytime, okay?"

It had felt good to talk, to get some of the regret off her chest. She'd never be free of the shame, but sharing it had somehow shaved off the ragged edges. "All right, thank you." That sounded ridiculous, so she added with a mock frown, "Now let's eat this ice cream before it melts."

"Sounds like a plan." He used a remote to scroll through the channels until he came across *Alien* with Sigourney Weaver.

"Oh, this is one of my favorites," Phoenix said.

Surprised, Cooper paused. "You like horror?"

She grinned at him. "My whole family *loves* scary movies. My grandma always claimed that my mom teased her with Ridley's name because it's *so close* to Sigourney's character, Ellen Ripley, but without being quite there."

One brow lifted. "Because your grandmother liked horror, too?"

"Of course. When Ridley and I would visit, we'd play outside all day, fish in the pond and stuff, then settle down with popcorn and homemade milkshakes in front of the TV. We got to take turns picking movies. Grandma's only rule was there couldn't be a lot of sex or nudity."

"That rules out most horror."

"I know." She leaned closer, as if sharing a confidence. "Ridley and I used to sneak and watch the forbidden movies whenever we got a chance."

Cooper laughed. "Hell of an education for a kid."

She grinned, feeling incredibly lighthearted as he settled in with her to watch.

They were engrossed in the movie, the ice cream gone, the room dark, when on the screen, a face-grabbing alien dropped on Ripley's shoulder. Phoenix didn't mean to, but she jerked so sharply, she almost cracked Cooper in the nose.

Mortification erupted in a strangled laugh. Good grief, she'd seen the movie a dozen times and knew that scene was coming...and still it got her. "I'm so sorry!" She cupped his face. "Did I hurt you?"

"Actually, you startled me more than the alien did."

Heat burned in her cheeks. "That scene gets me every time."

Now looking concerned, he asked, "Are you sure the movie won't bother you later?"

Phoenix batted her lashes at him, and said in her most innocent voice, "You mean because I'm a frail little woman who has to sleep alone?"

"You don't *have* to. You're more than welcome to—"

Knowing she'd accidentally put him on the spot, she interjected with, "Will it scare *you*?"

He grinned. "As long as no one is flailing next to me, I think I'll hold up okay."

Playfully, she punched his shoulder. "I didn't *flail*."

"What would you call it?"

"Mildly startled?" At his grunt, she couldn't help laughing. "If a scary movie doesn't leave you trembling, why do you think it would bother me? It's not like an actual alien will creep into my cabin tonight."

He gave her a firm kiss. "Point taken. Sorry if I offended."

Her heart swelled. "I don't offend that easily." Actually, it was nice to have someone who cared.

Someone other than her bossy and outrageous older sister.

They got comfortable again, staying quiet until the next commercial. Then he picked up as if there'd been no interruption at all. "Even though a horror veteran and a cheesy movie won't spook you, you're welcome to stay here."

Had he been stewing on that for the last ten minutes? Seemed so. And oh, how the idea tempted her.

But she knew she couldn't stay.

Not for much longer.

Soon, she promised herself.

Hoping for a casual air, she smiled up at him. "Thanks, but I'd rather not risk gossip. It's better if I come from my cabin tomorrow morning, same as I always do."

"Better for who?"

For you, she wanted to say, but didn't. "I'm sure everyone already knows we're seeing each other, but I'd rather they not know how fast we're moving."

"Fast? Seems to me it's been excruciatingly slow—but I won't pressure you tonight."

Tonight. Did that mean he planned to pressure her tomorrow? If so, she'd decide then what to do. She'd had such a wonderful time, she didn't want to chance spoiling the rest of the evening.

During commercials, they talked—and kissed a lot. Then when the movie returned, she sat in his embrace. He touched her hair, stroked her hip and occasionally palmed her breasts. She breathed in his scent, soaked up his warmth, while his chest repeatedly drew her curious fingers…and her lips.

In so many ways, the entire evening felt perfect.

She was so cozy, so content that by the time the movie ended, she was almost asleep. When Cooper caught her yawning, she saw in his eyes that he wanted to try to convince her to stay over.

It was a good thing he didn't, because with all her defenses down, she might have caved. She forced her feet to the floor and her butt off the couch. "Time for me to get dressed."

"Now, that is a crime." He eyed her legs. "Will you believe me when I say you'd look amazing in a bikini?"

Phoenix snorted a laugh. "Thank you, but I'll stick with my old reliable one-piece." After a deep stretch, she headed down the hall. Already, she felt familiar with his home. He kept it clean, but not necessarily tidy. He liked things a certain way, set up for functionality rather than presentation.

She, on the other hand, was all about how things looked. If she lived here, she'd—

Good Lord. Though Cooper was behind her, her face went hot. He'd offered her one night to stay over, but he wasn't asking for a roommate. She'd do well to remember that.

Sex, she reiterated to her tired brain as she stepped into the bedroom. Great sex. Phenomenal sex.

Sex…that felt like so much more?

No. No, no, no—

"What's wrong?"

In the middle of her silent denials, she spun to face him, mortified to think he might know her thoughts. "What do you mean?"

"Phoenix." He cupped her face. "Give me a little credit, okay? I can tell when something is bothering you."

Did he really know her so well? An unsettling thought—that also warmed her heart.

She forced a smile. "It's nothing. I was just worrying about Ridley."

Skeptical, he asked, "You'll miss her tonight?"

"She's bossy and she snores, so not likely."

Humor eased away his worry. "Is that so? Maybe I should warn Baxter."

She laughed, but ruined it with another yawn. "It's getting late. I need to go." *Before I give in to the desire to stay.*

He didn't argue, but she could tell he didn't like it, either.

They dressed together in near silence. When she was ready to leave, Cooper pocketed his keys and phone and walked with her.

Shoulder to shoulder with her, Cooper asked, "Want me to drive you?"

"Mmm." She looked up at the clear sky, velvet black with a million glittering stars and a fat, glowing moon, all reflecting off the surface of the lake. A light breeze teased over her face, stirring the balmy air. She spread her arms wide. "It's such a nice night I'd prefer to walk, if that's okay." She could extend their time together just a little longer.

"Sure." They were almost down the hill, the grass alternately slick with dew, then dry and prickly, when he asked, "Want to walk with me to get Sugar from Daron before I take you home? You could tell her good-night."

Aha, so Cooper also wanted to steal every minute he could. "I'd love to." She leaned closer, saying sotto voce, "Besides, I'm dying to see how things are going with Maris and Daron."

"Voices carry out here," Daron said from somewhere down the hill. "And I had no idea you were a voyeur."

Phoenix slapped a hand over her mouth. *Busted.*

There was a muted complaint from Maris.

Daron grunted and said, "Ow, damn."

Then Maris called loudly, "There's absolutely nothing to see… well, except for the dog piddling."

Daron objected to that, while Maris shushed him.

She shot a look at Cooper, and caught his suppressed smile. Sharing the moment, she leaned against him. He gave her a brief hug just before they stumbled upon Maris and Daron, standing a discreet distance apart.

Sugar was in the middle of peeing when she spotted them and she ran—in a half squat—yapping happily.

It was another twenty minutes before Cooper and Sugar finished walking her home. Unfortunately, her porch light was off.

"That's odd."

"What?" Cooper asked.

"I added a sensor to the porch light so it would automatically come on at dusk, but it's not on."

Just that quick, his good mood fled and dark suspicion brought his brows together. He handed her the leash for Sugar, saying, "Wait here," and went up to the dark porch, using his phone as a flashlight.

Heart pounding in dread, she watched as he checked the door first and found it still locked. After glancing back and seeing that she hadn't budged, he again circled her cabin.

This was starting to become a habit, but she was extremely glad for his help. It was late enough—into the park's quiet time—that no one else was about. Many campers had lights on the outside of their RVs and fifth wheels, and some of the people using tents had small fires out front.

And yet, it felt eerily still and quiet, when minutes before it had felt magical.

She stared hard into the heavy shadows, watching for Cooper to reemerge—and finally he did, stepping up to the deck from the other side, apparently finding nothing amiss.

His back to her, he checked the porch light…and his head turned slightly. "The bulb is broken."

"Broken?" She inched closer. "How?"

"I don't know." He met her before she could get one foot on the deck step. "Let me take a look around inside."

"This is starting to feel like déjà vu." She hoped the casual words belied her nervousness, because already her palms felt damp and her heart raced. *It's only a broken light bulb.* Logically, she knew it happened, but fear was seldom logical. Would she always immediately equate a simple problem with possible danger?

God, she hoped not.

She got the keys from her purse and handed them over. Because she was jumpy, she scooped up Sugar and held her close, taking comfort from the dog as she watched Cooper unlock the door and disappear inside, flipping on lights as he did so.

It wouldn't take him more than a minute to go through the entire place—

In a move far more startling than an alien dropping on Ridley's shoulder, Sugar launched into a furious tirade of barking and snarling. It was all Phoenix could do to hold on to her—and then she saw the vague figure racing away into the darkness, feet skidding on gravel.

Cooper rushed out—but it was already too late. Whoever had been there had raced for the woods so she caught his arm while trying to hold on to the dog at the same time.

Her heart thumped so violently, she could barely draw breath, but she choked out, "He's gone."

Eyes narrowed, Cooper stared at where the man had disappeared, then ushered Phoenix and Sugar into the cabin. Calmer than she, he said, "Good dog, Sugar. Good dog."

He said nothing to Phoenix, but drew out his phone and placed a call. When he spoke, she realized he'd dialed Officer Clark.

"Gibb? The fucker was just here."

Odd, Phoenix thought, that his voice sounded so calm in contrast to what he said.

"No, I didn't see him—just the back of a man running away." His voice lowered. "He was at Ms. Rose's cabin. Someone broke the porch light. No, no real damage other than a bulb, but if I hadn't been with her, she'd have been walking..." He cast a glance at Phoenix. "Right."

She looked back, trying to mimic his composed mood. But

damn it, this time her instincts had been right, even though she'd tried to ignore them. Given her past, it now seemed impossible to discern when she should and shouldn't be alarmed.

"Yeah," Cooper muttered, "I'll wait. Thanks."

That sounded like he might be hanging around for a bit. Phoenix sat on her sofa and folded her hands together. "Wait for what?" There, that sounded reasonable and calm…

As long as he didn't notice how her fingers were shaking.

"Waiting here with you until Gibb calls me back." Cooper paced, and the dog tracked his every step. "He's already out so he'll go by where the pricks live and see what's up."

"Oh." She cleared her throat. "How long will that take, do you think?"

"Not long." He looked again at Sugar, then picked her up. "You make a hell of a guard dog, baby." He kissed her on the top of her furry little head, making her whole body jiggle with joy. When he looked at Phoenix, his gaze assessing, she tried to look brave.

She must have failed.

He sat beside her, cupping a hand around the back of her neck. "You okay?"

Oh, that gentle voice just might do her in. She made her lips curl in the semblance of a smile and said with false confidence, "Of course. Why wouldn't I be?"

When he only continued to watch her, those beautiful eyes seeing too much, she began to babble.

"There could be a lot of reasons why someone was running around the park. We shouldn't automatically think something nefarious is going on. Maybe the bulb just blew. Bulbs do that, you know. It's not like the guy was actually at my cabin, just—" she waved a hand "—somewhere close behind it."

"Phoenix."

She rounded on him. "Are you upset? Nervous?"

"Actually, yeah."

Her eyes widened. "You are?" Well, damn it, that only made her more jumpy, giving her reason to think there was good cause to worry. To be sure, she asked, "Why?"

He started to speak, but then his cell phone rang. He set the dog on the floor and stood, pacing again as he answered.

"Gibb? Find out anything?" Cooper listened, his scowl growing darker by the second. "Bullshit." And then with even more heat, "How can you be sure?"

Phoenix watched as he rubbed the back of his neck.

"No," Cooper said. "There's nothing here to see. Yeah, I'm sure. It's okay, thanks."

When he disconnected, Phoenix waited.

After several seconds, he turned to face her, his expression still grim. "Harry and his two cohorts were in when Gibb got there. In fact, they were in the middle of a video game with about ten other guys."

"Meaning—"

"Lots of alibis. Gibb said it didn't look to him like they'd been anywhere. They were kicked back, shoes off, cans of beer everywhere and Harry was plenty pissed to have his game interrupted."

"Well then..." She stalled, unsure what to think. "I guess I was right. Not a big deal."

Cooper stood very tall, his broad shoulders looking even wider with his tension. "Come home with me for the night."

God, it would be so easy to give in, to lean on him. But she was an independent woman. She was strong.

She had this.

Smiling, a genuine smile this time because, damn it, she was proud of herself, she stood. "I can't." She hugged him tight, despite his stiff posture. "But if you wouldn't mind staying until I change that light, I'd really appreciate it."

A week later, Ridley sat across from Phoenix at the little wrought-iron table she'd purchased to go outside under her RV's canopy, a steaming cup of coffee in her hands. It was a beautiful June morning, the sky blue, the birds happily singing, children playing nearby, and she could even hear the quiet rush of water in the creek.

Bleh.

She needed to start work in another twenty minutes, and all she really wanted to do was crawl back into her surprisingly comfortable bed. But she wouldn't.

Coop had been thrilled to sign her on as a permanent employee, just as Daron had promised. He took every opportunity to tell her what a great job she was doing. Though she wouldn't admit it to him or Phoenix, she liked his praise, so she worked hard to always be on time.

"You look exhausted," Phoenix noted.

Ridley made a face at her. "I lie awake every night worrying about you."

With an eye roll, Phoenix warned, "Ridley—"

She was just irascible enough to grumble, "I get it that you wouldn't stay with Big Sexy..." She paused, plunking down her cup. "Actually, I *don't* get it, but fine, I'll respect your decision. Sort of."

"Gee, thanks."

She ignored that dry tone to continue on her tirade. "But to turn away your own sister?" Ridley concentrated on her ire, more than her hurt, over Phoenix's absurd insistence on independence. "What's up with that?"

The hot coffee left steam on Phoenix's glasses as she sipped. She removed them, using the edge of her shirt as a polishing cloth. "I think the fact that nothing else has happened proves there's no reason for everyone to keep fussing."

"I'll damn well fuss if I want to," Ridley snapped, though if she was being totally honest, her worry for Phoenix only accounted for part of her recent insomnia. "I should've never bought this stupid RV, should've never moved out of your cabin, never..." *Made plans for Baxter.* Damn the man, how dare he keep her twisted up like this?

"I thought you loved the RV."

Yeah, she did. "It was a waste of money."

Phoenix gave a noncommittal "Hmm."

"Hmm? What do you mean *hmm*?"

Her sister laughed. "You really are touchy today, aren't you?"

Ridley slumped back in her chair. The beautiful floral cushions made it a very comfortable seat—for a stylish RV that she actually loved. Everything inside the camper was well planned for functionality, not a single inch of space wasted.

She'd mostly bought it as a place to get busy with Baxter, and that dick was avoiding her. She hadn't seen him at all in the past week.

She eyed Phoenix, then sighed. It wasn't fair to take out her bad mood on her sis. "I need to get laid."

Phoenix choked on her coffee.

"Prude," Ridley accused, but she'd lost the heat of her anger. "You can afford to laugh since you're doing the nasty with Coop every damn night." Was she jealous? Hell, yes.

Quickly sobering, Phoenix asked, "Have you actually, ah... invited Baxter to your bed?"

"Of course not. The bum has to ask me, not the other way around."

A rich, male voice interjected, "Well, maybe someone should have told me that."

Both women swung around to find Baxter himself—still a dick—standing there looking good enough to eat. Phoenix went wide-eyed...and then grinned. Ridley scowled.

Morning sunshine stroked Baxter's fair hair. He wore only black board shorts with unlaced sneakers and God Almighty, his body was better than the coffee.

She looked at her own reflection in his mirrored sunglasses, saying succinctly, "Go away."

"Nope."

He couldn't take a seat—there were only two—so Ridley turned back to her coffee, intent on ignoring him.

Phoenix, the rat, had other plans. She hastily stood. "I should be on my way."

Ridley was really too tired to come up with an adequate insult for the deserter, so she said only, "Paybacks are hell, sis."

Smiling, Phoenix came around the table, bent for a hug and said quietly in her ear, "The cure is right here. All you gotta do is grab it."

"Oh, I'll grab it all right—"

"Shush." She gave Ridley a loud kiss on the cheek and stepped away. As she passed Baxter, she muttered, "Play nice. I'm partly to blame for her grumpy mood."

"I will if she will."

Shaking her head, Phoenix walked away.

An odd mix of expectation, dread and annoyance kept Ridley bitter. She gave all her attention to her coffee cup and did her best to ignore the stud-vibes coming off Baxter.

Of course, he refused to be ignored.

"The silent treatment is interesting." He spun the vacated chair around, straddled the seat and braced his bare arms over the back. Softer now, he added, "But I heard what you said, and there's no taking it back."

Temptation, that's what he was. Pure, hot temptation.

Ridley sniffed in disdain. "I may not be interested anymore," she lied, and went back to sipping her coffee.

Keeping her eyes off him took all her concentration. *The struggle is real.* When he said nothing else, she sighed dramatically. "Run along, Baxter."

Instead, he took off his sunglasses and placed them on the table.

Oh, unfair! Those stunning green eyes drew her like a damned magnet.

"I was away from the park the last few days."

Away? Well, damn, no wonder she hadn't seen him. She pretended only mild interest.

As if he knew her ploy, his eyes glittered. "I sometimes teach private classes in different locations. Coop has no problem with me adjusting the schedule here when I need to be somewhere else, especially since Kelly can fill in for me then."

"Kelly?"

"She's an assistant."

Only an assistant? Ridley wondered.

Again, he seemed to know her thoughts. "I have a scuba shop in town, too. Kelly's usually there—except for when I need her here."

She'd need to meet Kelly to decide how she felt about that. With any luck the woman would be sixty, leathered by the sun, and with an ugly temperament. Until then... She shoved to her feet. "Well?"

His brows shot up. "Well, what?"

"Ask already—and you damn well better make it pretty."

A slow, cocky smile sharpened his appeal. Slowly, he stood too, flattening both hands on the tabletop, and leaned toward her, his gaze on her mouth. With his voice whiskey-rough, he whispered, "Let me fuck you, Ridley. Pretty please."

Oh, yeah... She swallowed. That'd work. She folded her arms under her breasts. "Eight o'clock, here. Tonight."

His attention dipped to her cleavage, enhanced by her stance. "It's going to be a very long day."

Yeah, tell me about it. She lifted her chin. "Not for me. I'll be too busy to watch the clock." For a little payback, she added, "Daron is going to do some repairs to a cabin while I'm cleaning it—"

He came around the table so quickly, she almost squeaked.

Before she knew it, he had her chin caught gently between long fingers, his other hand pressing at the small of her back.

Somehow she was flush against his lean body and her senses rioted with pleasure. *Nice.*

"I'm all for keeping this casual."

Double dick. "You have no choice in that."

"But," he added with emphasis, "you're going to have to limit yourself to one man at a time."

Her eyes flared. Wow, he had a hell of an opinion on her stamina. Leaning into him more, ensuring that her boobs squashed against his naked chest, she purred, "One man is fine—long as he makes it worth my while."

His mouth landed on hers and before she had time to assess the impact, he had her lips open, his tongue dancing against her. *The man knows how to kiss.* Along with that thought she heard a laugh.

Baxter released her mouth, his expression dark as he looked off to the side.

Keeping her face hidden against him, not sure she had the strength yet to move, she asked, "People?"

"They've moved on, but the park's getting busy." He eased away from her. "I need to get down to the shop anyway. I have classes this morning."

"Lots of little hotties waiting for you?"

"Right now I'm only concerned with one hottie," he said.

Basically avoiding an answer.

She knew anyway. Baxter was always surrounded by admirers.

He stood there, breathing deepened, gaze intense. "Eight o'clock, Ridley." He pressed one more quick kiss to her mouth, and strode away.

Soon as he was gone, she fanned her face and fell boneless into her seat. Oh, it was definitely going to be a long day—that'd be worth it in the end.

She hoped.

Later that morning, Baxter was in the shop before classes, doing an equipment check, trying—and failing—to think about something, *anything*, other than Ridley, when Coop stopped in.

Knowing what he wanted, Baxter went to the door, flipped over a sign to read CLOSED, and turned the lock.

Since Gibb had been unable to catch the goons at any wrongdoing, Baxter had taken it upon himself to see what he could find out—after he'd gotten Coop's reluctant agreement first.

Unfortunately, he didn't have much to report.

"Phoenix is working?" he asked as he petted the little dog that now shadowed Coop almost everywhere he went.

"Yeah. She'll be busy until five or later." He unleashed the pup so it could explore. Hands on his hips, expression grim, Coop asked, "Anything?"

"Not much." Baxter propped a hip against the checkout counter. "I found the guys, even talked with them some, at a local bar."

"You didn't find out anything?"

He shrugged. "Nothing you didn't already know. They consider themselves badasses—which has to be the mystery of the year, because I doubt they have a complete spine between the three of them."

"Or a brain," Coop muttered.

He nodded in agreement. "After they left the bar, I chatted up a few other people. They claim Harry has been lying low, that some 'big dude' beat his ass."

Coop snorted. "I tapped him once."

"Apparently, it was enough of a tap to intimidate." Baxter hated to disappoint Coop, but he needed to know. "One guy, commiserating with Harry, said a cop tried to blame him for some 'shit he didn't even do.'"

"The night Phoenix's porch light was broken and she saw someone running?"

"I assume. Harry appears to be well-known in the bar, as an irritant to some and a buddy to others. But they all agreed that he's been sticking close to home lately."

"Fuck."

"Yeah, my thoughts exactly." Baxter would have loved to confirm Harry as the culprit, which would have given Coop leave to revisit the punk. But it wasn't to be.

"Did it cost you anything to get that info?"

With a grin, Baxter said, "Not really. A few drinks in a dive, a near brawl of my own, and some fast excuses to dissuade a couple of interested women. Overall, not a bad night."

"I can repay you for the drinks."

"The hell you will," he said, still grinning. "I enjoyed it." Except for the part about the women coming on to him. That had been awkward, and the cause for the near brawl.

Apparently, the locals didn't like seeing their ladies rejected, no matter how nicely.

Rejecting them hadn't made Baxter happy, either. Used to be that a one-night stand with a stranger would have suited him just fine. No strings. No familiarity. Satisfying sex, nothing more.

Unfortunately, he didn't want anyone but Ridley.

Coop reluctantly nodded. "Thanks."

"Anyway," Baxter said, shaking off his odd preoccupation with a woman who insulted him as often as she turned him on, "it sounds like maybe it was all happenstance, just as Phoenix claims."

"Maybe." Coop headed for the door. "Or there's another threat...one that could be more serious."

Damn. Baxter didn't like that idea at all.

If Phoenix was at risk, could Ridley be also?

11

PHOENIX HUMMED AS SHE RAKED, HER MIND ON MANY things—like her sister and Baxter. Were they working out their differences? Jumping into bed right now?

Still playing cat and mouse with each other?

Or had Baxter walked away?

She wanted to see Ridley happy, but wasn't sure which outcome would make that happen. There were times when Ridley could be very self-destructive. What she wanted wasn't always what she needed.

But then, Phoenix was the same.

Every night she joined Cooper in his home. She'd play with Sugar while Cooper grilled dinner. She'd help him with the dishes, and then they'd walk the dog around the resort, or play with her in Cooper's yard. Sometimes they watched TV, sometimes they just talked.

No matter how their evening went, they always ended up in bed and it was the most amazing thing she'd ever experienced, almost as if they were meant to complement each other. Every time felt new, hotter, better than the time before it.

And afterward, difficult as it might be, Phoenix insisted on returning to her cabin.

Her small home felt lonelier each time she did.

Yes, she wanted to stay with Cooper, to sleep curled at his side and wake with him in the morning. Share coffee. Share a shower.

Maybe share a life…

She wanted that a lot.

The sensible side of her brain, though, reminded her that she had important, personal goals, and they didn't include relying on others. Not yet, anyway.

She didn't need to prove anything to others…but she wanted to prove something to herself.

Needing a distraction, she pulled out her phone and texted Ridley.

How did it go?

While waiting for a reply, she put away the rake and tidied up the maintenance building, making sure every tool was in its designated spot. Organization was important to her because it made her job easier. She'd already lectured the high school boys who often helped with cutting the grass. Too many times, they'd left things out of place, always in a hurry to be on their way. They'd caught on quickly and now, almost by rote, they returned things to where they belonged.

Less than a minute later, her phone dinged. 8:00 tonight. Whoo hoo.

A smile twitched on her mouth. 8:00 you two are getting together?

Yup & I may just wear him out, so if he's not at the job tomorrow, you'll know he died happy.

Phoenix laughed aloud. What about you? Do you expect to expire with pleasure?

You betcha.

Still grinning, Phoenix shook her head. She'd always envied her sister's daring and exuberance. LOL. Have fun!

Gotta go. I need to hustle so I can finish early. Need time to make myself ravishing.

With her innate sense of style and slimmer figure, Ridley always looked great. Phoenix rapidly thumbed in: Love ya!

You too.

She slid the phone into her pocket, warm with happiness for her sister.

"Let me guess—that was Ridley?"

Shock brought her around so fast, Phoenix lost her footing and fell back against a wooden support post. The world seemed to spin around her; her heart went into her throat then dropped into her stomach.

Her ex stood there in the open double doors of the building, sunlight haloing his body and making his face difficult to see. But she recognized him all the same.

It took her three tries to find her voice, and then she whispered, "David."

He stepped farther inside, a smile fading off his face. "I didn't mean to startle you."

Startle her? Her reaction was so much worse than that. She swallowed heavily, forming the words carefully. "What are you doing here?"

Appearing wounded, he shoved his hands into the pockets

of his pants and exhaled a slow breath. “I wanted to see you, to see how you’re doing.”

He looked the same, his brown hair neatly trimmed, his face freshly shaved. She thought she even detected his cologne…or maybe that was just a memory powering through her surprise.

“But…how?” She hadn’t told him where she was.

Some odd emotion had him lowering his eyelids. He turned his head a little, giving her a sideways glance. “You’re not happy to see me.”

She didn’t know how she felt. “It’s a…surprise.” It was cowardly, but if given a choice, she’d have never seen him again. She didn’t want to face all the things stolen from her, the things she’d given up—and what she’d forced away.

The pole at her back became a welcome support as she slowly straightened, trying to hide her turmoil.

He spared a fleeting smile. “I still follow you on Facebook. You’ve posted enough photos of the place, finding it was easy.” He came forward a single step. “You seemed happy in your posts.”

Though he said it as a statement, she saw the question in his searching gray eyes. “I am.” *Why was he here?*

“Still jumpy, though?” He nodded, drawing his own conclusions. “I really am sorry for showing up unannounced. I just thought…”

Her heart hammered wildly. Did he think she was ready to get back together? That they could now move on as a couple? She waited, not sure what to say, not sure what to do.

Cautiously, he approached, his eyes now watchful, until he stood right in front of her.

“Phoenix.” When he reached for her hand, she resisted the urge to step away. She wasn’t afraid of David. Not ever that.

But she dreaded what he might say, what he might want.

She feared the reason for his visit, and the fresh hurt she might cause.

He wore his serious face, the one he usually saved for talks about their future. The one he'd worn while they'd chosen their house and made wedding plans.

David was a good man, and she'd hurt him so badly. The least she could do now was to greet him properly.

Something icy inside her seemed to crack. "David," she whispered, reaching for him, drawing him into a tight hug. "It's so good to see you."

Relief visibly rushed through him, and he crushed her close, his face in her neck, the cool brush of his hair against her cheek.

He was solid and familiar, and affection tugged at her heart. She squeezed tighter, saying, "I am so, so sorry for everything."

His arms loosened and, putting his hands on her shoulders, he pressed her back. "You don't need to apologize, Phoenix. Not to me. I'm just glad to see you looking more like yourself."

She smiled now, genuinely happy to see him—but still guarded. "How have you been?"

"Fine." A smile cracked, this one more authentic, somehow more *real*. "Actually, I'm better than fine." He took her hand. "Come here. I want to talk to you."

"O-kay," she said, putting wariness in the word.

"Relax, honey." He led her to the riding mower and indicated she should sit. "I'm not here to pressure you."

Unsure what he considered pressure, she didn't yet relax.

"You're happy?" he asked. "Because you really do seem happy in your posts."

Knowing she couldn't lie to him, Phoenix nodded. "I'm very happy."

He released a breath, followed by a wide grin. "See, I can still read you—even in a Facebook post."

"David—"

"I've moved on, too," he said quickly.

Hope bloomed. "Really?" And because she could still read

him as well, she suddenly knew. Her voice took on a teasing note when she asked, "Who is she?"

"I hope you don't mind, but your friend, Angie…"

Her jaw loosened. "Angie Perkins?"

"I know she was a friend of yours, but you were gone and she said she hadn't heard from you in forever. We were talking, and one thing led to another—"

Laughing, Phoenix launched against him. "I think that's wonderful!" She and Angie had been casual friends, but Phoenix hadn't spoken with her since the attack.

"So you don't mind?"

"Of course not." It amused her because Angie's opinion of David had been lackluster at best—unless… Phoenix grinned, wondering if Angie had pretended to be less than impressed to cover up her attraction. *Interesting.* She pressed him back. "You two are serious?"

"It's still new, but yeah, we're getting there. I just felt like I should check up on you before taking things any further."

"David, that is so sweet—but totally unnecessary."

He nodded. "Angie said if you were still interested, you would have been in touch. She's the one who pushed me to…" His voice faded into nothingness.

"To forget about me?" Phoenix asked gently. "She's right, and I'm so glad you have."

"No, I haven't. I never could." He held both her hands. "I'll always love you, Phoenix. We had a long history together and, at least on my part, a special closeness."

Such a good, *good* man. No, she'd never deserved him, but she was happy to count him as a friend, as *only* a friend, so she lied. "Yes, it was very special."

He lifted her hand, kissing her knuckles. "Now that I'm happy, I wanted you to be happy, too."

She was about to answer, to assure him that she was, but she didn't get the chance.

"Am I interrupting?"

She glanced over David's shoulder and met Cooper's gaze. Oh, his eyes weren't mellow now. Far from it. Despite his calm facade and the gentle way he held Sugar, she could read all the ways he'd misconstrued the situation.

"Cooper." She disengaged from David and went to him, taking his arm.

Realization dawned on David's face.

Doing the introductions, she said, "David, this is Cooper Cochran. He owns the resort. Cooper, this is my friend, David." She hadn't accurately introduced either man but she saw no point in clarifying that Cooper was more to her than just a boss, and David had been closer than any friend. Enough tension already choked the air.

Cooper shifted Sugar into one arm and stepped forward, eyes narrowed, hand extended. "David."

"Nice to meet you," David said, drumming up his usual congenial smile. "Beautiful place you have."

"Thank you." He reached back, looping his arm around her shoulders and bringing her alongside him. "Phoenix keeps it looking that way."

"She was always talented with anything that grew." David shifted his gaze from her to Cooper and back again. "I had hoped to visit for a bit, but I see that you're working."

"Cooper won't mind if I take off for an hour."

After a heavy stillness, Cooper looked down at her, his amber eyes direct, holding hers. "Of course not." He shared a strained smile. "Take off the entire afternoon if you'd like."

"I can't," she countered quickly. She didn't want to rudely send David packing, but neither did she want to take hours to reminisce. "Too much to get done today, but I would like to show David around."

Cooper nodded. "All right."

It seemed prudent, at least to Phoenix's mind, to make a few things clear to both men, so she put a hand to the side of Cooper's face, went on tiptoe and kissed his mouth. "Thank you."

Cooper damn well didn't want to leave them alone, but he wasn't the jealous type—not usually, anyway—and he wanted Phoenix to know that he trusted her.

The ex wasn't what he'd expected. He looked like a nice enough guy, clean-cut, athletic. It might be ridiculous, but he'd sort of imagined him as a creep, maybe a dude with a big head or a beer gut. He'd expected something about him to be offensive—which was stupid, because Phoenix wouldn't have been engaged to him if he wasn't a nice, responsible, handsome man.

Coop barely suppressed a growl. Knowing she'd been engaged and seeing her with the guy were two very different things.

It helped that, in subtle ways, she'd made it clear that David was only a friend now, and that Coop was…more.

How much more, that was what he'd like to know. He didn't like that she refused to stay the night at his house. Respecting her meant accepting her decision without argument—but it wasn't easy. He wanted her close, where he could watch over her.

No matter the logical conclusions and evidence to the contrary, he couldn't shake the idea that she was in danger. Gut instinct told him that someone had deliberately broken her porch light. And earlier there'd been those mud tracks all over her deck. He wasn't ready to let Harry off the hook.

And now her ex was here—meaning he'd known where to find her. Coincidence?

Cooper wasn't willing to chance it.

For that reason, he found several reasons to be in the same area as Phoenix and David. Not right next to them, but close enough.

He made a pretense of paying them no attention. Sugar helped with that by yapping happily at people they passed, chasing leaves and begging for pets. The little dog drew attention everywhere she went. Kids adored her, and she adored them. Women fawned over her, loving the expressiveness of her big brown eyes. Even men paused to scratch her behind her floppy ears.

He was paused near the private docks at the pond, two young women cooing over Sugar, when out of his peripheral vision he saw Phoenix approaching.

Her pale blue eyes were wide and watchful behind her glasses, her fingers tangled together, and David was no longer with her.

Sugar spotted her, too. With a bark, she abandoned the new admirers and ran—ears flopping wildly—to Phoenix, who knelt to accept the greeting.

Coop would have gone to her, as well—Sugar had her leash stretched as far as it would go—but the women had questions about the paddleboats for rent. As he politely answered them, he was aware of Phoenix sitting on the ground and Sugar crawling into her lap.

The pup was shameful in her demands for loving.

Coop wouldn't mind a little of that attention himself.

Finally, after another five minutes of what amounted mostly to chitchat, Phoenix said, "Cooper?"

Excusing himself from the women, he turned to her. "All done with your visit?"

She stared up at him, Sugar hugged close. "David just left."

He tried to read her face, to see how upset she might be—or how pleased, but he couldn't tell if the visit from her ex was a good or a bad thing.

"Can we talk?" she asked.

Since that was what he wanted, he smiled. "Sure."

She set Sugar back on her feet, then reached for a hand up.

Coop easily hauled her upright. Once she was on her feet, she didn't let go. In fact, she hugged his arm while urging him forward—away from the maintenance building.

"Where are we going?"

Her fingers teased over his left arm, mostly over his biceps. "Remember I said that I couldn't take the afternoon off?"

"Yeah." He'd been relieved that she hadn't wanted to spend more time with David.

"I've changed my mind." She paused, her brows drawn together as she looked up at him. "Unless you're busy?"

He'd had some errands to run, but he mentally canceled them without remorse. "Nothing that can't wait."

"You're sure?"

"Positive."

Her slow smile was somehow naughty. "Good. Let's go to your house."

The way she said that made his body tense—in all the best ways. "Are we going there to talk?" He had to make sure he was reading this right. So far, Phoenix had been beyond circumspect when it came to their relationship. To her, appearances mattered. He couldn't just assume, because of a visit from the past, that she'd suddenly changed her outlook on that.

"We can talk," she said, still hurrying him along. "After."

"After?"

They started up the hill, and she asked thoughtfully, "Will you think I'm taking special favors just because we're sexually involved?"

It was about more than the sex, but for once he didn't focus on the distinction, asking instead, "Special favors?"

Keeping her gaze straight ahead, she nodded. "Skipping work for an afternoon of sex." She waved her free hand. "I promise I can make it up later. Today was going to be a light day anyway. But I really should be on the clock, right? Not sneaking away—"

How the hell was it sneaking when anyone could see them?

"—to your house, to indulge a craving."

"A craving?" Damn it, he was starting to sound like a parrot, repeating everything she said. As they reached his house, he scowled. "I'm starting to wonder if I should be insulted."

She flashed him a glance. "Insulted? Because I want you?"

He unlocked the door and, once Sugar was inside, removed her leash. Then he turned to Phoenix. "Why now?"

Color crept up her neck. "Am I presuming too much?"

"No." He backed her into the door, then caged her there with his hands flattened at either side of her head. "But you have to admit, the timing seems suspect."

Confusion filled her gaze. "How so?"

"You get a visit from your ex, and suddenly you want me in the middle of the day."

Her eyes flared wide. "Oh, my God, you think I want you because of David?" She quickly shook her head. "Wait, I do—but probably not for the reasons you think."

"Why don't you explain it to me then?"

Instead, she said, "Maybe this was a bad idea."

"No." He bent to nuzzle her throat. "Sex with you, anytime, any day, is never a bad idea." He lifted his head. "David mentioned your special relationship."

"So you heard that?" She put a hand to his chest, lightly petting. "Just how long were you eavesdropping?

"Long enough to wonder if you were having a reunion."

Her lips curled sweetly. "Cooper," she whispered, her tone chastising. "How could you ever think that?"

He was starting to feel like an ass—an ass who had badly bungled accepting a sweet offer. "What did he want?"

"To tell me he'd moved on, and now that he's happy, he hopes I'm happy, as well."

Fuck. So the guy was gracious, too.

Phoenix held his face between her small hands and smiled up at him. "I didn't want to hurt David again, so I agreed that our relationship was special to me. But the truth is, I didn't know what special really meant—not until you."

Coop caught his breath. "Is that so?"

She kissed his chin, then his throat. "I hope I don't spook

you." Her lips touched the side of his neck. "I promise I'm not trying to push or make more of our relationship than there is."

Everywhere she touched, his skin burned. "I don't spook easily."

"Awesome." She lightly bit his shoulder. "Then please understand. I carried so much remorse for hurting David that it almost smothered me. Seeing him today, finding out that he's happy, that we can be friends—*only* friends—was so liberating. It's like I can finally take a deep breath, when before I was strangled."

He hated the idea of her feeling that way, and now he knew he owed David his gratitude. "Then I'm glad he came by." And that he'd set her free. "Come on."

Sugar followed them down the hall, but then slipped into the closet to sleep. Cooper quietly closed the door.

"Won't that scare her?"

He shook his head. "She lets me know when she wants out."

"All right." She reached for the hem of his shirt, then had to struggle to get it over his head.

The height difference was enough that Coop bent to help her.

She murmured, "Thank you." Then lowered to her knees.

Damn. Staring down at the crooked part in her glossy black hair, he felt his body hardening. It took him a second to realize that she'd untied his sneakers and was urging him to lift his feet so she could get them off him.

Wondering what else she had planned, he quickly helped with that. Barefoot now, he braced his legs apart and waited.

After flashing him a smile, Phoenix straightened her glasses… and reached up for the snap to his shorts.

Coop didn't say a word. Hell, he barely breathed.

She opened the snap, dragged down the zipper and leaned forward, her face against him as she inhaled. "I love how you smell."

His jaw clenched.

With her hands on the front of his thighs, she rubbed her

cheek against him. He felt her warm breath, and it was all he could do to stay still.

Through his boxers, she grazed him with her teeth.

"Phoenix—"

"Let's get these off you." She tugged down his shorts and boxers together.

He kicked them aside, then reached for her shirt, but she brushed his hands away. "Not yet."

Not yet? Tangling a hand in her hair, Coop tipped up her face. "You're making me crazy."

"Good. You deserve to go a little crazy." Her small hand wrapped around him. Holding him firm while she leaned in and pressed a kiss to the underside of the head.

His cock swelled more, his breath laboring.

The feel of her tongue, flattened against him, licking down his length made his body clench. He urged her upward again, relishing the wet, hot glide—she drew the head into her mouth, sucking softly.

Coop groaned, both hands now in her hair. He didn't want to steal her show, but he needed her to take more of him. He needed her to move.

He needed to fuck her mouth.

Almost against his will, he pressed forward, and Phoenix gave a small hum of acceptance, of pleasure. God, it was erotic and hot and it could only be better if she was naked, too. But for whatever reason, she seemed hell bent on driving him insane.

He was already halfway there.

Holding her still, he pressed into her warm mouth, loving how her lips closed around him, how she moved her tongue. Just as slowly he withdrew again.

Her hands went to his backside, her nails prickling his skin as she urged him in again.

No problem.

This time, when he was about to withdraw, she instead took

him deeper, the suction so sweet that his balls tightened and he knew he was in danger of coming.

As if she sensed it, one hand came around to his front, fondling his testicles while she went down again, not so slowly now.

A river of heat rushed through his veins. His eyes went heavy—but he couldn't look away from her. Wisps of dark hair came loose from her ponytail. Behind her glasses, her eyes were closed in a look of concentration. A flush stained her cheeks, hollowed from the suction. Her lips around his cock were wet.

Feeling the pressure rise, Coop feathered his thumbs along her jaw. "I'm going to come."

She gave a humming reply, her nails contracting on his ass—and she didn't stop.

Permission then.

The sensations, the visual, were both so sweet, he wanted it to last, his teeth clenched as he fought for control. She worked him as if she enjoyed it as much as he did.

That thought was his undoing.

He held her head, his hips moving, his body straining as release washed through him.

Phoenix drained him, her hands now gentle as she petted, soothed. As she accepted.

He was still semi-hard, his cock now glistening from her wet mouth, when she released him and looked up.

He watched her lick her lips. A deep breath didn't help, not when he realized the problem.

He was falling in love.

Odd that a blowjob would bring on the realization.

Phoenix watched the play of emotions on Cooper's face and wondered what he was thinking. There was a languid sensuality to his golden eyes, to the heaviness of his eyelids and the softness of his mouth.

Walking her fingers up his thighs, his hips and his abs, she offered her hands.

The slightest smile curved his mouth as he caught her wrists and lifted her to her feet. She put her arms over his shoulders and rested her cheek against his chest, unable to find the words to explain how different she felt.

David's visit was like a warm, leisurely shower after a long, sweaty day. It had revived her, washing away all the grimy memories and crippling regret.

She hadn't realized just how badly she needed David's forgiveness until he gave it to her.

Against her temple, Cooper asked, "Any reason why that just happened?"

She could understand his confusion. She was usually so insistent on maintaining her work schedule—as if that would keep people from knowing about their involvement. Cooper's Charm was like a big family, a big *nosy* family. Everyone knew everyone else's business.

After happily servicing Cooper, she felt swollen with need, but also soft with affection. She burrowed closer, liking the downy prickle of his chest hair. "I felt like celebrating."

He choked on a laugh. "I love the way you celebrate."

"I loved it, too."

He went still, then groaned. "Don't. Not yet."

Smiling against his shoulder, she asked, "Don't what?"

Sliding his hands down to her bottom, he pressed her closer. "Get me hard again so soon."

Phoenix wiggled, then sighed, "Ah, too late."

His laugh was rough and sexy and in two steps, he tumbled her to the bed. "Let's get you naked."

She stretched luxuriously. "Let's."

Taking his time, Cooper stripped her, and as he did so, his hands played over her skin—the insides of her thighs, her stomach, beneath her breasts, even the ticklish undersides of her arms.

His mouth followed his fingertips, sometimes biting gently, other times licking.

Sucking a time or two.

It was heaven, indulging all her senses without the past weighing her down.

With both of them naked now, Cooper lounged beside her, one big hand on her stomach as he blew warm breath over her nipple. "What were we celebrating, baby?"

She smiled. "Starting over."

That made him rise up to see her face, his expression curious. "Are we?"

"Yes."

He didn't laugh or frown. Instead, he pressed a soft kiss to her lips and asked, "Why?"

"Because now I'm more *me*." She put her palms to his chest, urging him to his back so she could crawl over him. "That doesn't sound right, does it?"

"I think I get it." Again, his hands settled on her bottom. "You're back to yourself, the woman you were before your life got turned upside down."

"Yes. I feel whole again, flesh and blood instead of a shadow."

"You were never a shadow," he chided.

Of course he didn't think so, because he didn't know the real her. She laughed, straddling his lap and bracing her hands on his chest. "Thank you. Condom?"

He studied her before reaching out one long arm, snagging the drawer on the nightstand and fishing out the protection. He started to hand it to her, then pulled it away, saying, "I have questions, but I think I'd rather wait to ask them."

"Okay." He could ask her anything. She'd decided not to worry about impressions or misunderstandings. Going forward, she refused to waste a single day. A single *minute*.

The past had imprisoned her long enough.

Still, he withheld the condom. "Will you be running off after this?"

Oh, he made it sound bad, the way she defected to her cabin each night. In so many ways, while trying to display independence she'd instead been a 'fraidy cat. But no more.

Unfortunately, she did still have work to do, so she said, "For a while. But if you want, I'll come back tonight."

His eyebrows knit together. "For dinner?"

"Sure." She spread her fingers over his upper chest, then slowly dragged them down over his flat brown nipples. "You're an excellent cook."

Cooper clenched all over, drew a big breath, and said calmly, "For sex?"

"If you're able, then sure, I can be convinced."

"I'll be able," he growled, and finally gave over the little silver packet—but only so he could cup a hand around her neck and tug her down, face-to-face. His eyes were darker, like rum over ice. "To sleep?"

It was such a wonderful invitation. She knew he was worried, that the unresolved situation with Harry and his cohorts left him feeling something bad would eventually happen. The offer wouldn't always be there—she couldn't make assumptions about the future, and didn't want to anyway—but tonight was all hers, so she said, "If you and Sugar want me here."

There was an infinitesimal widening of his eyes before he caught her in a heated kiss, his tongue taking possession, ramping up her need.

He wanted to take over. Coop was the type of leader that, even in sex, would be dominant. She liked that about him.

This time, however, she'd lead the way.

"Shh," she whispered. "Lie back."

His nostrils flared and he asked with suspicion, "Why?"

"Because I'm not done enjoying you."

It was slow to come, but his small, sexy smile told her that he wasn't intimidated. In fact, he seemed to like the idea.

"Now," she said, and rolled the condom onto him. He was fully erect again, throbbing in her hand. She recalled the taste of him and her breathing deepened.

Widening her thighs around his hips, she braced one hand against his body and with the other, she held him in place against her, moving the head against her own wetness, teasing herself and him with each glide against her swollen lips. Her breathing quickened. She wanted to make this last, but she wasn't sure she could.

Just as she nudged him a little inside her, he reached up to cup both her breasts, his rough thumbs drifting back and forth over her nipples.

No, she definitely wouldn't last. He, on the other hand, had already gotten off once, and now seemed plenty patient.

He caught her nipples, flattening them between a thumb and finger, tugging gently. She arched her back, her body flooded with sensation.

"Nice," he murmured, still tugging, twisting carefully. "Once you're done torturing us both, lean forward so I can get my mouth on you."

That did it. Phoenix closed her eyes and, rocking her hips, took every wonderful inch of him. She felt full, a little stretched, and she loved it.

Cooper gave a husky growl. "Come here."

Leaning forward only sent him deeper, stealing her breath. Groaning, she flattened her hands at either side of his head while pressing her hips to his, back and forth, back and forth, seeking, *needing.* When his mouth latched on to one puckered nipple, she knew she'd lost the game. "Cooper..."

"Let me," he whispered, and then his hands were on her hips and he took over, thrusting into her while working her nipple with his tongue. The position kept her open, her clitoris exposed to his every stroke. The relentless rhythm sent her glasses sliding down the bridge of her nose.

She didn't care.

The pleasure coiled. Her hands clenched into the bedding. She tipped back her head, groaning, reaching, wanting—and finally, *finally*, the climax rushed through her.

She heard Cooper's answering murmur against her breast, felt the tensing of his body beneath her, the way he pressed hard into her with his release.

God, it was so perfect, lasting until her thighs trembled and her arms refused to support her.

He released her nipple, his hands now caressing her hips as she sank down against him, her glasses almost falling off. She adjusted them quickly before sliding to the side of him, her limbs weak.

Cooper turned his head to see her. After several deep breaths, he said, "We should celebrate more often."

She huffed a laugh, not only happy, but also content. It felt good. *She* felt good.

Ridley was going to be thrilled.

12

WHILE THEY BOTH CAUGHT THEIR BREATH, COOP THOUGHT about Phoenix, her uniqueness, her sweetness blended with scorching sex appeal.

He'd never gotten a blowjob from a woman in glasses. The thought made him smile.

As if she sensed it, she peered up at him. "What?"

He traced the top rim of her glasses, from one arm, over her nose, and to the other. "It takes talent to do that wearing these."

Adorably prim, she stated, "I do everything in them, except shower and sleep."

"They're hot."

She made a sound between a full laugh and a silly giggle. That happy sound swelled inside him, chasing out shadowy remnants of grief. Almost from the first moment he'd met her, Phoenix had affected him that way. She'd kick-started his emotions when he'd thought them long dead. The sensation was a little uncomfortable—but he liked it all the same.

Rubbing his fingers into her silky hair, he tilted her face toward him and asked, "So David showed up, and he made this big difference in your life?"

Her brows pulled together behind her glasses. "It's hard to explain. It's like..." Her inky lashes swept up and she gazed at him. "I was dragging this rock. Uphill, you know?"

Coop nodded, encouraging her.

"It was hard, but I was getting there little by little. When I met you, you started helping me and so I was making more progress, getting that damn rock up the hill—for what reason, I don't know." She ducked her face, her lips moving against his skin. "But then David showed up, and it was like he told me there was no rock."

Oh, God, Coop heard the tears in her voice and it crushed him. He drew her full against him, his arms around her. "No reason for guilt?"

She nodded, and when she looked up at him, she was smiling, tears clinging to her lashes. "You've helped me so much, Cooper."

From everything she'd said, David should get the credit. "I'm glad."

"You don't realize, do you?" She scooted up until she could put her elbows on his chest.

It was a pose she favored, and one he enjoyed because it pushed together her impressive breasts, creating amazing cleavage.

"The things you do," she said, too seriously, "the way you give, even who you are—you have no idea how special any of that is, do you?"

It made him uneasy, all these extreme compliments. Anna used to say the same, almost in the same way, and that struck too close, making him want to sidestep.

"I'm not," he teased, turning her under him again. "But if you actually want to get any work done today, I suggest you get a move on." He put a love bite on her shoulder. "Before I recover enough to convince you to stay."

For one heart-stopping moment, her gaze searched his and he wondered if she'd feel slighted, if she'd misunderstand his reasons for dodging. She was opening up to him, sharing herself, and here he'd just—

"Right you are." She gave him a loud smooch and squirreled away from his hold. "I can make it back at 7:00, if that's okay?"

He stared at her back while she pulled on her panties. After coming twice, he should have been spent, but the sight of her perfect ass caused a spark of heat. "Seven is perfect," he murmured, watching as she hooked her bra.

Phoenix didn't wear expensive lingerie, but then, she didn't need to. Her body was enticing enough not to need decoration.

Sugar yapped, so Phoenix opened the closet. The dog peeked out, watching as she finished dressing. Coop knew Sugar didn't want her to go. Hell, he didn't really want her to go either, but he needed some time to think—and he wanted to find out more about David. Why had the man really showed up today? Was it as simple as the explanation he gave—or did Coop have reason to distrust the timing?

He'd do some research before he decided.

And he'd try his best not to let jealousy influence him.

Ridley, along with everyone else, knew that Phoenix had gone up to the house with Cooper, and then stayed long enough to have lots of fun.

Silently, she cheered her sister. *You go, girl.*

Any man who could bring Phoenix around was a hero in her book.

As she finished stacking fresh white towels in the small linen closet of the cabin, Ridley saw her sister through the narrow window. She was striding down the hill to the main path.

Phoenix wore a huge smile.

Hurriedly, Ridley finished what she was doing and darted out to catch her. "Phoenix."

She looked up, her smile widened, and Phoenix veered off so that they could meet at the lane opposite the scuba shop.

"Well, look at you," Ridley said as soon as she was close enough. "A little 'afternoon delight' agrees with you."

To her surprise, Phoenix said, "It really does."

Ridley fought the urge to gape at her, and instead grinned. "Oh, you naughty girl. You're getting as bad as me."

Phoenix sputtered a laugh. "Since you're wonderful, I'll take that as a compliment."

"Please do." Ridley had been keeping up with Phoenix's long stride, but now she hooked her arm through hers and drew her to a halt. "What's the rush?"

"I need to finish up for the day and now I'm behind."

"So you loosened up, but not all that much?" Ridley looked at her more closely, then tilted her head. "Something is different."

"Yup." Phoenix did a quick look around, and finding they had relative privacy, threw her arms wide. "I'm free."

"Free, as in?"

"David was here."

Well, knock her over with a feather. "Shut up. No way!" Phoenix didn't look upset over it. She looked…damn it, *free.*

Almost bubbling over with enthusiasm, Phoenix leaned in close. "He's moved on, Ridley. He's in love with someone else, someone I know will make him happier than I ever could, and I don't have to feel guilty anymore."

"You *never* had to feel guilty." She'd told her that often enough. Phoenix was one of the nicest, most caring and considerate people she knew.

"I did anyway." For only a moment, Phoenix's expression grew somber. "I felt so freaking guilty it sometimes choked me."

"Oh, honey." Ridley felt her throat closing up. When Phoenix hurt, she felt it, too. "Why didn't you tell me?"

"I wanted to work it out myself, remember?" She took Ridley's hands. "And you had your own junk to deal with."

Ridley shook that off. "Forget Robbie. He's not worth mentioning."

"He hurt you, and I'd still like to make him pay."

"I did," Ridley said with evil delight. "I made him pay big."

But Phoenix didn't smile at the familiar jest. "We both know he could afford it, and even if he couldn't, it's not enough for the way he treated you."

How the hell had Phoenix turned this around on her? Ridley huffed in exasperation. "I'm a big girl and I'm over it," she lied.

Clearly, Phoenix didn't buy it, but she did let it go. "And I'm a big girl too, which is why I wanted to deal with my issues on my own."

Ridley bit her lip. Everything about Phoenix was different, as if she were miraculously softer but more firm, accepting yet stronger. "And you have?"

"Yes."

Reaching for her, Ridley intended a giant hug—but Daron interrupted.

"Are you two arguing, gossiping or something different?"

Phoenix laughed. "A little of each, actually."

"Which is usually how we do things."

"Fascinating." He grinned at each of them.

Ridley cocked out a hip. "Did you want something?"

"Such a loaded question—"

Maris, who'd been walking past, gave him a shove and kept going.

He pitched forward, almost slamming into Ridley before whirling to see who'd pushed him. When he saw Maris, he broke into a big grin. Still watching her, he said to Ridley, "Shower is fixed in cabin five—and I still think your ex must've been a blind ass. Later, ladies." He took off in Maris's wake.

Phoenix shook her head. "Despite the way she always turns him down, he doesn't give up."

Ridley snorted. "Maybe because he knows she's fighting herself more than him."

That got Phoenix's attention. "You think so, too?"

Ridley countered with, "Absolutely."

"Hmm. It's possible, I guess, but I've been so busy working on me lately, I haven't paid enough attention to everyone else."

"Then trust me."

"You could be wrong, you know. In a lot of ways, they're polar opposites."

"So?" Ridley folded her arms. "I'll bet you fifty bucks they end up in the sack."

Phoenix gave it some thought. "When? It can't be indefinite."

"With those two, it's like a slow burn, so let's say…before the holidays." Ridley held out a hand.

Looking away, Phoenix asked, "Will we still be here for the holidays?"

"Hey, I'm not going anywhere. I'll have to have my RV winterized, but Daron says there are plenty of cabins available during the coldest months."

"You and Daron have done a lot of talking."

She leaned in to say, "It makes Baxter jealous."

Phoenix laughed. "You are so bad."

"Will *you* still be here?"

"Honestly, I don't know. I guess that depends on how things go with Cooper. I like it here, and they do plenty of holiday things to keep me busy." She looked up the hill toward Cooper's house. "Guess I'll have to wait and see."

"I vote we both stay." Ridley glanced around at the kids playing, the people visiting, the water and trees and…the *friendliness*. "I like it here."

"Me, too." She sighed. "I guess I better get to work or I'll never get done. FYI, I'm spending the night with Cooper."

Wow. That really was a big step for her circumspect little sister. Ridley replied by offering her a high five.

Phoenix slapped her hand and started to back away. "What about you and Baxter?"

She struck a smug pose. "He's coming over tonight."

"Just think, there'll be fireworks and it's not even the Fourth of July yet."

Ridley laughed as she waved goodbye. God, it was nice to see Phoenix so content. She turned to get back to her own work—and something hit her chest. When she looked down she saw the biggest, most hideous praying mantis ever…and it was looking at her!

The scream stuck in her throat. She frantically swatted at the thing, but it clung—*clung*—to her shirt with multiple legs and long, angular arms. Hysteria had her madly attempting to free herself, blind to onlookers and the consequent laughs.

Suddenly an arm came around her from behind, locking her close to a solid wall of muscle so she couldn't move. Warm breath brushed her ear with a soft "Shush" sound, and then a big, dark hand reached around her and easily plucked the insect free.

When the arm around her loosened, Ridley shot away, wanting as much distance between her and the bug as she could get. She sprinted to the opposite side of a cabin, then, panting in remaining terror, peeked around the corner to see Baxter carrying the gruesome thing to a decorative flower display edging a light pole.

Still she didn't emerge.

But at that point, she became aware of people still standing about, grinning at her, one kid dancing crazily as if to mimic her. When the mom saw Ridley looking, she tried to still the boy, but Ridley released a shaky laugh.

"It's accurate," she said, much to the mom's relief. With a shudder, she added, "I *hate* bugs."

The woman, who appeared nice enough, said, "Me too, actually. But you have me beat on the dance."

Baxter stepped in front of her. He wasn't laughing. "You okay?"

"Humiliation isn't fatal, thank goodness."

"No reason to be humiliated." He took her shoulders and drew her close. "Fear isn't a reasonable thing, and it's not easily controlled."

Loving the warm comfort, Ridley leaned into him. "Thank you for playing the hero." She couldn't suppress another shudder. "The monster wouldn't let me go."

His lips brushed her temple. "You do realize the park is full of insects, right?"

Ridley tucked her face against his chest. He was damp, his hair dripping as if he'd just come from the lake. His skin felt cool against her cheek. "Don't remind me."

"If it helps, it's rare for a bug to actually fly onto a person. You're not their first choice for places to land."

"Guess I'm just lucky then, huh?" Damn, he smelled good. His taut skin, lightly tanned, made her want to rub her nose all over him. Her mouth, too. And her tongue—

"You were nice to the kid."

Leaning back to see him, she asked, "That little rascal who was mocking me?" She couldn't stop the smile that bloomed. "He's just a kid being a kid. Pretty cute, actually."

Baxter stared at her, wet lashes framing those bright green eyes.

"What?" she asked, unsure why he looked at her so fixedly.

He shrugged. "That attitude surprises me."

Indignation growing, Ridley disengaged from his hold. "Because I'm such a bitch, you mean?"

"I never said—"

"Obviously, I'm the sort to kick puppies and harangue children who behave like—" she gasped dramatically "—*children.*" Frustration carried her as she turned to storm away.

Baxter caught her and spun her sharply back around.

When she started to blast him, his mouth silenced her. Cool lips on warm, coaxing, pressing.

Dangerous move, she thought. With both his hands now framing her face, he left his body vulnerable. She should stomp on his foot, tug his chest hair—or maybe even plant her knee in his crotch.

He deserved it, damn him.

She meant to do *something*—anything other than soften against him. Anything other than open her mouth for his tongue.

Anything other than moan quietly.

Still holding her face, he murmured against her lips, "I meant that fear can make people react without thinking. And you were scared shitless."

"Such a lovely description to apply to a lady."

"It's accurate. Jason Vorhees wouldn't have scared you more."

"Well, actually, he's one of my favorite monsters." When Baxter looked confused, she shook her head. "Never mind. You were saying?" If he had more of an apology to make, she wanted to hear it.

"That kind of fear can prompt us to say or do things we later regret."

"Yeah, well." She almost resented his understanding more than his implied insult. "I adore kids enough that I think I can refrain from ever hurting them, either by word or action."

Amused, Baxter repeated, "You adore kids," with just a touch of surprise. "And monsters, too—as long as they aren't insects?"

Eyes narrowing in renewed ire, she snapped, "Yeah, so?"

"So there's obviously a lot I don't know about you."

That gave her the will to push away from him again, only this time she didn't attempt to stomp off. "Let's keep it that way, okay?"

"Why?"

Her eyes flared in disbelief. *"Why?"*

"You're shouting."

Damn him. She brought her voice down to a growl. "Maybe because you turned to stone the other day over pizza at Coop's place?"

"I didn't—" he started to protest.

No way would she let him get away with that. "It was obvious to the rest of us that you didn't want to be there, not in a setting where you were expected to socialize with me." To punctuate her understanding of the situation, she stated, "Sex, yes. Getting to know me? Obviously a big *hell, no.*" Ridley realized she was almost shouting again.

Baxter didn't attempt another denial. He steadily stared at her, waiting.

Ridley faked a calm she couldn't feel. *Why* she couldn't feel it, she had no idea—except that he seemed to bring out the worst in her. "It's not a problem for me."

He gave her a look of irony. "That's not the impression you're giving."

"I was just accosted by a praying mantis! I'm frazzled." That certainly seemed like a valid excuse to her. "You can believe me, we want the same things." Patting his naked chest in dismissal, she said, "Thanks for the bug rescue. I need to get back to work, but I'll see you tonight. And Baxter?"

Appearing thoughtful, his gaze still far too perceptive, he asked, "Hmm?"

"Bring your A-game. I deserve it." And with that, she finally walked away.

Ridley liked kids. And she didn't mind laughing at herself, even over something so very real to her.

He'd just left the lake when, again, his gaze was drawn to her. When he saw her flailing about, he'd at first thought she'd been stung. He'd already been walking her way, ignoring questions from the class and a few attempts to flirt with him. The closer he'd gotten to her, the faster he'd moved.

Her face was white, her eyes unseeing as she'd uselessly batted at the poor mantis while drawing a crowd of onlookers who found her hilarious.

He'd said her name but she didn't hear him, so he'd done the expedient thing of holding her still and removing the bug. She could be an Olympic sprinter, she moved so fast once he'd freed her of it.

And still she hadn't been offended by a kid making fun of her. The boy, probably ten or so, had put on quite a show. When Ridley noticed, Baxter had expected any number of reactions from her—anger, tears, annoyance.

Instead, she'd been amused.

Even as she'd given him hell, practically vibrating with the need to attack him, he'd wanted to kiss her. He'd known she was holding back by sheer will, and he'd wanted her mouth. Badly.

Was it the insect, as she'd claimed, that had her overreacting?

Or was she that offended by his comment about the kid?

He wanted to know. Suddenly, in fact, he *needed* to know.

She was right that he didn't want to socialize with her. Not in a group. But privately? Maybe after a powerful orgasm made her more docile, he'd find out everything he could.

Assuming the woman was ever docile.

Baxter grinned as he headed back to his disgruntled guests, his thoughts on how fun it would be to tame Ridley Rose's prickly temper.

Damn, but she was proving to be the best sort of challenge.

Polished from head to toe, hair conditioned and soft, body sleek in scented lotion, makeup perfectly applied, Ridley tugged on a smooth camisole top, no bra, with thin harem pants over pretty thong panties. Barefoot, she walked to the blinds in the bedroom to peek out. It was fifteen minutes early, but Baxter was just walking up. He wore a snowy-white T-shirt that contrasted with his tanned skin, with his usual board shorts and sneakers. His fair hair looked as if it had dried in the humid air. Reflective sunglasses protected his eyes from the glare of the hot, summer day.

The sun wouldn't completely set until close to ten o'clock. Too bad she couldn't open the blinds and see Baxter's naked body in the natural light.

She planned to put him through his paces. Just thinking it made her heart trip in excitement. She would make him insane with lust, make him beg for release. She'd be in control from start to finish.

He would know that he'd met his match—and then she would decide the course of their relationship. Never again would she let any man hurt her.

His brisk knock brought her to the door. She strolled—leisurely—to the living room to answer. Even after she reached for the knob, she hesitated, anticipation ripening to an acute ache. After a deep breath and quick lick across her lips to wet them, she turned the handle and pushed the door wide, greeting him with a smile as the steps came down.

She'd already rehearsed what she'd say, how she'd play him along, make him wait until *she* was ready—

He came up the steps in one big leap and before she could make a sound, he had an arm around her waist, her body hauled close to his.

"God, the day was excruciatingly long." Then his mouth was on hers and Ridley forgot her plan.

She was vaguely aware of him shoving the door shut without breaking the kiss—vaguely, because most of her concentration was on his wicked tongue, exploring over her teeth, her lips, before plunging deep. When she tried to kiss him back, he sucked her tongue and lightly bit her lips until she couldn't breathe, could only hang on to him.

"So soft," he murmured.

She wasn't sure if he meant her hair, where he'd tunneled in his fingers, or her ass, which he currently squeezed, drawing her closer and closer to him, ensuring she felt the solid ridge of his erection.

Control. Right, she was supposed to be calling the shots.

With that in mind, Ridley slid a hand down his chest, over his flat abs to his straining cock in the loose shorts.

Mmm, nice. She liked the way he jerked, how he freed his mouth to hiss in a breath.

Yes, she could do this. She…immediately found herself backed up to the only available empty wall space in the RV. At first he ground himself into her hand, then he captured both her wrists and pressed her hands to the wall at either side of her head while he opened his mouth on her neck, directly over her fluttering pulse.

Her toes curled. Her stomach quivered. Mmmm, that felt *so* delicious.

Without her quite realizing it, he transferred both her wrists into one of his hands, so he could move his long fingers over her left breast.

"No bra," he whispered in approval. "Damn, you are stacked."

Yes, "the girls" had always been one of her best physical features. No surprise that Baxter would focus there.

Then he lightly touched his mouth to hers again. "I love this sassy, sarcastic mouth, too. Your lips are so soft."

The lips he teased parted in surprise.

"Mmm." His tongue traced just inside. "Do you know how hot you are when you're giving me hell?"

That had to be a joke…right? Hard for her to think clearly when he went back to kissing her while still cuddling her breast, occasionally scraping the tips of his fingers over her thrusting nipple.

Somehow—because he was diabolical—he also got his muscled thigh between her legs, pressing against her most heated spot. She inhaled sharply and he sealed his mouth to hers, deepening the kiss. He released her wrists, but she was so lost to sensation her hands merely slid down to his hard shoulders where she grasped him, needing some stationary support.

He closed his fingers on her already sensitized nipple, worrying it relentlessly while his other hand drew her along his thigh in small, rhythmic movements that rocked her sex against him in a torturous way.

Oh, God, if he didn't stop, she'd be coming in minutes.

And of course, he didn't stop. No, he amplified his efforts as if he knew she was close.

He left her mouth, but only to put his own to her throat, his teeth grazing her skin. He bent lower, and suddenly his lips were on her opposite nipple, a shock of sensation as he dampened the material of her top with his tongue.

She sank her hands into his silky hair, too breathless to protest. Too close to care that she'd completely lost the lead.

"Baxter," she whispered.

"Hush."

Ohhh, later she'd make him pay for that. But now, now she just needed his mouth on her naked skin. She released him to hook her fingers in the front of her top, then tugged it down, stretching the expensive material without care. "Here," she said, offering herself to him.

She felt his smile against the upper curve of her breast. If he teased, if he laughed, she'd—

His mouth latched on to her, sucking softly, then, before she could catch her breath, not so softly.

"Yes." She dropped her head back against the wall, her eyes so heavy she could barely keep them open. His fair hair brushed her skin, his mouth pulled, his hand continued rocking her…

She came in a rush, hard and fierce, the pleasure crashing through her in persistent waves that left her crying out, her whole body shuddering. Always in sex, she tried to be aware of how she looked, tried not to give in to "orgasm face." Now, with Baxter, she couldn't think, much less care about her appearance.

As the climax receded, she would have slid down the wall except for Baxter's embrace.

His husky voice whispered, "Nice," in her ear right before he tipped her over his shoulder and carried her down the narrow hallway without bumping her head.

He dumped her on the bed.

Not sexy. But he was stripping off his shirt—very, *very* sexy—and shucking his shorts, so she didn't complain.

Naked, he rolled on a condom, his fingers hurried but sure over his cock. Ridley licked her lips.

Could a man be more delicious? His body was lean, toned, cut in key places...like those mouthwatering muscles that led down to his erection. Flexing biceps, carved shoulders, long defined thighs. He was fit in a natural, oh-so appealing way and now, after the draining O she'd just had, she could spend an hour just visually exploring him.

When he finally looked at her, his eyes were like green fire burning over her body.

She smiled, enjoyed his obvious lust.

Jaw tight, color high on his cheekbones, he shoved her camisole above her breasts. He breathed heavily, muttering, "Jesus." Both hands cupped her breasts, kneading softly, but not for long. In a rush, he caught her harem pants and stripped them off her, along with the thong, in one long drag. Slower now, he coasted his big hands down her thighs, pressing them apart as he did so.

"Fucking gorgeous all over."

His voice was so low, so gravelly, she barely heard him.

His gaze lifted to lock on hers. "A hundred things."

"What?"

"A hundred things I want to do, but I need you now."

Ridley meant to welcome him with open arms, but he didn't give her a chance. He pulled her hips to the edge of the bed, hooked his elbows under her legs, spreading her wide, and then he was at her opening, nudging, moving in her wetness, finding just the right place before sliding deep in one long, sure thrust.

Her body arched up to meet him, every nerve ending suddenly alive again, wanting, needing.

"Look at me, Ridley."

She got her eyes open for the odd request, even managed a polite, "Yes?"

"Keep looking at me." He withdrew a little, only to drive in again, hard enough to scoot her on the mattress.

Oh, but that was too intimate, forcing her to feel what he felt—letting him know what *she* felt. No other man had asked it of her, so why should he?

She turned her head to the side...and he stopped, staying deep inside her, but utterly still.

She could feel him throbbing as her body squeezed around him, trying to encourage him, yet he didn't move.

Softly, he commanded, "Look at me."

Not being a woman who took orders lightly, she resisted.

He pressed over her, bending her legs back farther so that her knees would have pressed her breasts...if his hands weren't over them, holding them so that he could brush her nipples with his thumbs.

"Ridley," he sang insistently, and he tugged, sending sensation straight from her nipples to where she held him, hard and full, inside her body.

Ah, God... She opened her eyes on his face.

Instead of gloating, he leaned forward more—which sent him impossibly deeper—and put a butterfly kiss to her mouth.

After that, she could barely think enough to breathe, definitely not enough to defy him.

He slid in and out, each stroke a little harder, a little faster, until they were straining together. Gazes still locked.

It was the most personal, private, wonderfully invasive thing she'd ever experienced, heightening every sensation, both physical and emotional.

She gasped, "Baxter."

"Come for me." He held her nipples in his fingers, his thrusts causing a rhythmic tug there that matched the hot glide and retreat of his cock inside her swollen sex. "Come *now*, Ridley," he urged, his face darkening, his jaw flexing.

As if he could command it so, she did, almost screaming with the power of it, her fingers digging deep into his chest, her thighs locked tight over his shoulders.

Watching him made it more exciting, his raw, real expressions as release coursed through him.

As they both gradually stilled, he clumsily freed her legs and lowered his body to hers, his face beside hers, his breath fast and hot.

She luxuriated in the aftermath, her body still buzzing pleasantly, every emotion spent so that she seemed to float even with his weight pressing down on her. Minutes passed, maybe thirty or more, in that pleasant haze.

Ridley sighed in contentment. It was amazing, wonderful, the best sex—something *more* than sex—she'd ever experienced. She could so easily become addicted…

Wait, *what*?

Her eyes popped open wide with the realization of what had happened.

Frantically, she shoved on Baxter's shoulders. "Move!"

Unconcerned with her sudden mood shift, he grumbled a complaint, then rolled clumsily to the side of her.

She was damn near panicking—and Baxter looked ready to sleep.

13

WHEN RIDLEY FUSSED BESIDE HIM, HER MOVEMENTS agitated, he let out an aggrieved sigh. *Should have known the peace wouldn't last.*

For some reason, he almost smiled.

Obviously annoyed, Ridley sat up with enough angry movement to shake the whole bed. He could feel her glaring at him, but he didn't open his eyes.

Not yet.

She smacked his shoulder. "Don't you dare fall asleep."

Here we go. Baxter looked at her. "Problem?" he asked with admirable calm—a calm he knew would only fire her up more.

With wild hair around her face, her naked body rosy, she snapped, "That didn't go at all how I planned it."

"No?" Baxter crossed his arms behind his head and said reasonably, "I came. You came." He lifted a brow, eyeing her naked boobs. *Damn, she has a kickin' body.* Despite that, his attention was drawn back to her eyes. "You even screamed a little—and RVs aren't soundproof, FYI."

Her jaw dropped and fresh color stained her cheekbones. "Oh, my God."

Since he didn't want her shy about letting loose in the future—and he had no real plans of taking her to his house—he said quickly, "We both enjoyed ourselves. So where's the problem?"

It took her a second to gather her thoughts, then her beautiful blues fried him. "It was too fast."

He could have laughed. Fast, yes. But he knew that wasn't the lady's problem. No, Ridley had wanted to call the shots and instead he'd made a point of taking over.

At least, that was what he told himself, that every move, every word, had been deliberate.

He wasn't sure that was true. Once she'd opened that door, he'd lost sight of the long game in favor of just having her. Of finally getting her naked, touching her, tasting her.

He'd moved on instinct, on need, without a plan in mind.

Never would he admit that to her, though. "Give me five minutes and we can start over. I can maybe make it last a little longer the second time. Maybe. Might have to happen with the third—"

Her eyes narrowed. "No, I don't think so."

Another challenge? This time he did smile, openly, almost a taunt. "You don't have to make it more interesting for me, you know."

Her eyes flared wide. "Go home."

Deliberately, he yawned. "In a minute." And he closed his eyes...but kept his senses alert. Ridley was the type of woman who did unexpected things. She could attack at any moment and he had to be ready. Hell, he could feel the whole bed trembling with her ire.

Suddenly, she cuddled into his side. "I'll give you an hour. Prepare yourself."

Smug in the outcome, Baxter slipped an arm around her, kissed her forehead and said, "Yes, ma'am."

Today was not a good day to be running late. After opening the padlock on the maintenance building doors and stepping inside, Phoenix checked the time on her phone. It was already 7:15 and she still had a lot of things to put away before she could grab a quick shower and join Cooper.

Maybe, she thought with a smile, she'd just shower at his house.

Would that be too invasive? Would it signify growth in their relationship that Cooper didn't want? Sometimes he was so hard to read.

Regardless, now that she was more accepting of her feelings, she was anxious to see him again.

She stored the tools she'd carried in her hands, then turned to go for the cart that she'd left outside.

Suddenly the metal door slammed shut. With only a couple of small windows, heavy shadows immediately filled the interior.

Thoughts scrambling, she started forward. There'd been no wind, no reason for the door to—

A loud *bang* sent alarm screaming through her. Then another and another, until the rapid-fire pops registered in her brain.

Gunfire.

Dear God. An acrid scent filled her nostrils as she dove behind a tall toolbox, shaking uncontrollably, her heart slamming in her chest. Fear made her clumsy, and as the sound escalated, she covered her head, cowering in a tight ball, a scream strangling in her throat.

One thought cut through the terror.

She might die here…when she'd just started to live again.

Her poor sister—Ridley would be devastated.

And Cooper. Dear God, Cooper. How would he deal with this after losing his beloved wife?

"Phoenix!"

When she first heard the shout, Phoenix didn't understand. She was so mired in her fear that it took her a second to realize that the loud pops had dwindled, replaced by a new sound that closely resembled…fists on the door?

"Damn it, Phoenix! *Answer me.*"

Daron? She thought it, then she yelled in relief, "Daron!"

The doors slammed open and he charged in as if he'd thrown himself against them. As he searched the gravel-floored building, their eyes met, then he looked around again and with a curse, headed to the right of the doors, growling, "Firecrackers."

The fierce beating of her heart began to slow. Cautiously raising her head, she became aware of the gravel cutting into her knees and shins, of a small fire flickering on a bale of hay left over from the fall. And the smoke, so much smoke hanging in the air.

Now that she saw it, her eyes burned and she coughed.

Daron stomped, rearranged and smothered the flames before they could really take hold. Fresh air blew into the building.

She wasn't alone. Wasn't being attacked.

Her legs were too rubbery to stand, so Phoenix dropped back onto her butt—reminded again of that damn sharp gravel. She put her head on her knees and concentrated on drinking in big gulps of air.

Why did it keep happening?

She hadn't heard him approach, but then Daron's hands were on her shoulders and he pulled her close, offering comfort. "You're okay, babe. Some fucking asshole threw in some firecrackers and then locked the doors."

She'd been locked in?

"How…" She swallowed to remove the squeak from her voice. "How did you know?"

"I was heading up here to look for a fuse for a camper when I heard the noise. Fireworks aren't allowed in the park."

She suddenly realized his chest was bare, her hands fisted against him. He was incredibly warm, solid and safe.

But he wasn't Cooper.

His hand cupped the back of her head. "I was already irritated, but then I saw your cart and I…" He shook his head. "I just knew." Hugging her again, he kissed the top of her head. "Scared the bejesus out of me."

She choked on a laugh. "Bet it scared me more." Knowing she couldn't continue to cower against him, she pressed back and sucked in another deep breath, hoping it would help to loosen the restriction in her chest. "Sorry." Composing herself was so difficult. "I didn't mean to—"

"Hush." He stood and helped her up, frowning at her scraped knees. "I need to call Coop, and then I need to call the cops."

"Cops?"

He gave her an incredulous look, which he quickly softened. "Hon, someone did this on purpose. The door was locked from the outside."

"Oh, right." She felt sick as it all started sinking in. "But who?"

"No idea, but we're going to find out." He withdrew his cell phone.

Phoenix touched his arm. "Don't tell Cooper yet. I'll explain it to him."

His gaze sharpened. "Why wait?"

"It…might bother him. I'd rather he see that I'm okay first."

Daron considered her a moment, then nodded before thumbing in a few numbers.

Fretful, so many worries squeezing her heart, Phoenix waited.

"Coop? Hey, it's Daron. You busy?… No," he said quickly. "Everything is fine, but could you come down to the maintenance building? I need to show you something." He nodded, then added, his gaze on Phoenix, "Yeah, she's right here. I'll explain when you get here… Right. See you in five." He disconnected and shoved the phone into his pocket, again looking around. "We need a new lock."

Still feeling dazed, Phoenix looked at him.

Brows flat, he explained, "I broke the other one."

She thought of how he crashed inside. And if he hadn't? Eventually she'd have realized the problem, but would the straw have caught fire first? What about the fuel and other accelerants? There were so many tools and pieces of equipment in the building, she knew she'd have been jumping at shadows. Solemn, aware of what could have happened, she whispered, "Thank you, Daron."

He nodded. "We should wait for Gibb," he said, hands on his hips as he looked around, "before we touch anything. He's already aware of the problems."

She tipped her head in dawning realization. "I suppose you are, too?"

"You're one of us now, right? What affects you affects the rest of us."

Despite the awful circumstances, his statement warmed her. Being part of Cooper's Charm was a very nice feeling.

"Come on. We'll meet Coop outside, then you head up to his house and wash your knees, maybe put some antiseptic on them or something."

Phoenix looked at her legs and the superficial scratches. She'd done worse while working in brambles. "I'm fine. But this..." she said, indicating the building. Scattered bits of straw still smoldered on the floor. The doors hung open, one of them crooked on a loose hinge. "I need to clean this up after Officer Clark does...whatever he needs to do."

"Hell, no," Daron insisted. "I'll do it." Without waiting for her to argue—if she would have, given the way she still trembled—he led her outside, into the bright sun and fresh air.

Because the maintenance building was located at the end of a lane along the rustic tent camping area, few people were around.

She considered that a blessing, saving her some discomfort, but it also lowered the chances that anyone would have seen anything.

Daron pulled the doors partially shut behind him, then led her over to a bench situated under a decorative copse of trees. "Let's wait for Coop here."

Knowing he'd closed the doors so she didn't have to see inside, her mouth twisted. "Thanks."

He patted her knee while watching for Cooper to arrive.

In preparation, she straightened her shirt and her glasses, doing her best to look unaffected, to look *fine* when she felt anything but.

When she finally saw Coop approaching in a golf cart—going faster than was allowed—she felt ridiculous tears sting her eyes. *No, I will not do that.* She sucked in several fast breaths and concentrated on looking serene.

Coop pulled to a halt next to them. He stared into her eyes, then climbed from the golf cart. Without a word, he handed Sugar to Daron and strode to Phoenix.

She opened her mouth to explain, but he tugged her close, his arms folding around her, and she found she couldn't utter a single word.

Coop watched as Phoenix moved the spaghetti around her plate. She'd had only a few bites of it, less of her salad, none of her garlic bread.

He wanted to coddle her, but that wasn't what she wanted, and he tried to be conscious of her preferences. Twice she'd been close to tears; he didn't want to be the one who pushed her over the edge. It'd be tough for him to see her cry, but he knew it'd level her pride.

He glanced toward the door. *When would Gibb finish?* How long did it take to look around and question a few vacationers? There wasn't that much to see, not many people he could talk to, especially since Daron said no one was around when he reached the building.

Phoenix picked up her garlic bread. "Shouldn't Officer Clark be done by now?"

"Soon." *I hope.* If a man could be in two places, Coop would be there now, listening in, getting info firsthand—and insisting that someone go check up on Harry and his goons. The waiting, the not knowing, was excruciating for him.

How bad must it be for her?

That was why he'd opted to take Phoenix to his house. She'd tried to insist she'd be fine alone, and she was strong enough that he believed her. But Ridley was off somewhere with Baxter and though Phoenix hid it well, she was shaken. For him, she was the priority. So here he sat, waiting.

"Cooper," she said softly.

Finding her gaze on him, he forced away his frown and said, "Hmm?"

As if he'd done something to amuse her, she smiled. "You're sure you don't mind if I stay here tonight?"

If he had his way, she'd move in until…

His brain stalled. *Until when?* Until they found out who was harassing her? And then what?

Since he didn't know, he shook off the deeper question and answered what she'd asked. "I want you to stay. I'll feel better if you do."

In a corner of the kitchen, Sugar snored, but the rapping of knuckles on wood brought her awake with a jerk.

Phoenix jumped too, scowled darkly, then composed herself.

"Gibb," Cooper said, already up and striding for the door.

She nodded and, oddly enough, took a big bite of bread—maybe just to give herself something to do.

Sugar followed Coop to the door, and when she saw the officer, she sniffed his foot, gave him a look of dismissal and padded back to her bed to sleep again.

Not much of a watchdog after all, Coop thought.

Hat in his hands, Gibb gave Coop a brief nod before stepping inside. "Sorry that took so long."

"Doesn't matter if you found something."

"Unfortunately, I didn't." He turned to Phoenix. "You're okay?"

"It startled the heck out of me, but I wasn't hurt."

Coop would have disagreed, but once she'd cleaned her knees, the scrapes weren't bad. Still infuriated him, though.

"I can imagine." Gibb took a seat beside her. "You don't recall anyone around when you went into the building?"

Her mouth twisted to the side. "I'm afraid I was daydreaming, not really paying attention to my surroundings. I was just about done for the day and trying to hurry so I wouldn't be late for dinner." She indicated the food.

Gibb smiled. "Understandable."

Manners belatedly kicked in. "Hungry?" Coop asked, knowing his friend had likely missed dinner. "There's plenty left."

"If I'm not interrupting.?"

It was Phoenix who assured him, saying, "Not at all. You can eat while you tell us what we should do next."

Putting his hat on his knee, Gibb sat back. "Other than being cautious, which I know you're already doing, there's not much I'd add."

Coop set a plate of spaghetti in front of him along with a bowl of salad and a glass of tea, then took his own seat at the end of the table. "Will you go see Harry?"

"Already did." He twined spaghetti around his fork. "That's part of what took me so long. I didn't want to give him a chance to cover his tracks."

"And?" Coop's patience was at an end.

Gibb finished the bite, wiped his mouth and explained, "He was at his grandma's. She lives down the street, so I stopped in there." With a shake of his head, Gibb said, "He wasn't happy for me to interrupt. Neither was his grandma. She gave me all sorts of hell and said Harry had been with her for a few hours at least." He smirked. "According to her, he's a good boy."

"Jesus," Coop muttered, sitting back in his seat.

"I'm sorry, but there's not much more I can do." In between bites, Gibb promised he'd keep an eye on things, suggested Phoenix shouldn't be alone, and lastly, mentioned that it *could* have been a simple prank by a kid.

Coop stewed in silence. He wanted to mention another possibility but wasn't sure how Phoenix would react.

"Did you believe him?" she asked suddenly, her expression curious. "Harry, I mean. Did you believe that he'd been with his grandmother?"

Coop and Gibb both looked at her.

Gibb seemed to stall, taking a long drink of his tea. When he finished, he pushed back his plate and folded his arms on the table. "Honestly, I don't know. Harry's always been a troublemaker, and some trouble is bigger than others. He knows I'm watching him and he doesn't like it, but is he stupid enough to keep up a harebrained campaign against you anyway?"

"Stupid enough?" Coop said. "Yes."

Gibb grunted a laugh. "Yeah, I suppose he is. To be honest though..." Gibb glanced at Coop first, then at Phoenix. "This doesn't really feel like him. I think he's on his guard with Coop for one thing. He'd probably never admit it, but you scared him."

"If others think that too," Coop mused aloud, "maybe his friends, then he could be trying to prove something."

Gibb turned thoughtful. "True."

Phoenix cleared her throat. "I wonder if there could be another possibility."

Coop's gaze snapped to hers. Suddenly he knew they were thinking the same thing—David.

Her ex visits, and right after that someone decides to terrorize her? He figured that was one hell of a coincidence, and apparently she felt the same. He should have realized that she wouldn't shy away from it. "I wondered the same."

She shrugged. "I'd have a hard time believing it."

"I know."

"I don't *want* to believe it."

He could understand that, especially since the visit had ended well, and she'd felt so good about it.

"But I also don't want your property further damaged, so I think I should share everything."

Though he agreed, her motivation pissed him off. "Daron already repaired the doors."

Gibb added, "The place is locked up again." He finished his tea. "What other possibility are we talking about?"

Coop continued to watch, silently encouraging. Now that she'd brought it up, he'd prefer to let her share what she wanted about her ex and their backstory.

She looked away first, her entire demeanor composed.

His pride expanded.

"David is my ex. Before I moved here, we were engaged." She paused. "But I ended things."

"And he's bitter?" Gibb guessed.

"Actually, no. He has every reason to be, but he came by this morning and he was super nice."

It was subtle, but Coop saw Gibb go on alert. "He came here?"

"Yes."

"So he knew where you were?"

She shook her head. "I've posted photos on social media and he saw them."

Gibb considered that, then nodded. "Go on."

"David said he's found someone else and moved on. He's happy now and he hopes I'm happy, too."

"That's why he came? To tell you that?"

"Yes." Phoenix traced the top of her tea glass, her gaze averted a moment before she turned to Gibb again. "But it seems a little convenient that he was here, that he was so incredibly nice about everything…" She bit her lip. "It could seem surprising to most that he'd care enough for me that he wouldn't want me to feel guilty, even though he's in love with another woman now."

Damn right it was "surprising," Coop thought, but he didn't say it aloud.

"Hmm," Gibb said, being noncommittal. "Does he live in the same place?"

"He said he moved out of the house we chose together. He has it up for sale." She frowned. "I'm not sure where he's living now, though. Maybe with his new girlfriend."

"Is his phone number the same?" Gibb asked.

"Should be."

"Why don't you try calling him? You can tell him what happened today, ask him if he saw anyone hanging around—we'll see how he reacts."

Looking very unconvinced, but still agreeable, Phoenix got out her phone and dialed David.

Coop noticed that, while she didn't have him in her contacts, she still knew the number by heart.

"Hi," she said, a small frown in place, and then uncertainly, "Is David there? Oh. Oh, I'm sorry." After disconnecting, she checked the number she'd called. "That's weird. I had the right number…"

"So it's changed?" Coop asked.

"Apparently." She seemed to think about it, then shook her head. "But I still find it hard to believe David would try to scare me. He's not that way."

"Is he the type to seek you out, just to tell you to move on and be happy?" Gibb asked.

She gave him a wry smile. "Let's just say I believed him when he said it. He was—*is*—a nice guy. Everyone likes him."

They were all silent a moment, then Gibb stood. "Thank you for dinner." He grinned at Coop. "You're a good cook."

"He really is," Phoenix agreed with her own smile.

Coop stood too, his frustration extreme.

At the door, Gibb paused. "If you're interested, I have an idea."

"Let's hear it." At this point, Coop was willing to try just about anything.

Gibb turned his hat in his hands, then gave all his attention to Phoenix. "You say your ex found you because of social media. That goes both ways, right? You could try looking him up, see if you can figure out where he's staying, who he might be staying with."

"Oh, absolutely," she said. "I should be able to find him on Facebook, Instagram, maybe even SnapChat."

Unless he'd canceled everything, Coop thought, and that would be telling.

"I need to get back to work. But reach out to him and let me know how it goes."

Phoenix agreed, but reiterated again that she wasn't accusing David of anything.

While she talked with Gibb, Coop was thinking of another way social media might help.

He had the perfect trap in mind—but it'd be better if he didn't mention it yet.

Baxter stared down at Ridley while she slept. It amused him that she hadn't removed her makeup, and now she looked like a raccoon. And her hair, all that glorious mink streaked with red, looked like a rat's nest and yet somehow it made her even sexier.

Even asleep, she had attitude, her brows slightly pinched, her hand beside her face curled into a fist as if she might battle someone in her dreams.

If she'd let him, he'd do that for her.

She turned to her back, stretching with a low groan, one rosy nipple peeking out from beneath the sheet before she settled again with a sigh.

Baxter didn't move, content to just look at her, remembering how she'd snuggled next to him last night, surprising him.

And then they'd both passed out.

So much for his plans of having her again and again, of impressing her with his stamina and expertise. He silently snorted to himself.

She'd impressed him.

It was a neat trick, how she balanced her abrasive manner with the unconditional love of a devoted sister, the wildness of her passion with her cuddly nature.

And she was afraid of bugs.

He smiled, liking that human weakness.

Unable to resist, he caught the sheet in two fingers and very slowly drew it down until both her breasts showed, then her smooth belly, over her hips and the neatly trimmed triangle of hair, down to her knees.

She had a beautiful body.

A challenging demeanor.

A sexual drive that rivaled his own.

Mentally listing her assets meant he was already too involved, but he couldn't make himself care. Ridley Rose was the type of woman who'd make a long-term sexual relationship worthwhile—emphasis on the *sexual.* Today he'd explain things to her. With any luck, she'd agree with him.

Just then, her bluer-than-blue eyes popped open. She stared blankly at the ceiling, almost with dread, before letting her gaze slide over to him.

Baxter smiled and cupped the breast closest to him. "You could patent this look."

She swallowed.

"Sleep-rumpled sexy. That's what I'd call it. Thing is, I'm not sure any other woman could pull it off the way you do."

Her mouth flattened, then a glittering look of retribution entered those amazing eyes. "What," she growled in a grumpy morning voice, "are you still doing in my bed?"

"Enjoying the view, naturally."

Her face went blank, her head lifted to see her naked body, and he expected her to scramble.

Of course, she surprised him.

She dropped back to the pillow and said in vague complaint, "Perv."

"Come again?"

"I might." She glanced at him, then stretched luxuriously—no doubt to make him react.

Which he did.

"First, though, I have to pee."

He grinned. "Yeah, me, too."

She came up on one elbow, leg bent in a classic pose as old as time. "And I'd prefer to brush my teeth."

He liked this playful side of her. *No surprise there. He pretty much liked* everything *about her.* "If you insist."

She leaned over him…but only to see the clock. "I have half an hour. How good are you at quickies?"

Baxter caught her hips. "You've yet to see my long game. Now hustle it up."

The way she climbed over him was enough to stop his heart. He watched the sensual sway of her hips as she disappeared into the hall bath through the connecting door in the bedroom. While she was gone, he found his shorts and removed the small, clip-on sprayer he had attached to the belt.

He set it on the nightstand, then waited for her to leave the john.

She came out with her wild hair smoothed, her breath minty and a scorching anticipation in her eyes. Going in next, thinking it was the least-sexy morning after he'd ever experienced, he hastily took care of business, found mouthwash in her medicine cabinet and rejoined her in the bedroom.

"Ever hear of spontaneity?" he asked.

Her nose winkled. "Maybe when I was twenty. These days, comfort takes priority."

Baxter soaked in the sight of her on the bed, propped on an elbow, her breasts soft and full, her legs long and lightly muscled. "You make yourself sound old when I know you're not."

"Twenty-eight." She met his gaze with defiance. "Old enough to do what I want, the way I want it. And right now, I want you, here—" she pointed to the mattress beside her "—naked and willing."

"All right," he agreed as he stopped beside the bed. "But I have something for you first."

With her gaze on his junk, she cooed in a silly voice, "Oh, I see what you have for me. Thank you."

Knowing he was hard, Baxter laughed. "Actually, I meant this." He lifted the spray bottle and held it out to her.

If he'd offered her a snake, she couldn't have looked more wary. "What is it?"

"A personal sized, refillable, clip-on bug spray." He showed her the flexible clip on the back. "It can go onto a belt or just the waistband of your jeans or shorts. Maybe even a purse, though I don't think you carry one while working here."

Silence.

Baxter looked at her face and found an expression he hadn't seen before, sort of bemused and uncertain, and maybe...softened?

He cleared his throat. "With so many bugs around the park, I figured you could carry it on you. If another lands on you, just give it a zap and it'll head the opposite direction real fast—"

Her body landing against his ended his explanation. He dropped the spray to the floor and closed his arms around her. "What's this?"

She rained kisses all over his face. "That's the nicest gift I've ever received."

Frowning, Baxter tried to lean her away so he could see her face, but she clung to him. He felt her shudder, heard a sniff, and his heart damn near stopped.

"Are you crying?"

She bit his shoulder, not a gentle nip either, and said, "I'm not crying, you're crying." Then she laughed, and sure enough, when she leaned back to see him, tears swam in her eyes. "That really was sweet. Thank you."

With more questions to ask, Baxter tumbled her backward into the bed and pinned her down with his body. Somehow, by the luck of fate, her legs were around him, his cock perfectly aligned with her soft, warm sex.

Maybe he didn't have any questions after all—

"What?" Ridley smiled up at him. "You're looking at me funny."

So he looked *funny* while fighting the urge to thrust into her? Good to know.

"What?" she asked again, her hands stroking his shoulders, his neck.

Only because he thought this might be important, Baxter tamped down the lust—but it wasn't easy. "You're telling me that bug spray is a better gift than the usual, like flowers or dinner out?"

She snorted. "Clichéd crap. Who needs it?"

Was she wiggling against him on purpose? Maybe testing his willpower? Honest to God, it felt like he'd almost slipped into her just now.

He felt heat rising up his spine and had to concentrate hard to say, "Is that right?"

"A personal-sized defense against bugs, though…well, don't freak out, but that's personal. It's for me, not just any woman, and I appreciate it." Wearing the softest expression he'd ever seen on her, she leaned up to brush her lips over his. "And now we only have twenty minutes, so unless you plan to go bareback, how about finding a condom so we can get on with it?"

He smothered her teasing with a kiss, but damn, he was tempted. He was already right there, the head of his cock sliding back and forth against her wetness. No doubt she was on the pill, but there were other things to consider besides babies, so he did the responsible thing and moved off her, snagged his shorts, found a condom and rolled it on in record time.

When he turned back to her, she smiled, and he was on her like a marauder. Apparently, she loved it, because she opened her legs to him, then lifted to meet his first hard thrust.

Wet and hot and as ready as him.

Perfection.

He moved over her, in her, loving the clasp of her body on his erection, the way she tried to take him deeper, how she tilted her hips against him.

Every sound she made spurred him on. She was just as frantic, her hands grabbing him everywhere, her ankles crossed tight over his lower back.

"Baxter," she demanded, panting.

He put his face in her neck, breathing her in, doing his best to hold off while ramping up the pace, the pressure.

"Baxter," she cried again, gasping.

So close. So damn close. He ground against her.

"Baxter." Her body bowed beneath him, her face twisted in her pleasure, muscles straining.

"God, you're beautiful," he growled, then he let himself go, a flood of pleasure crashing through him. He collapsed on her, but immediately flipped so she was sprawled over him.

"Oh, my God," she whispered. "I'm supposed to move for work now?"

He swatted her very sexy rump and said, "We both do."

"Next time, we gotta wake up earlier. I haven't even had coffee!"

Next time. Nice to know she was thinking along the same lines as him. While his hand was on her ass anyway, he cuddled and asked, "Do I have to wait until 8:00 tonight?"

He felt her grin against his chest, then she lifted her head. "No."

He smiled, too. "Want me to go grab you some coffee while you get ready?"

That sweet but perplexed look flitted over her face again. "Just so we're clear, I'm not a woman who turns down nice offers like that, so don't say it unless you mean it."

He bit her bottom lip. "I mean it." Rolling again, he put her under him. "I always say what I mean." With one last kiss, he pushed off the bed.

They hadn't had the talk he'd planned, Baxter thought as he dragged on his wrinkled shorts and shirt, but getting that reaction—for bug spray, of all things—was probably better anyway. The sex was definitely better.

Ridley brushed past him on her way into the bathroom. "Thank you." He heard the shower start.

"Be back as quick as I can." After stepping into his shoes, he headed out the door, finger-combing his hair as he walked. It was early enough that only a few people were up and about, but Maris would have the coffee ready.

They could talk anytime; tonight—or even tomorrow morning.

Thinking that, he decided he'd need to run home for a change of clothes and probably a razor.

He was just about to step into the store when the gravity of his thoughts hit him.

Mentally, he backpedaled. He couldn't plan to stay over with her two nights in a row. He should be planning *not* to.

He knew where this path was headed and he didn't want to

go there. He'd already visited once, bought the T-shirt, and only sucky memories remained. Since he wasn't a masochist, he'd decided to never head that way again. Hurt, humiliation… no thank you.

Love 'em and leave 'em. That was the safe road. The comfortable road.

He'd been coasting that way with no problems…until meeting Ridley.

Just sex, he insisted to himself as he stalked into the store, his mood taking a nosedive into bitter territory.

Sex in the evening, great.

And if they decided on sex in the morning, then he'd just arrive at the park a little earlier.

Never mind that holding her all night had been nice, she didn't want things to get serious any more than he did.

"Good morning," Maris said, swinging her long blond braid off her shoulder. "Coffee?"

"Two please. To go." It struck him that Maris was always at the damn store, and she never seemed to be just arriving. No matter how early he rolled in, she was there, raring to go, never harried. "Do you sleep?"

She blinked at him. "Yes?"

"How, when you're always here?"

"I'm not," she protested, already filling the disposable mugs. "But time is money, you know, so I like to get here early."

"And leave late?"

She shrugged, then indicated the cups. "Two, huh?"

Baxter shook his head at the way her big brown eyes widened in question. "To save you from asking, one is for Ridley."

She eyed his unshaved face and rumpled clothes, then doctored one cup with cream and sugar, the way Ridley preferred it. "Since you commented on me being early, should I mention that you're…late?"

Daron saved him by dragging in, looking worse than Baxter

did as he said, "Maris, honey, I hope you made the coffee strong because after the night I had, I need it," around a wide yawn.

Her teasing smile disappeared and those big brown eyes narrowed.

"Ass," Baxter accused as he took the coffee and left.

He hadn't been gone long, so he wasn't surprised to hear the shower still going when he stepped into Ridley's RV. He put one cup on her dinette table and then rapped on the bathroom door. "Hey, I have to run. Coffee is out here waiting for you."

The shower shut off. "I'll be out in two minutes."

And I'll have already left. "Don't rush." If she stepped out naked, he was a goner. He needed to split while his willpower held firm. "I'm already running late." Damn, he sounded lame. "I'll see you tonight." Without waiting for her to answer, he hurried from the RV.

He'd see her again tonight because he couldn't resist, but he'd make damn sure to keep things on an even keel. No more gifts. No more getting waylaid by her personality shifts.

And no more sleeping through the night.

Wrapped in a towel, her hair dripping, Ridley rushed out of the shower and looked around. A steaming cup of coffee sat on her dinette. Baxter, the coward, was nowhere to be seen.

Oh, but she'd known. She'd heard it in his voice, the miserable jerk. And to think she'd been feeling… Damn him, she'd felt connected.

Stupid, stupid, stupid. Hadn't she learned anything since her divorce?

Would he come back tonight? She gave it a quick thought and decided that yes, he most definitely would. He wanted sex, after all.

Well, he wouldn't be disappointed. She'd give him that, but only that—and not a single thing more.

14

THAT AFTERNOON, PHOENIX TEXTED RIDLEY TO ASK, Lunch? She needed to catch her up on what had happened. As it was, Ridley would be pissed that she hadn't been told right away.

Ridley immediately messaged back, Yes! When?

I'm free in 5.

My place, Ridley returned.

Phoenix wondered if her sister actually had any food in her RV, but if not, they could walk down to the store. She wanted to talk to Ridley more than she wanted to eat, anyway.

Her sister was pacing under the canopy when Phoenix arrived. Ridley took one look at her, and grabbed her up close for a bruising hug.

"I swear," she complained into Phoenix's ear, "I see less of you now that I'm living yards away than I did when we each had our own houses."

It said a lot, Phoenix thought, that Ridley could joke about that and neither of them winced. After all, neither of them had left their houses under ideal situations.

"What's happened?" Phoenix asked, knowing there had to be a reason for Ridley to be so huggy.

"Baxter is still a dick." Stepping away, she gestured for Phoenix to precede her into the RV. "He made me swoon with sex, then ran like the craven jerk he is."

"Funny," Phoenix remarked, "I heard he spent the night."

"Right, he did. He also sexed me up good this morning—after he gave me a gift."

"That all sounds really nice." Phoenix dropped into a seat at the dinette table.

"It was—until he ran."

"Ran?" Phoenix asked. "Or merely went to work?"

Ridley snorted. "He literally fled while I was in the shower." Bending into the fridge, Ridley produced two loaded salads, just like Phoenix liked them. Blackened chicken, cranberries, pecans and lots of leafy greens.

"Mmm. Are we celebrating?"

Ridley put out two bottles of frosty raspberry tea next. "No." She pulled the top off her salad bowl, then pointed her fork at Phoenix. "I can't believe I was getting porked while some asshole was trying to terrorize you. And *you* didn't tell me about it! I had to hear it from Maris, who heard it from Daron."

Shrugging, Phoenix said, "I asked to have lunch so I could tell you now." She dug into her salad. "Oh, man, so good."

"You should have called me last night."

"So you could do what?" She chewed and swallowed quickly before Ridley could argue. "I didn't contact you because one, it was under control. Two, I wasn't terrorized." Much. "And three, you were getting porked."

Ridley made a face, then conceded the point. "Fine. So give me the firsthand version. What exactly happened?"

Not a problem. Phoenix needed her sister to have the details anyway. She filled her in, only skimping on how afraid she'd really been, then summed it up with, "So of course Cooper thinks David might have had something to do with it."

"Well, if Harry is ruled out—"

"He's not. Cooper isn't eliminating anyone yet, and he refuses to think it could have been a prank."

Ridley raised a hand. "For the record, I agree with Cooper. I hate to say it, hon, but it feels like you're being targeted."

Yes, it did, but what to do about it, that was the big question. "Officer Clark suggested I contact David, so I tried. But he changed his number."

Pausing in her attack on the salad, Ridley stared at her. "David changed his number?"

"It gets weirder." She explained the plan, how she'd searched him on social media last night. "David is either off everything, or he's set up his privacy so I can't see him."

"No way." Ridley produced her phone and started searching. After a minute, she said, "Huh. I can't find him on Facebook." She searched some more. "Not SnapChat, either." She feverishly scrolled again. "Instagram is a nope."

Phoenix sighed. "So it's not just me. As my sister, he's probably blocking you, too. Only…why would he? Especially after stopping by to say hi and wish me well?"

Ridley scowled. "Didn't he mention the woman he's with now?"

Nodding, Phoenix said, "Angie Perkins."

"Right. Weren't the two of you friends at one time?"

"We were friendly, but we were never close."

Ridley gave her a level look. "Do you have her phone number?"

"I…" Phoenix blinked. "Yes, I think so."

"Call her. Ask her what old David is up to, but be tactful. Sneaky even. Don't let her know we're suspicious of him."

"I'm not all that suspicious." Still, she had to admit that it was weird for him to disappear off social media.

"Well, I am," Ridley said. "Call her."

Phoenix bit her lip. "Now?"

"Why not now? Get it over with and then maybe you can put Cooper's mind to rest on at least one dude."

Actually, that seemed like a good idea. Her relationship with Cooper was new and she didn't like these side distractions.

Plus there was the very real worry that it was his protective nature guiding things. If there was no threat to her, would he still ask her to stay over?

To give herself time to think on what to say, Phoenix ate the rest of her salad before picking up her phone.

As she sat there, procrastinating, Ridley, the jerk, started making chicken noises.

"I hope you lay an egg," Phoenix grouched, then she called Angie.

On the third ring, Angie answered with a flat, almost antagonistic voice. "Phoenix."

Just that, nothing more. Phoenix drew a breath. "Angie, hi. How've you been?"

"Really great, actually."

A sneer? "I'm glad to hear it." To end the awkwardness, Phoenix said, "Listen, the reason I'm calling—"

"You want to talk to David."

Angie was so deliberately hostile that Phoenix wasn't sure what to think. Across from her, Ridley mouthed the word: *bitch.*

Phoenix shook her head. She remembered Angie as friendly, funny and easygoing. But that was then, and perhaps more had changed than she realized. "I did have a question for him," Phoenix said neutrally.

"You can ask me. David and I are together now."

The way she said it, Phoenix could tell that Angie expected to surprise her. Did that mean David had come to see her without

Angie knowing? Not a great way to start a relationship. "That's wonderful. I hope you'll both be really happy."

Since that wasn't what Angie expected, she was quiet a moment before snapping, "What's your question?"

"I was trying to find David on Facebook, but—"

"I had him cancel everything because of this exact reason! I didn't want you coming back around, causing more trouble."

"More?" she asked, starting to get annoyed herself.

"You hurt him," Angie accused.

Having the truth flung at her, Phoenix deflated. "I know, and I'm sorry."

At that, Ridley stiffened and shook her head.

Phoenix ignored her. "That was never my intention."

"It's too late for you to apologize to him now."

Apparently, it wasn't, since she'd just done so yesterday—and David had accepted.

"You're not going to worm your way back in."

"I wasn't trying to, I promise."

"If you mean that," Angie said, her tone flat, "then stay out of his life."

"I plan to." Best to just spit it out so she could end this awful call. "I just need to know, is he living with you?"

"Yes. He's moved on. *We've* moved on. You should do the same." The call ended.

Stunned, Phoenix stared at her phone, then slowly looked up at Ridley.

"Gee, is she jealous much?"

"Ridley." It seemed Angie felt very protective of David, and that made Phoenix reconsider just how badly it had crushed him when she'd ended their engagement. She sat back and pondered what to do next. "I still don't think it was David."

"If it's any consolation, I find it hard to believe too, but that doesn't mean we should rule him out. From now on, you shouldn't be alone."

Phoenix almost groaned. "You, too?"

"Yes, me, too." Ridley held up a finger to silence her complaints. "Think about how you'd feel if that crazy stuff happened to me."

"It hasn't been *that* crazy. Yes, the firecrackers were terrible, but bulbs do blow, so that might not have been all that significant."

Ridley dropped her hands and stared at Phoenix, her voice going all gentle and big sisterly. "I just got you back, Phoenix. Humor me, please."

Put that way, of course she would. "I'll be extra careful at all times. I promise."

"Thank you." She forked her last bite of chicken. "So where does grouchy Angie live? I can drive by there to see if David is really with her."

"No, you absolutely will not do that. It's stalkerish." She got up to throw away her empty salad container. "Besides, David knows you."

They both snickered over the real reason Phoenix didn't want Ridley going by the house, then Phoenix said, "I should get back to work."

"Me, too."

She paused, eyeing Ridley. "Is Baxter coming over again tonight?"

"Yup."

"Is he staying the night?"

"Hell, no." Ridley grinned. "I hope he tries just so I can throw him out, but my guess is he'll stay long enough to be polite, then make his getaway."

Folding her arms and leaning back on the counter, Phoenix asked, "Does that bother you?"

Ridley looked her right in the eyes and said with credible indifference, "Nope."

Phoenix still didn't buy it. "You said he bought you a gift?"

Lifting the hem of her shirt, Ridley showed off a small canister set inside a case that clipped onto her pocket.

"Mace?"

Ridley snorted a laugh. "Bug spray, actually." She flipped the little container. "My own personal defense against insects. Really sweet gift."

"Yes, very thoughtful."

She scrunched her mouth to one side. "I got all stupidly grateful when he gave it to me, but that didn't seem to bother him. At least, not at the time. I guess I should have just said, *thanks, jerk*, and left it at that."

Phoenix couldn't help but laugh. "Cut him some slack, sis. Diehard bachelors are always afraid of getting involved. If he's feeling tempted, he might be more defensive."

Ridley shook off her sour mood. "Whatever. Let's go before Big Sexy reprimands us for slacking on the job." On the way out the door, she said again, "Don't go off to that maintenance building alone, okay? It's too isolated. If you need to be there, let me know and I'll go with you."

"And if someone accosts us, you'll blast them with your bug spray?"

She nodded. "Followed by a knee to the nuts. Gets 'em every time."

That Friday night, Baxter lay next to Ridley, still sucking in great gulps of air, a sheen of sweat on his body, his muscles relaxed, and he wondered what the hell was going on.

With him, not her. Oh, he knew exactly what she was doing: giving him what he'd asked for.

And God Almighty, the lady knew how to give.

As usual, she'd drained him. He'd never known a more energetic, enthusiastic and creative partner.

Or a woman more remote.

He turned his head to see her. Like him, she rested on her

back, one leg bent slightly outward, a forearm over her eyes, her hair spread over the pillow.

His gaze tracked the line of her stubborn chin and soft, parted lips, down her delicate throat and over the slope of her extraordinary breasts. Her nipples were soft now, but still rosy from their vigorous activity.

Her other hand rested limply on her stomach.

He wanted her again, which was insane since his heartbeat hadn't slowed yet. In the past four days, he'd come to the conclusion that he couldn't stop wanting her.

He thought about her during instruction, when he was underwater with a full class. He thought about her when other women came on to him. He thought about her when he hadn't seen her for a few hours, or when he knew he'd see her soon, and like now, when he was still with her.

Suddenly she reached over and, without moving that arm from her eyes, blindly patted him—getting perilously close to his junk. "I'm about to fall asleep."

Which was her way of saying, *Hit the road, bud.* Well, screw it. He wasn't ready to go yet. Staying a little longer wouldn't hurt anything.

Having her one more time would only signify that she was sexy—which was something she already knew.

Besides, it was Friday. If ever he was going to stay, Friday would be the— *Stop trying to rationalize it.*

Abruptly turning onto his side, Baxter caught her hand and kissed her knuckles.

She went very still, her chest no longer rising and falling with her deep breaths.

"Do you plan to sleep like this?" he asked, carrying her hand, held in his, back to her belly, then lightly brushing over her midriff, down to that soft fluff of hair. His knuckles teased over her, finding her still damp and warm, and his dick shifted in interest.

Slowly, Ridley lowered her arm. Her eyes looked like blue

ice…that was quickly thawing. "No," she said with just a hint of sarcasm. "After sex, I usually pull on a ball gown to sleep in."

Baxter's mouth twitched. Ridley's prickliness was both amusing and adorable. "Is that right? Can you fit many ball gowns in that tiny closet?"

"One is all I need, right? Now if you'll go—" she tried to tug her hand from his, but he held on "—I'll get dressed and go to sleep."

Ignoring most of that, he asked, "Are you sleepy? Because I'm suddenly wide-awake."

She jerked, *hard*, and freed her hand. "Maybe you could jog around the park?" she said with a sneering smile. "That might help you expend some energy."

"I can think of a better way to unwind."

She glared. "I just unwound you, damn it."

"Yes, you did," he agreed, reaching out to trace a circle around one nipple—which immediately tightened. "But then you lay there looking unbelievably gorgeous and smokin' hot, and suddenly I was wound up again."

Her eyes went heavy, a flush climbing up her throat—then without warning, she scrambled out of the bed and stood beside it, feet braced apart, hands on naked—luscious—hips, frying him with the fierceness of her gaze. "Get out."

Baxter considered her before cautiously sitting up. "Get out now, but return tomorrow?"

She rolled one shoulder. "That's up to you."

"Doesn't matter to you either way?"

Her chin went up. "Hey, you're the one who is so squeamish about staying over. I'm just following your cues."

That bit of honesty surprised him. He would have bet money that Ridley would have gone the rest of her life swearing that she was the one who didn't want him sleeping over. Instead, she shamed him by putting it all back on him—where it rightfully belonged.

He gave her an apologetic look. "I'm a dick."

"No argument from me." She turned to walk away, a hard-ass to the bitter end.

He caught her wrist, *very gently*, and pulled her back around. "Let's talk."

"Sure. Tomorrow."

Admiration had him smiling. "Since you're being so upfront, do you really want me to go? You know I will. But if it's just that you're still rightfully pissed, then I'd like to explain."

"Ohhh, you have an—" she made air quotes "—explanation? Why didn't you say so?" Like a princess, all haughty and smug, she perched on his lap.

With them both naked.

Baxter sighed. "You don't make it easy."

Wiggling her ass, she smiled at him and said, "Don't you mean I make it *hard*?"

"So damn sassy." He turned suddenly, pinning her under his chest on the mattress, her legs still draped over his thighs.

Her mouth pinched and her slim brows drew together. "This is not a position for discussion."

"It is if we both try really hard." He waited, his expression a question, until she nodded. "Thank you." Why he was suddenly into self-torture, he didn't know, but this? This defined torture.

But what else could he do?

He felt caught in the middle of two impossible situations. Wanting Ridley, while not *wanting* to want her.

As if that made sense.

Hating the humiliation of his past, but for some reason, driven to explain it to her. Maybe because she hadn't pried.

Maybe because he wasn't sure if it would matter to her. To *them*.

He was tired of fighting her, while also fighting himself. So he manned up and started with, "I got dumped once."

Her bottom lip poked out in a silly, sympathetic pout. "Oh, poor baby." Then in a meaner voice, she asked, "Is that it?"

"Not entirely." Dropping his attention to her boobs made it easier. And besides, he liked looking at them. "I was getting serious, but apparently she was just confused."

"Well, you're confusing, so I can understand—"

"She was gay." He winced at how he spit that out there, but getting it over and done with was easier than dragging it out. He didn't want to tell Ridley about the girl's reticence even while insisting they had sex, or how disconnected she'd been—definitely not about how she'd cried afterward, or how fucking sick he'd felt about it all.

Silence, and then: "Oh?"

She said it like a question, as if she needed him to spell it out for her. Great. He tried for some flippancy. "Yeah, see, she wasn't sure, but apparently sex with me convinced her."

Ridley snorted. "Don't be an ass. I'd say if she gave up sex with you, then she wasn't confused at all. Macho, hot, well-hung studs with crazy, mind-blowing moves just wasn't her thing."

Baxter almost laughed. *Almost.* Ridley gave him hell with both barrels, and now she'd just defended him the same way. "Well hung?" he asked, to hide how pleased he was with her very Ridley-like reaction.

"Like you don't know it." She slipped her arms around his neck. "How old were you?"

To hide some of the embarrassment, he played it down, saying, "A very tender twenty-two."

"Tender? You?" She gave another rude snort. "But hey, I can see how that might kick your ego."

Talk about an understatement. He'd been madly in love for the first time in his life—and she'd told him he was part of an experiment. A failed experiment. "She dated a lot of guys," he admitted. "She definitely seemed into the opposite sex. Then she hooked up with me and turned to women."

Humor curved her sweet mouth. "Bet your buddies had a field day with that one."

To put it mildly. He'd been the butt of every joke for a damned year. None of it had been deliberately cruel, just guys being guys, and he'd done his best to take the gibes with chuckles...but it had still sucked. If he hadn't been personally involved with her, if he hadn't thought she was the one... "Yeah, everyone really yukked it up."

"If I'd been around then," she said, leaning up to nibble on his bottom lip, "I'd have taken advantage of your weakened state and used. You. Up." She sealed her mouth over his and kissed him in that scorching way she had, using lips and tongue and teeth. "No one would have dared to tease."

"Yeah?" The past slid away into the recesses of his mind, overshadowed by the present—with Ridley in it. "Why don't you show me?"

She dodged his reciprocal kiss. "We're talking, remember?"

Right. The talk. "We're not done?" Because he was definitely done.

Ridley rolled her eyes. "Where's that woman now?"

"In a happy five-year relationship." He smiled, thinking of the only good thing to come out of that time. "Great job, great partner, good life."

She tipped her head, studying him. "How do you know?"

"We live in the same neighborhood." Which, of course, since they shared some of the same friends, meant the jokes resurfaced every so often. Hell, sometimes even she told them. Sometimes he did, too. They were past it, he was happy for her...but it had definitely been a lesson learned.

"And you chat with her? You two are friends?"

"You realize there's no reason to be jealous, right? I mean, she's definitely not into me—proved that years ago."

Ridley smacked his shoulder. "I'm not jealous. I'm...awed."

That didn't make any sense. "Why would you be?"

"Because this woman impacted you, and not in a good way, right?"

"I got over it." Eventually.

"But you don't resent her for it?"

Ridley's boobs were *really* distracting him now. "Wasn't her fault, was it? She had a right to be happy, same as everyone else." He'd mostly blamed himself for falling in love—or at least as in love as a horny twenty-two-year-old could.

Something strange brightened her eyes. Her lashes half lowered and she wore this odd smile. "You're not such a dick after all."

"I have my moments."

"Well, if you were a saint, you wouldn't be nearly so appealing." She pushed against his chest until he rolled to his back so she could climb atop him. "Here's the deal. Are you listening?"

Baxter clasped her ass with both hands and pressed her closer. "You have my undivided attention."

"I'm not interested in a serious relationship, but like anyone else, I enjoy a good cuddle now and then. If you want to stay over, ask. I'll either say yes or no, but it won't be vindictive. If I want you to stay, *I'll* ask. If you say no, I'll assume you have a good reason and I won't be offended. But no more darting off unexpectedly. I don't like that."

"Yes, ma'am." Was she into him sleeping over? He got hard, or rather *harder*, just thinking about it. "How's tonight looking?"

"I don't know," she said, all sassy attitude. "Will you make it worth my while?"

He grinned. Somehow, in some bizarre way, having what should have been a very uncomfortable talk with Ridley had turned into a very relaxed thing, a *sexy* thing. Damn, she was unique. "You have a quick answer for everything, don't you?"

"Are you being evasive?" she countered.

"Not at all." Rolling, he tucked her beneath him. He kneed her legs farther apart, settling between them, then opened his mouth on her throat, her shoulder, down to her breasts. "I promise," he whispered against her warming flesh, "you won't have any complaints."

Slender fingers tunneled into his hair, holding him closer as she whispered, "You can stay."

With a little lurch to her heart, Phoenix noticed that the photo of Cooper's wife was missing from the bookshelf in the living room. She'd gotten used to seeing it there, and now the empty space between the books made the bookshelf look like a puzzle with a piece missing.

Wondering why he'd moved it, she sat on the couch. Immediately, Sugar began hopping, wanting up. The dog's legs were just a little too short to make the leap easy. Phoenix bent and lifted her into her lap. "Now that you're eating regularly, you've really filled out."

On alert, Sugar stared at Phoenix and flipped her head to one side. Her ears followed. She flipped it the other way, and her ears followed again. Phoenix laughed, holding the dog's face and kissing her furry little forehead right between her big dark eyes. "You don't understand, do you? Only we humans are self-conscious about weight."

Cooper strode in, his hair damp from his shower, wearing only loose shorts that hung low on his hips, leaving his chest and abdomen utterly bare. "You don't have to be self-conscious. Your curves are in all the right places."

She grinned at him. He said things like that often, as if he truly appreciated her extra pounds. At every opportunity he showed her how much he enjoyed her boobs and behind. Good thing, since she wasn't into strenuous exercise or crazy diets. "Cooper?"

"Hmm?" He sat next to her and picked up the TV remote.

That was standard for them, a comfortable routine that she'd come to cherish: work during the day, dinner after sex, sometimes sex again and if not, a movie on the television.

She looked forward to those quiet, private moments together.

He chose an old horror flick, *Evil Dead*—another of her favorites! He knew her tastes so well, but luckily, they meshed with his. Settling back, he rested his arm over her shoulders and propped his feet on the coffee table, his body relaxed.

"Where is your wife's photo?"

It was slight, but she saw the way he paused before turning to her. Wearing no expression at all, he said, "I put it away." While answering her, he stroked Sugar's ear, then went on to say, "Her ear is completely healed now."

"I know. And her coat is so shiny. She looks beautiful and healthy, but more importantly, she's happy." *Like me*, Phoenix wanted to say, but first she needed to make things clear to him. "The photo?"

He hugged her closer so he could kiss her temple, just above the arm of her glasses. "I put it away."

That much was clear. "You don't need to do that."

With a short laugh, he shook his head. "You're the only woman I know who would argue in favor of leaving it out."

"She was your wife. You loved her. She loved you."

"Yes." He kissed the end of her nose, then her chin. "But she's gone."

Phoenix turned her head to his big shoulder. So strong, so sturdy. She remembered when she'd first met him, how she'd made note of his size because it reminded her of the men who'd attacked her. Now she knew his strength would only shield her, never hurt her. Cooper wasn't a man who'd use his strength against another, only if it was in self-defense or to protect someone he cared about.

She knew he cared about her.

"You'll never forget her," Phoenix said softly. "It doesn't matter if the picture is there or not." Her hand moved over his chest until she felt his heartbeat. "She'll always be here." And she was okay with that.

"Yes." His hand covered hers. "She'll always be an important memory. But as you said, the photo doesn't need to be on my bookshelf."

She belonged there, though. Phoenix didn't want to be responsible for her image being tucked away. "You know I'm not the type of woman to be threatened by a memory."

"No, you're special." He nudged up her face. "Very special." The kiss he pressed to her mouth was soft and exploring, tender and revealing.

Sugar climbed up to lick their faces, and Cooper leaned away, laughing. "Cock blocker," he accused, resettling Sugar between them. The dog's tail swung wildly, her joyous expression bouncing from Phoenix to Cooper and back again.

Phoenix couldn't resist hugging them both. It got her face wet with more licks, but it was worth it.

Cooper held the remote, but he didn't start the movie. Instead, he looked down at her until she turned her face up to his.

The somber concern in his eyes alarmed her. She started to straighten. "What?"

His arm around her shoulders kept her close. "I realize nothing else has happened in the past week, and I'm willing to agree that dangerous nonsense with the firecrackers could have been no more than a prank."

If he thought that, why did he look so grave? "But?"

"But on top of David being impossible to reach, Harry has gone missing, too."

Whoa. "What do you mean he's gone missing?"

Cooper shrugged. "Gibb goes by there every so often and he hasn't seen him, so he asked a couple of his friends, and they all say they haven't seen him, either."

"Weird. Did he check with his grandmother?"

"He opted not to. He doesn't really have a reason to be checking up on him."

Just as she didn't really have a reason to check on David. "Try not to worry, okay? I'll continue to be careful, I promise." What she couldn't do was to continue relying on others to escort her around the park. It was getting absurd and was most likely unnecessary. "And since I'll be careful, I want things to go back to normal."

"Meaning what?" He straightened. "If you're talking about staying the night in the cabin, it's a lousy idea—"

"I wasn't."

Cooper visibly relaxed. "Good." With a crooked smile, he added, "I like having you here."

Other than a few overnight necessities, like a toothbrush, hairbrush and her favorite lotion, all her things were still in the cabin. Sometimes she showered with Cooper, sometimes she showered at the cabin. The arrangement was loose, but also convenient, and neither of them had pressed for more; for now, she didn't need more.

She loved her job, she loved the environment of the Cooper's Charm resort and she very much enjoyed sleeping with Cooper. How long that last part would continue, she didn't know, but she planned to savor every moment of it.

"I like being here," she assured him. "What I meant is that I need to take full responsibility for my job—a job I'm good at. A job I enjoy."

He waited, patience personified, and she realized that he was actually pretty good at that. He wasn't a man who pressured or tried to impose his will over everything. Oh, he had his opinions and he wasn't afraid to share them. But never, not once, had she felt disrespected, as if he discounted her thoughts on things.

The realization made her smile.

Which made him suspicious. "Am I missing something?"

"Only that I think you're wonderful." She stroked his face, feeling the rasp of his beard shadow and the warmth of his skin. "Believe me, whenever I go in the maintenance building now, I'll be on the lookout for shady people. I won't linger in there—" Even now, with someone always with her, she felt jumpy in the building. "And I'll make sure to go only during busy times of day, when vacationers are around. But I need to do my job—*without* a babysitter."

For Cooper, she knew the worry was real, especially given how he'd lost his wife. She could only imagine the scenarios that ran through his mind, the old, hurtful memories that intruded. She couldn't relent. The situations were entirely different, and she wasn't his wife.

"Cooper?"

He flexed his neck, his gaze averted.

Phoenix could see he didn't like it, just as she knew he'd agree anyway.

Finally, he looked at her. "You won't get distracted?"

"I'll be like a hawk."

"You won't text your sister while you're in there?"

She crossed her heart.

Cooper sighed. "That's all well and good, but I can't shake a gut feeling that something bad is going to happen."

Phoenix didn't mention that the tragedy with his wife likely caused that gut feeling. What he felt for her wasn't the same as the deep love he'd had for Anna, but it would still be natural for him to fear losing her.

"I don't want you to worry." She hated the thought that she might cause him any concern at all.

"Great. Then I'll add a security camera to the building."

"A security camera?"

"I should have had one anyway," he explained before she could feel too bad about the expense. "Now we know it's necessary. And how about we set up a schedule? If I know when you'll be in the maintenance building, that'll help. Do you think you could limit it to two trips a day? Maybe get everything you need in the morning, then return it by five or six at the end of the day?"

"Entirely doable," she promised, already thinking ahead to

how she'd work it. "And in fact, I could put the tools I use most often in the supply shed instead." While the maintenance building was at the farthest end of the property, out of the way, the supply shed was situated between there and the lake. Hookup sites for RVs and campers flanked it on two sides, with a playground and the lodge in front across one of the in-park roadways. The creek and woods were behind it, but she'd have no reason to go around to the back anyway.

Cooper tugged her toward him so he could give her a kiss. "Hell of an idea, and I'll help you move some things over in the morning."

"You have the time tomorrow?"

"I'll make the time."

Sugar must have gotten tired of all their talking and smooching because she stretched, then gingerly dropped down off the couch. They watched her go down the hall and knew she was going to bed.

"You know," Cooper said, "that's not a bad idea."

"Moving some things to the supply shed?"

Shaking his head and nuzzling against her ear, he whispered, "Heading to bed." He trailed a hand up her thigh, then over her bottom.

Teasing, she asked, "Can we watch the movie tomorrow then?"

"Or the day after." He opened his mouth on her throat. "Or next week." She felt the abrasion of his whiskers, the roughness of his tongue. "Or we can save it for Halloween."

Meaning she'd be with him months from now?

That thrilled her almost as much as the way he slipped his hand into her panties.

But in a very different way.

15

PHOENIX HAD JUST POURED THE COFFEE WHEN THE knock sounded. Sugar, who'd been sleeping peacefully, launched from the bed like a berserker, yapping furiously while keeping ten feet from the door.

It stalled her heart for a moment, the way the dog carried on. She hadn't been that vicious when Gibb visited, but maybe she wasn't used to visitors until the afternoon.

Phoenix glanced toward the hall, but she could hear Cooper's playlist blaring as he did his daily workout in the spare bedroom. Unwilling to disrupt him, she said to the dog, "Shh. It's okay," and crossed the kitchen to answer.

Shock ran through her when, through the window, she saw Harry standing there.

Their gazes met and he smirked, loads of attitude piled on his scrawny shoulders.

Fury kicked in. She yanked open the door, saying in accusation, *"You."*

Sugar yelped and jumped back, then snarled again as she crept up to peek through Phoenix's legs. It dawned on her that the dog, even while terrified of her abuser, wanted to offer her protection.

In that moment, she could have attacked Harry herself.

"Hush, baby, you're okay." It took a little maneuvering, but she got Sugar off her heels so she could lift the reluctant dog into her arms, soothing her as best she could. With a glare at Harry, she promised, "I won't let anyone hurt you."

Harry scowled at the dog, then at her before looking beyond her. "Where's Cochran?"

For an answer, she demanded, "What do you want?"

His lip curled. "So you two are sharing sheets, huh? I figured as much."

With her impatience deliberately plain to see, Phoenix patted the dog and waited.

His glower darkened. "Stop sending people to check up on me. It's fucking harassment and I'm sick of it."

The crude language irritated her. "I have no idea what you're talking about. Last I heard—" *Which was just last night.* "—you were nowhere to be found."

"That's bullshit," he snapped, his demeanor defensive. "My grandma's been sick and I've been staying with her."

Phoenix sniffed. "That's convenient."

Heat crept up his neck and turned his bulging eyes red. "It's convenient that my grandma isn't feeling well?"

Phoenix made a face. "If that's true—and I have my doubts—but if it is, I'm sorry to hear it." Guilt nudged her. *What if it is true?* "Is she really?"

"She's seventy, so yeah, something is always wrong." He took a half step into the open doorway.

She didn't budge. Maybe her bravery was inspired by Sugar, but Cooper being close enough to be her backup was the more likely explanation. Whatever the reason, Harry didn't scare her. Not here, not now.

His voice lowered to a snarl. "My friends are starting to ask questions I can't fucking answer."

Holding Sugar closer, Phoenix thrust up her chin. "You will stop cursing at me, Harry, or you'll be speaking to a slammed door."

He blinked, then narrowed his eyes. "So the little mouse isn't so jumpy anymore?"

"I was never jumpy," she lied. "But I was concerned for the dog—a dog you will never again touch."

His hands fisted. "I haven't been paid."

"After what you've done?" Incredulous, she accused, "You could have burned down the building!"

Blank surprise temporarily wiped the anger from his flushed face. "What building?" Suspicion growing, he asked, "What the fuck are you talking about?"

"Your little prank with firecrackers?" She gave a mean laugh. "Don't pretend it wasn't you."

Looking truly bewildered, he shook his head. "I have no clue what you're talking about."

"Sure you don't." Sugar snapped at him, so Phoenix quickly stepped back a few inches. "Someone," she explained, while watching his expression closely, "locked me in the maintenance building *after* throwing in a string of firecrackers."

Arms spread wide, face tilted in, he growled, "I don't even know where your maintenance building is!"

Damn it, she was starting to believe him. "So why have you been hiding from Officer Clark?"

He grunted. "I don't hide."

"The officer couldn't find you."

"I told you, I was with my grandma a lot, but last night I was at the bar—which you know since you sent that goon to check up on me."

It was her turn to be surprised. "I didn't send anyone."

"Then your boyfriend did."

Her boyfriend. Was that how people saw Cooper? Would they be wrong?

True, their relationship was still relatively new, or so it felt to her. She was still thinking in terms of loose and casual—yet something more would be nice.

Very nice.

Either way, she didn't think Cooper would have sent someone after Harry without telling her. She gave it some thought, then suggested, "Maybe Baxter—"

Harry cut her off with a shake of his head. "No, not him. That other asshole."

So he knew Baxter? Curious now, she asked, "What, er, asshole do you mean?"

"Oh, way to play stupid, honey, but I'm not buying it. You know damn good and well who I mean."

"Actually, I don't." She eyed him up and down. "Sounds to me like you have a bunch of enemies."

"You," he said, pointing a finger at her, so close that only an inch separated his finger from her nose, "don't know shit about me, so don't stand there thinking—"

Sugar took exception to his theatrics and tried to bite him again!

For that reason only—or so Phoenix told herself—she backed up a few steps more. "Get out."

His lip curled. "I am out."

"Good." She closed the door in his face.

From outside the kitchen, he said, "You're blaming me for shit I didn't do!"

She leaned close to the window, saying loud enough that he'd hear, but without his edge of anger, "There's plenty you *did* do, so deal with it."

Throwing his hands in the air, Harry turned and stalked away. She watched until she couldn't see him anymore, then she sat down on the floor with Sugar in her arms and tried to reason through what he'd said.

That was where Cooper found her when he walked into the kitchen, showered, freshly shaved and dressed.

He did a double-take on his way to the coffeepot. "What's going on? Why are you sitting down there?"

She idly played with Sugar's left ear. "Harry was here."

Almost in slow motion, Cooper pivoted, an empty mug in his hand, to stare at her. "Why didn't you come get me?"

"It was fine," she said, reassuring him. "But it upset Sugar." That probably sounded dumb since Sugar was now lounged back in her arms like a baby, ears hanging down and eyes closed.

Cooper didn't move. In fact, he seemed glued to the spot. "Why didn't you call me?"

"I'm surprised you didn't hear the arguing."

At that, he thunked down the cup and came to crouch in front of her. "There was arguing?"

"A little." She looked at his face—a face that every day became more dear to her. A weird sort of pride had her mouth quirking. "Know what?"

He waited.

"I argued as much as he did. Maybe more. I think that took him by surprise."

He searched her face, then his softened. "So you weren't afraid?"

"I was cautious," she promised, not wanting him to worry about her. "But no, I wasn't afraid. When I first saw him, I was furious. Odd, I know, but Sugar was freaking out and that reminded me of how he'd mistreated the dog. More than anything, I just wanted to smack him."

Cooper looked down at the dog, now peacefully asleep. His mouth quirked, too. "She feels safe with you."

Just as Phoenix felt safe with Cooper. "I'm glad."

"So." His gaze rose to meet hers. "What did old Harry want?"

"He was offended that we're blaming him for things he says he didn't do. I mentioned the firecrackers to him, and Cooper…he looked honestly confused, like he really hadn't done it."

"No doubt he's an excellent liar."

"Probably, but I think I believe him. He also said something about us sending a goon to harass him last night." She further explained everything Harry had said. "Do you think David might've somehow known about Harry and visited him?"

"I suppose it's possible." To her surprise, he sat back and draped his wrists over his knees. "If he'd been watching the place, he might've seen Gibb here and known something was up. If he followed him—"

"Then he could have seen Gibb talking to Harry." But that would require a lot of coincidence and perfect timing.

When her cell phone rang, she set Sugar aside to lift a hip and draw the phone from her back pocket. The dog plopped down beside her with a sigh, already dozing off again.

Phoenix didn't recognize the number, so she answered with a polite, "Hello?"

"Phoenix? It's me, David."

Coop nodded his thanks when Phoenix, appearing staggered by the unexpected call, pushed the speaker button so he could listen in.

"David, hi." She cleared her throat. "Um, what's up?"

Her effort at casual banter, which sounded strained to Coop, must have convinced David.

Her ex blew out a breath, then said in a rush, "I owe you a big apology."

"Oh?" Her gaze locked with Coop's. "An apology for what?"

"Angie told me you called. She also told me that she wasn't very nice." David sounded tortured with that admission. "I'm sorry."

"It's fine, David. I understand."

"Do you?"

"Well, not really."

His laugh was sad and strangely exhausted. "She didn't know that I'd visited you. I figured she wouldn't understand, but I knew it was wrong to keep it from her. When I finally told her, she admitted that you'd called."

Phoenix licked her lips, thinking. But she was smart, so Coop wasn't surprised when she said, "I hope I didn't cause any problems. I want only the best for you."

"I know. I feel the same about you." There was a beat of silence, then David asked, "Why did you call? I admit I wasn't expecting it."

"I had wanted to ask you something, but you changed your number and I couldn't connect on any of the familiar places like Facebook."

He sighed. "Fact is, after what happened to you, I was pretty shook up." He hesitated, then rushed on, saying, "I loved you, Phoenix, but then you broke things off and—don't feel bad, but I was a mess. If it hadn't been for Angie, I'd probably still be sitting in the house you chose, moping about things I couldn't change and making myself a miserable bastard."

Coop watched her close, guilt in her eyes. "I am so sorry."

"Please don't be. Things were rough, I admit, but if they hadn't played out as they did, I wouldn't be with Angie now. Honestly, Phoenix, I'm happy. That's why I visited, to make sure you knew because, hon, I know you and I figured you'd be feeling bad. I didn't want that."

She nodded, swallowing hard. "Thank you."

"I also knew Angie wouldn't understand. She thinks I'm still hung up on you."

"But you're not," Phoenix said fiercely.

To Coop, it only sounded a little like a question.

"I'm not," David confirmed. "I love Angie." He laughed, then added, "I'm working with her dad now and it's great, and

I'm living with Angie until we have our house built. We've bought the land and we're working with the architect. It's exciting and fun and…" His voice trailed off. "I guess you don't need all the details. But if you ever want to reach out, you can use this number."

Gently now, Phoenix said, "Thank you, David."

"So why did you want to talk to me?"

Coop saw her thinking fast, and he knew the minute she thought of a good reason other than the truth: that they'd thought he might've been there to cause trouble.

"That day you visited, something weird happened."

"Weird?"

"It's not important, but I wondered if maybe you saw anyone, I don't know—*suspicious*—hanging around?"

Concern edged his voice, making him sound urgent. "What happened? Were you hurt?"

"Not really, just scared." She gave the bare bones of the incident. "It was the noise that startled me the most. I thought it was someone shooting."

"Jesus, Phoenix. After what you went through, you had to be panicked."

"A little," she admitted.

Coop frowned. Why did David have to press her? If he truly knew her at all, he'd know showing fear was a problem for her.

"You don't have any ideas?" David asked.

"Unfortunately, no."

There was a heavy pause, and then he said with dawning concern, "You thought it might've been me, didn't you?"

Looking pained, she said, "Not really, no." She bit her lip before adding, "Others mentioned the possibility."

"Honestly, I can see why. But I swear to you, I wouldn't—"

She interrupted him to say, "I never really believed it, David. I promise."

"I'm glad." Except for the sound of his breathing, David was silent a moment. "I wish I could help, but that day I was so focused on seeing you, on making sure you were okay, I didn't really pay attention."

"I understand."

"We're still friends, honey. If you ever need me, please let me know, okay?"

Softly, Phoenix pointed out the obvious. "Angie wouldn't like that."

"I'll make her understand. Just promise me you'll call if—"

"No," she said, her voice gentle. "I appreciate it, David, I really do, but as you said, we've moved on. We each have other, more important people in our lives now." At that, she met Coop's eyes.

He smiled, enjoying the way she'd just claimed him to her ex.

"I'm glad to hear it. Take care of yourself, Phoenix."

"Same to you." As she set the phone aside, Phoenix frowned. "If it wasn't him, and it wasn't Harry, then it must have been no more than a stupid prank."

Coop wasn't yet ready to rule out either man, but he said, "Let's hope so," then lifted her into his lap. Sugar gave them both a look for disrupting her sleep, moved a few feet away and went back to sleep.

Phoenix got comfortable against him, her head on his shoulder, her hand resting against his chest.

"Am I important to you, Phoenix?"

As if surprised by the question, she tipped back to see him, her incredible blue eyes widened behind the lenses of her glasses. "What?"

"You told David that you now had more important people in your life." Gently, he straightened her glasses for her, then tucked back a wisp of her sleek, inky black hair. "Am I one of those people?"

A little uncertain, she asked, "Do you want to be?"

"Oh, yeah." He let his finger trail across her cheek, down her jaw to her throat, then to the upper swells of her breasts. "I've been working at it, you know."

She smiled at his teasing. "You don't have to work for it, and yes, you're very important to me." She caught his hand, pressing it to her chest. "I don't know how it happened so fast when I was trying my best not to get involved. But there you go."

His grin was slow and satisfied. Naturally, his fingers curved around her, enjoying the fullness of her soft flesh. She hadn't mentioned love, and that was okay. When he thought of how far they'd come, it didn't seem fast to him at all, but he'd take what he could get.

God knew that each day, she became more important to him, too. He didn't want to take it for granted, having her in his house, in his bed.

In his heart.

For now, being important to her seemed like a big enough step.

As the weeks went by and nothing else happened, they all accepted that the trouble was behind them, allowing them to move on without worries.

July turned into August with a heat wave that scorched the grass and turned the leaves on the trees brittle. The lake and pool became the most popular hangout—and Phoenix actually broke down to swim.

She felt more daring these days, so on a shopping trip with her sister, she splurged and bought a new modest two-piece. The bottom wasn't nearly as minuscule, nor the top as skimpy, as the suit Ridley chose, but then her sister always did have more daring—and the body to make it work.

Phoenix's suit, a pale blue that Ridley said matched her eyes—never mind that Ridley's eyes were the same color—had a wider top that adequately supported her breasts, and bottoms with a ruffle around the hip bone–level waistband. It was pretty, but she felt silly in it; her belly was pale compared to the light tan on her legs and arms. But seeing Coop's face when she came out wearing it took care of her reservations.

"Damn," he growled, slowly rising from his seat. "We're going swimming?"

"It's a nice night for it." She loved how his gaze moved all over her. "That is, if we can use your private dock?"

"Yeah, sure." He came toward her. "We should make a calendar with you on the cover. We'd be rich in no time."

Laughing, Phoenix turned to show him the back—then felt his hands on her waist, hands that quickly slipped down to her hips.

Against her ear, he asked, "You sure you want to swim?"

Oh, it was nice to be wanted by Cooper Cochran. "Yes, absolutely."

His lips played over her neck. "All right. I'll consider it foreplay." He gave her bottom a pat before stepping back. "Give me just a minute to change into my trunks. Don't go out without me, okay?"

Her brows went up. "Why?"

Like a lecherous wolf, he eyed her up and down. "I don't want you tempting the masses." After that outrageous comment, he headed for the hall.

Grinning, Phoenix found Sugar's leash. The second she lifted it, the little dog went nuts, knowing it was a signal that they'd be going outside.

"Cooper is pretty awesome, isn't he?"

Sugar answered with a quick circle around her feet.

"I know what I look like, and yet he makes me feel like a sex symbol. No one has ever done that before. Not that I'm hung up on body issues or anything."

Stopping to stare at her, Sugar seemed to be listening.

"But it's different with Cooper."

The dog gave a bark of agreement.

Phoenix attached the leash, gave the dog a full stroke down her back, then turned as she heard Cooper reenter. He wore loose black swim shorts, a white T-shirt and he carried two towels with a plastic pouch for his phone and wallet.

Crazy how much she anticipated swimming with him.

After she added her phone to the pouch, he looped one towel around her neck and kissed her soundly on the mouth. "I'm good for an hour, no more." He coasted the backs of his knuckles over her lower stomach. "Besides, I don't want you to sunburn."

"It's almost 8:00."

"And still sunny." He snagged up a few water bottles and a dish for Sugar, and they headed out.

When they reached his dock a few minutes later, she knew he was right. The sun remained a blazing fireball in the cloudless sky. They could hear the laughter and splashing at the beach, but no one intruded beyond the buoys that marked his private area.

Cooper leashed Sugar in the only shady spot with a dish of water, then made a clean dive into the lake.

Phoenix, feeling a little unsure, put her glasses safely with the towels, then waded in off the sandy shoreline. In only a few steps, the tepid water was past her knees, and a few more after that, it lapped at her breasts.

She felt the movement of the water, then saw Cooper rise in front of her. This close, she could see him, and he looked gorgeous with his hair slicked back.

"You're okay?" he asked, taking her hands and leading her farther out.

"It feels wonderful."

"Baxter and Daron are looking this way."

She laughed at his grumbling tone. "I bet it's not just them."

"Maris and your sister, too," he admitted.

"Are they all swimming?"

"Mostly your sister was flaunting, but Baxter just picked her up and, with Daron egging him on, tossed her in."

"In the lake?"

"Yeah."

"Oh, wow." Phoenix tried to look serious, but couldn't repress her grin. "She'll get even in a diabolical way. She always does."

"Yup. She's already talking to a few other guys while ignoring Baxter. But it doesn't appear he'll allow that for too long." Cooper shook his head, then leaned close, his body further warming her in the water. "I'm glad you don't bring it as hardcore as Ridley."

Loving the feel of his wet skin, she slipped her hands up and over his wide shoulders. "Meaning?"

"She loves making Baxter jealous, and the poor schmuck falls for it every time."

"That 'poor schmuck' *did* throw her in."

"True." Rough fingers slipped under her chin, tilting up her face. "I like your sister a lot. I especially like how much she loves you. But I'm not a game player."

Phoenix wrinkled her nose. "Me neither." She had a hard enough time keeping up with what was real without adding confusing games of one-upmanship to it.

"I know, and I appreciate it. So let's make a deal. Any misunderstandings will be discussed. I'll never give you reason to doubt me, and you never give me reason to be jealous." He didn't wait for her reply. "And if one of us does get jealous, we'll talk about it so it doesn't become an issue."

"Deal," she said immediately, but with all the discussion, she wondered if jealousy had been an issue with his wife. Personally, she wasn't the type for it. She either trusted someone or she didn't, and if she didn't trust Cooper, she wouldn't be with him still.

Should she bring it up? Until she decided, she tried a different tack. "I think we're already doing that, right? Maybe not about jealousy, but a few weeks back, when I wanted you to trust me not to take chances—"

"And I told you it had nothing to do with trust—but I understood you didn't like being coddled."

"Not when it feels like an insult to my intelligence."

"Which would never be my intention." His breath teased her ear as he whispered, "Your brains are as attractive as your kickin' body."

Phoenix shivered, and his teeth tugged at her earlobe. To give her brain something to focus on other than his big gorgeous body and subtle seduction, she asked, "What's my smart-ass sister doing now?"

He turned his head to look—and laughed. "She and Baxter are in much the same position as us."

Good. Ridley deserved to be happy. "I guess Baxter convinced her to forget her payback."

"Apparently." He scooped his hands down to her bottom below the water. "We need to try this again some evening when no one else is around and it's too dark for others to see us."

"Swim at night?" The idea didn't sound appealing at all.

"Have you ever had sex in the water?"

"Actually...no." But suddenly his suggestion seemed more appealing. "Cooper?"

Lips to her neck, he murmured, "Hmm?"

"Was your wife the jealous type?" As soon as the words left her mouth, Phoenix cringed. She hadn't meant to blurt it out like that, but the way he touched her, the warmth of his mouth, scattered her thoughts.

For only a heartbeat, his body stilled against hers. In the next second, he leaned away, his hands now holding her waist, their bodies no longer flush together. "Why do you ask?"

He appeared more defensive than offended. "It does seem to be an important matter to you."

Two more beats passed, then he leaned in for a fast, firm kiss. "Yes, she was jealous a lot, though she never had any reason to be. She'd have hated the resort."

"Because you deal with a lot of female customers?" Many of them, Phoenix silently added, dressed in skimpy summer clothes or even bikinis. And of course they often flirted with him. Why wouldn't they? He was big, buff, gorgeous—and single.

Cooper nodded, and then he surprised her by hugging her close, his chin atop her head. "We had a good marriage. But like most couples, we had our problems."

"Things are never perfect in any relationship."

"True. I never talked about it before, though, because it would have felt disloyal." His laugh was rough, and filled with irony. "So odd that it doesn't feel that way with you. It's even odder that you don't mind talking about it."

No, she didn't mind. "I'm glad you had her." She meant that with all her heart. Cooper deserved happiness, and Anna had given him that. "I'm just sorry that you lost her so soon."

With a groan, he held her out the length of his arms. "Phoenix..."

"Yoo-hoo."

Recognizing her sister's voice, Phoenix turned toward the shore. She could just make out Ridley's outline—alone. "Where's Baxter?" she asked her, worrying that they might have gotten into another disagreement.

"Some new guests had scuba questions for him." Sotto voce, Ridley confessed, "Two old dudes, so I happily left him with them. It's the hoochies who come on to him that I don't trust." Hands on her hips, Ridley asked, "So Coop, how involved are you two in that water?" She peered at them skeptically. "The water is so dark, it's hard to tell."

While Phoenix choked on a laugh, Ridley asked, "Any chance I can steal my sister for a few minutes?"

Taking her arm, Cooper started her back toward shore. "I was whispering sweet nothings in her ear, but I suppose I can give you five minutes."

Regretfully, Ridley said, "Might take fifteen. Is that okay?"

Phoenix heard a note of...*something* in her sister's voice. "Everything okay?"

"Fine." But she added in a rush, "I think."

"You *think*?"

"Normally I wouldn't intrude when it's clear Coop is getting his romance on."

Tone dry, Cooper said, "I was that obvious, huh?"

"Yeah," she replied. "You're not a subtle guy."

Phoenix squeezed the water off the ends of her hair as they climbed to the shore. "Towel?"

"Anyway, I really do hate interrupting." Ridley rushed to hand her a towel and her glasses. "It's just that if I don't talk to you soon, I might explode. Or worse, do something stupid." As an aside to Cooper, she confided, "Phoenix is the supplier of commonsense."

"True enough."

With her glasses on now, she could see the tender look Cooper gave her. "Do you mind?"

"Not at all." To Ridley, he asked, "Will you have enough privacy if I take Sugar into the lake to teach her to swim?"

"How good are your ears?"

He laughed. "I won't be straining to listen, if that's what you mean."

"Then I suppose it's fine." She shifted her feet, antsy in her impatience. "Thank you, Coop, seriously."

"No problem." He went to Sugar, who'd been dozing peacefully, and scooped her up.

Phoenix could hear him talking softly to the dog as he waded into the water hip deep. Already Sugar's legs were pumping even though she had yet to touch the water. Seeing the dog was excited, but not afraid, Phoenix turned to her sister.

"Come on." Ridley grabbed her hand and dragged her away from the shore, toward the shade of the tree where the dog had been.

"What's going on? You're sure you're okay?" Phoenix spread out the towel and started to lower herself.

"I'm pregnant."

Shock took out her legs and she plopped down hard on her backside. *"Pregnant?"*

"Shh." Ridley sat beside her, her back to the tree, her eyes closed as if by finally sharing, she'd exhausted herself.

"But...are you sure?"

"Positive. I did the whole home check then—"

"And you didn't tell me?" Phoenix pushed her shoulder, but immediately snatched back her hand, horrified by what she'd done. "Oh, hell. I didn't mean—"

Ridley rolled her head enough that she could glare. "I'm not breakable, sis. Just knocked up."

Pregnant. Phoenix had a hard time taking it in. "But Robbie left you because you couldn't conceive."

"Yeah." She closed her eyes again, but she was smiling. "Apparently the problem wasn't with me."

Phoenix sat sideways to face her. "Apparently not." With her heart starting to pound in excitement, she gently stroked her sister's hair. "Ridley, are we happy about this?"

Still with her eyes closed, Ridley nodded, then gulped.

"We are?" Phoenix gulped, too. *A baby.* The smile came with a bloom of happiness. "We are!"

"I should have known Baxter would be more potent."

A snickering laugh escaped Phoenix before she could stop it.

Ridley bumped her with her shoulder and finally looked at her.

She had tears in her eyes, but she looked... "Radiant," Phoenix breathed.

"Come again?"

Phoenix threw her arms around her. "Oh, Ridley, you're beautiful."

Ridley laughed. "Thank you?"

"We're going to have a baby." She started to bounce and couldn't stop.

"We are." Ridley began bouncing, too.

Phoenix noticed Cooper staring at them, a lopsided smile on his face as he watched them hugging and laughing.

"We're drawing attention."

Quickly, Ridley cleared her throat, wiped her eyes and resettled against the tree. "You can't tell anyone yet."

She nodded. "What does Baxter think?"

"Well..." Ridley plucked at a dandelion, twirling it between her fingers. "I haven't exactly told him yet—and before you blast me, recall that I told *you* first, and that's how it should be."

"Okay, I'll give you that one." She was honored to be the first to know. "But you *are* going to tell him, right?"

She shrugged. "Eventually."

"Ridley Rose." Phoenix sat back, her hands on her hips.

Smirking, Ridley looked her over. "That indignant pose loses something when you're sitting on a beach towel in a bikini squinting from the sun."

"You have to tell him, sooner rather than later."

Slumping, Ridley mangled the weed. "What if he's not happy? What if he's the opposite of happy? We're not you and Cooper. We're not—"

"Me and Cooper?"

With a roll of her eyes, Ridley said, "Don't play at being surprised. You two have it worked out. You're the perfect couple, for crying out loud."

It took Phoenix a second to find her voice after that crazy claim. "Cooper is still in love with his deceased wife. Yes, we have a great relationship, but it's all very uncertain."

"Oh, my God," Ridley complained, much aggrieved. "That is such bullshit and you know it. He's crazy about you. You're crazy about him."

Beyond crazy, actually. She loved him. "But his wife—"

"Is *gone*," Ridley stressed. "And you're here."

Was it enough though, just to be present?

Ridley peered at her. "Everyone grieves, Phoenix. Change is hard. But Cooper isn't the type to live in the past. You know that, right? Or are you really that far in denial?"

Denial? No, she wasn't. Not anymore. Yet... Phoenix shook her head and got them back on track. "We're talking about you." They could sort out her complicated relationship with Cooper on another day.

"Me—and junior." Ridley put a hand to her flat belly. She exhaled and smiled. "I don't know jack about being a mother."

Strangling on a laugh, Phoenix asked, "Are you kidding me? You've been mothering me forever."

"You," she said, "don't need to be fed or have your diapers changed—"

Phoenix snorted.

"—and God knows you don't depend on me."

"Do, too." Unwilling to let Ridley hark back, Phoenix grabbed her hands. "You are the most witty—"

"You mean sarcastic."

"—smart and caring—"

"Sharp and intrusive?"

"—and generous person I know." With a look, Phoenix dared her to insult herself again.

In reply, Ridley pretended to lock her lips.

Satisfied, Phoenix continued. "You're a wonderful person and that baby is going to be very, very lucky to have you."

"And Baxter? Will he be lucky to have me?"

"He'll be the luckiest of all because he'll have both you and a baby."

"There's a hitch, though." In a very uncharacteristic show of timidity, Ridley looked down and whispered, "I'm in love with him."

As far as revelations went, that one failed. She'd known for a while that her sister was hooked. "That's wonderful, Ridley." Wonderful that she'd finally admitted it!

"Is it? What if he doesn't feel the same?" She groaned loudly. "God, Phoenix, I've beat him over the head with the dogged assertion that ours is just a sexual thing. And he's agreed with it! What if he wants the baby—" she blinked fast as if fighting tears "—but he doesn't want *me*?"

It was an unusual thing, seeing her headstrong, snarky sister so vulnerable. "I'm betting he does. After all, he's not a fool. But if not, we'll deal with it together."

Ridley slanted her a look. "Promise you won't run away a second time? Because hon, I need you."

That was a big admission for Ridley, and it damn near made her cry. "Never again," she vowed. "You have my word." Phoenix cupped her face in her hands. "Tell him, Ridley. Today. Right now even. Go interrupt the old dudes and drag Baxter away someplace private and *tell* him."

Looking unconvinced, Ridley said, "You forgot to add chickenshit to my accolades."

"Brave," Phoenix corrected. "You're brave enough to do this."

In agreement and resolve, Ridley stiffened her shoulders and lifted her chin. "You're going to be such a terrific auntie."

At that, they both started giggling again.

16

COOP HAD DISCREETLY WATCHED THE CONVERSATION between Phoenix and her sister, and he knew that whatever they'd discussed, it had pleased Phoenix. Even when she'd been talking seriously to Ridley, or hugging her in sympathy, she'd looked ecstatic. He was curious, but figured she'd tell him when she was ready.

That didn't stop him from asking, "Were you and Ridley having your own private party?"

Another very sweet smile curved her lips, and a rosy glow colored her cheeks. "Something like that." She peeked up at him as they walked to the house. "I can't tell you anything yet, but soon, I promise."

He didn't mind waiting. As long as Phoenix was with him, as long as she was this happy, he had what he needed. For now.

Eventually, he'd want more, but he hoped to ease her into it.

They paused in front of the house while Sugar took care of business near a bush.

"Look at that sky." Shielding her eyes, her nose scrunching, Phoenix gazed toward the setting sun.

After Ridley had left, they'd played together with Sugar in the water for another half an hour. The dog had taken right to swimming, but still they'd kept her in the shallows. Now as the sun dropped in the sky, it splashed watercolors of purple, pink, crimson and yellow across the horizon.

"Pretty," he agreed, looking more at her than the scenery. In so many ways, she seemed an intrinsic part of the resort. A very special, most important part.

"It's breathtaking," she whispered.

If she liked it enough, maybe she'd be content to stay forever.

When Sugar finished, Coop opened the door for her to go in. She made a beeline for her dishes, gobbled up some food, then trotted down the hall to sleep. Apparently, swimming in the sunshine exhausted everyone, even high-energy dogs. Since her fur was still damp, he was extra glad that she didn't want to sleep on the bed.

Giving up her admiration of the sunset, Phoenix started to follow the dog inside.

Though she must have missed it earlier, the second she stepped over the threshold, she noticed that Anna's photo wasn't on the desk.

Halting, she stared fixedly at the spot where it had always been. Her towel slipped in her hands, dropping loosely around her hips, her hair in dark, wet hanks over her bare shoulders.

Her gaze cautiously sought his. "You put that one away, too?"

Having thought about it a lot, he'd expected the question and saw no reason to pretend he didn't understand. Phoenix wasn't like other women. She was so far out of the realm of other women that she constantly took him by surprise. He knew he could be up-front with her, and he was.

Smiling, he rested his hand over his chest. "It's here."

"In your heart?"

"Yes." He'd never forget Anna, but he could move forward now without anger, without anguish. Thanks to Phoenix, he could love again. "I don't need or want a daily reminder of her." Hoping she'd understand, he moved his hand to her cheek. "Not anymore."

She stared up at him, her eyes big and glassy, her lips trembling. "I don't want to come between—"

"You're not." She couldn't be between him and a memory, not when she came first, before anything or anyone else. He wanted to say more, so much more, but he feared rushing her. In many ways, she was still shy of commitment. Part of that, he knew, was out of deference to him and the love he'd had for Anna.

It was up to him to show her that now, with her in his life, everything was different. That started with the removal of reminders of his past.

She leaned against him, her face tipped back so she could see him. "You're sure, Cooper?"

"Very sure."

Her acceptance was tremulous and heartbreakingly beautiful. "All right."

His blood fired, and he hugged her closer, lifting her off her feet while taking her mouth in a hot, deep kiss. To his libido, it seemed like she'd just agreed to a lot.

She kept one arm locked around his neck and with the other, she held on to the plastic bag holding their phones and his wallet.

Sliding a forearm under her bottom, he carried her down the hall, then let her slide down his body until she stood before him. The plastic bag got tossed aside—he didn't really care where it landed.

He dropped his towel, stripped away hers, then also removed her bathing suit top and bottoms. God, he would never tire of her body, of the soft, abundant curves. He adored those as much as the eager way she approached their lovemaking.

Every time with Phoenix felt both new and yet familiar; comfortable, but unbearably exciting. It was special, because *she* was special.

Whether she knew it yet or not, he'd already accepted that he wanted her, now, tomorrow…and for the rest of his life.

Baxter didn't know what to think when Ridley finally sidled up to him. She'd been hanging back a few yards, watching him while he not-so-patiently waited to make his escape. The two men before him had inexhaustible curiosity about diving, the park and the lake. Like many elders, they had stories and adventures to share, and apparently they wanted to share them all with him. He'd tried to concentrate on adequate replies, but it was getting late, well past his work hours, and he wanted Ridley.

As usual.

Now, as she approached, the two men lost their trains of thought, too busy staring at her to continue speaking.

She'd pulled on a cover-up but hadn't closed it in the front, meaning her very sweet body was still easily seen by all.

True, every woman on the beach wore a suit…but every woman wasn't Ridley.

When Ridley realized they were all three staring at her, she gave her patented "make a man drool" smile and said, "Excuse me, gentlemen, but I need to borrow Baxter if that's okay?"

The old goats nearly fell over themselves assuring her it was fine.

She hooked her arm through his. "Inside?"

If she planned to seduce him in the scuba shop with dozens of people still hanging around, he'd…*what*? Count himself a lucky bastard? Probably.

"Sure." Damn it, he was already getting semi-hard just thinking about it and even with the top half of his wet suit turned down, that wouldn't do. He tried a deep breath, but despite the weeks they'd been together, she still did it for him. God, he had it bad.

Ridley could give him a look, or that killer smile, or hell, she could just be walking away from him—even after giving him hell—and he wanted her.

Instead of her effect wearing off, it seemed to amplify each day. What he'd thought would be a quick affair that burned out naturally was instead an attraction that flamed brighter and hotter than ever.

It'd be unsettling if he wasn't having so much fun. Ridley was so damn honest he never had to guess about her motives. Even when she tried to make him jealous, she let him know what she was doing.

Better still, he trusted her. The games were fun because he knew, deep down in his...*fuck, his heart*? Yeah, his heart knew she wasn't a cheater. If she lost interest, she'd tell him so to his face. No confusion. No guessing.

There was something very reassuring, very addictive, about knowing her so well and trusting her so completely. Ridley told him what she wanted, when she wanted it, how she wanted it. She also listened when he did the same, and then she took wicked pleasure in giving it to him.

Huh. Was he falling in love with her?

Baxter stopped so suddenly that Ridley ran into him with an "Ompf."

He turned to stare at her, boggled by the notion that he wanted a lifetime with her.

"Hey." Scowling, she bumped him with her hip. "Why'd you put on the brakes like that?"

All he could do was shake his head. Seeing that particular disgruntled frown on her face—even *that* made him hard.

Put a fork in me, I'm done.

Hands on her hips, she snapped, "What's going on, Baxter? Why are you looking at me like I'm naked?"

Slowly, the grin spread. "That's how I usually see you, now that I know what's underneath the clothes. Not that you're wearing anything even close to resembling clothes today."

"Oh? Do you like it?" Smirking, she struck a pose, breasts out, hand on the dip of her waist, leg turned just so. Then suddenly her scowl was back. "Don't get too used to it. Things are about to change."

He stiffened from head to toe. "What the hell does that mean?" If she planned to end things when he'd just realized he wanted forever, he'd... Well, he didn't know yet, but he wasn't about to let her call it quits.

Exasperated, she put both hands on her hips. "I'll explain if you'll get a move on. Or would you rather we stay here drawing attention?"

True, people were starting to stare. He glanced at the scuba shop, but he'd rather not make it too easy on her, so instead he led her over to a vacated picnic table. It was far enough away that no one could overhear if she thought to dump him.

Somehow he'd change her mind—even if he had to carry her off to bed.

That was where he was most convincing anyway.

Ridley waited until Baxter stopped at the table. Wearing a black scowl that, okay, she had to admit was a bit intimidating, he gestured for her to sit.

She paced instead.

Baxter gave her a look, then sprawled onto the bench seat, arms crossed over his bare chest, legs parted.

At least he wore his reflective sunglasses. Somehow, not seeing his eyes made it less nerve-racking to say, "I'm pregnant."

Other than his jaw going slack, he turned to stone.

Damn. She hadn't meant to blurt it out like that. Now that she had, anxiety dampened her palms and made her heart hammer.

When Baxter didn't say anything, she leaned in and snarled right into his handsome face, "Pregnant. Knocked up. Bun in the oven." To punctuate all that, she added with a sneer, *"Dad."*

He came to his feet so swiftly, she didn't realize he was moving until suddenly he towered over her.

His lips moved, twice, before he choked out, *"How?"*

He sounded more stunned than angry. Ridley could feel heat pulsing in her face, feel the prickling of the skin on the back of her neck. *This won't do.* She wouldn't let herself be this nervous.

Now that he was on his feet, she sat, legs crossed, arms spread out on the table behind her. "I didn't figure you for the type who'd need an anatomy lesson."

Chest heaving, he faced her and warned, *"Ridley..."*

"Fine." She was too stressed herself to drag it out. "I've been thinking about it. I mean, we've been careful, right? Even though I didn't think I could get pregnant, there are other things to worry about. Not that I was still worrying about them with you, but my middle name is 'responsible,' so—"

"Wait." He twirled a finger in the air. "Rewind that."

She lifted her brows. "Which part?"

"You didn't think you could get pregnant?"

Oh, yeah, she'd never really explained that, had she? Shrugging, she said, "That's why Robbie divorced me. He and his parents wanted an heir, but it wasn't happening. Not even after three years of boinking without protection. I was willing to try some medical routes, but he refused." She scowled, thinking. "Maybe the dick knew he was the problem, not me. Could be why he didn't want a reproductive professional's input. I mean, he lives off the largesse of his haughty—"

"Ridley," he said again, and she noticed that his hands were clenching and unclenching into fists.

Fascinating. "So anyway, he wanted out so he could find some other, more fertile lady to give him a brood of kids. He and his parents were happy to pay me off to make the divorce easy. I was...hurt. I mean, not that I was actively wanting kids back then...or really, even since then. But eventually I figured I would."

"Ridley," he said again, his voice even softer.

She sighed. "So anyway, it hurt me to be told I was defective, to be discarded because of it, to learn that Robbie never really loved *me*." Defensively, she added, "When I hurt, I get even."

He stood over her. "Good for you."

Crazy how much his understanding meant to her.

"So," he said, "Robbie was an asshole who didn't want the truth exposed. How come you didn't get medical confirmation?"

She shrugged. "I didn't know I wanted kids, so why bother? I was all butt-hurt about his defection, invested in my revenge, then things happened with Phoenix and..."

He stared at her, his brows raised above the rims of his sunglasses.

That got her back on track. "Anyway, you remember way back at the beginning, we were fooling around and you hadn't yet rolled on a rubber? I distinctly remember..." She coughed for emphasis. "Contact." Though her pulse seemed to be on a race, she fashioned a smile. "Delicious contact. Apparently, you're such a potent stud, that's all it took."

"I'd say that makes you potent, as well."

"Yeah. Take that, Robbie."

His chest rose on a big breath, then he eased himself down beside her and breathed in wonder, "A baby."

"Yup."

It startled her when he jerked off his sunglasses. Those green eyes of his were downright incandescent with some emotion she couldn't quite read. "We're having a baby." His nostrils flared. "We *are*, aren't we?"

Time to come clean. "Yes, I am." If he heard the clarification, he made no mention of it. "Baxter..." This was the hard part. Best to spit it out quickly. "I'm in great financial shape. You know that. I can care for the baby on my own—"

His body jerked toward her. "Fuck that. You're not cutting me out, so forget it."

"—but I…" She blinked at him. "What?"

"I said forget it. I want in."

Ridley blinked. "In…on dad duty?"

"Damn right. Long haul. Birth to college and beyond."

Well, he was certainly thinking ahead. "Okay, fine." Relief lifted some of her worry. "But—"

"No buts." His shoulders tensed as he leaned into her space. "In fact, I think we should get married."

Whoa, somehow she'd totally lost control of this convo. "Married?"

"Stop repeating everything I say, damn it!"

"You won't let me finish what *I* want to say!"

His jaw flexed and his eyes narrowed. "Because you're trying to dump me."

"Wrong!"

He paused. "Wrong?"

Throwing up her hands, Ridley stood again. Nervous energy made it impossible to stay still.

Baxter snatched her into his lap. Much more softly, he asked, "How am I wrong, babe?"

She couldn't look at him this closely, so instead she stared at his chest. "I love you."

This new silence cut deep.

"Baxter?" She peeked up and found him grinning, the jerk.

He started to speak, and then suddenly Daron was there, pausing only long enough to say, "Fire at the maintenance building! Joy's calling Coop. Maris is calling the fire department. It looks bad." And off he went in a fast jog.

They both stood and sure enough, smoke visibly filled the sky at the far end of the resort.

Baxter cursed. "I'll come find you as soon as we get things under control."

Ridley started after him. "I'll help."

Pivoting fast, Baxter pinned her with an incredulous glare. "You're pregnant!"

Oh, good grief. "Doesn't make me lame."

"No." He grabbed her shoulders, kissed her hard and said, "Please, for my sake, stay at this end of the park, okay? Maris will need help with the store anyway."

Wondering if this was what she'd have to put up with, Ridley nodded. "Fine. I'll stay. But we'll talk about this later."

"No doubt."

She grabbed him before he could go. "You better be careful, Baxter McNab. I'm going to be really pissed if you get hurt."

"Because you love me," he said with a grin, then he turned and ran after Daron.

Ridley huffed out a breath. Life was about to change big-time.

She was pretty sure it'd be awesome.

Grinning, she headed to the store to help Maris.

The ringing of Coop's cell phone sounded from somewhere down on the floor. Still trying to catch her breath, Phoenix lazily kissed his sweaty shoulder and asked, "Should you get that?"

"Probably." Yet he didn't move, except to fondle her breast.

Lightly, she bit his shoulder, tasting the salt of his skin, relishing the heat of his body and his scent, intensified from their fast, urgent lovemaking.

They were both very mellow now, and for Phoenix, it felt as if everything were fresh and new.

The ringing stopped, but not for long.

When it started up the second time, Cooper groaned and turned away from her, glancing around the room as if trying to locate it.

"Sounds like it's coming from under the bed."

"Yeah." He stood, giving her a nice view of his broad back, narrow hips and taut behind before he knelt and located the phone.

Propping up on her elbow, she watched him as he answered the phone before sitting on the side of the bed.

The straightening of his spine told her something was wrong even before his side of the conversation registered.

"Damn it, they should all stay clear." Already up and struggling into shorts, he added, "No, don't go near it, Maris. I'll take care of it. Yeah, I'm on my way. Thanks." He disconnected, saying to Phoenix, "Fire at the maintenance building."

"Fire?" She slid from the bed.

"I have to run. Daron and Baxter are on-site, and the fire department should be on the way, but I need to make sure our guests keep their distance."

She tugged on her panties, then a T-shirt, not bothering with a bra. "I can help with that."

Cooper grabbed her shoulders. "Think about it, honey. This could be a trap."

"A trap?"

He let her go to shove his feet into shoes. "I'm willing to bet the fire was deliberately set. And that means whoever's been hassling you is back."

"Oh." Slowly she sank onto the side of the bed, her thoughts spinning. "But there has to be a large crowd out there."

"Exactly. How are we to know who did it, or who we can trust? It's going to be chaotic and I'll feel better if you stay here, with the door locked."

He was ready to go, his expression stern, concerned, and the last thing she wanted to be was a distraction.

"All right. But please be careful."

He nodded, and she followed him to the kitchen. Only a handful of stars lit the sky, so Cooper flipped on the outside floodlights.

Just then they heard the siren.

"Lock this behind me," he said as he went out the door and

over to his golf cart, which would get him there quicker than walking.

"Seriously," she called after him. "Be careful, and please let me know how bad it is as soon as you can."

"I will. Don't worry."

Through the closed door, she watched him drive down the hill in the grass. In the distance, colored lights flashed from the fire truck.

If it was a deliberate fire, that would mean she'd brought even more trouble to his door. The thought made her sick.

When she heard a noise behind her, she assumed it was Sugar and turned to greet the little dog, ready to comfort her—and take some comfort of her own.

She saw only a shadow in the hallway. A big shadow.

Her heart jumped into her throat, strangling any sound she might have made. She edged toward the door, quietly opening the lock and turning the doorknob, but just as she got it open, the shadow merged into a man.

A very large man.

Despite the smothering summer heat, he wore a ski mask.

Coop stood back as the firefighters quickly got the blaze under control. With spotlights aimed at the building, he saw that it was a loss with two burned sides, the others singed, the roof severely damaged.

The damned security camera had all but melted.

At least no one had been hurt.

Baxter and Daron had done an admirable job of blocking curious guests outside the perimeter set up by the firefighters. Joy had quickly created a makeshift play area for kids well away from danger, but unfortunately still within view of the chaos. The lodge was already in use, so she'd gotten them as far away from the smoke as she could. Frazzled parents alternately gawked and reassured their children. One of the firefighters had walked over there, equally flirting with Joy and leaving the kids in awe. He passed out badges and plastic helmets, so at least the children weren't upset by the destruction.

Coop, however, was outraged.

With the entire park up and awake to witness the spectacle, he kept his rage under wraps.

Standing beside him, Gibb silently studied the building, his arms folded, hat pushed back, expression thoughtful.

So others wouldn't hear, Coop kept his voice low. "It was deliberately set."

"I'd say so."

They both watched as a female firefighter inspected the area where the fire originated. She'd already informed them that a flare, placed against paper and wood at the back of the building, had been deliberately set up. Apparently gasoline or some other accelerant had been splashed on the exterior walls.

The big question remained: Why?

Gibb's eyes narrowed more. "Does Phoenix ever work this late?"

"No. And even if she did, she wouldn't be at this end of the park alone at this time of night. We've discussed it, and while she considered the threats over, she agreed to be extra cautious."

"So this wasn't to trap her, then."

Something, some odd sense of alarm, dug into Coop's spine. He stiffened. *Phoenix was alone now.*

Gibb looked at him, a reciprocal unease on his face. "Where is she?"

"In my house." Already turning, Coop took off at a run. He wouldn't risk the motor on the golf cart possibly alerting their firebug to his approach. That is, *if* the man thought to get to Phoenix. *If* he'd set the fire to distract Coop.

If, if, if.

Why didn't I keep her with me?

Fear left a sick churning in his gut, a cold sweat on the back of his neck. He heard Gibb calling to him as he darted in and around RVs, mindless of the privacy of others as he took the most direct path to the house.

Halfway up, he saw that the kitchen door was open. *Oh, God.*

A hand grabbed his arm and he turned, fist already cocked back.

"Don't you dare!"

Ridley. He tried to shake her off. "I have to—"

Baxter grabbed his other arm. "Hold up one second, Coop." He sounded strained, urgent. "We need to think about this."

There was no time to think, no time to talk. "I have to get to her."

"Agreed," Baxter said. "But if you charge in, she could get hurt."

The rationale sank into his pounding brain.

Ridley still held on to him as she spoke in rapid, jumbled chatter. "Sugar came to me. The poor little thing was frantic. Soon as I saw her, I knew something was wrong. Phoenix would never leave the door open for the dog to get out, so I put her with Maris and was ready to call you when Baxter showed up. Then we saw you running…" She stopped to inhale, sucking air. *"What are we going to do?"*

Gibb reached them. "I'm going up, the rest of you are going to stay here."

"Like hell." Coop shook them all off.

"Fuck," Gibb growled, then quickly rallied before Coop could get far. "Fine—here's a plan. I'll go around to the front of the house, see if I can get in that way and come up behind him. You two cover the back. Do *not* barge in. That's dangerous for everyone, including Phoenix."

Coop started forward, making no promises at all. He'd do whatever was needed to keep Phoenix from being hurt.

Behind him, he heard Ridley and Baxter in hushed disagreement with each other, but a second later, Baxter caught up to him.

Staying low, they crept to the open kitchen door.

And then Coop saw it: Phoenix in her T-shirt and panties, her hair still tumbled from their exuberant sex, her expression pale and stoic behind her glasses.

Across from her stood a man as large as Coop himself, a face shield covering his face and neck.

In one beefy hand, he held a bed pillow, and in the other, he gripped a gun—aimed at Phoenix's chest.

Even as she stared steadily at the masked man, Phoenix prayed. She prayed for herself, desperately wanting to live, and for Cooper. He needed her, she sensed that now. If something happened to her, if she died in violence as his wife had, would he be able to recover? Yes, he was a survivor, but by his own admission he'd retreated from life, hiding in the masses, living partially in the past with only memories to sustain him.

He deserved so much more than that.

He deserved everything.

If she lived through this, she'd see that he got it.

"You didn't think I'd find you, did you? You thought you were safe now."

The hard beating of her heart caused a physical ache in her chest. She shook her head. "Who are you?"

Though she couldn't see his face, she heard the smirk in his voice when he said, "Come on, now, sweetheart. You're not dumb. Who do you think?"

"Not David," she said, confident about that. "Not Harry, either." He was too big to be either of them… She gasped as shocking recognition clawed past her fear. In a strained whisper, she said, "You robbed me."

"Now she's catching on."

She clutched the counter behind her with both hands, determined not to crumble. "There were two of you."

He tilted his head in assent. "My friend has no spine, no sense of completing a task. I say fuck him." His voice softened. "Just as I say fuck *you*."

"But I did nothing to you!"

All calm fled him and he roared, "You got away!"

Flinching back from his anger, Phoenix tried to think, but drew a blank. At least Sugar wasn't in danger since she'd fled out the open door in a panic. Maybe, with any luck, someone would notice the little dog, notice the open door and help would arrive in time.

"No one will save you this time," he crooned, quashing her hopes. "The fire will keep everyone busy. I made sure of that."

So it had all been part of a plan—a plan to kill her? "How did you get in?" Through the throbbing panic, she thought that if she could keep him talking, maybe she could buy some time.

"A window around front." He strolled closer, his head tilted to the side, the gun getting closer and closer to her. "That entrance that's never used, since it faces away from the park. I found that out my first day here—more than two months ago."

"Here…in the resort?" Dear God. Knowing he'd been around that long sent shivers up her spine.

"It was easy to rent a spot in the primitive tent area." His gaze moved over her and she became painfully aware that she wore only a T-shirt and panties. "Nice of you to welcome me like this." He used the gun to gesture up and down her body. "Unnecessary, but appreciated all the same."

Her breath strangled in her lungs. No, she wouldn't play his sick game, wouldn't uselessly attempt to cover herself or even reply to his crude comments. "You've been here all along?"

"In and out." He stopped about ten feet from her. "Often enough to see the cop coming and going. I followed him when he went to talk to that punk, Harry, who, by the way, will have to go now that he knows what I look like." In a vague voice, almost as an afterthought, he murmured, "I'll be visiting that sad excuse for a man later tonight."

Phoenix had never thought to feel sorry for Harry, but now she did. "Why did you talk to him?"

"To feel him out, and let me tell you, he doesn't like you or your boyfriend. Blamed you both for sending me around." Amusement entered his tone. "He spilled his guts with little prompting from me, complaining that anyone who could afford this camp setup should damn well be able to pay for a chicken."

Phoenix almost groaned.

"Took me a bit to figure out that nonsense, but knowing your boyfriend owns the park factored into my end game. See, it makes sense that he'd run to greet the firefighters and take responsibility for his guests, right? And since he's involved with you I figured he'd leave you behind. I wasn't wrong, was I?" Voice smooth, he said, "You're here, and he's not."

Phoenix was somewhat thankful for that. At least Cooper was safe.

A laugh, raw and mean, filled the air as he came closer still, the gun held down at his side. "But don't delude yourself. I'm here now because I don't leave loose ends. I'll get him eventually. Maybe not right away, but—"

Something inside her snapped. Phoenix didn't think about it, couldn't weigh the risk against the blazing anger that gave her strength. She simply reacted, launching herself at the man, her curled fingers aiming for his face.

Surprise took him backward in an awkward lurch and he almost fell. The gun exploded, shattering a window on the wall behind her, and while she heard it, while she felt bone-deep fear, her body seemed to be on autopilot...set in attack mode.

She clawed at the mask, half ripping it from his face. Screaming like a banshee, she kicked for his groin—until his fist caught her temple, knocking her to the floor. Her glasses skidded away, stars dancing before her eyes. Panting in pain, she waited for the gunshot that would end her life, but instead she caught sight of a large body charging into the kitchen, taking down the masked man in a vicious tackle. The entire floor shook as the men landed hard.

Someone crouched in front of her, and when she started to scuttle away, Baxter said, "It's me, Phoenix. Stay still."

She grabbed for his back, offered as a protective shield. If Baxter was here, Cooper must be also.

Fear choked her.

She struggled to sit up—then screamed in horror at a second gun blast.

No, *oh God, no.*

Tears spilled from her eyes and sobs burned her throat—until strong, familiar arms folded around her. "Shh, don't cry."

She gasped in great gulps of air. *"Cooper."* He was alive, warm and vital, and safe.

"It's okay, baby." His hands stroked her hair. "I've got you." Warm lips brushed her face where she'd been struck. "Are you okay?"

"Me?" She clutched at him, remnants of terror remaining. "I heard a shot! Are you hurt?"

"I'm fine. Gibb shot the bastard."

From somewhere in the kitchen, Officer Clark muttered, "Better than you beating him to death."

She ran her hands up Cooper's body to his neck, then his face. "Is he dead?"

Baxter choked on a startled laugh.

"No." Cooper gently drew her closer against his chest. "He's hurt, but not dead."

"Oh." She tried not to sound too disappointed. In rushed explanation, she said, "He set the fire. And he was going to kill Harry and then you."

"He won't hurt anyone else."

Beside them, Baxter said, "Here."

She felt Cooper reach out, and then he settled her glasses on her, tenderly tucking the arms over her ears, nudging the frames into place on her nose.

"Cooper." Finally, she could see him clearly, could see that he wasn't hurt at all, although worry ravaged his features, making his eyes dark, his jaw tight. She peered past him and saw the man, now without his mask, absolutely demolished. Blood covered his nose and swollen mouth and ran down his throat. His brown hair, matted with more blood, stood on end. He had only one slightly dazed eye open.

As Phoenix stared at him, he groaned raggedly, attempting to roll to his side. Since he wore handcuffs, Officer Clark helped him to sit up.

"You, um…" She transferred her attention back to Cooper. "You pulverized him."

"I love you," he said as if the words weren't life-altering. "The bastard is lucky I didn't kill him."

Her eyes went wide. They sat on the kitchen floor, Baxter, Officer Clark and a near-unconscious evil creep nearby, and Cooper chose *that* moment to make a major declaration?

Cooper leaned in to kiss the end of her nose.

"I love you, too." Her eyes flared even more. *She hadn't even meant to say that!*

But now that she had… Her voice broke and she reached for him, grasping, *needing*. "God, Cooper, I love you so much!"

With his arms around her, his face bent down to hers, she felt surrounded and safe and so happy it almost hurt. She stifled a watery laugh.

The man who had attacked her at her shop so long ago, the man who'd paralyzed her so badly that she'd spent months hiding in a hotel room, that man was only feet away and she didn't care. He was nothing now, not a threat, barely a memory.

"Are you getting hysterical on me?" Cooper asked with mild interest.

"No." She clutched him tighter. "I'm just happy."

"I'm glad."

She lowered her voice. "I hear more sirens, which means more people showing up, and I'm in my panties."

A shirt dropped over her. Baxter, his chest and shoulders now bare, discreetly turned away as she wrapped it around herself like a skirt.

A new flurry of activity drew her attention to the doorway and then Ridley ran in, her face filled with shock and worry as she searched the room, seeing the battered goon, the officer… and finally Phoenix.

Hanging on to the doorway, she asked, "You're okay?"

Phoenix nodded. "Absolutely fine," she promised.

"Oh, thank God." Her relief was so strong, she nearly sank to the floor.

Baxter caught her. "What the hell are you doing here?"

Eyes closing, her sister snarled, "Don't yell at me."

"I wasn't," he protested with heat, then asked more softly, "Are you insane? I thought we agreed you would wait in the store."

"No, you ordered and I mostly ignored."

Baxter glowered even as he wrapped his arms around her. "You shouldn't be running in your condition."

Cooper's expression went comically blank. "Her condition?"

Oh, how Phoenix had hoped to tell him in a gentler, more private way. Cooper had lost his own child with the death of his wife. How would he react to Ridley's pregnancy? Would it dredge up all the heartache and loss, make it fresh and painful again?

She prayed not, because she loved Cooper, and she loved Ridley, and honest to God, she already loved the baby her sister carried.

Baxter had already spilled the beans, so Phoenix quietly explained, "Ridley is having a baby."

His brows shot up so high, they disappeared under his disheveled hair. But he didn't look upset, just surprised.

Phoenix touched his face. "I'm getting a niece or nephew."

Cooper looked at Baxter first, then Ridley.

Her sister said, "We're in this together. Auntie is a very important role."

Baxter didn't object to that, but he did add, almost like an afterthought, "We'll be getting married, too."

It was ridiculous under the circumstances, but Phoenix thrust a fist into the air. "Yes!"

With a strained laugh, Cooper hugged her so tightly she squeaked.

Ridley cocked open one eye for a lopsided glare aimed at Baxter, but anything she might've said got cut short as an ambulance arrived and paramedics hurried in. Maris and Daron showed up with Sugar, who went berserk when reunited with Phoenix and Cooper.

How odd that there could be so much joy on such an insane, dangerous night. Phoenix had a feeling that as long as she was with Cooper, it would always be that way.

17

SEVERAL HOURS LATER, DAWN PLAYED ALONG THE horizon, reflecting off the placid surface of the lake. A breeze ruffled the tops of the trees. Slowly the stars faded from the sky.

Beneath the lounge chair where he and Phoenix sat together, Sugar dozed, her soft doggy snores drifting on the quiet air. So far, she'd refused to be more than a few feet away from Phoenix. The pup was incredibly protective.

Coop knew just how she felt.

Despite the beautiful, peaceful setting, the scent of smoke lingered in the air. If he thought too much about what had happened, how close he'd come to losing Phoenix…

Shaken anew, he hugged her closer, her back to his chest, his face against her neck. Luckily, she didn't seem to mind. She reached back to tangle a hand in his hair, turning her face so that her lips brushed his upper arm.

The bruise on her cheek would be there for a while. Every time he saw it, rage coursed through him. The man who'd attacked her had a name now—Potts McDonald—and it was attached to a long list of priors. Gibb promised that McDonald, who was wanted in two other states for robberies, wouldn't be a problem for a very, very long time.

Across from them on padded lawn chairs, Ridley sat with Baxter. After the long night, they'd all been too wired to sleep. There'd been endless questions and confusion, not only with the attack against Phoenix, but with the fire. After McDonald was taken away, the four of them had worked with Maris and Daron to calm the guests and ensure the safety of the resort. Joy had also wanted to help, but with a young son, they'd all agreed she had more important priorities.

They'd ended the long night with cold sandwiches, chips and tea, eaten outside.

Sugar stirred, crawled out from under the chair and peeked at Phoenix. Seeing her, she wagged her butt—not just her tail, but her entire bottom half—then went under the chair again, collapsing with a contented sigh.

Phoenix gave a tired smile. "Poor baby. She's still shaken."

"We all are," Ridley said, lounging limply against Baxter. "I swear, my heart about stopped when I realized what had happened."

Baxter stroked Ridley's arm, but he was looking at Phoenix. "How did the dog get out, anyway?"

"I saw McDonald's shadow in the hallway before he reached the kitchen. I opened the door to try to get out but he reached me too quickly. Since he had a gun—"

Coop squeezed her, and she patted his arm.

"I didn't dare run. But luckily, Sugar did." She reached down with her other hand to rub the dog's head. "I was hoping she'd go down to the store and that someone would figure out that there was a problem."

Baxter nodded. "I guess she did, but before that happened, Coop had already realized it was a setup."

Coop wanted to stay calm for Phoenix, but thinking about that moment of charged panic wouldn't help, so he changed the topic, saying to Baxter, "The chapel here at the park would make a nice setting."

Ridley frowned. "Setting for what?"

"For the wedding," Baxter explained.

"I haven't agreed to marry you."

Baxter grinned and kissed her temple. "But you will."

"I don't know—"

"I do," he insisted. "You love me. I love you. We're having a baby, so—"

"You love me?" She twisted to face him, all kinds of doubtful. "That's the first I'm hearing it and you have to admit, given the timing, it seems suspicious."

"I could say the same to you. Recall that you told me you were knocked up and that you loved me almost in the same breath."

Ridley drew herself up, glaring. "I recall that you didn't return the sentiment."

He groaned. "Use that sharp brain I admire so much, okay? I didn't get a chance to reply because Daron interrupted us to say we had a building on fire."

"I love you," she said fast, then cocked a brow. "Huh. That took like, what, two seconds? But you're saying you didn't have time to—"

Baxter kissed her. Not a little kiss, but a long, openmouthed, bend-her-over-his-arm kiss that successfully silenced her.

Coop chuckled. He'd wanted a switch in topic, and now he had it.

Soon as Baxter released Ridley's mouth, he said, "I more than love you. I like your company. I admire your gutsy attitudes. I lust for you nonstop. I relish your arguments as much as I do your laughter. And I'm already anticipating having a baby with you. If I was a little slow to say all that, I promise to make up for it every day for the rest of our lives."

"Aww," Phoenix whispered. "So sweet. Come on, Ridley, cut him a break."

Ridley, still draped back over his arm, said, "It can't be that easy. Nothing is ever that easy for me."

"Only because, until now, you didn't have me." Baxter kissed her again, softly this time. "Marry me. If not here, then anywhere. But soon. I don't want to wait for months."

After a deep breath, Ridley smiled sleepily. "All right." She turned to Phoenix. "What about you?"

"I'm thrilled for you." To Baxter, she said, "Welcome to the family."

Because that wasn't at all what she'd meant, Ridley aimed an imperious look at Cooper.

He grinned, happy to take the bait. "I'm sorry, Phoenix."

She twisted toward him, her brows pulled together. "Sorry for what?"

He lightly touched the bruise on her cheek, his heart breaking all over again. "When we heard about the fire, you wanted to go with me." He had to clear this up before they moved forward. So he admitted, "I thought I knew what was best for you and I was dead wrong. If I hadn't insisted you stay behind, none of this would have happened."

"Oh, Cooper." She sat up to smile at him. "Don't you see? If I'd gone with you, that goon would still be loose, still harassing me, still a threat. Yes, it was scary for a few minutes, but because you're protective, because you were thinking of me, because you're *you*, you realized what was happening." Phoenix put her small hands on either side of his face. "You not only saved me, you ended the threat."

He swallowed heavily. "Are you saying that you don't mind my overprotective tendencies?"

"I love you, everything about you, especially how much you care."

Smiling, so content with life it was almost scary, Coop put his forehead to hers. "I love you the same."

"Now it's my turn." She gave him a sweet kiss. "I'm sorry for bringing so much trouble here."

"Don't." He couldn't bear it.

Softly, her words a breath of sound, she said, "I love you, Cooper. I'd like to spend the rest of my life showing you how much."

Because he wasn't sure he could do anything else, he kissed her. Mindful of her hurt cheek, he kept the contact extremely gentle.

Smiling, Baxter stood and tugged Ridley to her feet. "I think that's our cue to grab an hour or two of sleep before we get our day started."

Coop managed to end the kiss. "Thank you both for your help today."

Ridley leaned down to give him a hug. "Thank you for saving my sister." To Phoenix, she said, "I'm going to be extra clingy for a while and you're just going to have to put up with it."

Phoenix stifled a grin. "I'll do my best."

"Thanks." Her expression softened. "I love you, sis."

Nodding, choking back emotion, Phoenix whispered, "I love you, too."

With that settled, Ridley turned to lean on Baxter and together, they walked down the hill.

Once the other couple was out of sight, Coop kissed Phoenix again. He had to keep touching her, reassuring himself that she was okay, that they were still together.

As if she understood and maybe felt the same, she burrowed close.

Feeling as if he had to cement things, he held her face between his hands and stared into her beautiful eyes. "Not to steal anyone's thunder, but will you marry me?"

Without any hesitation, she said, "Yes." Then again, with more excitement, *"Yes."* She squeezed him so tightly, he could feel her heartbeat.

"God, I love you, Phoenix." It was enough, more than he'd

ever expected, but he needed to know, so he tipped up her face yet again. "You and Ridley are content to stay here? At the park, I mean."

"Of course." She smiled so bright, so beautifully, he caught his breath. "Cooper's Charm is more than a good place to get away. It's also a perfect place to stay."

"And to raise a baby?"

She touched his face. "Will it bother you?"

He understood her meaning and appreciated her consideration. "Babies are always a blessing." Turning his face to kiss her palm, he said, "I'd like it if we had a few of our own."

Her expression lit with a smile that showed in her light blue eyes. "They could all grow up together. Close cousins. Oh, I love that idea."

"I'm glad." They'd both come to the resort to escape their pasts, but in the process had found a way to live again. Cooper's Charm…it was more than a getaway.

It was a future, as long as they were together.